Praise for the Novels
of Rob Thurman

Deathwish

"The action is fast-paced and exciting, and the plot twists
are delicious."   —Errant Dreams Reviews

"A solid addition to a suitably dark and gritty urban
fantasy series."   —Monsters and Critics

"Readers will feel the story line is moving at the speed of
light as the Leandros brothers move from one escapade
to another adventure without a respite. . . . They make
a great team as they battle against overwhelming odds,
leaving the audience to root for them to succeed and
wait for their next misadventures."
                                    —Alternative Worlds

"Suspenseful. . . . Readers are assured of copious
amounts of gut-wrenching action and creepy thrills."
                                    —*Romantic Times*

Madhouse

"Thurman continues to deliver strong tales of dark urban
fantasy. . . . Fans of street-level urban fantasy will enjoy
this new novel greatly."   —SFRevu

"I think if you love the Winchester boys of *Supernatural*,
there's a good chance you will love the Leandros brothers of Thurman's books. . . . One of *Madhouse*'s strengths
is Cal's narrative voice, which is never anything less than
sardonic. Another strength is the dialogue, which is just
as sharp and, depending on your sense of humor, hys-
terical."   —Dear Author . . .

continued . . .

Chimera

Rob Thurman

A ROC BOOK

ROC

Published by New American Library, a division of
Penguin Group (USA) Inc., 375 Hudson Street,
New York, New York 10014, USA
Penguin Group (Canada), 90 Eglinton Avenue East, Suite 700, Toronto,
Ontario M4P 2Y3, Canada (a division of Pearson Penguin Canada Inc.)
Penguin Books Ltd., 80 Strand, London WC2R 0RL, England
Penguin Ireland, 25 St. Stephen's Green, Dublin 2,
Ireland (a division of Penguin Books Ltd.)
Penguin Group (Australia), 250 Camberwell Road, Camberwell, Victoria 3124,
Australia (a division of Pearson Australia Group Pty. Ltd.)
Penguin Books India Pvt. Ltd., 11 Community Centre, Panchsheel Park,
New Delhi - 110 017, India
Penguin Group (NZ), 67 Apollo Drive, Rosedale, North Shore 0632,
New Zealand (a division of Pearson New Zealand Ltd.)
Penguin Books (South Africa) (Pty.) Ltd., 24 Sturdee Avenue,
Rosebank, Johannesburg 2196, South Africa

Penguin Books Ltd., Registered Offices:
80 Strand, London WC2R 0RL, England

First published by Roc, an imprint of New American Library,
a division of Penguin Group (USA) Inc.

First printing, June 2010
10 9 8 7 6 5 4 3 2

PUBLISHER'S NOTE
This is a work of fiction. Names, characters, places, and incidents either are the
product of the author's imagination or are used fictitiously, and any resemblance
to actual persons, living or dead, business establishments, events, or locales is
entirely coincidental.

The publisher does not have any control over and does not assume any responsibility for author or third-party Web sites or their content.

To Lucienne, who believed

Acknowledgments

To my mom, who suggested I give my old dream of writing a go. If I become a victim of artistic Darwinism, I blame her. Also to Shannon—best friend and sister with a black belt in tough love; to my patient editor, Anne Sowards; to the infallible Kat Sherbo; Brian McKay (ninja of the dark craft of copy writing and muse of a fictional disease we won't discuss here . . . but did discuss at length in *Roadkill*); Agent Jeff Thurman of the FBI for the usual weapons advice; talented artist Aleta Rafton; Lucienne Diver, who astounds me in the best possible way at every turn; and great and lasting friends Michael and Sara.

What a chimera then is man! What a novelty! What a monster, what a chaos, what a subject of contradiction, what a prodigy! A judge of all things, a feeble worm of the earth; depositary of truth, a cloaca of uncertainty and error: the pride and refuse of the universe.

—Blaise Pascal (1623–1662)

Death hath a thousand doors to let out life.

—Philip Massinger (1583–1640)

Prologue

He dreamed of sun, wind, and horses.

He always did.

Strange. He'd never touched a horse, much less ridden one, but that was the dream all the same. It was the same every night since he could remember. There was the sweet green smell of grass and the smooth motion of the mount between his legs. The wind was cool in his face as the buttery sun beat down like a warm hand on his head. There was a handful of mane tangled in his fingers. Black and coarse, it was rough silk against his skin. It was a feeling so familiar, so right. The sky stretched overhead, the endless blazing blue seemingly as close as the hand he raised toward it. He could almost snag it in his grip and trail it along behind him like a kite.

Pretty words.

Pretty, but that wasn't what made the dream so vivid. The unmistakably pungent smell of ripe horse manure, not to mention the equally pungent smell of his own sweat—they were the details that brought it home. He had other dreams, not as often, but on the rare occasion that he did, he never picked up scents. It made him wonder. And if there was one thing he hated, it was pointless wondering.

Why did he dream in such rich detail of things he'd never done, never known? He wasn't saying that it wasn't possible, a dream such as that. If he'd learned anything, it was that the strange was always possible; maybe not desirable, but possible.

But in the end, so what? Dreams were just dreams, no matter their origins. Maybe this dream was a substitute for a memory he'd never made . . . a life he hadn't lived. He'd never ridden a horse across a swelling hill of waving grass. He'd never chased a summer day and taken it for the ride of its life. He'd never reached, wild and free, for a handful of the sky. He'd done none of those things.

And he never would.

He had been born a slave. Some said "prisoner" instead; others, in white coats, lied with the gloating label of "student." But he knew. He was born a slave, and he would die a slave.

The dream faded along with sleep. He opened his eyes to a reality all too full of smells of its own. They were worse than the relatively honest ones of sweat and horses. He detected alcohol and disinfectant; industrial detergents that bleached cheap cotton sheets; the occasional sharpness of urine and vomit. That was just this room. Outside was a hall that led to other rooms, other smells. Outside was a whole number of things, none of them pleasant.

Grunting, he rolled over onto his stomach and ignored the eye-watering whiff of bleach and the blackly unbleachable thoughts; he'd had much practice. It was never completely dark in the room, just as it was never completely private. The dim lighting recessed at the base of the wall let him see that the bed beside his was empty. A boy younger than he, with hair the color of a carrot, had spent the past seven years in that bed. Peter. Not Pete or Petey. It was always Peter. Precise, rigid, he had been a walking study in anal retention, controlling every gesture, every word; controlling everything he possibly could in a place where the ultimate control would never be his.

Peter always made his bed too—obsessively. If he went to the bathroom in the middle of the night, he made his bed before going. Could you believe it? It wasn't made now. There was only a messy tangle of blankets and sheets that would've had the boy sweating with anxiety.

Peter wasn't coming back.

The boy had been there when he'd fallen asleep and now he was gone. Expunged, the staff would say, and never mention him again. Peter had made that last great escape.

He could've said he'd miss the other boy, but it would have been a lie. In this place, people came and people went. Get attached and you'd go crazy. Detachment was a survival skill . . . the first true lesson here. And he was a good student.

As far as he was concerned, he was alone in that small world. It couldn't be any other way; not here, not now. Not ever. He laid his head back on his pillow and waited for sleep. He'd read that some did multiplication tables in their heads, some sang silent lullabies, and some counted sheep. Not him. He counted horses. They galloped through fields, racing a golden sun. Counting on, he slipped into sleep. There he dreamed . . . of sun, wind, and horses.

He always did.

Chapter 1

"A picture's worth a thousand words." Jesus, how often have you heard that old saying? Slathered across sickeningly sweet greeting cards, beaming from manipulative TV commercials, it was a time-honored classic. A picture's worth a thousand words. . . . Yeah? Right now I could think of only one.

Goddamnit.

Behind glass, framed in velvety rosewood, the photograph was one I hadn't seen before. Not that I didn't recognize it; I did. I might not have remembered ever seeing the picture, but I recalled all too clearly the moment it captured—the last Christmas. Not as in the one last year—no, it was a helluva lot more momentous than that. Think "the Last Christmas" as you would "the Last Supper." In some ways it was much the same—an ending, a betrayal, and lives that would never be as they once were. I might have been an unwitting Judas, but the result had been the same. Consequently, I hadn't felt much like celebrating on the twenty-fifth in the past ten years. You could keep the twinkling lights and the tree, but screw the presents and the eggnog; I didn't want any part of it.

All those things were in the five-by-seven photo . . . along with two boys. One was fourteen; one, seven. There was no guessing involved in that. I knew those ages to the day, if not the minute. The older kid was obviously a cocky son of a bitch with black hair, mocking pale brown eyes, and a grin that just wouldn't quit. My grin . . . I hadn't seen it in a long, long time—not that version. The one I flashed these days had all the warmth of a jagged shard of ice.

The younger boy in the picture occupied a different end of the spectrum, in appearance and personality. He had unusual eyes, unique in their innocence and color. One green, one blue, they looked out calmly from beneath the fringe of pale blond bangs. His smile was smaller than my grin, but pure and happy. I touched a finger to the glass over that smile. It was my brother, Lukas.

We sat under a ridiculously huge tree. The lights sparkled among a thousand silver icicles and a thick coating of artificial snow. We'd insisted on the cheap and tacky spray despite our father's snort of derision. It would be the only snow we were likely to see that year. Southern Florida wasn't much for the white stuff—not that kind anyway. I had my arm slung around Lukas's smaller shoulders and both of us sported eggnog mustaches, yellow and foamy. Mom had started the habit of making us alcohol-free nog three years before, and even though she'd died only a year later, the tradition was kept up. It kept her alive and with us for the holiday. And it made Lukas happy.

Kid brothers were always a pain in the ass. Any older brother or sister would tell you that. They tagged after you, asked a thousand questions, and bugged you endlessly. They took your crap without asking and narc'ed you out every chance they got. Lukas did all that, sure. He also looked up to me, brought me things—a sea-polished stone from the beach or a comic book he bought with his allowance—and didn't think any cootie-ridden girl was good enough for his brother. If making eggnog made him smile, what the hell? I'd do it. And for those two years I did. Dear old Dad was always too busy, and the housekeepers . . . well, they weren't Mom. The creamy drink pretty much sucked, but Lukas and I drank it anyway before opening our presents.

Of course, that year was the one the presents were

too big to open. That year was the year we had to go to
the newly built stable to see them. They came with fancy
names, I'm sure, but I never learned them. I called mine
Harry, after Dirty Harry. That was the year I wanted
to grow up to be a cop. I'd never seen my father laugh
before; not like that. "A *mussor*," he'd choked, darkly
amused. "I couldn't show my face again, Stoipah." He
shouldn't have worried. It had been a dream that didn't
have a prayer of lasting very long.

Lukas named his Annie for our mother, Anya. Those
were our presents. Horses, two of them . . . a mare and
a gelding. It would've been natural to blame it all on
them, the horses, but it would've been a lie. And while I
could lie smoothly without conscience to anyone I came
across, I'd never figured out the art of lying to myself. It
damn sure would've made things much easier. But if I
knew one thing in this godforsaken world, it was that I
didn't deserve easy and I didn't deserve to forget.

Others though . . . For them it seemed much easier to
forget. The framed picture had come through the mail,
boxed neatly with a short note from my father. *For you,
Stefan.* It wasn't signed, but it didn't have to be. I recognized the bold slash of ink, the roughly spare sentiment.
Anatoly Korsak had to pick and choose his words very
carefully—an occupational hazard. You never knew who
might be reading your mail or listening to your phone
conversations. Actually, that was a little less than true.
Anatoly was all too aware of who was reading his mail
these days—and thanks to our connection, mine. Let
them. Aside from my monthly *Playboy*, they weren't
going to find anything of interest. As for the postmark
on today's package, you could bet your ass that Anatoly
was states away from that location.

The day before had been my birthday. The picture
was my present. Maybe it was meant as a memorial, a reminder of better, sweeter times, or maybe Anatoly was
just cleaning out his goddamn attic. Either way, I didn't
give a shit, because in reality it was none of those things.

It was a gravestone, pure and simple. Unconsciously, my hand had already tightened on the smooth wood of the frame, a split second away from slamming it against the wall. It would've been a petty piece of violence wrapped around a large chunk of raw pain, but in the end I couldn't do it. That smile, my brother's smile . . . Smash it? I just couldn't.

Sliding it carefully back into its sheltering box, I placed it in the bottom drawer of my computer desk. Out of sight, out of mind; not exactly, but for now it was the best compromise I could make. Leaning back in the leather swivel chair, I closed my eyes and tugged the tie from my hair and massaged soothing fingers into my scalp. I could feel the black waves brush my shoulders and felt my lips curl ruefully. I needed a haircut. One of the guys had called me *malchik privlekatelnayo*; pretty boy. It was a joke, of course. Despite the hair, I was anything but pretty. The scar that ran from the corner of my left eyebrow along my jaw to the point of my chin hadn't precisely healed in a manner a plastic surgeon would've approved. Couple that with eyes as bleak and cold as a killing frost and I didn't exactly make children run for their mother, but I definitely gave them second thoughts—mostly about the boogeyman and things that went bump in the night, I imagined.

I could've gotten my face fixed. Well, not fixed, but improved, yet I didn't see the point. I'd learned it certainly didn't hurt me in my current profession. Before that . . . I'd wanted to keep the scar. I wanted to be reminded . . . every time I looked in the mirror and every time I saw my reflection in the face of others.

My head continued to throb and I gave up rubbing it to go into the bathroom. Opening the medicine cabinet, I popped three Tylenol and chased them with a handful of sulfurous water from the tap. Through the wavy glass of the privacy window I could see splinters of a pounding slate blue surf and dirty white sand. I lived in a condo on one of the less-desirable stretches of the

Miami shore. Even a life of crime wouldn't pay for a beach house, not when you were on as low a rung on the ladder as I was.

Anatoly had been grudgingly impressed that I wouldn't take his money, that I wanted to make my own way working for one of his allies. That wasn't it, though. If I was going to take blood money, I wasn't going to pretend it was anything but what it was. I wasn't going to remove myself from the process and live like the prince I'd been born; a prince of crime and death, but a prince all the same—at least to my father's peers. In the eyes of the police and the government, I was a little less royal. In the eyes of the victims, I was nothing more than a thug.

They were right.

But, hey, that was just my day job, so to speak. In the end I hadn't been able to escape destiny. Dirty Harry was forgotten and I fell into the family business without much of a struggle. It was all secondary anyway, random noise that didn't have a chance of interfering with my true calling of finding him . . . finding Lukas.

Bringing my brother home.

Changing into sweats, I moved into the kitchen to whip up some supper—"whipping up" being a nice euphemism for nuking leftover Chinese. As the microwave hummed, I considered picking up the phone to let Anatoly know how I felt about my birthday present. I could let him know what I thought of his giving up on his younger son. I could also beat my head against the wall; the result would be the same. It wasn't worth the effort. Tracking him down now that he was indicted could take hours if not days, and that was if he was even answering the phone. Anatoly had numerous safe houses and refuges, and no one but he knew where they all were. I was no exception to the rule. And even if I did manage to find my father, I already had that particular conversation thoroughly memorized. My mouth flattened and I turned back to the microwave to pull out the steaming carton gaily decorated with red, green, and blue dragons.

I'd learned over the years that the majority of families of missing children never give up. They always look and they always hope . . . if not for a happy ending, at least for an answer—a resolution, peace.

Anatoly had obviously made his peace long ago. I'd never understood it. He hadn't been the most demonstrative of fathers, but as ruthless crime lords went, he wasn't so bad, I thought dryly. He'd been proud of Lukas and me, generous with presents if not with his time. At the age of fourteen, I wasn't quite aware of what he did or who he was, but I was aware he wasn't your average working Joe. And I had known he had resources that far outstripped those of the police. Why he hadn't used them more after Lukas had first been taken and why he didn't use them even now, I didn't know. Damn it, I just didn't know. Every time I brought up the subject, it ended in the same way.

I jammed the fork into soy-soaked noodles and twirled it savagely. Lukas was gone, he'd say implacably. We had to accept it and move on. Living in the past was useless and it was weak. It had no place in men like us.

He'd given up so easily, so goddamn easily. In ten years not a day had gone by that I hadn't thought of Lukas. I had no illusions that it was the same for Anatoly. Taking the noodles to my computer, I sat down and clicked onto the Net. There were hundreds of user groups devoted to those left behind and those still searching. They offered support, a shoulder to lean on, and the words of those who'd lived through the same nightmare. Those were things I didn't need or want. What I surfed for was information and techniques that could help me find Lukas.

These days, I mainly used the computer for e-mail, and I no longer searched alone. Money could buy anything. That wasn't news to me, and now most of mine went to buy what Anatoly could've given me for free. And when the money ran out . . . well, let's say I wasn't a stranger to working out things in trade. I had skills. They weren't the kind you bragged about in your alumni newsletter, but they were still valuable to certain people. Pulling up my e-mail program, I scowled. I was happy with my dick size, thanks so much. Deleting the spam, I moved on to the only entry that looked promising. It was from Saul.

Saul was the best at what he did, and what he did was find people. For those who loved them or for those who hated them—he made no distinctions. If you had the cash, he was your bloodhound of choice. Amoral as a shark and unstoppable as the IRS, they didn't come any more relentlessly efficient than Saul Skoczinsky. It was nice when your friends shared your work ethic. The e-mail was short and succinct, scheduling a lunch meeting for tomorrow. I didn't get my hopes up. Some days it seemed as if Lukas had never existed. If it weren't for the picture resting in the drawer, today would've been one of those days.

Interrupting my train of thought, my beeper vibrated like a cheap motel bed, skittering across the surface of my coffee table. "Shit," I said, exhaling. Neither rain, nor sleet, nor snow . . . The expression was coined for a mailman, but it covered the slightly shadier of us as well. Turning off the computer, I made a call, changed, and hit the street just as the sun started to go down.

Koschecka, the Pussycat, was a club located downtown. With twisted pink and green neon lighting, concrete walls, and a doorman straight out of the gorilla cage at the zoo, it wasn't a place for tourists or timid locals. "Vas," I drawled, lightly slapping the hulking shoulder, "how's it hanging, *cherepaxa*?"

Sevastian ignored the greeting and opened the door for me. I wasn't too hurt. Once I'd thought the man had the walking-talking-gum syndrome. With his lowered furry brows, shaved bullet head, and a neck that was long missing in action, it would be easy to peg Sevastian as one neuron-challenged son of a bitch, incapable of wrapping his tiny mind around more than one task at a time. But as I came to know him, I'd realized pretty quickly that wasn't the case. Sevastian wasn't stupid; he was a snob. Born and raised in the old country, he had little use for those of us born in the United States. And he had even less love for me and my winning personality. Hard to imagine, but there you have it. The fact I called him turtle didn't seem to help matters much. But with that round, shiny head and bulked-up body as impervious as any shell, who could blame me? Apparently, a grudge-hungry poster boy for steroid rage, that's who.

Inside, the bar was wall-to-wall sour sweat and horny, potbellied men. Colored lights blossomed, swam in circles, then slammed into the walls like suicidal fireflies. The stripper on stage, a gorgeous girl named Cleo, seemed to suddenly come down with a bad case of the measles as the cherry red disco ball on the ceiling spun into action. Slightly stomach churning, it didn't appear to bother the guys next to the stage, who were rubbing greasy dollar bills between their fingers.

At the bar I stopped and caught the attention of the guy pouring the vodka. "The boss here yet?"

Dmitri nodded a hello at me and jerked his chin toward the back. "Yeah, the whole crew's there. You're the last."

Great. That was bound to go over like a Gay Pride parade at the Vatican. Sevastian had been the one to call me, and you could bet your ass he'd put me at the bottom of his to-do list. Swearing under my breath, I motioned to the bottle in his hand. "Have a peace offering I could take back? Something a little better than that piss you're pouring? What is that anyway, a specimen for your doctor? Damn, Dmitri."

Dmitri had known me long enough to let that roll off his back, water to a soused duck. "It's good enough for these jack-offs," he grumbled, waving a hand at the Thursday-night crowd. It wasn't a designation he gave frivolously either. There was many a customer who had one hand hidden from sight. Pity the waitress who had to take the tip from *that* hand later on. "Here." From beneath the bar, he hoisted up two bottles of Mosko Crystall, one of the best Russian vodkas on the market. "A friend of mine smuggled them from his last trip to Moscow."

That was the good stuff all right, almost impossible to come by here, and I was going to have to pay through the nose if I wanted it. Pulling out my wallet, I dropped a hundred on the bar's scarred and sticky surface. Dmitri pursed his lips and looked over my shoulder, bored. Hissing in annoyance, I deposited another hundred on top of the first.

That got his attention, just barely. "I don't know, Stef," he said dubiously. "Do you know how hard it is to get this? The bribes, the risk . . . The backache alone is hell. Dragging a suitcase full of bottles can give you a hernia the size of a grapefruit—I shit you not. Not to mention—"

Reaching across the bar, I took the bottles from his hands and fixed him with an unblinkingly patient stare as his mouth finally flapped to a halt. "Dmitri," I offered amiably, "I'm not in the mood to play bargaining babushka, got it?"

Perhaps not the brightest bulb on Broadway, he still knew enough not to press his luck. "Okay, okay." Scooping up the money uneasily, he folded it and jammed it into his pocket. *"Zhatky."*

Cranky. Shit. Maybe Dmitri hadn't known me as long as all that then if that was the worst label he could put on me. Carrying one bottle in each hand, I headed toward the back without much enthusiasm. Konstantin Gurov, my boss, wasn't the most forgiving of men. As the immortal Ricky Ricardo had once said, I was going to have some 'splainin' to do. It was safe to say, however, that Ricky had probably never rammed a screwdriver in Lucy's ear for any of her escapades, much less just for being late.

Sevastian hadn't explained the reason for the unscheduled meet, and as I passed into a dingy hallway, the only thing I could immediately bring to mind was the trouble back in New York. Operations had spread from there to Miami many years ago, but as time went on, relations had begun to fray between the old school and those who'd once been seen as pioneers in a sunnier clime. Since I did mostly bodyguard work for Gurov, it was hard to reason why my cheerful self would be needed. Whatever the reason, I'd find out soon enough. At the end of the hall I nudged the door silently open with my foot and walked in, bearing gifts.

It would've been better if I'd been bearing a gun.

The room was where Gurov conducted most of his business and was soundproofed for all the obvious reasons. That was how three of our own could be lying on the floor with no one out in the bar any the wiser—lying there, motionless and bloody. Copper was thick in the air, saturating every molecule with slippery, gleeful fingers. It would've been easy to choke on the metallic taint and even easier to freeze at the sight before me. Luckily, my sense of self-preservation was stronger than that.

With my hands full, the gun resting in my shoulder holster may as well have been at home in my underwear drawer for all the good it did me. With the killer's back to me, I had a split second to make my move. And I made it before I even consciously realized the identity of the one who propelled the motion. The vodka bottle in my right hand swung to a high arc, then plummeted down just as Gregori started to turn. It hit him at the base of his skull and dropped him instantly. The Glock in his hand was released by nerveless fingers and skittered across the tile floor.

Gregori . . . I'd like to say I didn't believe it, but hell, I'd learned to believe anything. That loyalty could be bought and sold was a given on these streets—on any street for that matter. I recognized the killer just as I recognized everyone in the room. The three dead or injured on the floor were men I worked with almost every day.

The one I'd laid out with the bottle, Gregori Gurov, was Konstantin's cousin. Family. Konstantin himself didn't look any more surprised by that than I did.

"You're late," came his gravelly voice. As I bent over to retrieve Gregori's gun, the icy gray eyes fixed on me. Without a blink he'd stood facing certain death from his cousin. As Gregori had aimed his gun at him, Konstantin had calmly met his fate without emotion. When I'd walked through the door, there hadn't been a twitch to betray my presence. Konstantin didn't have ice water in his veins; he had Freon. Coolant for blood and a vacuum for a soul; that was the man who signed my paycheck— so to speak.

"Sevastian seems to have a problem remembering my number," I said, kneeling to feel for a pulse on the guy nearest to me. "I guess we both owe the shithead, huh, boss?"

The skin beneath my fingers was cool to the touch and unruffled by a beating artery. I gnawed at my lower lip and shook my head. Paulie, goddamnit. This had never been the life for you. You should've taken that pretty girlfriend of yours to Vegas, married her, and made lots of fat babies. He'd been a happy-go-lucky son of a bitch who'd been born into the business, same as I. Always one to go with the flow, he'd drifted here, drifted there, and now had ended up facedown on a sticky bar floor. When you drifted, you risked getting caught in a riptide. Paulie had been sucked down and gobbled up by a merciless sea. If it hadn't been for that pain-in-the-ass Sevastian, I'd have probably gone down with him.

The other two were just as lifeless, and I rubbed a hand hard across my face. For all my big talk, I hadn't seen much death before, not like this. Before becoming a *byk*, a bodyguard, for Gurov, I'd gone to college for a few years and done some drifting of my own. In the end I hadn't fought the recruiting of "Uncle" Konstantin. A friend of my father's, he hadn't cut me any slack. Clever and with an iron fist of control, he was a potent mix, and it tended to ensure that wholesale slaughter didn't often happen. That sort of thing, he'd said on more than one occasion, wasn't good for business—entertaining, but not profitable. The man had a style of management; there was no denying it.

"Go. Tell Sevastian to bring a cleanup crew." Those transparent eyes moved from me to the stirring form of Gregori. "I wish to speak with my cousin." The ice abruptly was stained the color of shadows. "Apparently he is unhappy with his current position."

I left without a backward glance. One killer, two killers . . . and a bloodstained bottle of expensive vodka. It was like a very nasty version of a nursery rhyme, and I wasn't particularly wild about catching the live show. It only struck me halfway to Sevastian and the door that I was still carrying one bottle of Mosko. Cracking it open, I took a swallow as I kept walking. It was going to be a long night.

Chapter 2

Watching the sunrise was a tradition for lovers, nature enthusiasts, or poets. It wasn't for the likes of me. But I sat there anyway, on the beach with sand gritty between my toes. Rays the color of a beautiful woman's hair spilled across the horizon, strawberry blond silk gleaming bright. Crimson and gold, it reflected onto the ocean, transforming it into a fractured kaleidoscope. The colors of the peacock and phoenix mingled into an incomparable whole. I laughed without humor. Maybe I was a poet after all.

I'd discarded my shoes, worn black loafers, at the water's edge. They were probably halfway to Cuba by now. I had spent nearly a half hour standing in the water, the salt scouring the skin of my ankles and feet cleaner than they cared to be. If it would've helped, I would've dunked my head and let the salt scrub my brain. Last night was a memory I wouldn't have minded having wiped clean—four bodies wrapped in plastic tablecloths and duct tape. I hadn't been in the room when Gregori was "promoted," but I'd felt the heavy weight of an erased life in my hands when I helped load his still body into a car trunk and watched as he and the others were carried away. Death no longer rode astride a pale horse. He'd traded up . . . Mercedes, Jags. The Grim Reaper had expensive taste.

Now I sat, my legs unwilling to carry me back home. Drifting, I'd gotten carried into some damn black water, and I wasn't sure I cared enough to try to swim out.

Almost half my life had revolved around finding my brother. I hadn't paid attention to much else, and this was where it had landed me.

And I wasn't sure there was anything I could do about it.

Lukas wouldn't have gone this way—never; not even if things had been reversed and something had happened to me. If I'd been stolen away and he'd blamed himself, he still wouldn't have fallen into a violence of convenience. Lukas had been made for better things. He'd been made a better person. He was only seven, but you could still see that difference in the tranquillity of the eyes, a quality that seemed to belong to someone much older.

Ignoring my stubborn legs, I stood as sand cascaded off me. Soon it would be time to meet Saul for lunch. It could be he had information pointing to Lukas. And if not? Head down, I trudged on, long strands of hair hanging in my eyes. If not, maybe I would go back to the bar and kick the *dermo* out of Sevastian . . . just for the hell of it.

By the time lunch rolled around, it felt as if the sand I'd showered off had ended up beneath my eyelids. I hadn't slept and I was sure it showed in the lines bracketing my mouth and the annoyed twist of my lips. I was old at the age of twenty-four. Saul didn't comment on my rough look; he just raised his ginger eyebrows and returned to checking out his menu. Feeding the man could be a chore. He was a vegan—meat or any animal products whatsoever were verboten. Breaking a finger or two for information, that was no problem. Scrambled eggs with cheese? That was a blasphemy against God and nature. Yeah, you had to respect a man with morals.

Not that I was in any position to judge. "Jesus," I snapped as he lingered over the choices. "Go with the fungus of the day and let's get this show on the road, Saul."

"Temper. Temper." He snapped the menu shut and motioned for our server. "Does baby need a nap?"

Our server arrived just in time to receive the full force of my scowl. Understandably, she turned to take Saul's order first. Skoczinsky had no problem with that. Running a hand across his highlighted auburn hair, he flashed a blinding smile framed by a prematurely white-streaked goatee. I waited impatiently as he and the equally interested blond waitress flirted endlessly. Finally, I rapped my order, cutting off the mutual drooling. Offended, improbably aquarmarine eyes narrowed at me as she scribbled on a pad, and, pushing out her equally improbable breasts, stalked off on heels high enough to give that stalk a helluva bob and sway for Saul to watch. Watch, he did, too . . . on my time and my dime.

"You need to get married," I grumbled. "It'd keep these meetings shorter if you got your rocks off at home."

"The things I'm thinking about her aren't legal, even if I were married. There are still a few states lagging behind the times," he said, putting the leer away as he turned his attention back to me. "No leash for me. A stallion's gotta run, baby."

That line, so old and hackneyed, had me snorting into my ice water. "Yeah, you're a real beast, Skoczinsky. A walking cologne commercial, tackled by women wherever your ass goes."

"The day I see you wearing something you didn't buy at Wal-Mart . . . then you can mock me. You couldn't pay a woman to screw you, much less get her to give it up for free," he shot back the barb with the good-naturedness I'd gotten used to from him. Switching to a much soberer mode, he massaged the back of his neck and straightened in his chair. "We'd better get down to business, Stefan." That was my cue. I slid an envelope plump with cash across the table and watched it disappear like a rabbit in a hat. But while the payment-up-front process was familiar, Saul calling me by my real name was not. As his work was only slightly more legal than mine, he gave his clients nicknames. That meant if he was in public with them or someone of a federal nature was listening in, the client's identity was protected.

He usually called me Smirnoff. Russian vodka. Big leap, but I didn't care. With Saul's lethal verbal jabs, I was only grateful he hadn't gone with Rasputin. The most infamous death in history: poisoned, shot, beaten, stabbed, his dick cut off, and then what was left of him heaved into an icy Russian river. Good luck couldn't go with a nickname like that, and I needed all the luck I could get.

"Give," I said impassively.

Saul and I weren't friends. I wasn't sure either of us was equipped emotionally in that department, but we did have a mutual respect for each other. It tended to be oiled by my money and his skill, but it was there regardless. In the past it had him making a gruff attempt to ease the blow when he came up empty. This time he didn't make an effort. This time, for the very first time, he didn't have to.

"Don't get your hopes up." The hazel eyes were grim, but the finger he tapped repeatedly against the table gave away his excitement. "But I think I might have found something."

Under the right circumstances a moment can last forever. This was that moment. There was an eternity of clinking glasses, midday chatter, and the soft strumming of a sidewalk musician lounging against the patio rail. I was a fly stuck in an empanada-and-paella-scented amber. Not twelve hours ago I'd seen death come and go, barely missing me in the process. It had been more than a hiccup in my routine; I had the bloodshot eyes to prove it. But this . . . This staggered me. This rocked me at every level in a way nothing else could.

"What?" The word fell between us, hoarse and choked. Clearing my throat, I went on flatly. "What did you find?"

Did you ever hope for something so fiercely, with such

devotion, that when you closed your eyes you could all but feel it in the palm of your hand? I never had. That was the kind of faith usually only children possessed. I'd lost my childhood the second I'd lost Lukas. And it had been me—only me. Losing my brother had been a responsibility I'd never shirked, not even to myself. So, as a sinner did penance, I looked for him; I always would.

But not for one moment did I imagine I would find him.

Searching for Lukas had kept my mind occupied. It kept me from thinking of things that couldn't be changed, past and present. Now my excuse might disappear. It had my fingers tightening on the water glass, the rough cut-diamond pattern pressing into my flesh. Hope was a four-letter word all right; the most profane I'd ever heard.

I'm not sure what it was that Saul caught a glimpse of in my eyes, but he seemed relieved that our food arrived so promptly. Sizzling portobello mushroom fajitas were slid in front of him, and I didn't have a clue as to what I was given. I didn't remember what I'd ordered, and I didn't bother to look. "Tell me. What did you find?" I repeated.

Saul picked up a fork and speared a mushroom. "Fungus o' the day as ordered," he said with a faint grin as he began to assemble his fajita. Taking a bite, he chewed, then swallowed before exhaling. "Okay, this is the drill. Since you hired me three years ago, I've done a bit of subcontracting in addition to my own investigating. It wasn't much, but I paid some people to keep an eye out for a teenager who matches your brother's description. I plugged his picture into my own age progression program. It beats the feds' any day of the week. Pumped out some prints and gave the info to the guys. Normally I wouldn't have bothered going that route on a case as old as this one. Spotting a kid after ten years, it just ain't gonna happen. But Lukas with his different-colored eyes could be the exception to that rule. So I said what the hell."

"Who are these people? The ones who look?"

"Could be anybody." He shrugged. "Anybody I find reliable. Best ones are women who work in the mall. They have the eyes of eagles and the boredom of the ages driving them. The second best are people working at the schools or hospitals. Most kids go through there one way or the other when it comes to my business." He didn't have to elaborate; I understood all too clearly the hospital reference. Tilting his head slightly, he said honestly, "It was a long shot, Smirnoff, you know? I had no idea it might turn anything up. Chances are if Lukas is still alive, he'd be far from his original abduction site." He drained his glass, eyes gleaming with the thrill of the chase. "One big-ass long shot that just might have paid off."

I liked Skoczinsky well enough, I did. I didn't have any particular urge to do the man harm . . . not until now. Right then I could've cheerfully pounded his head to a bloody pulp against the table without an ounce of remorse. Narrowing my eyes silently, I waited. It was something I was good at by now. The poker face I wore came with long years of practice, but card games had little to do with it.

Regardless, Saul seemed to take the hint. Uneasily, he shifted a bit in the chair. "One of the girls in the International Mall spotted someone yesterday who looked like the picture—not exactly, but close enough. One green eye, one blue. Hair was brown, not blond, but that wouldn't be unusual. A lot of blonds get darker hair as they age. Kid looked about sixteen or seventeen, as Lukas would be. Paloma's young, nineteen, but smarter than most anyone has a right to be. I trust in her. If she says he matched our specs, then he did."

I was stunned, literally. A hammer slamming between my eyes wouldn't have produced a much different reaction. A mall—he'd been in a mall. How could that be? It was as if the Holy Grail had shown up in a crane-operated arcade machine, surrounded by stuffed animals with the mechanical claw poised right above it. I simply couldn't wrap my mind around it.

"In fact," he continued, "I trust her enough to have followed him. She called me and I was there in fifteen. I picked them up before they hit the parking lot."

"Them?" I was surprised my vocal cords were still working. For that matter I was surprised any of me was still working.

"It looked like he was on some sort of field trip." He frowned, striking his fork lightly against the edge of his plate. "Some sort." I could tell something had puzzled him as he'd watched the group. Before I could ask what, he elaborated. "There were fifteen of them—quiet, well behaved. Weirdly so. Not at all like normal kids turned loose in a mall. I thought private school maybe, something parochial with those ruler-wielding nuns." Shaking his head, he instantly refuted his own theory. "But that wasn't it. Their teachers weren't nuns, that's for damn sure. Not unless they were drill sergeants on their days off. These guys looked like guards. Yeah, sure, they were wearing typical teacher crap. Polyester blazers, cheap button downs, bad shoes. But it was just a look. Whatever link they have to the educational system is damn slim at best. Most of them looked like you." He grimaced and added, "Sorry, minus the polyester of course."

"Thugs, in other words." With a shrug, I cut off whatever else he was going to say. That was just Saul, thinking the fashion commentary was more of an insult than comparing me to a *chainik*, a professional bully. I knew what I was. It would be rather futile to get pissed off when someone pointed it out. Plus, Saul was more than on the shady side himself when it came to "physical persuasion." He simply concealed his a little better than I did. Maybe it was all about fashion sense. "Where'd they go?"

"That's where it gets weirder." Saul's gaze was frank on mine. "Lukas . . . If this is Lukas, he wasn't the victim of an ordinary child abduction. At least not ordinary in any sense I've seen before. They came to the mall in two vans, not a bus. I followed them about two and a half hours west to their school. Hell, if you could call it that. It was more like a compound, a fucking miniscule military base." While my appetite had long disappeared, his was still in full force. Efficiently rolling another fajita, he made quick work of half of it in two bites. "I looked it over all I could, which wasn't much. They got a gate straight out of Dade Correctional and a wall that would put that one in China to shame. The president should have their security."

What did that mean? What did all of this mean? "Government?" I couldn't imagine how the hell the government could be involved in Lukas's disappearance. That made no sense whatsoever.

"That's what I thought at first, but . . ." The waitress chose that moment to come back for a second round of water and flirting. The black scowl and flash of bared teeth I turned on her had her rethinking that in a hurry. Saul watched her go with a wistful glint in his eyes, but he knew better than to complain. Knowing how pivotal a moment this was for me and how unexpected, he also knew I was hanging on to my control by a fast-unraveling thread. "Keep it together," he ordered quietly. "We might finally be there, so don't lose it, okay? Stay with me."

If anything was ever easier said than done . . . Never mind the world had disappeared beneath my feet and left me in dizzying free fall. Swallowing against the chunk of dry ice burning in my throat, I consciously unclenched my fingers on both hands and uncurled my fists. Placing my hands flat on the table beside my plate, I sucked in a deep breath and said calmly, "I'm okay." At his skeptical snort, I qualified, "Really. I'm okay as I'm going to be. So, let's get on with it. Not the government? How do you know?" It wouldn't be long before the shock wore off and reality set in. Reality didn't have a history of playing well with others.

Saul went on to tell me just what he had found out.

He'd run a title check on the land where the compound resided. There was a series of dummy corporations, but Saul had cut his teeth on that kind of duplicity. It'd slowed him down, but it hadn't stopped him. At the end he'd run into a company he simply couldn't crack, but it wasn't federal. That didn't mean there might not be federal ties, but the organization was privately owned. Although he couldn't find out what the organization was, he could find out everything that it wasn't. They weren't owned by the government and no one in the business world had any idea they existed. They had no stocks; they weren't insured; they had no accounts with any bank in this country. And as far as Saul could determine, they didn't pay taxes. So either the government didn't know they existed, or they turned a blind eye for some reason.

It didn't make any goddamn sense, none of it. And the more Saul talked, the less sense it made. A compound in the boonies, a school that wasn't a school, security that back in the old days would've made the KGB say, "Damn, where you been shopping?"

Eventually Saul ran out of things to say, and in many ways I was as lost as I'd ever been. Bits and pieces made up a jigsaw puzzle designed by a schizophrenic. I wasn't missing a few pieces; I was missing an entire frame of reference. I wasn't sure I was any closer to knowing what had happened to Lukas, save for one small difference.

Now I could ask him.

Chapter 3

It happened Christmas Day.

It was the same Christmas Day that was captured in that goddamn photograph—people all eggnog and smiles, never seeing that the moon was tumbling from the sky; unaware that the sun had gone black and the earth itself trembled under their feet, hungry to devour them. I guess that's how people made it through life . . . by the God-given grace of ignorance. If you knew what was coming, I had my doubts you'd stick around this vale of tears to experience it firsthand.

If ignorance is bliss, I was the happiest dumb fuck around that day.

Christmas for a kid was always the best day of the year. It was even better than Halloween. Yeah, okay, Halloween did have costumes and pounds of tooth-rotting candy, but at fourteen, I'd been far too old for that; not that Lukas and I'd ever had much of an opportunity for trick-or-treating. Our home, the one we'd lived in all our lives, wasn't the kind that rubbed shoulders with its stuccoed neighbors. The nearest house to us was at least a half mile away. You could say we lived in a gated community, only the gate started at our driveway. There was a modest wall of crushed coquina shell that while nearly indestructible was easily scaled. How'd I know? I'd done it many a night, just for the hell of it. I'd also gotten my ass busted each time I was caught. The true security lay in the most up-to-date system on the market—two German shepherds and a few rotating "friends" of my fa-

ther's. He had a lot of friends, Anatoly. All that wasn't as
easy to get around as the wall. No, not easy.

But not impossible.

We'd spent most of the day with the new horses,
riding them inside the walls, which was a good ten or
twelve acres. It sounded like quite a bit when you said
it, but on horseback it may as well have been the corral
at a pony ride. We wanted to run flat out, gallop as long
as the horses would go. We wanted to hit the beach and
kick up clouds of sand and water. It wasn't an extraordinary request. I was good on a horse, thanks to lessons,
and Lukas may as well have been born on one. He was
a throwback to our Steppe days, our father liked to say;
our own little Cossack. On most days the Cossack and I
would've gotten our way.

That day was the exception. Anatoly's annual Christmas party was in full swing before noon and would most
likely last until past midnight. People would come and
go all day. Thoroughly vetted at the front gate, they'd
wine, dine, and suck up to the almighty Korsak with all
the lip-smacking capability in them.

With the festivities, no one had the time to take us
out and keep an eye on us—as if we needed that. It was
the typical sneering complaint of the average teenager.
And for all that went on in my father's business, I was
still as average as they came. Unforgivably stupid would
be another label that fit to a T. Life can be like that, for
an adult or a kid. You look away from the road for one
moment, one reckless, idiotic moment, and your car is
careening directly into Hell. It could be that you go over
a cliff or ram a school bus full of children. It might even
be convincing your little brother that sneaking your
horses out of the back gate for a ride is the best idea
since peanut butter and *Playboy*.

The wall hadn't been much of a challenge for me, and
it wasn't one at all for the horses. They sailed over it,
flowing smoothly as a quicksilver shot of mercury. We'd
gone to the far back wall and escaped unnoticed. It was

an innate skill. Lock a punk-ass teenager in Fort Knox and given enough time he'd find his way out to the nearest trouble. It was what we were bred for.

"Just like Zorro," Lukas had said, beaming, his hands entangled in mane.

For my little brother, however, it wasn't sneaking around. It wasn't breaking the rules. It was an adventure of two heroes, no more and no less.

We rode bareback, and as I pulled a ferocious mock scowl at Lukas, I felt the warm liquid glide of horse muscle beneath me. "If you're Zorro, then who am I?"

"My loyal sidekick," he said solemnly. Our mounts, Annie, the sorrel mare and Harry, the big bay gelding, moved over dry ground and stubby grass toward the path that led down to the beach.

"Okay, I see where this is going." Narrowing my eyes, I nudged Harry's sides and propelled him into a trot. "So, if you're Robin Hood, I'm . . ."

"Little John," he finished with delight, urging Anna after us.

Counting myself lucky he hadn't said Maid Marian, I continued the game. "Butch?"

"Sundance!"

"Batman?"

"Robin!" he crowed, laughing at the image of me in green tights.

I couldn't decide whether to howl in outrage or laugh. I laughed. It was an easier choice to make then—far easier. "No more old reruns for you, Lukasha." And then we were on the trail and rocketing down it to the beach at a pace that would've turned any adult's hair white instantly. When we hit the bottom we were at a full gallop. Sand plumed in the air and burned pale gold in the December sun. Salt stung our nostrils as we sent Anna and Harry into the water, but it was a good sting. It was the kind that let you know you were alive and made memories that refused to fade. Until the day I died, the smell of the ocean would always be intrinsically linked with the scent of horse. As much as the rest of that memory sucked, the beginning of it I still cherished. It had been the last perfect moment in my life—the last instant I hadn't been one of the walking wounded. It was the last time I'd been whole.

"Slowpoke," Lukas called over his shoulder as he raced his mare along the shore to leave me in the proverbial dust.

I let him go, not realizing just how true that was. I let Lukas go, never knowing how permanent a surrender it was. Directing my mount deeper into the water, I hissed at the chill that soaked through my jeans. Harry snorted at the sensation, tossed his head, but kept going. I would chase after Lukas later. After all, we had all day, right? Child that I was, I believed that . . . right up until I heard the first gunshot.

It was the first I'd ever heard. And although I'd heard a few since, the sound would never rip through me like the first. It couldn't. The bullet didn't hit me. It wasn't even aimed at me, but it staggered my heart as if the lead had plowed through it dead center. When I saw Annie fall, I started to suspect that it might as well have. And when Lukas tumbled onto an outcropping of rock, I wished it had. I wished the blood staining my brother's pale hair were pumping from my chest instead.

I don't remember how, but I managed to get the gelding out of the water and gallop him down the beach. I was in the water and then I was almost to Lukas, limp on his back, with no passing of time between. I was close enough to see his hand lying half on sand, half on rock. It was turned palm upward, the fingers curling slightly, unmoving; a piece of flotsam washed in with the tide, lifeless and still. As the next shot took Harry between his intelligent, dark eyes, Lukas's hand was the sight I carried with me.

I wasn't knocked out, although I may as well have been. Harry took me down as quickly and thoroughly as any tidal wave. The fall crushed the air from my lungs and for several agonizing minutes all I saw and all I breathed in was blackness. Blind and deaf, I struggled against the vise locked around my chest. When the darkness finally parted, I blinked up at an intense blue sky. Not a cloud . . . not one. It was beautiful. The sun was warm and heavy on my legs; so damn heavy. I reached down and felt it under my hand. It was soft, silky, and tickled my skin with the caress of butterfly wings. I frowned. It wasn't the sun. Warm, yes, but it wasn't the sun.

Harry.

Pulling ragged gasps of air into aching lungs, I pushed up on my elbows. Ominously motionless, the gelding lay across my legs, pinning me to the ground. In my life less than half a day, Harry had now moved on. Reaching over to pull myself up with handfuls of glossy bay fur, I saw someone else moving on as well.

The man had his back to me. All I could see was short dark hair, a black Windbreaker, and a gun tucked in the back waistband of the man's jeans. He didn't look at me, not once—not even when I began yelling at him, when I screamed for help; when I screamed for my daddy in a way I hadn't since I was a baby. The shooter ignored it all. Stooping, he scooped Lukas up in his arms and began walking away. Thin arms and dangling legs, my brother was the puppet turned into a real live boy, only this time it was the other way around. I screamed until my voice was gone, but the sound of crashing waves and screeching gulls was my only answer. The house was too far, the party too loud. I clawed uselessly at the sand, trying to dig my way out from under the horse.

When the man disappeared up the trail with Lukas, I was left with nothing but a throat torn to silence, a jaggedly bloody slice along my jaw, hands scraped raw, and a burden of guilt far heavier than the dead horse across my legs.

There were times, even ten years later, when I woke up in the middle of the night and still felt Harry weighting the lower half of my body down against the mattress.

Tonight was one of those. Considering the news Saul had broken to me at lunch, it wasn't much of a surprise. Brushing a hand over my legs, I almost felt the rasp of horsehair against my palm. "Sorry, Harry," I murmured.

Pushing against the invisible weight, I sat up and slid out from under the sheet. The clock on the bedside table read just past three a.m. Not your usual digital alarm, it was a fancier, chrome-and-silver-chased timepiece. A gift of my last girlfriend, Natalie, I'd wondered whether it had been her way of telling me our time was running out. In the end, I never got the message, as it had stayed longer than she had managed to. She was the exception. I wasn't much on long relationships. Blaming it on my "work" would be easy enough, but the true bottom line? The search for Lukas took up so much of my resources, including the emotional ones, that I simply didn't have enough left over to live a life.

So I screwed around with the type of women who didn't mind my unpredictable hours or what I did with that time. Most were dancers at the club or friends of girlfriends of the guys I rubbed shoulders with. Consequently, most had a moral elasticity that more than rivaled mine. They weren't any more invested in me than I was in them. Screwing around was the right term on both sides. Our kind weren't into relationships. Natalie though ... Natalie had been different. I'd gone to college with Nat and even dated her off and on my sophomore and junior year. When I ran into her three years later, we had picked up where we'd left off without missing a beat. There was the same banter; Nat had a wit sharper and more delicately cutting than glass. There were the same habits of late-night pizza and early-morning runs, which was one helluva sacrifice for me. Sleeping late wasn't just a hobby; it was a God-given right. Only Natalie could've prodded me out of bed as quickly as my frequent nightmares did, but her way tended to be much more pleasant. Long red hair, that natural kind almost as orange as a carrot, laughing blue eyes, and freckles that bloomed like tiny scarlet poppies across the tops of her milk-pale breasts, she was beautiful, intelligent, quick-tempered, and honest to the bone—so honest, in fact, that she became the first woman I lied to.

It was pretty much a doomed effort from the very beginning, and I knew it. But the weeks we had together gave me a glimpse into a life that might have been ... if I hadn't lost my brother ... if I hadn't fallen in with thieves out of sheer apathy ... if I'd been a man instead of an obsession-driven tin soldier. Wind me up and watch me go, blindly marching down a path without end.

Nat had found out soon enough what my life was all about. Obsession she could've lived with, I think. But dishonesty and only a passing acquaintance with the law-abiding world, that wasn't a life she would embrace—or tolerate. She had loved me, but she'd loved something else more ... her soul.

At least she left me the clock.

Giving up sleep as a lost cause, I padded in bare feet over to the living room window to watch moon-spangled waves. I had a lot of planning to do, and watching the tide's hypnotic show helped my brain disassociate to do its job. Saul was my first thought. I needed his help, his expertise, and he wasn't being too cooperative. At the restaurant he'd slid back in his chair, held up his hands, and shook his head adamantly. "Sorry, buddy," he had said in a tone remarkably lacking in apology. "I found him, just like you wanted. My job is officially over."

Maybe it wasn't such a leap for me, but it was something of an assumption for Saul ... being so certain that this boy was Lukas. The sight of that compound had unquestionably put him on edge. Whatever was going on within those walls, he obviously wanted no part of it. But if my less-than-distinguished career had taught me anything, it was that everyone had their price. The look he'd stolen over his shoulder at me as he'd left the restaurant had shown a darkly annoyed glimmer. Yeah, he knew it wasn't over between us.

Folding my arms, I leaned toward the window and rested my forehead against the cool glass. Five stories down I could see empty tide-washed sand. There were no dead horses, their legs curved slackly in a running position; no little boys with pale and limp starfish hands. "Lukasha," I murmured, the nickname still natural on my lips after all these years. "You out there?"

The moon continued to pass through the sky and I imagined for the very first time that I might actually hear a reply.

Chapter 4

Konstantin had many favorite restaurants, but not a single one of them was Russian. Too much borscht and cabbage as a child had humbled better men. I'd seen the sight of a beet cause Gurov's left eye to twitch uncontrollably. Embracing the favored local cuisine wholeheartedly, he ate more Cuban food than Castro himself. Payasada was his most frequent choice, and I was more than familiar with the setup there. The front door, the fire exits, the back door through the kitchen; I'd checked them all out on more than one occasion.

"You look like *dermo*," Konstantin observed coolly after sipping Cuban coffee from a tiny cup cradled in his palm. As strong as the drink was, I was surprised it didn't dissolve the china between itself and freedom.

I was working. The glass of iced tea before me was for appearance only. I kept my hands below the level of the bright red and yellow tablecloth and my eyes scanning the lunch crowd. "Noisy neighbors," I replied blandly, shrugging my shoulders lightly under my jacket. Lukas was my business and mine alone. Anatoly had made that clear.

A razor-thin white eyebrow arched skeptically, but he returned to his coffee without comment. The source of my sleeplessness didn't interest Gurov. His only concern was that I performed my duty and kept him alive. Anything else was simply an empty distraction between him and his paper. Normally lunch duty was no real hardship. Despite what the movies said, it was a rare occasion indeed that a hit went down in a perfectly well lit and respectable restaurant.

The line of my back was as tense as the rest of me. Shifting minutely, I rolled my shoulders in a futile effort to relax. There were a hundred things I wanted—needed—to do. Lukas could be out there, and here I sat, watching my boss suck down gallons of coffee. Time was moving so slowly that I could actually feel my arteries harden from the cold pizza I'd had for breakfast. I wanted to go stake out the "compound," as Saul had labeled it. I couldn't make a move until that was done.

But more than that, I wanted to see him. I wanted at least a glimpse of the boy who could be my brother. Hell, who was I trying to kid? He was my brother. He was Lukas. . . .

He had to be.

For a few hours, however, I was stuck. And while I had plans to make before I could hit that place even for simple observation, the sooner I could do something concrete, the less likely I was to put my fist through the nearest wall—or the nearest waiter. This had not been my week for those in the challenging field of food service. I raised a hand to catch the attention of our server as the level of dark coffee in Konstantin's cup dropped. The waiter was lounging against one wall with arms folded and one foot lazily tapping along to the overhead samba beat. If there was a hurry to be found, he didn't seem to be in it. He was probably a model/musician loathing his day job.

Gurov didn't enjoy waiting for his coffee . . . or anything for that matter. And I didn't enjoy what he might have me do if his needs didn't get immediate attention. As I added a laser-sharp glare to my gesturing hand, the waiter pushed away from the wall and headed our way. His bored look was now mingled with a slight hint of unease. It seemed he wasn't quite as thickheaded as I'd thought.

"Never mind, Stefan. I must cut this lunch short."

Konstantin was folding the newspaper with quick, precise movements. "Perhaps you'll have an opportunity for a little education with our *preyatel* upon our next visit. I have an appointment to attend to."

Taking care of the bill, I rather hoped the next time we came back, the rock star wannabe would have gotten a new job. For his sake. Gurov didn't hold grudges; he'd invented them. Kicking the shit out of some waiter, I didn't need a fortune-teller to read that in my future.

I led the way out of the restaurant, pausing in the doorway to check the sidewalk and street. Clear. Konstantin tapped a finger against his watch impatiently. A glittering gold and diamond piece, it cost more than my condo. My priorities in life would be viewed as askew by some, I knew. I was more than a little fucked up and there was no denying it. But when it came to material things, I'd learned the hard way. Money couldn't buy the things that mattered. If I spent that much on a watch, it shouldn't just keep time; it had better let me travel through it too.

Moving down the sidewalk, I fished in my jacket pocket for the remote to Gurov's car and started it while we were still half a block away. Our guys weren't much on bombs, but the Colombians lived and breathed explosives. Fortunately for the fire hydrant we were parked next to so blatantly, the car started without incident. Opening the door for the older man, I scooped the ticket off the windshield and stuffed it in my pocket. As I headed around the front of the shiny black hood, I spotted them. There were two big guys wearing similar Windbreakers. I was sure Saul would've said it was a fashion disaster, but even in the winter Miami's warm weather made you work to cover up your gun.

Rocking back casually on my heels, I did another quick visual check. Yeah, just the two, and amateurs to boot. Not *Mafiya*; I could tell that at a glance. They were most likely punks out to jack a car. About eighteen or nineteen, one white, one black, they had identical empty

eyes. I saw a blade flick to life in one tattooed hand held
close to a leg. Someone hadn't listened to their guidance
counselor any more than I had.

I didn't bother with planning or subtlety. That sort of
thing would be wasted with these guys. Within seconds
they were in front of me, faces as predatory as the vul-
pine face of any wolf. I hit the one without the knife first.
His empty hands were even more threatening. A knife I
could deal with; a gun out of nowhere would be a little
trickier. Flashing a cheerful grin, I leaned against the
closed driver's door. "Nice jackets. Can I help you guys?
You lost? Out to spread the word of God maybe?" I
couldn't look innocent. Life had made damn sure that
was something my face would never be able to wear.
But I gave it my best shot only to see it reflected back at
me in a sudden uneasiness in the face of the man with
the switchblade. Wolves recognized their own. On the
other hand, the one I kicked in the stomach didn't look
uneasy. In fact, he didn't look anything but nauseated.

One hand on the car supporting me, I twisted sideways and planted a foot in the abdomen of the one whose
empty hand had suddenly darted toward his jacket. Before he hit the asphalt, I gave him another on the point
of his chin, taking him out of the game then and there.
No flies on him when it came to self-interest, his buddy
had already lunged at me. With sharp silver metal and
teeth bared in a twisted face, he slashed at me while hissing curses like a foul-mouthed pit viper.

Kids.

I blocked his arm with my left one, my hand fisted.
My other hand was wrapped snugly around the grip of
a Steyr 9mm. Yeah, flies weren't exactly roosting on me
either. I planted the end of the four-inch barrel firmly in
the center of his pimply forehead. Could be he'd planned
on stripping the car and trading the parts for zit cream.
He froze, the shiny black eyes no longer empty. Fear,
pure and simple, shone clearly, along with a desire to be
anywhere but here. Tough love worked wonders.

"Go home, Junior," I said flatly. "You're not ready to play with the big boys yet." Only five or six years separated me from this piece of shit barely out of diapers—half a decade, but it may as well have been a lifetime.

The knife clattered on the asphalt, shortly followed by his ass. Scrambling backward for several feet, he then flipped over to a crawl before lunging to his feet and running down the street. Half in front of the car, his friend still lay unconscious and obviously forgotten. There's no honor among thieves and apparently no loyalty either. Sighing, I holstered the semiautomatic and bent down to slide my hands under the slack shoulders to drag him to the sidewalk. He was lucky. Some guys I knew would've driven over him and raided his wallet for the car wash money.

It had all taken less than thirty seconds, but as I slid behind the steering wheel, Konstantin still pinned me with an expression of sharp annoyance. "*Tat?*" he demanded, fingers drumming on his suit-clad knee.

"Yeah," I confirmed. *Tat* referred to common thieves, unworthy of the respect given to their more murderously organized brethren . . . us. "And pretty shitty ones at that." Pulling away from the curb, I raised a hand in a casual wave to the small knot of tourists gaping from the curb. This had been more fun in the sun than they'd bargained for, I was thinking.

"Pity." Gurov leaned back against the butter-soft leather of the seats. Closing his eyes, he linked fingers across a stomach amazingly lean for a sixty-year-old man.

Raising my eyebrows, I repeated the word, curious.

Face serene, he said, "Pity. If your heart was with your family, your work could be truly phenomenal."

Being phenomenal in a career of brutality; I wasn't sure the two belonged in the same sentence . . . or in the same man. As for family, I knew who it was, and who it wasn't.

Gurov and the others didn't even come close.

Chapter 5

"I hate you, you son of a bitch."

Unimpressed, I kept the night-vision goggles up to my eyes and replied absently, "No one held a gun to your head, Skoczinsky."

"Bullshit." Beside me, he shifted on his stomach and with a snarl swatted at a buzzing mosquito. "It may as well have been and you know it."

He was right, even if I hadn't known it at the time. The amount of money I'd offered Saul had made it almost impossible for his mercenary soul to refuse, but *almost* is just that—almost. What carried it beyond that was the question I'd asked, a simple one: What if it were your brother? It was a fairly desperate attempt on my part, and I hadn't expected it to do much good. Some people don't give a damn about the brothers they do have and some don't have any at all. But sometimes those desperate attempts work best of all.

It wasn't a gun to his head, that question, but to Saul, combined with the money, it had been every bit as convincing. I'd seen it in the tightening of his jaw and the ice behind his glare . . . a brittle ice running with cracks in all directions, ready to break. If you were a bodyguard, reading people was a crucial skill. I didn't know exactly what had changed Saul's mind, but he had changed it and that was all that mattered. I wasn't going to waste time feeling guilty about it, I thought obstinately, doing my best to promptly squelch the supposedly nonexistent emotion. After all, with the chunk of change I was giving him, he could stock up on plenty of long spoons for the next time he supped with the devil.

"Yeah, yeah. I'll cry for you later." I needed Saul for this. If that meant manipulating him, I would do it. I would do it and deal with the consequences to my questionable conscience later. I would also give anything I had to get him on board. That anything came to pretty much every penny I had to my name and then some, but I didn't have any doubt it would be money well spent. "Make yourself useful. Take the east side, and check back in fifteen."

With another grumbled curse, he slithered off into the night with an alacrity that would've done any soldier proud. It might be a job he regretted taking, but he would do it to the best of his ability nonetheless. His morality might reside on a level far more shadowy than that of your average upright citizen, but Saul did have principles he followed rigorously and questions he wouldn't answer. The principles might always come back to that bottom line, the almighty dollar or euro, but they did exist. And because they did, he had led me personally to the "school" he'd followed the children to two days before.

He'd been on the nose with his description of the place. If this was a school, then Stalin was the headmaster. The compound, and it was that without a doubt, was smothered in concealing gloom. There was none of the garish orange glow that blanketed the sky over Miami to lighten the night. The lack of moon or urban lights led to a blackness as thick as the depths of a tar pit— thick, sticky, and virtually impenetrable. Despite that, the NVGs provided by Saul let me see the details of the place. In fact, I could see them clearly enough that I swore silently.

Walls topped with razor wire and a twisted iron monstrosity of a gate that belonged at Dr. Frankenstein's castle, it was one goddamn impressive setup, I was forced to admit. Nearly three hours from the city limits and on the edge of the Everglades, you'd be hard-pressed to find a more inhospitable spot if you had years to search. With sand, scrub, and low-lying water filled with creatures more ill-tempered than my boss, it didn't make for a real estate agent's dream. More important, it didn't bode well for a fast escape.

Exhaling, I dropped the goggles onto the ground and rubbed my eyes with a thumb and forefinger. The sand gritted under my elbows and aside from the croaking of frogs, it was the only sound to be heard. This wasn't a job for two men; hell, even the ATF would've been screwed. Not that that was saying much.

It didn't matter. I didn't have the ATF. I had Saul, myself, and a set of balls that would've impressed even King Kong. It would have to be enough. Saul hadn't bothered to ask why we didn't just call the cops and have them investigate. He was smarter than that. Lukas was still listed as a missing child, true. And if we'd gone to the police with our information, skimpy as it was, they would've looked into it. But by the time they made it past that massive gate, I seriously doubted there would be anything left to find. I had no idea what we were dealing with, not one goddamn clue, but it was safe to say the police might be every bit out of their depth as we were. It was a risk I wasn't about to take. If this teenager was Lukas, I wasn't giving any advance warning that might lead to a second disappearance. I had one chance to pull this off . . . one chance to save him. I wasn't going to blow it.

Not this time.

Grimly, I took another look at the place. Normally the resources needed for a place the likes of the one before me would've made me think government, but Saul had already discounted that. They had to be private, but that didn't tell me a damn thing about who they were and what they were doing. Regardless, sitting spinning my wheels trying to figure it out wasn't going to get me any closer to getting inside the walls. What we needed was a good measure of boldness and a shitload of luck. And there was no time like the present to get started. Doing a little slithering of my own, I headed down the slope for an up close and personal look at the walls of Jericho.

The walls didn't fall that night. They didn't quake; hell, they didn't even shiver, but at least we'd taken stock of what we were up against. That was something, right? I knew because as we had walked back to the car, Saul kept telling me so—repeatedly. I think he was concerned that I might have a psychotic break and try to scale the wall with my bare hands. Maybe it was an exaggeration, but truthfully he wasn't far off the mark. All those years. I clenched the steering wheel until my knuckles blanched bone white. All those years, and the best I could manage was slinking around in the dark. Lukas was there; he was right there. But he might as well have been on the moon . . . distant and unreachable . . . solitary and untouched . . . untouched. One could dream anyway. Jesus.

I rested my forehead on the wheel, exhaled once, twice, then straightened. "So, daylight surveillance tomorrow?" I asked mildly. The calm was hard won, as I tucked every bit of despair, frustration, and rage into a mental box and closed the lid tight. That box had been with me a long time now. Born on a windswept beach, whelped on the blood and pain of child and horse, this box had teeth. Considering what I fed it, it needed them.

The car in which Saul and I sat was a good two miles from the compound; a safe distance we'd thought, and so far we'd been right. The whites of his eyes glimmered in the darkness as he considered his answer. Fiddling with the volume control of the silent radio, he finally sighed and leaned back in his seat with a snort of self-disgust. "What the hell was I thinking? There is not enough money in the world for this cluster fuck." Jerking impatiently at the seat belt, he fastened it, then drummed the

dashboard with his fingers. "You and your stupid questions. I didn't have a brother. I had a sister. Rosemary.
Rosemary and Thyme, only she didn't have a lot of time.
We grew up poor as hell." He rubbed his face. "I grew
up anyway. We shared one room. I made her teddy bears
out of old clothes. Ripped them to pieces and tied them
in knots. They didn't look anything like a damn bear,
but . . . she was little. She didn't know differently and she
loved them. Loved me. You take that for granted when
you're a kid." He looked out the window at the night.
"She died of meningitis when she was five. Our parents
were useless. They didn't care or just assumed she'd get
better. They wouldn't even stay with her in the hospital.
I did. It was my hand she held when she was sick. It was
my hand she held when she died."

And he didn't have to look for her, because he knew
where she was . . . which plot of grass she lay under. Fuck.
At least I'd had some hope all these years, not much, but
Saul had nothing. I wanted to tell him he didn't have to
come, but the cold, hard truth was if he didn't, Lukas
might end up like Rosemary . . . or lost again. And Saul,
money or no money, Saul with his Rosemary living only
in his shadow and in his memories couldn't let that
happen.

Resigned himself to his fate, he went on. "So, tomorrow it is. You bring the sunblock; I'll bring the strippers
and margaritas. It'll be a party."

It'd be a festival, all right—no lights, no music, no
dancing. But if we managed to walk away unshot, I'd
still consider it nothing but gravy.

Chapter 6

It was six days before we spotted it—our in. Six miserably endless days. Hope, determined but no fool, had taken to lying low, leaving me with nothing but a frozen and empty calm. I still did my job, more or less, on the days I absolutely couldn't weasel my way out of it. It wasn't as if I had personal days coming to me in my line of work. Fortunately, nothing too annoying reared its head. With my level of distraction, it was doubtful I could've foiled a hit man any more clever than your average third grade delinquent. But now it was suddenly over. The walls hadn't tumbled, but they had opened up. It was a tiny hole, the fleetest windows of opportunity, but it was there—one minute chink in the armor.

It was all we needed.

Ever dug a pit before dawn, covered yourself with the sandy soil, and lain in it until dusk? Ever had sand mites set up camp in places a scrub brush couldn't touch? Ever burrowed down in your homemade grave while large men with even larger guns prowled less than a hundred feet away? I wouldn't recommend it. Using stiff and knotted muscles, I kept watch through miniature binoculars, and hoped my bladder wouldn't swell to exploding over the long hours. I'd done it three days in a row while Saul had pulled the previous watches. He hadn't enjoyed it any more than I did. From the bitching and moaning, he seemed to doubt he'd ever be able to satisfy any woman again, much less his flavor of the week. Apparently the stallion wasn't so much running now as limping pathetically.

It was nearly seven p.m. on the sixth day that I received some genuine joy. And it was just that, a heat that unfurled at the base of my brain and traveled as tiny jolts of electricity throughout my body. I could all but feel the warm fingers that squeezed my heart into a heavy, racing thump. This is it, it whispered. This is what you've been waiting for. Watch and see.

A food delivery truck usually wouldn't make such late stops, but this one did. And it was expected. Four men were waiting at the gate nearly fifteen minutes before it pulled up. Big men with short haircuts in identical khaki pants and black T-shirts that labeled them guards in all but the name tags. They were duly efficient and strictly professional with no laughing or unnecessary talking among them. One of them opened the back. It was a small truck, panel sized. The amount of food it could haul wouldn't hold the personnel required to run a setup like this for any more than seven days. That indicated a pattern, a delivery once a week and hopefully on the same day.

After checking out the inside of the truck, the guards waved it on through and closed the gate behind it. Twenty minutes later it returned. This time in addition to checking the back, the guards ran metal poles topped with mirrors along the undercarriage. That was odd, damn odd. They seemed concerned someone might get in, but a helluva lot more so that someone might get out. The place was shaping up more and more like a prison the longer the surveillance dragged on. The kids inside might be the toughest little monkeys outside *Lord of the Flies*, but this place was less like juvie and more like Alcatraz—hard to get into and impossible to get out of. I could feel the smile that curled my lips. It was savagely triumphant even if it tasted of grit and the blood of an abraded lip.

Difficult to get into maybe. Impossible to get out of? Not anymore.

Chapter 7

"Where you going, Stef?"

It was a question I'd heard a hundred times before. You could search the world, any country or culture, and it was a good bet you'd hear the same words or a version of them anyway. It was the siren call of little brothers far and wide. Lukas, for all that he was a great kid, was no different there. Rolling my eyes with all the long suffer-ance I could scrape up, I stuffed another pair of wadded-up jeans into the duffel bag resting on my bed. "Football camp, runt. Remember?"

"No, you never said." The corner of his mouth plunged down and a stubborn glint bloomed in his bicolored eyes. "You didn't. I would remember."

I thought it was more a matter of his not wanting to remember that led to his sudden amnesia. It was easy enough to understand even wrestling against the self-centered nature that was a biological by-product of being a teenager. It wasn't as if we could simply run out the front door, grab our bikes and our buddies, and race off down your typical neighborhood street. This wasn't a typical neighborhood, and we weren't your typical kids. Those kids didn't have "friends of the family" fer-rying them back and forth to a private school exclusive enough to put a Kennedy on the waiting list. Those kids lived far from our stretch of beach, and if I thought they were the lucky ones, I kept it to myself. Our father wasn't much on ungrateful children and had a spearing gaze that had even the smartest mouth snapping shut instantly. His brown eyes were mine, but I'd not seen any mirror reflect my irises paled to an ice-covered muddy pond. It might be a talent that came with age or it could come from something else entirely . . . something that I wasn't sure I wanted to think about, not even at the ripe old age of fourteen.

I knew what Lukas was feeling. I'd felt it myself. It was easy to get lonely. There were only so many school activities you could do and only so many times a week Anatoly was willing to have us driven to friends' houses. At the end of the day it came down to Lukas and me. With seven years' difference between us, we didn't have much in common. Video games and riding lessons; there wasn't much more. That was all right; it was enough. Never mind that Lukas read encyclopedias as if they were comic books and I read whatever I was forced to for English class . . . or porn if I could sneak it. And it didn't matter that he wanted to grow up to be a doctor or a chemist while, despite my father's amused disdain, I still had crazy thoughts about the police academy.

All the differences between us didn't matter a damn. We were all each other had. If it were the other way around and Lukas was off to camp, I'd miss the little shit. I'd die before I'd admit it, yeah, but I would miss him. Tugging at his olive green T-shirt, I pulled him down into a sitting position on the bed. "It's just two weeks." I might as well have said two years for the stricken look he gave me. Two weeks was forever when you were seven, and when you were a lonely seven, eternity wasn't just a concept. It was a cold, hard reality. "You want me to write?"

"Would you?" He seized on the offer immediately, his face brightening to a sunny glow.

Yeah, that wouldn't sentence me to two weeks of endless wedgies—writing my kid brother faithfully like the biggest dork on the planet. Swallowing a sigh, I managed to do the almost impossible and leapfrog a nicely

healthy egocentric core. "Every day. How 'bout that?"
Hooking an arm around a small, sturdy neck, I rubbed
my knuckles lightly across his head in the ever-classic
noogie.

He yelped, struggled, then collapsed laughing to rest
against my side. When he regained his breath and qui-
eted, he repeated the vow fervently, "Every day." Twisting his head, he looked up at me. He was close enough
that I could count the freckles on his nose, a gift from
our mom. "You won't forget? Like you forgot the Cap-
tain Crunch was mine? Like you forgot me at David Fe-
dorov's birthday party?"

Shrewd pup; his memory worked just fine when he
wanted it to. That had been two years ago and I *had* forgotten him. It had been for only a half hour, but it had
been a pretty scary half hour for a five-year-old roaming
around lost in a house bigger than the governor's mansion. We'd all trooped outside after cake for volleyball
and swimming, and it had never crossed my mind Lukas
had disappeared into the bathroom only minutes before. The housekeeper found him later sitting forlornly
on the sweeping stairs and led him out to the rest of the
party. He hadn't been mad. Lukas never got mad at his
oh-so-amazing older brother, but he hadn't forgotten
that *I* once had.

"Elephants have nothing on you, do they?" I rested
my chin on his head. "I won't forget, kiddo." Screw the
guys at camp. Let them make fun all they want. "I won't
forget you again. Promise." I meant it too, with an unshakable resolution I couldn't have dreamed would
have to last so long.

So damn long.

I couldn't say what brought that particular memory
to mind, but it wasn't surprising that my mind was boiling with every moment that I could recall of a seven-
year-old boy's life. It was just too bad for the guy whose
throat was under my shoe that the flash of guilt storm-
ing through my brain happened right then. It certainly

didn't put me in a very happy or forgiving frame of mind. It was a piece-of-shit world that took what should've been sweet nostalgia and turned it into nothing more than bitter regret. I had a feeling a small portion of that regret was about to be passed on.

Leaning a fraction harder, I let gravity take my weight until the distressed squawking died out beneath me. "Dipping into the till, Vasily." I shook my head, bored. "You think I have nothing better to do than kick your *preklag*?"

Normally this wasn't my job, punishing the stupid. I was a bodyguard, not random muscle, and I wasn't too wild about this new detour in my career path. No matter how temporary, this was not what I wanted to do. Maybe none of it was. What had once seemed as inevitable as the tide now seemed nothing short of criminal insanity. Everyone was born with a soul; when had I decided to throw mine away?

It didn't matter because I knew exactly when I was getting it back—two more days. Two more days and I wouldn't be the person I had been, but I would be better than I was now. It wasn't saying much, I realized with a dark twist of my lips, but it was better than nothing. I'd lived ten years with the nothing, and I had few illusions there was worse than that.

"How much did you take, *sika*?" The demand was harsh, the voice itself cut glass and shattered ice. It was my father's voice, clearly . . . unmistakably. And yet it managed to find its way from my mouth with a natural ease.

"Perhaps our dear friend Vasily would be more forthcoming with a crushed testicle." Konstantin crossed his legs, tugging carefully at the crease of his elegant slacks. "Or two." He was balanced on a barstool with the grace of a much younger man. With one arm resting along the polished wood and glass counter, he tapped his index finger imperiously against its surface. "Black tea, sugar and milk." Our beloved leader had a trace of a sweet tooth and preferred his tea milky and as cloying as honey in contrast to the strong Cuban coffee he favored. With shaking hands, the guy behind the bar scrambled to obey.

The restaurant belonged to the man on the floor, Vasily Bormiroff, who was soon to be a eunuch if Gurov had his way. Correction—the restaurant belonged to Vasily in name only. In reality, the Samovar, as with so many other businesses, existed to launder money for the organization. When some of that money went missing, it was taken personally. Poor doomed Bormiroff; he must have thought himself pretty damn clever, taking only a little here and a little there. He wasn't clever; he was a moron. Even a wayward penny would have snagged Konstantin's eye. Vasily was nothing but a hen in a fox house and a hen that was well and truly caught.

It was my bad luck that I was snared just as thoroughly with him. Not by virtue of the money, no. Thou shalt not steal was an easy commandment to obey when the Lord's wrath was so much more immediate. I preferred my balls unsmited; too bad it hadn't been so simple a decision for Vasily. And because it had not, I was very likely going to have to do something I would regret. Removing my foot from his neck to place it on his crotch, I thought Vasily might accept the regret happily if he could trade places with me. His mouth hung open as he gasped wetly for breath. Just as moist, his eyes were the apprehensive velvet brown of a dog caught pissing on the carpet.

Yeah, a bad, bad boy, but he wasn't escaping this with a swat on the muzzle. "The money," I prompted, applying pressure. Up until then Vasily had been playing dumb, an act at which he excelled with true Oscar quality. As his opportunities for children began to dissipate beneath my heel, he abruptly decided owning up to it and taking his medicine was the best way to go. Once he began to talk, he couldn't spill the location of his ill-gotten gains fast enough.

"Please . . . please, Mr. Gurov. Please. Sorry, so sorry. Never happen again, swear. I swear." Still pinned to the floor, Bormiroff babbled on in that vein for some time as Konstantin drank his tea, undisturbed by the pleas or tears. Seeing a grown man cry from pure terror wasn't enough to spoil a good cuppa. It might even add to the pleasure, if I correctly read the glitter behind the older man's wire rim glasses.

"Yes, Vasily, my friend, I believe you. It truly shall never happen again." Carefully patting his lips with a linen napkin, Konstantin stood and removed his glasses to tuck them away beneath his suit jacket. "Who knew you possessed a knowledge of the future to such an astounding degree?"

It was coming. It was coming and there didn't seem to be a damn thing I could do about it. I felt my mouth go dry and my ears ring lightly as the air in the room went dead. But as stagnant as the atmosphere was, it still carried Gurov's next words with uncanny clarity. Simple and innocuous, a casual bystander wouldn't have guessed them for the death sentence they were.

"Stefan, we shall take a taxi."

Implied was that the car was at my disposal for a disposal. With that he was gone, not a glance spared for the convulsively trembling man on the floor. In his mind, Vasily no longer existed except as a trunk accessory to be sandwiched between the spare tire and the jack. Trailing behind Gurov, Sevastian gave me a wink and a puckered smack of his lips. A bastard by any definition of the word, he was doing my customary job today, and he delighted in seeing me taking his. He and others thought I was overly fastidious about the wet work . . . that I didn't like to get my hands dirty. Shaved head gleaming, thick lips curled in a gloat, he couldn't wait to see my cherry popped because, frankly, he didn't think I had the stomach for it.

I was beginning to think he was right.

The sharp smell of ammonia hit the air and I lifted my foot with a grimace. "Jesus, Vasily." As I wiped the sole of my shoe on threadbare carpet, his hand moved to cover the now-wet crotch of his pants. Shame and despair had twisted his face into something primitive and unrecognizable. A Neanderthal watching a tornado form out of the sky above him would've worn a similar look: terror, disbelief, and a crushing realization of his own mortality.

"Don't." The incoherent prattling had stopped as Vasily's face went putty gray. His chest hitched as the air whistled through his stiffened throat. His brain had locked down along with the rest of his body. He had one word and one word only left available to him, and he said it again with the voice of an aged and brittle rubber band stretched long past its breaking point. "Don't."

Goddamnit. I was fucked, and I was fucked but good. If I didn't take out this embezzler, Konstantin would make sure I suffered what should've been Vasily's fate and most likely before the sun went down. Only two more days and this shit storm had to come now. It was enough to make you believe in God, because random fate simply didn't have the poisonous ingenuity for something this nasty.

Reaching down, I took a fistful of his shirt and pulled him upright. His legs gave out immediately, the muscle tone but a distant memory. Out of the corner of my eye I could see the white and staring face of the bartender. I ignored him; he was just another piece of the furniture. He belonged to Gurov the same as the restaurant did, and the possibility of his causing any trouble was nil. Giving Bormiriff a brisk shake in an effort to restart his engine, I ordered not unsympathetically, "Stand up, Vasily." He tried; I have to give him that. He did try. Unsteady as a newborn foal, he did his best to straighten his traitorous limbs beneath him. After several seconds in which my grip was the only thing holding him up, he managed to stay up with only a little help.

"Good, Vasily. One foot in front of the other." Heavy hand on his shoulder, I steered him toward the back exit. He nearly fell again as he realized we were headed toward the back alley, but I stabilized him and kept him moving. In the surrounding hush his choked wheezing was the only sound to be heard. He was walking to his death, staggering really, but the end result was the same. He knew it. I knew it. What could fill that silence? What the hell could you possibly say?

"I have a brother," I stated in soft contemplation as his shoulder spasmed beneath my steadying grasp. "Did you know?" Of course the poor bastard didn't know. All he knew of me was my role as Konstantin's shadow. It didn't matter. I wasn't talking to him. "His name's Lukas, after our grandfather." I pushed at the exit, paying little attention to the buzzing alarm. Passing out of the gloom into a brilliantly sunny Miami morning, I continued with a numb tongue that was flying solo and out of control. "He needs me, Vasily. He needs me alive. Can you understand that?"

From the gasping sobs that vibrated his frame and had him dropping to his hands and knees on the asphalt, I had to assume he didn't. I couldn't blame him; I don't think I would've understood either. He was crawling away from me now, the pathetic, terrified son of a bitch, over pavement littered with broken glass that tore at his palms. I could see the blood in a scarlet handprint on a discarded fast-food bag.

"Vasily." I didn't remember drawing my gun, but the crosshatched rubber of the grip filled my hand as cool plastic teased my trigger finger. It was the only thing I could feel. My arms, legs, even my face, felt numb and lifeless, but my palm felt the imprint of the gun as if it were a brand, red-hot and marking me for life. "Be still," I said gently. "It's over."

And it was over. Once I put him down, it would be

all over . . . for the both of us. But Lukas would live. Lukas would be free. Whether that made it worthwhile depended on your point of view. I raised the 9 mm. It was unfortunate for Vasily that his point of view no longer counted.

Chapter 8

Saul leaned loose and relaxed against the rear bumper and watched as I cleaned the trunk with Formula 409. He was the second person to watch me do it. The first had been Sevastian, who'd growled low in this thick throat when I'd shoved a handful of crimson-stained rags stuffed into a plastic grocery bag at him with the emotionless command to dump them. Profoundly disappointed that he couldn't report back to Konstantin any news that would've permanently removed me from sight, he'd left me in the condo garage with a wad of spit beside my shoe. Less than five minutes later Saul showed up with take-out sweet and sour tofu that included a sauce the unhappy scarlet of fresh blood.

It was not one of my better days.

Raising curious eyebrows, Saul bounced a fortune cookie in his hand as I continued to scrub. "Should I even ask?"

"No," I answered shortly in a tone that had made lesser men think twice. Saul, unfortunately, was not a lesser man.

"So much for scintillating conversation," he said dryly. Cracking open the cookie, he extracted the small slip of paper and gave an audible growl. "Do you believe this shit? It's a hard sell for some time-share scheme. It's not bad enough we get this crap in bathroom stalls. Now they're screwing with our cookies." At any other time his outrage would've been amusing, but not too much was tickling my funny bone today.

"You want a fortune? Here's your fortune." I slammed down the lid of the trunk. "Life is short, so get to the goddamn point."

His eyes dropped to the wad of paper towels clenched in my fist. I'd cleaned up most of the blood with the ones I'd pawned off on Sevastian, but there was still a faint splotch of red fading to wet pink on the one I held now. A ripple of unease passed through the mobile face before disappearing under a smooth mask. Saul had a definite nodding acquaintance with violence himself, but the implications here . . . a bloody trunk . . . might be more than even he cared to consider. "How about we go upstairs and eat while we talk? Having a picnic in an underground garage isn't my idea of class."

Giving his green, blue, and purple kaleidoscope silk shirt a disparaging glance, I drawled, "Yeah, you're all about class." I shrugged and led the way to the elevator. Upstairs I let us into my place, tossed the paper towels in the garbage, and washed my hands. As the warm water washed over my skin, I let it also carry the morning's events with it. I couldn't afford to be distracted. If that meant mentally burying the vision and consequences of what I'd done, that's what I would do. It wasn't as if they wouldn't be in good company. I might have to look into a bigger box. It was getting tight in there.

"Bring me a beer, would you?" Saul called from the living room.

Seconds later I tossed him a cold bottle with a jaundiced growl. "Don't you hate it when your ass gets superglued to the couch? Lazy bastard."

He caught the bottle and disregarded the barb with aplomb. "Hope you can use chopsticks."

He couldn't have told me that while I was still in the kitchen with the forks. I had many skills, some of which involved pointed objects, but wielding chopsticks wasn't one of them. It didn't matter. Hunger was the last thing on my mind at the moment. "It's all yours, Skoczinsky. Eat up."

"Your loss." He put his feet up on the coffee table and opened a carton of rice. "Don't come crying to me that you didn't get your daily dose of MSG."

I knew better than to think I could go toe-to-toe with the perpetual motion machine that was Saul's mouth. "Did you get all the equipment?" I didn't sit, instead walking over to the window to take a look at a view with which I was already intimately familiar.

"Everything but the weapons. You said you would handle that."

We'd been planning for five days now. In that time I'd managed to gather enough guns to give the NRA an orgasm. I'd also obtained Tasers, tear gas, and stun grenades, all police quality. My friends of the semiofficial capacity weren't exactly in high places, but they didn't have to be to get their hands on what I needed. "I took care of it."

"Sure you got enough?"

The side of my mouth crooked. "You'd better bring a back brace."

Saul had no complaints. He liked his skin in one piece and keeping it that way was of paramount importance in the Skoczinsky scheme of things. "I'll bring a wheelbarrow if I have to." Popping a clump of steamed rice into his mouth, he chewed and swallowed. "Have you given thought to what the hell you're going to do if we manage to pull him out of that place?"

Had I given it thought? I'd given it nothing but. I could go to the police. None of my past indiscretions were known, not even today's. What a versatile word, indiscretion . . . and how amazing the amount of dark and ugly territory it could cover. Most of that territory was invisible to the cops, and that meant I could take Lukas to the nearest station and scream for help like any other law-abiding citizen. And within an hour I'd be yelling again as those beefy guys in khakis dragged us back to the compound. Not government, but the government ties we so strongly suspected could come into play to pinpoint us in a heartbeat. The police were out of the question; probably the FBI as well. Call me suspicious and paranoid. It was better than being called dead.

My best bet was to go underground. Konstantin wouldn't be exactly thrilled to have me use the family network as a place to hide, but he would go along with it. It wouldn't be for my sake so much as a gesture for Anatoly. For protecting his ally's long-lost son, he could and would expect to be rewarded. Whether in measures of money or power, Gurov would come out far ahead of the game. I had never known him not to.

Taking this to my father now wasn't an option I'd wasted any time entertaining. At best he'd think me crazy; at worst he'd interfere. Aside from that, the possibility of finding Anatoly could take more time than I had. But once I had Lukas and could prove he was my brother, then I could go to my father. Out of sight within the family, hopefully I would have the leeway to track him down. Whoever ruled that armed structure might have the authorities on a choke chain, but fucking around with my less-than-easygoing pop was on par with sticking your dick in a shark's mouth and asking for a blow job. It just wasn't a good idea.

"Don't worry about it." I turned and watched as Saul broke into the second carton. Red sauce thickly coated the tofu clump and I shifted my gaze to over his shoulder. "If worse comes to worst, we'll crash at your place."

The disquiet evidenced in the sharp knitting of his eyebrows dissipated as he realized I wasn't serious. "Asshole," he grumbled around a mouthful of sweet and sour.

"Better you don't know anyway."

"Better for you, yeah," he countered cynically.

He was right. It was better for me. They shouldn't be able to hunt down either of us if we did our jobs correctly. But if by some bizarre twist they did find one of us, specifically Saul, I didn't want them to be able to get a scrap of information on my escape plan. With enough incentive anyone would talk. I knew the truth of that from personal experience seeing that today for an unforgettable time I had been the incentive.

Dumping the warm container on the coffee table with no care for the fine fake wood veneer, Saul appeared to have lost his appetite. "I put your money in my happy place. Funny. If anything, it made it less happy."

I knew he was worried about getting out of this alive. He would be an idiot if he weren't, and Saul was anything but an idiot. "Stay quick and smart, and you'll live to buy leather pants again."

"At least I'd look good in them. I can't say the same for your flat Russian ass," he sniped before finishing off half his beer in two long swallows. Saul's much-vaunted fashion sense came from the disco era, but it didn't seem to slow him down with waitresses who dreamed of one day making the big time: exotic nude masseuse. Who was I to say anything? If it worked, it worked. How it worked could remain a mystery. I was fine with that.

It went on that way for the majority of the night as we ran through the scenario again and again. Caustic quips and sarcastic swipes kept us from dwelling on what an incredible long shot this was . . . both for rescuing Lukas and maintaining a healthy pulse for ourselves. Near dawn, Saul dozed off, sprawled loose limbed and at ease across my sofa as if he owned it. I ended up at my computer desk, fiddling with the handle on the bottom drawer. After several minutes I gave in and pulled out the picture I'd received in the mail two weeks ago. Running a thumb lightly across the glass, I wiped away a nonexistent speck of dust.

"One more day, Lukasha," I promised, the whisper a bare breath of sound. "One more day."

Chapter 9

The key had been the delivery truck—a cursory search going in and a more detailed one coming out, all made on the inexplicable assumption that the true threat was behind the walls. I didn't know what lay at the core of that reasoning and I didn't care. What I did care about was stretching that loophole to the screaming point and beyond.

The large dead tree limb lying haphazardly across the road was the beginning of the stretching. There were many dead or dying trees in this area, but we'd decided against an entire tree. The driver might have been tempted to call for help in moving it. But one branch too big to carry but light enough to be dragged off if he put his back into it—that should do the trick.

With twilight falling just before seven this far into the year, the headlights of the truck were already on as it rolled past our hiding place. It was one week after I'd first spotted it—one week and right on time. There was the gentle squeal of brakes and a less gentle cursing floating out the window as the driver spotted the obstruction. A blond guy with a beer belly and hairstyle best left in the sixties, he climbed out of the cab. By the time he, with hands on hips, was studying the branch, Saul and I were on the move.

Dressed in black shirts, pants, gloves, and silk masks similar to a balaclava, we ran unseen to the back of the truck and slithered underneath. Fist-sized powerful magnets equipped with handles let us cling to the undercarriage as our combat-booted feet dug for purchase. Saul had come up with most of the more esoteric equipment with a flash of a brief and bitter line of a smile. "Connections of an ex-military life. Don't ask, don't tell," had been the beginning and end of his conversation on the subject.

As we silently hung there with arms straining, I could hear the driver puffing and swearing as he cleared the road. Then he was back in the truck and the asphalt began passing beneath us. The entire thing had taken less than five minutes, which was essential. If too much time passed, the guards would be suspicious and start to grill the driver, and that wouldn't do. As it stood now, this event barely registered with our blond, not especially bright Elvis and wasn't worth imprinting on an alcoholic brain cell, much less mentioning to the khaki crew.

The five miles passed and if we'd been walking rather than riding, it couldn't have passed any more slowly. By the time we reached the compound's gate, the muscles in my arms were howling in agony and I had a mild headache from the exhaust and the adrenaline. Turning my head, I could see the hyped glitter of Saul's eyes through the narrow opening of his mask. We were both feeling the rush, although neither one of us seemed to be enjoying it. I felt the truck jerk as the driver put it in park. Several pairs of big feet in leather sneakers approached as I heard the driver's side door being opened. This was it then.

"Open the back."

The voice was dispassionately professional, just a man doing his job. I hoped he did it precisely the way it had been done last week; otherwise we were stuck outside the gate with a couple of dead guys in tan pants, which was not the sign of a well-executed plan. Suddenly the truck's shifting on its tires as someone got a leg up on the bumper was followed by the sound of double doors in the back being opened. With a mouth dry and gritty as sandpaper, I waited for one of the inevitable thousand things that could go wrong. They could change their routine and look under the truck. Elvis could mention the unexpected stop a few miles back. There was no end to the shit that could befall us. Waiting was always the worst. Whether for ten seconds or ten years, it didn't matter. Waiting could shrivel the soul.

But despite my dark expectations, everything went like clockwork. It made me wonder if someone was paying attention up there or if they weren't and we'd slipped under the radar.

Within moments the rummaging was over, the doors were shut, and the feet were in retreat. I closed my eyes and forced the churning acid back down where it belonged, eating a hole in my stomach. Elvis settled back into his seat, lowering the chassy by several inches, shifted into drive, and we were inside—just like that. It couldn't have gone more perfectly if it had been scripted by fate itself.

The truck moved on at barely fifteen miles an hour for a short space until it pulled up next to a building; I could see the concrete base of the wall, plain and spare, in a dingy yellow artificial light. With the damn thing finally parked, I was able to unclench my fingers and with trembling arms let myself down to the ground. Every muscle in my body had taken on the consistency of overly boiled cabbage. Rolling over onto my stomach, I slid along the gravel to the edge of the undercarriage. I caught a glimpse of Elvis standing in an open door chatting up this place's version of the lunch lady. Improbably red hair, pear-shaped butt, and thick hose on thick legs, she didn't float my boat, but apparently she did something for Elvis. I didn't judge. I simply recognized the chance and took it.

Propelling myself on my elbows, I crept out from under the truck and lunged into the shadows. Saul was hard on my heels, so hard in fact that he nearly ran me over. With a healthy sense of self-survival combined with

those cutting-edge fashion skills of his, Saul was a true
Renaissance man. With the building wall gritty against
my back, I moved fast until I took a corner and passed
into a deeper darkness.

"And that, Smirnoff, is why I refuse to marry. Once
the ring is on, the ass immediately triples in size."

The disgusted hiss was a puff of air against my ear.
His comment on the mating habits of food servers and
ex–Kings of Rock and Roll couldn't have been heard
from more than five inches away, but it didn't stop me
from jabbing a warning elbow into Skoczinsky's ribs.
It had passed from full twilight into early night and
we were fairly well concealed by it, but there was no
need to press our luck. Moving on, we found a stairwell
framed by straggling bushes and concrete. It was thick
with grime and dirt, indicating it hadn't been used for
some time. Settling down into it, we prepared to wait
four or five hours until the place was tucked in for the
night. There might be a few khakis on patrol on the inside of the walls, but at least the other personnel, including the maligned lunch lady, would be asleep. It made
the process of breaking and entering a little less dangerous for us.

The hours passed. And that's about the best that
could be said, that they did pass. After ten years, you'd
think a few hours was something I could handle; that in
comparison it would be nothing—less than nothing; a
drop in an angry, churning ocean. But it wasn't. It was
ten years all over again.

Finally a hand on my shoulder brought me out of a
reverie of nothingness. "Time to go." With his voice tight
and controlled, Saul was all business now. He moved to
the metal door and went to work with a skill that had
me whistling low under my breath. Whatever branch of
the service Skoczinsky had served in, he hadn't spent
his time peeling potatoes. It took nearly forty minutes,
but he got us in, bypassing an alarm system I doubt I
would've detected and cutting the glass from the tiny

window set high on the door. After that it was a simple matter to manipulate a dead bolt with a long wire, and then we were in.

Out of the night and straight down the rabbit hole

It looked like a hospital operating room. There was the glitter of metal everywhere in the form of needles and probes, clamps and gurneys. Monitors upon monitors and trays of instruments put the finishing touches on the theme. And if that had been all in the room, it could've passed as a medical facility. But that wasn't all; that was only half the picture. Recessed security lighting showed computers on standby, softly humming in oddly comforting song. It wasn't one or two either, but an entire bank of them lining the wall. Screen after screen filled with a slowly rotating DNA strand shed a sickly green glow onto the shiny linoleum floor. That kind of tan and white checkerboard-patterned tile was cheap and easy to clean—especially of blood. I'd seen that theory proven true firsthand in the basement of Konstantin's bar. A bucket of a water and bleach mixture and a mop and it was as easy as that . . . except for the cracks.

Close to the operating table, I knelt down and pressed a gloved finger to the thin brown line that ran between the tile. This place wasn't just for looking pretty; they used it. Why was it I didn't believe they were performing tonsillectomies down here?

"This is one creepy motherfucking place."

I looked over at the whisper to see a child-sized hospital gown cascading from Saul's hand in a fall of pale turquoise. It was an oddly forlorn sight, that scrap of material. Despite its cleanliness—there wasn't a drop of anything on it, including blood—the sight of it made my stomach twist all the same. "Anything on the computers?" I asked, shifting my eyes to the safer target. I knew enough to surf the Net, but that was about the extent of my knowledge. On the other hand, Saul's business depended on his expertise with the technical as well as the physical.

Out of the corner of my eye I saw Saul shrug and move to take a seat at the nearest computer. Grunting at the spinning screen saver, he started typing. "Reminds me of biology class. Bacteria and fetal pigs; I've had better times," he said.

Then and now, I was assuming. Remaining silent as he worked, I explored the rest of the room. I was loath to call it an infirmary. People were meant to be healed in those types of rooms. I didn't see healing going on in this place. Along the far wall I found a massive refrigerator, easily the size of a restaurant walk-in model. But while the size might be similar, there was one immediately noticeable difference: the lock. This unit was sealed with a computerized pad that awaited a code key. Hissing in annoyance, I turned back to Saul. "Well?"

With some annoyance of his own, he slapped his hand on the side of the terminal. "It's locked up tighter than grandma's panties. I need either a password or a good week to work on it. Since we don't have either, I suggest we get moving."

It shouldn't have mattered, the impenetrable computer and tightly sealed refrigerator. It wasn't why we were here. I was here to retrieve Lukas, first, last and everything in between. Finding out who had taken him and why would be useful, damn useful, but we didn't have the time to spend on anything more than a quick and dirty search. We'd already done that now and it was time to move on. That didn't stop me from looking over my shoulder at the firefly glow of the computer monitors and thinking I was making a mistake walking away so quickly. That DNA molecule, boldly displayed, gnawed at me. What the hell were they doing here?

Saul's hand on my shoulder pushed me on through the next door. This one was locked as well, but from the inside . . . our side. I was able to handle that without resorting to Skoczinsky's felonious talents. From there we went upstairs to the first level. The level of illumination remained the same: shadowed gloom interspersed

with dim security lights near floor level. We had come
out into a long hall. There were doors scattered evenly
on either side and the floor was the same bland tile. Past
midnight, the place appeared deserted, but I decided it
still was time to bring my favorite boy out to play. Some
equated guns to women. That bald bastard Sevastian
called his Glock Lolita. Not only was he a bastard but a
pervert as well. I never saw weapons that way. The ability to do violence isn't exclusively linked to the male
gender, but I couldn't deny I thought we had a leg up on
it. I had never named my 9mm, but I did think of it as
male—ruthlessly, amorally, unapologetically male.

Jerking a thumb toward one end of the hall, Saul
drifted that way on silent feet with his own gun at the
ready. I took the other end and the strength it took to
hold the Steyr in my hand was only a fraction of what it
took to trigger that first door latch. Aside from the basement, the building, although sprawling, was only one
level. The children had to be here, if not in this hall then
in the next—or the next. What had been a dream for a
good portion of my life had become a reality just beyond my fingertips. Whatever I found here, for good or
for bad, was going to irrevocably change who I'd been. It
made opening that first door a little like dying.

The metal might have been cool to the touch, but I
felt nothing through my glove. Even without the shield-
ing material I don't think I would've felt anything but an
icy ghost of a sensation. My nerves, mental and physical,
had gone into hibernation for this excursion. It was the
only way to function, the only way to survive. And when
I opened that first door to see two sleeping boys with
coal black hair, I did survive. I survived, breathed in and
out like the living do, and then closed the door quietly to
move on to the next one.

Each room was equipped with two beds. Sometimes
both were filled with either boys or girls and sometimes
one would be empty—until I tried the fourth room. As
I pulled open the door there, someone was waiting for

me. Out of bed and just within reach of the doorway, a little girl looked up at me. She couldn't have been more than seven, eight at the most. Petite and dressed in plain white pajamas, she had a sweet, heart-shaped face and silver blond hair that was phantom pale in the low light. Innocent and lost, she belonged in a four-poster bed cuddling a furry teddy bear. She belonged with her mother and father, not here; not in this sterile and clinical prison. I clenched my jaw. Goddamnit. She wasn't my brother and could very well be a distraction that doomed us, but I couldn't stop myself. She wasn't mine and she wasn't Saul's Rosemary, but she was some-one's. Someone's heart was ripped out, their life ruined beyond repair because she had been taken. I holstered my gun and held out my hand to her. She didn't move, didn't cry out or scream, but only watched me with im-passively shadowed eyes. It was unnerving. What kid when faced with a gun-waving man dressed all in black wouldn't scream her lungs out?

Stripping off my glove, I tried again. Palm up, I let it lie unthreateningly between us with an inner patience I was far from feeling. "It's all right, sweetheart," I as-sured her softly. "Come with me. I'll take you home." She didn't blink at the words or move, but continued to study me with an assessment that was anything but childlike. It almost seemed to hold the cunning of an adult or . . . a wary animal. My hand began to grow cool, then cold, far colder than the temperature warranted. Confused, I pulled it back and turned it over. My nails were dark blue, the skin of my fingers blanched an un-natural white. What the fuck? When I looked back up, the door was shut once again. The girl was gone. Not much to my credit, I wasn't completely sorry.

Shaking my hand hard, I put the glove back on and gritted my teeth as the blood began to tingle fiercely back into my fingers. I had no idea what had happened and less time to think about it. Resolutely, I moved on to the next door.

I don't remember opening it.

I don't remember walking into the room. I only remember facing the boy sitting on the edge of his bed. Boy, young man, whatever you wanted to call him, he sat there wearing the same style unisex white pajamas and a face that bore only the faintest traces of curiosity. Without instruction from my conscious brain, my hand switched on a tiny penlight to see him more clearly. I stood, paralyzed, and looked—just looked. The line of the jaw and the slope of the nose were blurred by time. Ten years would change the map of anyone's face. But the eyes—they were the same. The colors, yes, but more than that; it was what lay behind the blue and green. It was Lukas, completely and utterly; the amazing directness, the clarity of spirit, the look of which I'd never forgotten.

They were my brother's eyes.

He had brown hair, I noticed dazedly. I hadn't expected that. I thought it would stay blond like our mother's. Medium length, it was a light chestnut with the occasional pale streak. He looked a little younger than the seventeen Saul had described and with a face as pale and tranquil as a snow-covered pond. He looked—my God—he looked like salvation.

"Lukas?" Raw and shaking, his name came out more a fractured sound than an actual word. It was less recognizable as letters strung together and more like a visceral grunt of pain. I tried again. "Lukas?"

His head tilted slightly and he corrected politely, "Michael." He didn't raise his hand to shield against my light but instead stared into it without hesitation as he repeated, "My name is Michael." Like the little girl, he didn't show any sign that he found any of this out of the ordinary. There was a man dressed all in black, armed and masked, and no one found that worth comment.

His voice was as his face, changed. The light tenor of childhood was gone, replaced by an adult's deeper tone. "Is this a test?"

I was still struggling to process the different name. It made comprehending his question difficult, perhaps impossible. I didn't even try. "Test? Lukas, it's me, Stefan. Your brother." It had been ten years, more than half of his life. In the back of my mind the realization that he might not know me had been present, but present and acceptable were two entirely different beasts. Emotional trauma or the physical trauma of his head injury when he had been kidnapped, the reasons for his memory loss were something I didn't have the time for now. "I'm your brother," I repeated.

I saw his confusion. It was suppressed and muted, but it was there. He opened his mouth, then closed it again without speaking. I used the opportunity to push on and say to crushingly familiar eyes, "I'm here to take you home."

As I talked, I shook like Vasily had when he had begged for his life. It was appropriate, because now I was begging for mine. It was easy to forgive myself the adrenaline and long-buried emotions wreaking havoc within, and when the moment of truth came, the shaking stopped. That moment happened when the alarm went off.

"Shit."

It was a silent alarm, at least in this section of the building. The only evidence that our break-in had been noticed was the sudden blinking of the security lights. It was enough to chill my blood; I didn't need a wailing siren or rotating red beacon. The simple strobing of the strips of fluorescence near the floor brought the catastrophe home clearly enough. Swearing again, I lunged over to the bed and circled my fingers around Lukas's wrist.

"Lukas, we have to go." I yanked at his arm, pulling him to his feet.

"Go?" he echoed with eerie calm. "Go where?"

"Right now out of here is good enough for me." Towing him along unresisting behind me, I ran into the hall and scanned it hurriedly for Saul. Even in the midst of it, the running and the alarms, I marveled at the solid feel of his flesh within my grip. For so long he had been a ghost that I could barely believe he was real and true to the touch.

"Smirnoff, haul ass!"

I whipped my head around to see Saul waving frantically by the same door through which we'd made our entrance, not using my real name, which I appreciated. Seeing that I'd spotted him, he wasted no time in beginning his escape. Obviously devil take the hindmost wasn't a phrase he took lightly. Following his lead, I ran toward the door. Lukas had been keeping up without difficulty until he saw our destination. He didn't stop or try to pull away, but he definitely slowed. Considering what lay below, I didn't blame him. "It's all right," I reassured him quickly as I fumbled at my belt. "We're just passing through that medical torture chamber downstairs. We're not sticking around."

It was hard to tell with only the fast glance I could allow him and his strangely unemotional façade, but I thought he seemed relieved. My attention was jerked away as I saw two men, the ever-present khaki brigade, enter the other end of the hall. Shoving Lukas before me when we reached the door to the basement, I whirled and tossed the grenade I'd taken from my belt. It was a standard smoke one. I had tear gas as well, but I was hesitant to use it so close to the other kids. As heavy white smoke billowed and blocked the men from view, there was the sharp bark of guns being fired. I didn't wait to see how good their aim was in whiteout conditions. Diving through the door after Lukas, I slammed it behind me and rushed headlong down the stairs. I caught up with him halfway down and took a handful of his pajama top to hurry him along.

He didn't complain or protest. He barely reacted at all, as obedient as a programmed robot. I didn't like it. It was unnatural, wrong, but as with other things, I didn't have the luxury of thinking about it right then. Staying alive and getting my brother out of this place made up my entire to-do list at the moment. Hitting the bottom, I saw Saul facing us several feet away. He had double handfuls of the more serious firepower: tear gas and stun grenades. "Move your shit," he snapped.

My shit and I complied with alacrity and took Lukas past the medical equipment and computers and out into the night air. The sound of hissing gas and ear-ringing explosions followed us as Saul heaved his grenades up the stairwell. I knew he would be pushing us out of the way from behind like a fullback if we didn't get going, and I charged up the concrete stairs with Lukas like a runaway train. I didn't even break stride with the first man I shot. The second one, unfortunately, didn't go down quite as easily.

Halfway across the pseudo–hospital room I'd once again drawn my gun. I'd known from the beginning that I would do what was necessary to free Lukas, no matter the cost. But I had thought I might hesitate when it came to pulling the trigger, if only for a second. I had thought I would pause before sending a bullet into a warm, living son of Man.

I didn't.

The first one went down with lead in the stomach. That's the way you were taught to shoot a person. Aim for the biggest target; aim for the torso. The police learned that, as did the rest of us who had less-admirable excuses for our violence. Whatever my justifications, I was already firing again as the first man hit the ground and his gun went flying. His partner, beefy and broad shouldered, was quicker on his feet. He twisted and dodged for cover toward the corner of the building. I was lucky to get one in his thigh and luckier that the bullet he squeezed off in our direction was only an evil buzz past my ear.

Giving Lukas a hard shove, I commanded, "Run!" As before, he did as he was told, without question. From behind us came another detonation, a much larger one than before. Saul had brought the genuine explosives into play. No one would be coming after us through the basement, because by now it was nothing more than a smoking ruin.

I kept just behind my brother as we ran. Saul, who passed us within seconds, kept ahead by a few feet. The son of a bitch could run like the wind, whatever his crappy taste in shirts. As for taste, no one could fault him his preference in weapons, an MP5 submachine gun. Granted, I was the one who had scored it among many others, but he'd had the good sense to choose it. And the good sense to use it.

Reading hard-core mysteries these days, I'd heard the clichéd description hail of bullets countless times. I'd scoffed at it then and I cursed it now. It wasn't hail. It was a fatal swarm of enraged hornets, whose slightest touch would kill and whose speed couldn't be captured by the eye. They flew both ways, those hornets, but it didn't make me feel any better. As one of the two guards posted at the gate began firing in our direction, I tackled Lukas to the ground. The air burst from his lungs in an audible grunt as I landed on top of him, but he didn't move beneath me as I returned the fire. Saul had thrown himself down to do the same with much more effect than I was having with my handgun. One guard fled for his life and one didn't have a life left to worry about. As I was getting to my feet, I caught a whiff of shampoo and toothpaste from the still figure beneath me. It gave me such a staggering flood of homesickness for a time long gone that the free hand I used to urge Lukas up clenched on his shoulder a little harder than necessary. He didn't react or wince. His focus was elsewhere, eyes fixed on the downed guard as he murmured, "Just a test."

I ignored the incomprehensible words and, relaxing my grip as best I could, pushed him back into motion. Saul was already at the gate and opening it. Lukas and I rushed past to one of the vans Saul had described from the children's "field trip." Saul and I had thought about leaving a car down the road for our escape but dismissed the idea instantly. We'd never make it that far on foot without being caught. The best next thing we'd decided was to make use of the transportation available. Then we could drive to our getaway vehicles that would be less likely discovered farther from the compound.

Inside the van I went to work unscrewing the steering column. I'd not actually stolen too many cars. Considering how I'd grown up and my father's position in the hierarchy, that wasn't all that surprising. By the time I turned sixteen, I already had two cars waiting in the garage for me. The necessity had not been there, but you never knew when a little knowledge would get you out of a huge mess. So I kept my hand in because practice does make perfect. The proof of that came thirty seconds later when the van started. Over my shoulder Lukas was watching me work, still calm and still in a place I couldn't understand or touch. "Did you lose your key?"

"Something like that," I muttered. "Sit back, Lukas, and hang on."

"Michael," he said with the first hint of stubbornness I'd seen in him. He settled back into the seat behind mine. "My name is Michael." As much as it hurt that he didn't know himself, or me, I was paradoxically relieved to know he wasn't an empty machine. He was human and he could be reached. Physically I had him; with time, I would get him back mentally as well—but first things first.

Peeling out, I sent gravel spraying as the van tore its way toward the gate. It was swinging slowly open as Saul pelted over to the passenger door and yanked it open. Half in and half out, he turned and emptied the rest of his clip into the three other vans and two cars still parked behind us. Tires burst like overripe melons as punctured gas tanks released streams of acrid gasoline onto the ground. "Flare," he demanded.

With one hand on the wheel I used the other to pull a group of two flares from my belt and slapped them against his palm. The resulting inferno was more than big enough to roast a few marshmallows. The explosion and flesh-melting orange flames lit up the sky sunrise bright as we passed through the gate. "Boom." Saul grinned at me as he slid into the seat and slammed the door. I couldn't see his mouth through the mask, but I didn't need to. It could be heard as easily as seen. I was on the verge of giving my own triumphant grin in return when there was another boom, this one from the back of the van. I turned to see that the doors had been yanked open. I also got a look at who'd opened them, whose feet had hit the van floor hard enough to imitate a silencer-muffled gunshot.

This man wasn't wearing khakis. He wasn't wearing anything but black, which blended so well into the darkness of his skin that he appeared nude. He hung in the open space, primeval and preternatural as a gargoyle rising from the sluggish waters of Genesis. Close-shaved hair was a pelt reflecting ambient light while the black eyes sucked it in. Tall and broad, he was a Greek statue carved in onyx . . . part myth, part monster. Muscles writhed as he stretched out a hand and spoke. And just like that he became a man. "Michael." The baritone was deep enough to vibrate bone. "Take my hand, boy."

The hand hung curved in a frozen position. Although it was the same color as the man's skin, it looked somehow off nonetheless. But it was less important than what was in his other hand. It was a gun. At the moment he couldn't use it because he was bracing himself with the fist curled around its grip. I didn't plan on giving him time to steady himself enough to put that gun into play, not when I could beat him to it. "Lukas, stay put," I rapped. It wasn't necessary. As amiably cooperative as he was with my orders, he was less inclined to listen to this guy. He didn't move as I stretched my arm back, steadying my elbow on his shoulder. It was a shoulder that had gone trembling and tense as iron. Before I could fire, the van chose that moment to remind me why "eyes on the road" had become the well-known adage it was.

Careening off the road, I cursed and turned my attention back to driving. The bullet that burned the skin of my jaw before shattering the windshield didn't help matters. "Saul, get that son of a bitch!" In the rearview mirror I could see that he was all the way in the van now, half naked and as unconcerned as if he'd been wearing body armor. His gun was pointed at the back of my head as Lukas slid over to press up against the window. My brother didn't seem to like this man any more than I did. "Saul . . ."

The prongs of the Taser imbedded themselves in the ebony chest before I had a chance to get another word out. As the current hit, the three hundred thousand volts dropped our unwanted visitor instantly. His gun discharged and blew a hole in the metal ceiling as he fell balanced precariously on the back edge. I took the van over one more hard bump and the man was gone, tumbling slack and limp out of the back. "Should've saved a bullet for that asshole," Saul muttered. He dropped the Taser on the floor and clambered into the back to pull the doors shut. "Who'd he think he was? Superman? Jesus." On the way back to the passenger side seat he paused to study Lukas. "You doing okay, kid?"

In my peripheral vision I saw the brown head tilt until it rested against the window glass as Lukas said bleakly, "I failed the test, didn't I?"

I shook my head as Saul's gaze slid my way. I had no idea and this wasn't the time to delve into it. Shrugging philosophically, Skoczinsky patted the white-covered shoulder. "Hang in there, buddy. We're here to help you." Settling back into his seat and replacing the empty clip in his MP5, he murmured, "Too bad we couldn't do the same for the others."

"We didn't have a choice." It was true, but it tasted bitter coming out of my mouth. It was a surgical strike, in and out, and the only chance we'd had. Trying to shepherd a group of children out would've taken more than twice the time and double the firefight. That was assuming the kids all cooperated, and one little girl came instantly to mind to refute that theory. My hand still vaguely ached as I did my best not to think about the weirdness of that. If we'd stayed any longer, we would've faced at least triple the force and against that all our fun little toys might not have meant squat. "Make the call."

After fastening his seat belt, Saul used a cell phone, disposable, paid for with cash, and untraceable to us, to call 911. Reporting a fire in a building full of children, he gave the address and then tossed the phone out of the open window. It was the quickest way to get a whole lot of people to the compound and fast, but I still had my doubts there would be a child left there to find. It would be fifteen minutes, maybe twenty, before the fire trucks would arrive this far out—not long, but I had the dark feeling it would be long enough for the people running that place.

"No one's behind us yet, but it won't be long." Saul twisted his neck to watch out the back window. "Can't this piece of shit go any faster?"

"Maybe if we lightened the load by dumping your bony ass." Pessimistically, I put more pressure on the gas pedal and was rewarded by a slight surge of the engine and rattle of the van body. With one hand on the steering wheel, I used the other to skim off my mask. "Burn that, would you? It has a nice helping of my DNA on it." I touched a finger to the still-wet blood on my jaw. Luckily it was the side of my face that was already scarred. Not much more damage could be done there. "Chances are they'll guess who I am soon enough, but better safe than sorry." If they were the ones who had originally taken Lukas, they were bound to know something of his family. And who else besides his family would come looking for him?

Fishing for his lighter, Saul set the mask on fire and

let it slip out of the window to follow the cell phone. It was a small comet trailing sparks as it was swallowed by the night. As he pressed the button to raise the window, I looked into the mirror again to see Lukas tilting his head to get a look at my face. The fleeting warmth I felt at the first sign of normal curiosity in him melted to nothingness as I saw the complete lack of recognition in his eyes. I don't know what I'd expected. He had no memory of his own name. Seeing my face so changed from my fourteen-year-old self wasn't likely to trigger a recollection, but . . . shit, hope springs eternal.

Turning my head, I said lightly to him, "Don't worry, Lukas. You always were the pretty one in the family."

He didn't return my forced smile but only leaned back in his seat as Saul sniped, "Speak for yourself. If pretty's in this van, he's sitting right here. Clooney's got nothing on me."

The chuckle that hung like an aborted sneeze in the back of my throat was unexpected. There were no two ways about it; I was going to miss Saul. Hurtling down the road in a shot-up van with a brother who didn't know me from Adam and with pursuers who couldn't be far behind, I should've had nothing but anxiety, desperation, and the black and red sketched images of fallen bodies in my thoughts. We weren't friends, Skoczinsky and I, I'd told myself a few times before, offhandedly blaming it on an inner lack in us both. Maybe that was true, or maybe I was fooling myself and any deficiency lay solely with me. If Saul and I weren't friends . . . well, I suddenly wished like hell we were. I was going to miss the son of a bitch.

If I lived that long.

Chapter 10

We dumped the van a few miles out. The two cars, non-descript blue with conveniently muddied license plates, were waiting where we had left them down a side road. A dirt trail was a better description, one filled with holes that rattled our bones before I put what was left of our ride into park. We moved quickly with the ever-present thought that time was ticking away faster than water swirling down a drain. Stripping off my black shirt, I revealed a long sleeve gray shirt. It was damned sedate compared to the stomach-churning spin of colors Saul seemed to prefer in his shirts, and I pretty much expected the automatically disparaging curl of his lip.

The all-black outfit might not attract the attention of a cop in the same way as would a gun resting on the dashboard, but the cat burglar look still might snag an extra glance. Lukas would be fine in his white scrub pajamas. From a distance it was indistinguishable from a T-shirt. If that hadn't been the case, I had a duffel bag full of my clothes in the backseat. I could've given him a sweatshirt, although it would've swallowed him. Only one or two inches shorter than my five foot eleven, he was a much slighter build—not skinny, but definitely lean. If our babushka Lena were still alive, she would've been stuffing him with food, trying to fatten him up.

"Lukas, get in the car." I wadded up the black shirt and tossed it onto the back floorboards.

He stood beside the van, watching as Saul and I moved around—always watching. By turns he seemed like a child, innocent and confused by the ways of the world, or an old man, uninterested and not particularly astonished by the turn of events. There were quite a few people in him, and not one of them was the Lukas I remembered; It was yet one more thing I simply didn't have time to ponder, not now.

"Michael."

I looked up from stashing my gun beneath the driver's seat of the car. The sheer determination projected behind the response caught my attention when I thought nothing less than gunfire would have. "What?"

"My name is Michael." From the obstinate set of his jaw I realized we'd reached a glitch in what so far had been a fairly successful run. "Test or not, call me by my name. Call me Michael."

I hesitated at the car door, then took a step toward him, halting when he took the same telling step backward. I knew what to say, because, after all, it was the truth. Look, I know you have no idea what's going on, I could tell him, but you have to trust me when I tell you that you are Lukas Korsak. You're my brother, and I've come to take you home. P.S. Great jammies. See there? Easy as pie. Delusional I was not, and I didn't need Saul's murmur of "Not the time" to know better than to get into it all now.

"Okay, Michael it is," I conceded, and was rewarded with a slight loosening of his wiry frame. I continued with a hard-won casual tone. "Could you hop in the car, Michael? We're in something of a hurry here."

His yes or no on that didn't matter. I hadn't come this far to have him go pelting off into the darkness like a jackrabbit. If worse came to worst, I'd bundle him up in a blanket with some duct tape and toss him in the backseat. His frame of mind right now couldn't be counted on to be anything but a little askew. It would be nice if he made the right decision if only for future trust issues, but it wasn't strictly necessary. I would do what I had to.

Studying me with fathomless eyes, his face gave nothing away as the scrutiny stretched on. Saul, an obviously budding diplomat, shifted his weight urgently, checked his watch, then growled, "Kid, it's simple. You can go with him or wait for the nut ball ninja in the jockey shorts. Make the call already, would ya?"

As he bowed his head, Lukas's lips thinned, and I heard his soft exhalation. "Simple." There were myriad emotions in that echo. Most were so fleeting, I could barely get a feeling for the flavor of them, but none of them were childlike—incredulity, resignation, and the blackest of black amusement. There were more, but it didn't matter. . . . Lukas had chosen his path. Without looking at either of us, he trudged across the dirt and climbed into my car.

Following him, I slid in behind the steering wheel and slammed the door shut. Saul leaned into the open window. His mask was still in place, but I could see his eyes, bloodshot from sleepless nights that had no doubt started the day he'd made his bargain with me. I hoped he enjoyed the money I'd given him. He deserved every penny and then some. "Thanks, Saul." Inadequate didn't even begin to cover that statement, but it was all I had left to my name. "I owe you, Skoczinsky."

"Yeah, like that's news." Once again I could hear the grin. "Send me a stripper-gram every year on my birthday and we'll call it even."

Saul had given me all the help I could pay for. Even more, he'd given me all I could ask for, and he'd given me a friendship I thought I was beyond. In our world it was nothing short of goddamn amazing. "Stay low, Saul. For a while at least." It wasn't much of a good-bye, but I'd never developed the talent for that—not with the practice I'd been given.

"You're preaching to the choir, Korsak," he drawled, and slapped the top of the car. Here he could use my actual name for the last time, as this was most likely also the last time he'd see me. "Now get out of here before you drain my will to live with that god-awful boring shirt."

With that and a short two-fingered salute, he turned and walked away. Pushing my hair behind my ears, I started the car and put it in motion. I didn't look back to see Saul get into his own car. If I had faith in anything, it was in his competence when it came to survival. I simply drove, into either a new life or the dark mirror version of an old one; I wasn't sure which.

"Fasten your seat belt," I said absently as I kept an eye out for pursuit. "Michael," I added belatedly. Jesus, all of a sudden I was a soccer mom—perhaps the most lethal soccer mom in the tri-state area.

There was the quiet snick of the latching mechanism and I spared a glance for my brother, sitting detached and classroom straight in the passenger seat. "Are you all right?" I asked with quiet concern. If there were a more stupid question to be asked, I couldn't think of it at the time, but it was sincerely said and sincerely felt. Lukas appeared to realize that. At least I hoped he did, maybe so much so that I was fooling myself into seeing something that wasn't there.

"This is no worse than the other tests." A long strand of brown hair fell across his forehead to the straight and uncompromising line of his brows as he looked at me, then away. His gaze lost out of his window, he queried evenly, "What will my punishment be? For failing?"

This test bullshit was turning into a broken record, a damn perturbing one. A disturbing piece to an ugly puzzle, it made me wonder for the thousandth time what was going on in that compound. What had happened to Lukas and the others? "Why do you think you failed?" It was the only question that wouldn't lead to a cascading domino of others that neither of us was ready for.

For the first time I saw my brother's composure falter. I could still see only the back of his head, but his shoulders jerked once before he managed to relax them with an effort that was obvious in the tense line of his neck. "Why, Michael?" I prodded, the name unwieldy and strange on my tongue. I was going to have to use it for a while, and the best way to do that was to start thinking of him as Michael in my mind. It hurt. God, did it ... voluntarily giving away one of the few slices of Lukas I'd had left. I just had to keep in mind I had the real thing now—physically. Mentally I would work on, no matter how long it might take.

"I didn't hurt you." He was barely audible, and I wasn't sure I heard him correctly until he said it again, more loudly and more strongly. "I didn't hurt you."

I couldn't believe it. A skinny kid and he thought he could hurt me. Worse, he thought he *should*. My road to Hell was paved not with good intentions but with indifference. The things I had ended up doing weren't the result of making bad choices, but rather of making no choices. I had no one to blame but myself. I could, however, blame someone when it came to Luk ... Michael. I didn't know if I'd killed those men I had shot during the rescue, but with a savage passion I suddenly wished I had.

"You didn't fail any test," I stated firmly. "There is no test, Michael. I'm here to help you, nothing else." He didn't reply, and I let it slide for the moment. "You hungry? There're some candy bars in the glove compartment. Help yourself."

I didn't expect him to immediately go for it and he didn't. It was almost fifteen minutes before he would even look away from the side window and face the front again. His face was smooth and unruffled. I knew that he wasn't frightened of me; I had my suspicions that he wasn't frightened of anyone except the man who'd invaded the van. I was relieved he didn't feel threatened by me, but I did wonder at it. You didn't have to know me to think I was one scary son of a bitch. You only had to look at me. The scar, the gallows behind my eyes— Prince Charming they did not make. It was strange, damn strange, that he wasn't more wary, but for now I was grateful.

"They're Three Musketeers," I coaxed. "You used to

eat those by the pound." I'd bought them at the drug-store the day before. They had been on the bottom row in their cheerfully shiny wrappers. It was ludicrous and a little pathetic, but bending over to pick them up was one of the harder things I'd done in my lifetime. Two candy bars that should've weighed literally nothing—why were they the fucking *Edmund Fitzgerald* in my hand? I'd almost dropped them back into their card-board container.

I had bought them anyway, fighting against the su-perstitious certainty that I'd also just bought myself some bad luck. And now I watched as Michael finally opened the glove compartment and took out one of them. He turned it over cautiously in his hands as if he were defusing a bomb before ripping the wrapper neatly. The bite was just as neat and economical. A trace of surprise showed in the quirk of his eyebrows as he chewed and swallowed. It was as if he'd never tasted one before. He ate the rest of the candy bar quickly, and as an encore he polished off the second in fewer than four bites.

"Good?" I ignored the ripple of unease that passed through me. It was his favorite snack; yet he obviously didn't remember it. Everything of Lukas was gone, large or small . . . gone. "Guess you didn't get too much of the sweet stuff in that prison." Moving my eyes from the stranger sitting next to me, I shifted my attention back to the road and reminded myself that it wasn't forever. We'd get those memories back or we'd make new ones, whatever it took.

"You talk a lot."

I couldn't help the jerk of the wheel beneath my hands. It was the first genuinely unprompted comment that my brother . . . that Michael had made that didn't involve the mysterious "tests." "Yeah?" That was not a statement that normally would have applied to me, but in this situation he was right. I didn't know what to say. How did you talk to a kid you couldn't know, no matter how much you wanted to, and who'd been plucked from bizarre circumstances that you didn't understand?

"It's a sign of insecurity. All the more classic psychology textbooks say so." He peered into the glove box once again. There was no sign of disappointment on that inscrutable face when no more chocolate was to be found, but I knew better. He was a teenager. Raised in a combination of a school, prison camp, and laboratory, that might be true, but some part of him was still a teenager, no matter how suppressed or denied.

"And what do you know about psychology, junior Freud?" Guiding the car with one hand, I dug under my seat. Bypassing cold metal, I pulled out a box of Double Stuf Oreos. We might be on the road for a long time and I'd stocked up on instant sources of cheap energy. Tossing them into his lap, I instantly heard the rustle of cellophane as he opened the package.

"He's not the type of psychology we study. His way of thinking isn't useful." There was the soft crunch of a cookie. "But I'm sure he would've had something to say about the size of your gun." There it was again, the mixture of child and man. The ravenous inroads he was making into the Oreos was the picture of a hungry Little Leaguer after the big game. The psychological point of view combined with a swipe worthy of Saul himself put him in the range of a cynical and caustic forty-year-old.

Bemused, I felt my lips curve. "Keep up with the sarcasm and I'll take my cookies back." I didn't mean it of course. If anything, I was happy, fucking delirious to see a hint of humor in him. It made him seem a little less than a galaxy length out of reach.

"I wasn't being sarcastic," he said seriously, flattening my cheer instantly. "The weapon is obviously an attempt to overcome your insecurity in many areas." Fingers prying the next cookie from its row, he finished matter-of-factly, "You're vulnerable. You should watch that."

Now what the hell could you say to that, I thought, nonplussed. And my 9mm was a perfectly normal-sized gun, no bigger than . . . shit. Cutting off that train of non-productive thought, I frowned with confusion. "Aren't you at all curious, L . . . Michael? I swoop in and drag you off in a scene straight out of a movie. Don't you have any questions about that?" Just one normal question to let me feel as if I had some control over the situation?

"No." Finally done with the cookies, he'd placed them carefully on the floor by his feet. "Either this is a test and you'll lie or you're an enemy and you'll lie." He rested his head back on the seat. From the corner of my eye I watched as he closed his. "Or you're a crazy man and you really do think I'm your brother. It's still lies, only then you're lying to yourself."

Our first conversation in ten years was considerably different from our last regarding sidekicks and sandcastles, heroes and horses. Right then I was more than ready, cowardly enough, for the grown-up in Michael to be gone and the child to reappear. The child I could handle, but this unwavering brick wall of a young man—I wasn't sure I could. I wasn't even sure I could see him . . . truly see him at all, not as he really was. That would involve letting go of the vision of a seven-year-old tag-along who had shadowed me silently into adulthood. I didn't think I would ever be willing to do that.

Beside me I could see him chew his bottom lip, leaving a smear of chocolate. The motion didn't last long, not with this self-possessed kid. His mouth relaxed as his jaw conversely tightened. He was tired; with the night he'd had it wasn't any surprise. The one thing, the only thing, he needed now was to rest. No one had accused me of having a soft heart . . . not the ex-girlfriends and not the men who'd ended up on the wrong side of my fists or gun. But this was my brother, no matter what he thought. For him I had a number of emotions. They were ancient ones and rusty from disuse, but they were there and chief among them was a mile-wide protective streak.

"Go to sleep, Michael," I directed, not ungently. "It's

a long drive." Especially when you had no idea where you were going. I'd picked a direction and gone with it, not that I had much choice in that. There weren't many options this far down in the state. For now I was simply running. Determining the destination would come when I was positive there was no pursuit.

He opened his eyes to give me a searching glance. There was no fear, but there was no trust either. "Come on, Freud," I assured with rueful patience. "You've been kidnapped, shot at, and fed cookies. What else could possibly happen? Take a nap already."

From the skeptical narrowing of his eyes I realized he thought that argument lacking, but he slid down in the seat, twisted onto his side as much as the seat belt would allow, and rested his head against the door. It wasn't long before I heard the deep and regular respiration of sleep. Looking away from the road, I took in the sight of his loose shoulders and the lax line of his spine under the white cloth.

He was here. He was really here. I could stretch out a hand if I wanted and lay it on his arm. I could touch him, flesh and blood that held genetic hands with my own. I could, but I didn't. He might have woken up or he might have disappeared . . . a soap bubble popping under reality's touch. I wasn't willing to risk either option.

I drove for nearly half the night. Around four a.m. I pulled off the interstate and checked us into a cheap little motel. Shabby and run-down, it had about twelve rooms and a night desk guy a few short chromosomes away from Norman Bates. He grunted, took my money, and didn't bother to ask for the fake ID I was prepared to fork over with the registration. Within ten minutes Michael and I were behind a locked door and at the visual mercy of ancient shag carpeting and orange and turquoise striped bedspreads. I dumped the duffel bag on the bed nearest the door and asked, "You want something to drink? There's a machine outside."

He shook his head and sat on the other bed, his toes

digging curiously into the long strands of the carpet. His toes were uncovered. Frowning, I switched on the bedside light for a better look. Was that . . . ? "Ah, shit." Kneeling on the floor in front of him, I took his ankle firmly in one hand and lifted his foot for a better look. He was in bare feet, not that I'd given that consideration even once as we'd run across dirt and sand, gravel, and shards of rock. The sole of the foot I held was crisscrossed with cuts and abrasions and colored a dark rust by dried blood.

Giving a pained hiss under my breath, I demanded, "You should've said something. Jesus." Out of the corner of my eye, I saw that his hand was hovering by my head. It was palm down in a fairly harmless position, so I ignored it. He very likely felt threatened; I would've in his shoes. This time I moved more slowly as to not startle him further and his hand slowly dropped back to his side. Lifting his other foot with painstaking care, I saw that it was in the same shape.

"Why?" he asked blankly.

He had no idea, literally none, as to why he should've called attention to his discomfort. "Because hurting you was never part of the plan," I snapped despite myself, guilt and self-annoyance bubbling up within. "And neither were feet that look like roadkill."

Setting the foot down gently, I headed straight into the bathroom and started water running in the tub. Taking one of the tiny shampoo bottles, I dumped the contents in as well. After seven inches of warm and soapy water filled the bottom, I turned off the tap and went back out to retrieve Michael.

As he sat gingerly on the edge of the tub, I had him roll up his pant legs and immerse his feet in the water. "Soak them for a while. I'll be right back." Out in the room I opened up the first aid kit and spread it out on my bed. I'd packed the kit before I'd packed anything else, but I had no idea I'd be using it so soon. Shaking out two ibuprofen into my palm, I took them back in

the bathroom and handed them to Michael. Running a
plastic cup of water, I offered that as well. "Take those.
It'll help with the pain."

He studied the pills side by side in his palm while I
held the cup. Finally, I nudged his shoulder. "Michael," I
prompted, "take the pills."

"I don't like pills." He looked up at me, a mutinous
set to his mouth. I could tell that if I'd pushed the issue,
he would've given in and taken them. He was shockingly
obedient for a teenager, at least in comparison to the
one I had been. Still, I decided pushing was not the way
to go—not on an issue so small. After seeing that basement room, it was easy to believe he had every reason to
dislike pills or anything remotely medically related.

Sighing, I thought for a moment, then gave him
a crooked smile. "Okay then, pick one." His expression was understandably dubious, but I persisted. "Go
on. Choose one. I'll take it and you can take the other.
They're harmless, Michael. Honestly."

The honesty didn't matter, but my offer to take one
did. Hell, I had a raging headache coming on anyway
and I swallowed the indicated pill without complaint.
Cautiously, Michael waited twenty minutes to see the
result before he took his. He was many things, this kid,
but stupid was not one of them. The warm water had
sluiced most of the dried blood from his feet by then
and I finished cleaning the rest of it with gauze and per-
oxide. Drying them with a towel, I slathered antibiotic
ointment liberally on both soles and then presented him
with a pair of clean socks from my bag. "Cover them
up. God knows what you could catch off this carpet—
Ebola, the plague, there's no telling."

He'd sat military straight on the bed while I'd performed the first aid and watched my every move. Furrowed brows said that care such as this wasn't exactly
what he was expecting, but he said nothing as he straightened and pulled on the socks.

"Go ahead and crash, kiddo." I cleaned up the first

aid kit and shoved it back in my bag. "We'll sleep a few hours before we hit the road again." It wouldn't be much of a rest, but I wanted to make sure those assholes weren't going to pick us up somehow. If they had government ties as we suspected, it would be easy enough for them to have a finger dipped into the local authorities' pie as well. There could be an APB out for Michael at this moment. No one had seen my face or Saul's, but it was safe to say they had an excellent description of my brother, both inside and out.

Once again I saw a glimpse of a shadowy and jaded humor as the last word passed my lips. "You really have no idea what I am, do you?"

I was going to have to adjust to his denial, at least for a while. Doing my best to massage out the pang of tension stabbing at the base of my neck, I answered with weary quiet. "You're my brother, Michael. And I'll prove it to you, I swear. Now get some sleep."

Bicolored eyes were as opaque and vigilant as those of a wild animal, but he stood to turn down the blankets. Sliding under them, he pulled them up to his neck and shifted over onto his side. It wasn't too long before he drifted off, his hair a brown tangle on the pillow. He was tired, I knew, but as had happened in the car, questions were passing through my head. He didn't trust me; as far as I could tell he didn't trust anyone, including those with whom he'd lived. Even factoring in exhaustion, it was unsettling how quickly he dropped off. It was as if he were so used to a life filled with menace and uncertainty that it was the norm for him.

I stood by the bed and watched him sleep for a long time. To look away seemed like the worst invitation to fate . . . as if he were only a dream conjured by nothing more than years of guilt. Stupid, but my gaze lingered on him as I turned off the lights and went over to recline in the garish orange chair by the window. I left the world inside the room and turned my attention to the one outside the window. If I wanted to keep my brother, I had to act like the professional I was. Arranging the blinds until a small space showed between each slat, I kept watch on the parking lot until the sun came up.

It was about then that I realized what Michael had said before he'd gone to bed. "You really have no idea who I am, do you?" That's what I'd assumed he had said, but my assumption had been wrong. It hadn't been the word "who" that sat in the middle of that sentence. No . . .

It had been "what."

Chapter 11

Michael woke without help from me. Rolling over, he tossed around for a few minutes before murmuring something. It sounded like a name . . . Peter. The sound of his own voice must have stirred him from sleep, because his eyes opened and the firm grip he had on a wad of sheets loosened. Blank and confused, his face smoothed out when he saw me. I didn't fool myself into thinking the sight of me was reassuring in any way. My image simply triggered his brain into catching up with the events of last night and letting him know how he'd ended up in a strange hotel room.

"Hungry?" I stretched my legs as the twinge in the small of my back reminded me of a night spent in a chair designed by the most sadistic carpenter alive. "We can get some drive-through later, but I have jerky or peanut butter to tide you over until then." Running a hand over fly-away hair, he sat up and slanted me a less-than-thrilled look. I supposed even institutional food was better than what I was serving. Giving a tired but heartfelt grin, I added, "Or there are still some Oreos." Our mom had to be spinning in her grave over my idea of nutrition for the teenager on the run.

The mention of the cookies went over much better than my other offerings. Blankets pooled on the floor as he climbed out of bed to give me a demandingly expectant look. "Good morning to you too, sunshine," I said, snorting. Within minutes Michael was munching his way to hopefully a more communicative mood. At seven he'd been a morning person, but then again, who wasn't at that age? There were lands to explore, dragons to slay, worlds to conquer.

"I'm going to grab a shower." I hesitated. "You're not going to take off, are you?" He wouldn't have gotten more than three steps outside the door if he had, but I wanted him to feel as if he had choices. He'd been a prisoner so long that I didn't want him feeling the same way with me.

"Is that even an option?" he asked with a marked lack of faith. My question was as glass to him. My intentions didn't matter, and he saw all too clearly what my actions would be.

I might as well be honest. Whether it was whatever psychology course he'd been fed or merely natural talent, he would be a hard kid to fool. It could be both. Lukas at seven had been both innocent and wise . . . and an impressive judge of character for such a young child. "Not really, Michael." I rubbed a hand over a bristly jaw and said regretfully, "Sorry."

He shrugged. "This is no worse than the Institute." Finishing his last cookie, he went over and began to make his bed, hospital corners and all.

I'd heard the capital I in institute. That must be what they called the compound. Filing it away for a later subject of questioning along with his odd use of the word "what," I took a change of clothes into the bathroom and showered. I left the door open to hear if Michael changed his mind and decided to make a break for it after all. The trickle of lukewarm water did little to drive the fatigue from my body or mind and I hurriedly soaped up. Climbing out ten minutes later, I dried off and wrapped a towel around my hips. The open door had kept the mirror from fogging and I shaved with a few quick strokes. Slipping on jeans and a sweatshirt, I pulled my wet hair back tightly. Before we left I would stuff it up in a baseball hat. I hadn't been seen, yeah, but it didn't hurt to change the look. If we were somehow

traced to this motel, they could easily get a description
of me from the desk clerk.

"Michael, you're up." I walked back into the room
and gathered some of my clothes for him. "Here're some
sweats and more ointment for your feet. And I think I
packed some sneakers that'll do. They might be a little
big, but I don't think we'll be doing much hiking."

He accepted the bundle wordlessly, went into the
bathroom, and closed the door behind him. I guess he
had no fear that I might make a run for it. By the time he
returned with damp hair and sweat clothes that bagged
on him, I was nearly ready to go. Handing him the ten-
nis shoes, I took the white pajamas from him. Taking out
my penknife, I began to methodically shred the cloth to
small, easily flushable pieces. "How are the feet?"

Sitting on the edge of the bed, he put on the shoes
and tied the laces neatly. "Fine," he said. He still didn't
know how to react to the concern, and it showed in the
faintly mystified glance that he shot my way. It made me
sincerely wish that Saul had used a real gun instead of
the stun variety on that son of a bitch in the back of the
van. That something so simple and basic as concern had
been lacking from Michael's life, it didn't do much for
the inner fire that had been smoldering since I'd seen
that first room in the compound basement. "Let's go,
Misha," I said gently. "There's greasy food out there
with our name all over it."

"Misha?" He stood in shoes that surprisingly seemed
to fit. Big feet had always run in our family.

"Michael is a mouthful," I lied. If I couldn't use the
name I'd known him by since the day that he'd been
born, then I wanted a name we could share . . . a name
that wasn't one those bastards had given him. The di-
minutive for Michael would do. "Misha is a nickname
for Michael." I cocked my head, deciding to go into our
Russian heritage later. "That okay?"

He thought about it, then nodded. As always, he
wasn't exactly swimming in enthusiasm, but I counted

it a win regardless. He did as well, I imagined, getting to keep at least a portion of the name he was attached to.

After disposing of the pajama remains down the toilet, one less thing to use to trace us, I hefted my bag and we headed out into the pastel dawn light.

Even the soft yellow and pink illumination stabbed at my eyes and I put on a pair of sunglasses the minute I entered the car. The brim of the baseball cap helped as well. After the nearly constant adrenaline rush of last night followed by no sleep, I had what was as bad as any hangover.

"Sleep deprivation can cause a significant decrease in performance and concentration," Michael said absently as he watched a portly family of five through the passenger side window. Early risers as well, they were unremarkable in all but size, shockingly loud tourist wear, and a large chocolate cruller wrapped in each pudgy hand. And I knew for a fact which of those three had caught Michael's attention. The kid had a jones for sugar like I'd never seen, and I had no one to blame for that but myself. With an almost wistful sigh, he turned back to me. "You didn't sleep last night, did you?"

"No, I didn't." I liked that he was beginning to ask questions . . . waking up to the new world around him. I also hoped it meant he might be willing to listen to a few questions of my own. "I wanted to keep watch. But I'll sleep tonight." I wouldn't have much of a choice. By tonight I would be too exhausted to fight it. Puzzled, I added an observation. "You're full of fun little facts, aren't you? Like the sleep thing. What kind of freaky classes did you have in that place?"

We were on the road again and had gone several miles before Michael finally spoke. "I've never talked with anyone outside of the Institute. I don't know what to say." It was hard for him to admit, as evident in the strained patches of white beside his mouth. "If this is a test, I'm doing badly. So badly." He shook his head.

"And if this isn't a test?" We had to get this misconception out of the way before we could make any progress, but Michael was hanging on to it hard.

"What else could it be?" There was a defeated note to his voice.

I tried for a reassuring smile. I doubt I succeeded. My job hadn't required that look very often. "Like you said, maybe I'm just some crazy guy who thinks he's found his brother. Sometimes, kiddo, you just have to go with the flow. So, tell me what they taught you. I think I'm sensing a theme."

Tracing a finger along the dashboard, he considered as more miles passed and then he began to talk. I listened to every word, hoping to hear the key that I could use to unlock the mystery of my brother. He talked about multiple classes. There were the usual basics such as history, math, chemistry, and others, but they were supplemented with psychology, law—both domestic and international—languages, and acting. There was a theme all right; a very definite one.

"And how are you in acting?" I flashed him a more natural smile as I reached up to adjust the rearview mirror. If he could pull a De Niro, I hadn't seen any signs of it yet.

"According to the Instructor, the worst he's ever seen," he replied without concern. Impressing the Instructor with his Oscar-winning ways apparently didn't interest Michael whatsoever. Once again I heard a capital letter where normally none would be. If Michael had any idea what the acting instructor's name actually was, I would be astonished.

"No big deal. There's more to life than Hollywood." Not that Hollywood had anything to do with the acting classes he had been taking. Spotting a sign indicating heart-stopping cholesterol at the next exit, I decided to make a stop. "They were training you to be a spy, weren't they? Espionage." Maybe Saul had been wrong about this not being a government project. It sounded more like a project better suited to the old Soviet regime of the Cold War, but all ruling parties had their secrets, even here.

"Spy?" He laughed too, but without humor. "No, not a spy." And with that the subject was closed. Crossing his arms, he closed his eyes to indicate this particular conversation had soured for him.

Having received more from him than I expected, I gave him a break. As I took the exit and hit the first generic fast-food place I saw, I decided against asking him what he wanted. I would hate to get my brother back, only to lose him to terminal dental caries in the first month. A breakfast sandwich, biscuits and gravy, and orange juice should be enough, I thought, before weakening to add pancakes to the order. I personally hated drive-through breakfast crap and ordered nothing but a large coffee for myself. I'd make up for it at lunch.

Back on the interstate, Michael took no prisoners on that bag of grease. The sandwich he tolerated, the gravy he loved, and the pancakes lifted him unto Heaven. They'd been labeled a new addition on the order menu: chocolate chip with a gallon of pseudo maple syrup. As I watched, he devoured every bite and then licked the fork. This kid, grave and educated in damn peculiar ways, was going after every molecule of sugary goodness like a five-year-old with a bowl of icing.

"What the hell did they feed you in that place anyway? Bread and water? Gruel?" I asked.

"Nutritious meals to keep our bodies at the peak of health," he replied. It sounded like a quote. I could picture it now . . . straight-edged grim words emblazoned on a wall above a pear-shaped cafeteria lady doling out boiled chicken, boiled potatoes, and boiled cabbage.

"All right," I said with determination. "For supper we have pizza, a liter of Coke, and a shitload of ice cream. Rocky road. So what if our teeth rot out? It'll be worth it."

"I know those are all very popular. Do they taste as good as chocolate chip pancakes?" There was definite interest in the question.

"Better," I promised. I wondered how it worked in that concrete prison. I imagined heads bowed over test papers. Circle A if pizza tastes good. Circle B if it does not taste good. Speaking of not good, that entire picture left a foul taste in my mouth—all those children leading the lives of small prisoners of war. I'd listened to the radio for any news on a police raid on the compound. Nothing. Big surprise. Either the entire police department was in their back pocket, not a very realistic proposition, or the Institute had been evacuated. Either way, the kids were gone.

Since the full stomach seemed to have relaxed Michael some, I decided to try more questions. "Misha, you said you were taught languages. Do you know Russian?"

"*Da, ya govaru pa russki*," he responded absently as he involved himself in returning all trash to the large white bag and carefully folding the top down, once then twice. *"Vy gavarite?"* So he must have known Misha was short for Michael, not that he'd shared the information.

"A little." I took the last sip of nearly cold coffee as I steered with one hand. "Probably less than you since you've studied it. What I picked up isn't exactly for use in polite company." It was a fairly good bet that he knew more proper Russian than I did. I could get my point across, but it would be a hard, ungrammatical road. My fluency was in the language of the job and those were not pretty words. "Our father's from Russia. Our mom was too."

"Was?" he repeated neutrally.

"She died." I crumpled the cup and let it drop from my hand. "A long time ago."

He considered that with eyes on a distant point; then he shook his head. "Your mother, not mine. I never had a mother or a father." His gaze moved to fix on me as he went on implacably. "Or a brother."

Hey, square one . . . How you doing?

It shouldn't have hit me as hard as it did. Since we'd pulled him out of that place, I'd known it was going to be an uphill battle. I'd known and I still knew, but . . . ah, fuck. "Eyes like yours aren't a dime a dozen, Misha," I said quietly. I didn't know if he was listening to me or not as he sat beside me as still as a stone, but I pushed on as best I could. I was working without a script, flailing in unknown territory. My line of work hadn't done much to train me in the ways of gentle persuasion. Now I had to learn the hard way, and at a time it had never been more important that I not fail. "They took you when you were seven. We were on a beach riding horses, and this man"—I swallowed against a nightmare that was as fresh now as it had been then—"this goddamn son of a bitch with a gun took you."

"Horses." It wasn't said in a questioning tone, but more in one of contemplation.

I didn't care how it was said. He was listening. He was hearing me. I grabbed on to the sliver of optimism and refused to give it up. "Yeah, we had horses. They were Christmas presents." I didn't think it was necessary to tell him they'd both died the same day he was taken. It was a detail that wouldn't help him to hear. It wouldn't do much for me either.

"What kind of horses?" He was curious despite himself, poor damn kid—my poor goddamn brother.

It'd been so long that I couldn't recall if they'd been Morgans or Quarterhorses. "Harry and Annie. Annie was yours. She was a sorrel mare, a tiny and frisky thing. Harry was a bay gelding, a big lovable guy." It might've been that Harry loved apples like all other horses, but Annie liked only carrots. Could be Annie wanted the soft, sweet velvet between her nostrils rubbed while Harry liked his ears scratched. I never had the opportunity to find out the small details of affection before they lay dying on the sand. "We rode them to the beach. We talked about . . . oh, hell . . . kids' things. Who was the hero and who was the sidekick." I flashed him a look of mock annoyance. "Somehow you were always the hero. Go figure."

He gave me a look of his own—utter and complete dismissal. The curiosity had vanished. "That's a story you should tell your brother, not me. If he's alive." Resting his head back against the seat, he ended without emotion. "If there ever was a brother."

I didn't lose my temper, not at him. He was a victim in all of this. I saved my anger for those responsible. "Can you drive?" I asked abruptly.

He straightened, startled by the curt question, then said, "What did you—"

I cut him off. "Can you drive?"

Nodding slowly, he said with a trace of uncertainty, "Theoretically."

Whatever that meant, it would have to be good enough. "Fine. Take the wheel." As he hesitated, I took his hand and put it on the steering wheel before twisting around to reach the duffel bag behind my seat. Ignoring the sudden weaving of the car, I searched until I found what I was looking for. Sitting back up, I reclaimed the wheel just in time to keep us from riding up the ass of a semi. "Whoa." I applied a light foot on the brake and peeled Michael's hand free of the wheel. "Thanks. I've got it now."

Blinking and a little pale, he said with faint dismay, "It's harder than it looks."

"Most things are, kiddo." And that was perhaps the truest thing I'd ever said. Without any further comment, I dumped the picture frame in his lap. He stared at the back of it for a moment. The crisp black velvet had the sheen of a smugly healthy cat and he ran his fingers along it in a stroking motion. Thanks for the Christmas present, Dad, I thought with grim satisfaction. It's going to help me after all.

It was the portrait of a knife-edged moment lost in the greedy maw of time; two children who could've grown up to become anything at all. Instead one was now a criminal and the other a teenager lost, in body and mind. And both of us might very well be damaged beyond repair. All that and more was waiting behind velvet.

"Turn it over," I commanded softly, hoping what was at once painful and wonderful to me might trigger something similar in him.

With one last petting motion, he did. There we were ... in all our glory. And it was a genuine glory, despite the ache that hit me every time I saw it. I didn't know what I would see in his face as he took it in. An explosion of memory that opened a floodgate in his mind? No, I didn't think it would be that easy; nothing in life ever was. The most I could realistically hope for was a small sliver of recognition or a flash of yearning for something just beyond his reach—the tip-of-the-tongue syndrome, that he knew something was there even if he didn't know what that something was.

I didn't get any of those. What happened was a shade to the left of that and one step lagging. It wasn't what I'd hoped for, but in many ways it was close to what I'd expected. You know what they say: Expect the worst and be pleasantly surprised. Not so. Expect the worst and find out your imagination is sorely lacking; that was my philosophy.

Confusion was the primary emotion that washed across skin that saw far too little sun. He truly hadn't believed there was a brother at all, much less one who could be him. "He doesn't look that much like me," he murmured with automatic denial. The same finger that traced the velvet now touched the glass gingerly. "Just the eyes, that's all."

"Isn't that enough?" He didn't want to look past age-regressed features or the light hair of childhood. He wanted to hold on to something familiar, no matter how horrible the familiar was. It was understandable, the fear, but I wasn't going to allow him to overlook the more obvious similarities. "That and the age. How many seventeen-year-old kids in southern Florida are running around with those eyes and are lacking parents? Go on, Misha, take a guess. How many?" It was a coincidence even too great for him to deny ... or so I thought.

He hesitated, then turned the frame over again, the picture safely hidden against his legs. Our history was dismissed just that quickly. "I don't know that I'm seventeen." Strangely, it seemed as if he'd been about to say something else at first. What did finally come out was meant to be logical, I could tell, but it had more of a stubborn ring to my ears. It made the corner of my mouth twitch upward until the meaning of those obstinate words hit me.

"What do you mean by that?" I demanded. The semi was still ahead of us, ambling along, slowly and placidly, like an elderly elephant on Prozac. "Are you saying you don't know how old you are?" I didn't know why that surprised me. The Institute undoubtedly didn't spend much on birthday cakes or clowns with balloons . . . unless the clown was hiding a hypodermic in one Day-Glo orange glove.

"No, I don't." He pushed up a sleeve that had slid down over the heel of his hand. "Nearly old enough for graduation, that's all I know."

"Graduation? What . . ." I wasn't able to finish. The widening of Michael's forward-facing eyes had me jerking my attention back to the road in front of the car. The back of the truck had opened to reveal five men, four of whom were wearing disturbingly familiar tan pants. It was hard to believe that I'd come to a point in my life where the sight of a pair of khakis or passing the Gap gave me the same surge of adrenaline than a hit attempt on my former boss once had. Marginally worse than the pants were the guns pointed in our direction. HK assault rifles were serious weapons, and I wondered if the concern was to get Michael back alive or simply get him back period.

The fifth man answered my question by pointing at us and saying something I couldn't hear through the glass. It was our pal from the van. He was dressed this time and not in goddamn khakis either. A dark gray suit and black shirt set him apart from the others almost as much as the ferocious intelligence in his dark eyes. Then I decided to stop with the fashion assessments and try avoiding a shitload of bullets instead.

Yanking the wheel to one side with one hand, I took the car into the emergency lane. With my free hand I grabbed Michael's shoulder and shoved him down into the small space between the seat and the dashboard. "But they've already seen me," he protested, wincing as I crammed him pretzel fashion onto the floorboards.

"It's not about the seeing. It's about the shooting." I rapped as the driver's side mirror was torn away by a bullet. "Keep your ass down." I wasn't about to let it get shot off, not on his first full day of freedom. Ducking low behind the dash, I felt frantically for the gun under my seat. "How the fuck did they find us?" I muttered to myself. It certainly hadn't been by a trail of cookie crumbs. Sugar-shark Michael would've taken care of any one of those, no matter how small.

The windshield shattered into gummy green safety glass. It showered over my shoulders and rained down on the brim of my hat. Straightening, I rested my hand on molded black plastic that had long lost the new car smell and pulled the trigger of my 9mm. One of the men spun around, his white shirt blooming crimson on the right side of his chest—lipstick red, but it wasn't the kind of kiss anyone would welcome. Jamming the gas pedal flat to the floor, I tried to take the car up past the truck. I saw the lips of the obvious leader, in all things including couture, move as he spoke into the mouthpiece of a slim headset similar to those worn by SWAT. The truck immediately swerved and cut me off.

Swearing, I tried the other side. Most of the cars around us had braked or halted altogether at the gunfire, but I still managed to send one oblivious driver yammering on his cell phone spinning out of control into the median. As the truck began a move to counter mine, I rethought my plan. "Hang on, Misha," I gritted as I twisted the wheel and the car into a one-eighty.

"Not really necessary," came the exasperated response. He was packed down there tightly enough that it was unlikely anything less than the Jaws of Life would pry him free. Beneath the irritation I heard the same dread that had first surfaced in the van. He might not be afraid of me, but Michael was afraid of someone. Sooner or later, I would find out why. When I killed that child-stealing, malevolent son of a bitch, I wanted to know each and every reason to equal each and every time I pulled the trigger.

Dodging haphazardly stopped cars with white-faced, gaping drivers, I stuck mainly to the emergency lane as I sent us speeding the wrong way up the interstate. Once or twice I had to detour into the main lanes if some shaking motorist was already hogging the side strip of gravel. Behind, the semi had stopped and the four men who were still mobile had jumped out onto the asphalt. Either they had a car that had been pacing them or they would commandeer the nearest one at gunpoint. I wanted to be at the last exit we'd passed before that mystery was solved. Barely two miles away, I began to run into moving traffic just as we reached it. If I had thought I could have made it across the median, I would've made the attempt, but the chances of getting bogged down in stagnant water and thick mud that grew reedy swamp grass was high. This was a low-slung machine we were traveling in, not an SUV. Political correctness—it'll get you killed every time.

In a blare of horns and metal scraping metal I grazed a light green Volkswagen and sped onto the off ramp. Narrowly escaping being crushed by a gasoline tanker, we bounced off a guardrail, skidded, and managed to get on the right side of the road. A quick look in the mirror showed a white Ford following the same perilous path, but with less success. Colliding with the front cab of the tanker, the white hood crumpled and a tire smoked from the friction, but the car kept coming. The bastards had commandeered their own car and were determined. Let them be—their resolve wasn't a drop in the deep blue compared to mine.

Looking left, then right, I made a split-second decision that had Hog Heaven barbecue patrons running for cover. Engine growling, the car jumped the parking lot curb and spun wildly in the crushed-clamshell stretch behind the seafood restaurant next door. Next to that was a gas station with a tiny alley framed by the back of the cinder-block building and undergrowth-choked trees. As we barreled through it, I caught a glimpse between buildings of the Ford rushing down the street toward the barbecue joint.

"Can I get up now?" Michael asked patiently with glass glittering in wind-tousled hair. Other than the look in his eyes when he'd first seen the man from the van minutes ago, he was as abnormally calm as if we were simply making a run to the grocery store. Maybe that class had followed the one on acting . . . calm in the face of certain death. Bring a number two pencil.

"No," I answered instantly. "Keep the balls of steel out of sight."

There was the quizzical quirk of light brown eyebrows before I put my attention back to driving for our lives. The car banged loudly into a green Dumpster at the back corner of the gas station and sent it chasing after a bald man with a beer belly who had just exited the bathroom. He fled promptly, his legs pumping and toilet paper fluttering from his shoe. I followed, bypassing him and the metal box on wheels before taking a sharp corner at the front of the building. After dodging a row of pumps, I took out a flock of plastic pelicans and then an equally gaudy fake purple pig.

That put me right behind the Ford as it smoked its way through the parking lot I'd just vacated fifteen seconds ago. Slamming into it, I propelled it several feet into a three-foot-high metal drainage pipe that marked the back boundary of the lot. The Ford flipped. There were sparks flying from the metal striking metal and a distinct crunching accompanied by the cacophony of smashing glass. The sound of a catastrophic wreck wasn't one you could mistake, but it usually didn't give you a warm glow.

Shifting into reverse, I could see a modest group of diners boiling out of the barbecue joint. It was a good thing I'd chosen an older model car or I wouldn't have seen much at all. It was generically inconspicuous, so the eye slid away from it naturally and it had the added bonus of no airbags. Instead of breathing in powder and plastic, I could see the pig crowd. I could also see something else, something a whole lot less pleasant than slightly greasy pork lovers.

Colors of gray, black, and red coalesced into the driver crawling with painfully slow deliberation from the overturned car. The man was as indestructible as a New York cockroach. "Who the hell is this guy?"

"Jericho."

With a pale face even paler, Michael had straightened enough to see out of what remained of the windshield. "Jericho," he repeated before sliding back down to wrap arms around his legs. Eyes far away, he rested his chin on his knees, to all appearances completely disinterested, completely gone; the poor goddamned kid. If there had been fewer people in the parking lot, I would've stopped the car, walked over, and taken the shot from a distance where missing wasn't possible. I didn't care if I was seen, but as far as I'd fallen, taking a chance on hurting an innocent if deluded bystander still was beyond me—I hoped.

This Jericho might still be moving, but he wouldn't be going anywhere anytime soon. For this moment, that would have to be good enough. His name was ironic, considering that when I'd first seen the compound I'd thought of the biblical walls of the same name. It was ironic and not a little goddamn spooky, but now wasn't the time to dwell on creepy coincidences.

Within minutes I had us back on the road. The interstate was a challenge with cars still snarled and sirens approaching, but it cleared out after the first few miles. And then we were just one more car in a flowing stream of them. Granted we were missing some glass and were pocked with bullet holes, but no one's perfect. Jesus, as conquering heroes went, I left a lot to be desired.

"We're going to need a new car," I commented brusquely. Looking over, I added in what I hoped was a more encouraging tone, "You can get up now, Misha. We've lost them."

Blue and green, a fog-bound and frozen lake, he wavered, then focused on me. "We have?" If it had sounded doubtful, I wouldn't have blamed him, but it didn't. It wasn't even politely skeptical, merely mildly indifferent. Michael had gone back to the safest place he knew . . . inside himself.

Reaching out with slow and infinite care, I brushed granules of glass from his hair. I knew I was seeing a child that was no more, but knowing and feeling don't always go hand in hand. "Yeah, kiddo, we have."

The unspoken "for now" I kept to myself.

Chapter 12

We ended up sleeping in the car.

I didn't want to take a chance of Jericho and his crew checking the local hotels with our descriptions. The son of a bitch might be in a hospital bed right now, but I didn't think that had much chance of stopping him. Slowing him down was the best I could hope for, and I'd long used up my hope for better things. I chose a small town off the interstate and eventually found a road that started as asphalt, wound its way to gravel, and finally ended up as a dirt track through kudzu-choked woods. The sun had gone down several hours ago by the time I parked. Stepping from the car, I stretched and grimaced as bones and tendons popped. Michael followed, hauntingly visible in the yellow spill of the car's dome light. As the scattering of blond in his hair was haloed into a phantom nimbus, he folded his arms and scanned the area with a frown. It was the most emotion I'd seen out of him in hours.

"What's wrong?" The bullet burn on my jaw from the night before itched fiercely and I gave it a soothing rub of my knuckle. "You still hungry?" He'd put away two cheeseburgers, a large order of fries,, and a chocolate shake for supper, but I'd seen his stomach in action. That may not have been enough. Godzilla descending on Tokyo had nothing on the ferocity of a teenager's appetite, and if Michael didn't behave as a teenager in anything else, he did in that.

"No, I'm not hungry." The frown deepened and he shifted from foot to foot. "Is this where we're staying?"

The corner of my mouth twitched ruefully at the faint dismay in his voice. "It's no worse than that rattrap from last night. We have fresh air, stars, and crickets to sing us to sleep. It's practically a commercial for camping gear. What else could you want?"

The reason for his two-step became apparent as he snapped rather desperately, "A bathroom."

"Ah." I fought against the laugh that wanted to spill free. After the day we'd had, I enjoyed the warm swell of humor, but I had a sneaking suspicion Michael wouldn't appreciate it if he thought the laughter was aimed at him. "Well, that's easy enough." I waved an arm. "Pick a tree."

"A tree?"

I'd dragged him here and there, nearly gotten him killed at every turn, and he hadn't blinked an eye. But tell him to take a leak in the great outdoors and he was as outraged as an eighty-year-old nun. "Watch out for snakes," I warned with only partially suppressed glee.

His wasn't a face made for scowls. It was too smooth, too serene a mask, but that didn't prevent him from giving it the old college try. As he walked into the trees, I could still see the pale smear of him in the dark. The waves of annoyance that I could feel radiating in my direction weren't pale at all. Pulling off the baseball cap, I grinned and tilted my head back to see the pink glitter of Mars. If I wanted to pretend it was like the old days, I could. Who was going to stop me? Teasing a younger brother, what could be more natural? What could be more treasured? I closed my eyes as a stream of cool air, pure and clean, washed over me. "If you have to wipe, try to avoid the poison ivy," I called.

"If you want me to believe that I'm your brother," the tart voice came from my elbow, "you have an odd way of showing it."

He'd moved up on me in utter silence. I was impressed, but not particularly surprised. Genes would tell. Our family had three generations of reason to be swift and soundless. Although I still was of the thought that Lukas . . . Michael . . . would've been the one to choose a different path from Korsak tradition. It was even possible that had he never been taken, I too might have turned out differently. Turned out better.

"You survived the deep dark woods, Grizzly Adams." I tossed the hat onto the hood of the car and gave him a quick whistle of mock respect. "I'm impressed. How do you want to celebrate? I think you've made your way through all the snack food, but you could lick the wrappers."

"I think," he said with narrow-eyed deliberation, not exactly enthused with my humor, "that a blanket would be fine."

Swallowing another grin, I fetched an armful of cotton from the trunk and put it in the backseat. "There you go, kiddo. Fold up one of them and make a pillow." I restrained an urge to ruffle his hair. It was so strong that it was painful, but it wasn't the thing to do. Seven-year-old Lukas would've tolerated it, only just, with a laughing protest, but Michael at seventeen wouldn't remotely enjoy the gesture. Most likely he would retreat, and I didn't want the day to end like that.

Michael settling down for the night gave me the chance to make some calls. I wasn't prepared for him to discover what I'd made of my life. It could be I'd never be entirely ready for that, but that was a problem for another day. The first call I made to Dmitri. He was more than a bartender; he was the next best thing to a mob yellow pages. If he didn't have the information I needed, he would know who did.

I tried the bar first. Unless he was off sick, Dmitri was usually there, six days a week. Konstantin was not one to concern himself with overtime regulations or the Fair Labor Standards Act. The phone rang several times before it was picked up and a voice said without preamble, "Koschecka. We're closed. Call back next week."

"Closed?" I drawled as I walked away from the car to

lean against a tree. The bark scratched roughly through my shirt. "Damn, Dmitri, who died?" There was silence in my ear. No glasses clinked, no music boomed; the only sound to be heard in the velvety quiet was the rasp of Dmitri's breath against the receiver. It was eerie enough to have my senses sharpening instantly. Something was wrong.

Ah, *shit*. Konstantin had found out about Bormiroff. It didn't get any more wrong than that. I had known that moment of morality was going to come back to bite me in the ass. I'd known it as I'd looked down at the man on all fours, his bloody hands trying to carry him away from death, trying to carry him away from me. I didn't try to fool myself with false memories. I'd had every intention of pulling that trigger. There was no doubt it would've effectively destroyed what was left of my soul, making the generous assumption I had one to begin with, but I hadn't seen any other option. Vasily had to die so that Lukas might live. It wasn't a fair choice, big surprise, but it was the one I had to make. That my finger refused to move had stunned me. That I'd lifted Bormiroff unceremoniously off the asphalt and hidden him in the trunk of my car before driving away had done more than stunned me. It had shaken me to the core, and not in a positive manner.

I hadn't been proud that I hadn't killed. Far from it. I was furious with myself, choking on guilt as corrosive as sulfuric acid. I had been risking Lukas's life for the life of a thief, and, at that, one stupid enough to steal from murderers. Vasily had sworn he wouldn't be seen in the state again, his hound dog eyes terrified in the gloom of the trunk. He'd promised he'd vanish. It could be done, especially if you were assumed dead. Whether that sad loser could pull it off was another story. But I'd given him the chance while simultaneously reducing Lukas's. The only thing that made the situation any less disastrous was that I planned to disappear myself days later. I hadn't anticipated needing help so soon. If Konstantin had found out about Vasily, help would be one of the few things he didn't visit upon me.

"Stefan?" Dmitri asked slowly. "Is that you?"

My attention was shifted from the recollection of helping Vasily from a bloodstained trunk in the bus station parking lot and giving him a fistful of money. "Yeah," I answered cautiously. "What's going on, Zakharov?"

"Nothing much." There was another pause, not as long as the first. "Where are you, pal?" Such a casual question and so very casually posed. I was fucked all right, thoroughly fucked. Dmitri was not especially adept or clever, and he was as aware of that as anyone. That he was attempting to be other than what he was brought home the tense nature of the situation.

"None of your damn business," I responded flatly. "Now tell me what the hell is going on, Dmitri. I don't have time to screw around here." The discomfort of the tree bristling against my back, the ache of the scrape on my jaw all faded. Every nerve ending I had, every sense I possessed; all were centered on the voice in my ear. And then the next three words shocked those senses numb.

"Konstantin is dead."

Konstantin? Dead? How could that be? People died, but Konstantin? He was a malevolent force of nature; the tidal wave that wiped out cities, the lightning storm that decimated the church picnic, the wildfire that destroyed half a state. How could someone . . . *something* like that die? My job had been to protect him and I had, but not at any time had I ever been able to picture him actually dying; not even when in the basement of Koschecka when I'd taken out his cousin with a vodka bottle. It just wasn't conceivable.

"Dead?" I said hoarsely. "What do you mean 'dead'?" Because that was such an ambiguous word, wasn't it?

"I mean that someone splattered his brains all over the inside of his car. Give me your fax number and I'll send you a sketch. Jesus Christ, Stefan, what did you do?" he hissed, the sound oddly hollow from the hand

I could so easily picture cupped between his mouth and the phone.

"Not a goddamn thing," I snapped back. "What the hell, Dmitri? You know better than that. You know who my father is. I'm loyal." As if there was any other choice for me.

"You don't show up yesterday and Konstantin ends up a *trip*. I ain't the only one connecting those dots."

A corpse. I still couldn't summon the image. Immaculate gray hair awash in blood and brain matter proved elusive to my imagination. "I had family business to take care of. I had to move fast." And asking for a leave of absence for what anyone would have classified as a wild-goose chase hadn't been precisely practical. I couldn't see my boss dead, but I had no difficulty picturing the expression on his face at the bizarrely mundane request for time off.

"So come back and explain it then. They'll listen to you, Stefan; they'd have to. You're Anatoly's kid." It was the same wheedling tone he'd used two weeks ago bargaining over the vodka. Getting me back would be some kind of feather in his cap. He had delusions of grandeur, did my pal Dmitri. He yearned to step out from behind that bar to bigger and better things, oblivious to the fact that those very things would swallow him whole. He didn't have the balls for the work or the brains to recognize the lack thereof.

In one respect, however, he was right. They would have listened to me because of Anatoly, "would have" being key words of the past. At one time I would've been untouchable, but with my father pulling a disappearing act that had lasted well over a year, that was no longer true. His dominance, once bedrock solid, was now on the wane. He still had his contacts, but the tentacles of influence had become like phantoms. He was the monster under the bed . . . terrifying, but given enough time, he could be forgotten in the light of day. If I went back, the Korsak name wouldn't save me and neither would the truth. I had called for help, but I would no longer find it here.

I disconnected, not bothering to spout protests of innocence. Dmitri wasn't the one I had to convince and the one I did wouldn't believe me. Konstantin's son was a chip off the old diabolical block but with a looser grip on his temper. He would put me down before the first word left my mouth. It was entirely possible that he'd been the one to pull the trigger on his father. I hadn't shown up; he'd seen his chance and next thing you knew, the head of Gurov senior was popping like a party balloon. It could have been him or it could've been one of Konstantin's many rivals. Whoever was genuinely responsible didn't matter. My ass was now grass in the city of Miami, if not the entire state.

I had made the call looking for names, for contacts that could provide us with a safe house for a night or two. That plan was shot to hell. I hadn't planned on going back, even once Lukas was safe, but neither had I planned on having bridges burned so thoroughly. I wondered whether I was making a mistake by not contacting the police, but in the next second I changed my mind. They had found us. . . . That man Jericho had found us so quickly, so effortlessly, I found it hard to believe he didn't have some government resources to draw upon.

My resources weren't nearly as high-flying, but I still had them, although locating the one I had in mind wasn't going to be easy. Anatoly hadn't vanished from only the authorities and the Family; he'd disappeared from my life as well. He was still in the country, I was fairly certain. He would've let me know if he was leaving. I did receive the occasional message, such as the Christmas picture, but Anatoly had made it clear before he went on the run that even I had to stay mostly in the dark. Whether it was a matter of trust or he actually wanted to keep me out of his legal troubles, the bottom line was I had no idea where he was—not yet. But I did have a list of places memorized where he might go. My father hadn't given me specifics, but our history had given me a place to start.

I made the first call.

Two hours later I gave up for the night. I was on day two of no sleep and even punching in numbers on the cell became a drunken fumble. Walking back to the car, I tripped twice and only once was from navigating the darkness. If I didn't get some rest, Michael's theoretical driving would be the only thing getting us around. Blissfully unaware of his potential chauffeuring duties, he slept on in the backseat. He was curled up all knees and elbows under the muffling blanket, and his brown hair shone in the overhead light. Deceptively pale, it looked almost as blond as I remembered it.

Sliding clumsily into the driver's seat, I closed the door with quiet care. The huddled form in the back shifted but didn't wake. I reclined the seat and folded arms against the raw breeze drifting through the empty windshield frame. It was in the fifties, unseasonably cold as it had been all the month of January. I let Michael keep both blankets. With exhaustion dragging me down with every heartbeat, a little cool air wasn't going to keep me awake. It didn't. I fell asleep between one breath and the next. It was as swift as a stumble and fall into a chasm. Slick fake leather grazed my cheek as I exhaled, and then I was gone.

Dreams of Konstantin followed me every step of the way. With a bloody hand resting on a seven-year-old Lukas's shoulder, he smiled at me coldly through scarlet-stained teeth. Unaware of the crimson fingerprints that marred the white of his Spider-Man T-shirt, Lukas waved solemnly.

The chill that chased me through the night had nothing to do with the cold.

Chapter 13

It was raining when I woke up. I could hear it drumming steadily against the window glass. I luxuriated in it for a moment. There was nothing more satisfying in the world than to lie in a tangle of warm blankets and hide from a wet and dreary morning. I turned over on my side, moving my hand to tuck it under the pillow, when I realized something. There was no pillow, there were no blankets, and the rain wasn't spattering on the window of my condo. It was hitting the roof of the car, and it was hitting me.

With a groan I straightened stiffly and rubbed a hand over my wet face. Through the tops of the trees I could see a sky the cloudy white of a freshwater pearl. The sun was the same color only a shade brighter . . . milky glass held to a fire. The rain, a warm drizzle, apparently had been drifting in for some time; my shirt was nearly soaked. At least it had warmed up to a more normal temperature for southern Florida. When I turned my head to check on Michael, I saw that he'd tossed his blankets aside. He was dry as a bone, the back windows still being intact. Shuttered eyes met mine as he pillowed his head on a folded arm. "You snore," he said in the hush.

"And you like to point out the obvious. I guess that makes us even." I ran a hand through snarled hair. The ponytail holder had disappeared sometime during the night. The first opportunity that came along I'd get it all cut off anyway. New car, new look; it was all part of the plan—the one I was making up as I went along. Disappearing wasn't as easy a trick as my father had made it seem, not with this guy Jericho sniffing the trail. I was going to pull out all the stops. Drastically changing our appearance was the first step. Maybe I'd scrounge a dress and wig and change Michael to Michelle.

"So," I said with a grin, "how do you feel about the color pink?"

Suspicion ripe in the narrowing of his eyes, he sat up and began to neatly fold the blankets. "In exactly the same way I think of making a bathroom of a tree."

He was back in his "old man" phase. The child was bound to resurface at the next fast-food joint. The thought sobered me, not because I didn't enjoy his amazement at experiencing things that I took for granted, but because it reminded me. I couldn't begin to imagine the life that had produced such an odd dichotomy in what had once been a normal if precocious kid.

"Misha," I started, ignoring the clammy sensation of the wet shirt sticking to my chest. "About this Jericho . . ."

"No." The flat denial sliced knife sharp through the air as Michael doggedly doubled the second blanket.

I didn't want to push him. I didn't want to do anything but make things as easy as they could be for the rest of his life. Making up for the past ten years wasn't practical or even possible, but it was an instinct difficult to fight. "Okay," I said exhaling with wry self-deprecation, "I know I look like some kind of superhero here, but I need all the help I can get. I need to know who this Jericho is. What he's capable of."

He kept his eyes on the cloth in his lap, hands smoothing the material. Just as I thought he would ignore me entirely, he said without emotion, "Anything. He's capable of anything."

Progress, but it was a progress that made my stomach tighten into a fist. He didn't look up as I reached over the seat and took the blanket. Shaking it back out, I used it to dry the passenger seat before inviting lightly, "Why don't you hop on up here, kiddo? You're giving me neck strain."

Silently he obeyed. The rain had halted except for the occasional drop, and he was mostly dry when he sat beside me. I started the car and cranked up the fan anyway. "I'm sorry to push you on this. I wish it could come out in your own time, Michael, I do. But we're in trouble here. I need to know anything that could help us." Tapping a finger on the wheel, I spoke more to myself than to my brother. "Such as why didn't they wait until we'd stopped for the night. It wouldn't have been nearly as public as the shit they pulled yesterday."

"They didn't want to take a chance that someone might see what I . . . that someone might see me." A brittle smile curved his lips. "Time is of the essence for them. Isn't that what they say in all the movies?"

"They let you see movies?" I asked, distracted by the thought of strangely quiet children dressed in institutional white pajamas. They were lined up in chairs before a television screen with their hands clasped in their laps as they watched images of a world beyond their reach. It was a scene from a darkly sterile future, one that I hoped not to be around to see.

"Training." The smile faded to a much smaller but more genuine one. "The only training I actually liked. And no one in the movies used a tree either."

"You just didn't see the right movies." I returned the smile and was surprised—and pleased—to see his deepen, but a sudden movement had the emotion melting away and my hand jerking toward the gun tucked between the seat and center console. The overhead V of geese honked and flew on. Relaxing, I pulled my hand away, but the shared moment was gone. "Tell me about Jericho, Misha," I urged quietly. "Tell me about the training."

The kid didn't have a nervous bone in his body from what I'd seen. His nerves, if not absent altogether, were knit of steel and titanium wire. But now I saw from the taut line of his spine and the tense clamp of his jaw that he wasn't happy with the subject at hand. They were subtle clues, barely visible unless you were looking and looking hard, but they were there. "I've been at the Institute all my life." The fleeting frown that came and went like heat lightning indicated that perhaps he wasn't as sure of that statement as he would've been two days ago. "I've been with you a little more than twenty-four hours. I'm not sure what I should do."

It was a hard-won admission of uncertainty from a shockingly self-contained boy. I treated it with the respect it deserved. "Would you go back to the Institute if you could?" It didn't seem conceivable, but I knew better than that. Some animals and most people get used to their cages, whether the bars were made of iron or something less tangible. Swing the door open and let them smell the freedom. A few would make a break for it, but the majority would turn their backs on it. Try to drag them free of their trap and they would kick and scream bloody murder. Freedom is hard, and dependence is so very easy. It's simple human nature. No one knew that better than I did. For the past ten years I'd lived in a cage built of bone, blood, and guilt, and I would've very likely have killed anyone who tried to force me out of it.

"Would you?" I repeated.

"No!" The answer was carried on an explosive burst of breath and it proved one thing instantly. Michael at seventeen was a stronger man than I had ever been. "No," he went on more calmly, "I won't go back. Not ever."

"Then trust me. Tell me what I need to know."

"Trust you?" The blackly amused cynicism that glittered in his eyes made me abruptly feel as if he were the older one. I was one day out of the family business, a grimly dark and violent business, and this kid had me feeling wide-eyed with dewy innocence. "Trust you," he echoed, shaking his head as if he couldn't believe I had the audacity to even say the words. Rolling down the window, he propped his elbow on the sill and his chin in his hand. "We had classes on that as well."

Waiting him out, I started the car and jounced our way back to the road. He would tolerate only so much pushing; I would have to be patient. It was nearly fifteen minutes before he spoke again. Eyes still gazing out the window and hair whipping in the wind, he began to speak in a voice indifferent and detached. He may have been aloof to it all, but the more he talked, the sicker I felt.

The Institute was precisely that from his description—twisted and horrific, but with the goal of education all the same. It wasn't what the students were being taught that triggered my gag reflex; it was the motivation behind it. Psychology and biology were part of a normal high school curriculum, but not the way they were presented there. They were teaching psychology to children to instruct them in manipulation and biology to illustrate the body's vulnerability. On and on it went. Every class was presented in terms of attack or defense.

Except for the occasional field trip, the kids weren't allowed any interaction with the outside world. Videos, prerecorded television programs, and computer programs were used to immerse them in real life. It was just another class. The field trips were to allow their instructors to observe the students, to see if they could blend in . . . be taken for normal children. All of this elaborate program, all this perverse training was for the purpose of . . . what? Michael had laughed when I'd guessed it was aimed at turning these kids into spies, even though programs like that had existed in my grandfather's time back in Russia, not to mention in the cheap novels I'd read in junior high.

"Why?" I demanded when he wound down. The details he had given me had been sketchy at best, and I could tell there were huge chunks of information he'd skipped over without touching on at all. "What's the point of all this sadistic bullshit? What's supposed to be the end result?"

"I'm the end result," he said without emotion.

And that, apparently, was the end of that topic. Either he couldn't face the rest, didn't trust me enough to tell me, or both. And since I already knew where he stood on the trust issue, I drew my own conclusions. But I gave it one last effort.

"Misha, the only thing I want to do is help you. As far as I'm concerned, that ranks above breathing in my book, but how can I if . . ."

"Do you want to hear about Jericho or not?" he cut in sharply, shifting and pulling at his seat belt as if it were too tight.

"Yeah, kid. I do," I relented. His customary calm might not be healthy considering his immediate past, but stripping it away all at once would leave him mentally defenseless. I wasn't sure that was the smart thing to do. I knew it wasn't the kind thing. "You can tell me over breakfast." I wanted to give him a chance to regain his balance. He might not trust me, but I wanted him to be comfortable with me . . . as much as he could be. "We'll even find you a real bathroom, nature boy. How about that?"

From the expression on his face and the set of his shoulders as he folded his arms, he let me know that was the very least I could do. He might not realize he was a teenager with all the personality traits that went with that, but at least he could pout like one. It was a start. Swallowing a smile, I kept an eye on the rearview mirror and started looking for a place to stuff the bottomless pit in the seat beside me.

Twenty minutes later we were seated in a mom-and-pop joint I spotted before we reached the interstate. It wasn't too much of a risk. We were off the beaten path. If Jericho had any bizarre form of APB out on us, I found it hard to believe it could reach into the grease-smoked depths of Mrs. Testimony Delgado's kitchen. She was the mom; we didn't see the pop. He may have been banished to washing dishes or peeling potatoes.

"No, no. Not this table, *perritos*. Scoot." She bustled out of the kitchen, her enormous breasts arriving two steps before the rest of her. Not old enough to be grandmotherly, she gave a good impression of an eccentric aunt. She would hug you, feed you with cookies and chocolate until you were as plump as she, then send you back to your parents while she put her feet up and drank a solid slug of scotch.

Waving a faded red and white kitchen towel at us, she herded us to another table in the corner. "Hope you don't mind, but that one's saved for four of my regulars." She bent over and continued in a whisper that probably didn't carry much past the parking lot. "Older gentlemen. They need to have the spot close to the convenience. Prostate troubles, poor old farts." She had prematurely silver-streaked black hair piled high on her head in a mass of carefully constructed sausage curls, amber skin with a handful of freckles, and amazing green eyes. They were large, snapping, and the color of sea glass washed on the beach. The best of many worlds combined into one beamingly glorious whole, she snatched the laminated menus from our hands and gave Michael's stomach a motherly pat. "These . . . They're not for you. Growing *muchacho* like you, I know exactly what your *panza* needs. *Flaco*." Shaking her head with disapproval, she pinched his chin. "*Perrito flaco*. Skinny puppy."

In a whirl of her green and red patterned muumuu she disappeared into the kitchen, her thick and sturdy ankles moving at a blur. Michael watched her go with something close to disbelief. I didn't bother to hide my grin. "Somebody has a girlfriend." A black glare was turned my way, and I jerked a thumb in the direction of the table we'd just occupied. "There's the bathroom you've been pining for. You might as well take the opportunity to clean up while you're in there. You need my comb, puppy?"

He slid out of his chair and gave me a scornful look that would've meant more without the confused flush over his cheekbones. Without a word he held out a hand to accept the comb and headed toward the indicated door. I poured a glass from the pitcher of juice on the table. It was strawberry, orange, pineapple, and something else mixed with crushed ice. It wasn't bad . . . not at all. I was on my second glass by the time Michael returned. I didn't feel the need to tell him I'd made a quick trip outside to check for an escape route from the bathroom. The only window I'd seen was far too small for even a lanky teenager to get through, and I made it back to the table long before Michael finished washing up.

Freshly combed hair was threaded back damply with only one strand springing free to curve and touch his eyebrow. He'd apparently run the comb under the tap before taming the fly-away strands of brown hair. I hoped he wasn't too attached to the color. "Looking good," I said approvingly, accepting back the comb. "You're going to break Mrs. Delgado's heart." I knew her name from the face beaming from a framed picture over the cash register. Letters carefully painted on the glass read TESTIMONY DELGADO, PROPRIETOR AND EMPLOYEE OF THE CENTURY. She was a woman who knew her own worth, our hostess.

The flush that had filled his face with color before he went to the bathroom reappeared. "I thought you wanted to hear about Jericho," he snapped defensively.

He wasn't used to being teased, that was easy to see. Hopefully, that would change, along with so many other things he'd been denied. "Yeah, I do." Pouring him a glass of the breakfast elixir of the gods. "But drink your juice first. I don't want a swat with the Delgado dish towel."

Lifting the glass, he gave the contents a doubtful sniff before taking an experimental swallow. "It's good." He sounded surprised, no doubt thrown off by the lack of chocolate syrup.

"*Si, perrito*, and it's good for you." Bustling up to the table, she slid two heavy white plates overloaded with food in front of us. Scrambled eggs mixed with peppers, mushrooms, and tomatoes, fried potatoes coated with cheese and onions, thick slices of ham and even thicker toast slathered with butter and jam. I felt my heart stagger in midbeat just at the sight. Serve it to a man over fifty and Mrs. Delgado would be considered an accomplice to murder. Pulling a bottle of ketchup and a jar of salsa out of her apron, she placed them on the table, smoothed a stray hair on the crown of Michael's head, and rushed back off. The woman was a whirlwind in a muumuu, a whirlwind with a black belt in cholesterol.

Michael looked down at his plate, then back up at me with round eyes. "Holy shit."

"Hey, watch it," I laughed. "Where'd you pick up language like that?"

"Movies." He picked up his fork and started on the eggs. "And you."

He had me there. I'd tried to keep it clean once we made it out of the compound, but how foolish was that? Michael had faced much worse in his life than a few dirty words. Besides, when I was seventeen I was playing football, smoking behind the gym, and my mouth had been anything but pristine. And I'd been a fairly good kid. Given that I had a father like mine, the little rebellions of a normal teenager had seemed innocently naïve . . . even to me. How could you be tempted to worse things when your father ordered men killed between dinner courses? Cheating, graffiti, vandalism—what the hell would be the point to those?

They were old thoughts and I shrugged them off to dig into my own breakfast. I ran out of steam about halfway through, my stomach uncomfortably full. Michael kept going to finish every bite on his plate and then eyed mine. The kid could eat and that was no lie.

I thought about giving him my leftovers, but the image of his spewing eggs and ham in a manner not even Dr. Seuss would approve of stopped me.

"About Jericho," I prodded as I leaned back in my chair, hoping against hope for a quick digestion.

"Oh." He stalled by helping himself to another glass of juice. That the subject of Jericho was harder to face than the Institute didn't give me a warm, fuzzy feeling. "Jericho." He took a swallow, his throat convulsing as if the juice were much thicker than it looked. "Jericho . . . He oversees the Institute. The students, the classes, everything."

"Even that room in the basement?" That ghastly room. "Does he oversee that too?"

Hand clenched tightly around the glass, he lowered his gaze into the icy red liquid. "Jericho has been at the Institute as long as I can remember. He's a scientist. All of the instructors called him Doctor." The curl of his lips was brutally bitter. "Or stuttered and wet their pants."

The memory of the shadowy figure from the back of the van was all too clear. The man had no fear or a surreal belief in his own immortality. Either one made him a dangerous man, not to mention a demented lunatic. But . . . he hadn't looked like a loony. He'd looked cold, hard, and completely in control.

"A scientist, huh?" I commented with the image of that rotating DNA helix I'd seen on the compound computers flashing through my mind. I had no difficulty picturing this Jericho involved in medical experiments on children. Of all the violent shit I'd seen in my life, nothing had turned my stomach as that thought did. "And what kind of science did the son of a bitch practice? What'd he do?" Something with a genetic flavor to it, I was presuming, but the two biology classes I'd taken in college hadn't exactly prepared me for any educated guesses.

He pushed the glass back and forth. The squeak of that and the sloshing juice were the only immediate sounds. There was the murmur of the other diners and Testimony Delgado's humming "Amazing Grace" in the background, but at our table there was silence. "Misha," I started, trying my best not to pressure him. "I'm trying to help. . . ."

The slamming of the glass on the surface of the table shut me up as it was intended to do. "Trying to help me. Trying to save me. I know." His voice was raw. "You keep saying so." From his tone it wasn't easy to tell whether he possessed any confidence in my ability to pull it off. "But you don't know. You can't know."

"Then tell me." I eased the glass from his grip and set it aside. "Explain it to me."

His shoulders slumped and he gave in. "He made us special. Jericho made us special."

That was the last I was able to get from him. Mrs. Delgado interrupted to drop the check on the table, but I had my doubts that he would've said anything more even if she'd kept her distance for a while longer. For the moment he'd reached the end of his rope; the strain was evident. He needed time to recuperate and regain a little distance.

The fact that I had questions boiling, hot and unsettled, would have to be put on the back burner for the time being. Special . . . made them special, what the hell could that mean? Misha was special to me; he was my brother. What could Jericho do to him that would make him special in a way that had Michael's voice breaking on the very word? Distracted, I dropped a few bills and a generous tip on the table. I might have been caught in my own thoughts, but I still appreciated what Mrs. Delgado had done for Michael. It had to be the only mothering he could remember receiving in his short life. There were a thousand things I wished he could recall, but our mom was at the top of the list. Chances were he wouldn't have remembered much about her anyway; he was five when she died. There would have been only scraps that remained, bits of warmth and emotion, but

I would've given anything for him to have those scraps back.

In the car I tried to focus. We needed a new car. We needed a new look. We needed a destination other than just "north," and we definitely had to find out how Jericho had picked up our trail so quickly. It was a list all right, and I knew how to accomplish only two of them.

For those two we'd need a town.

Chapter 14

The parking lot of the drugstore was nearly full, clogged with cars, and the store itself was full of people—good signs, both of them. It had taken a few exits to find just the place I had in mind. Shoving my gun into the back waistband of my pants, I got out of the car and made sure my shirt concealed the weapon. "Come on, kiddo. Be good and I might buy you some ice cream."

He was torn between outrage and desperation for a sugar fix. Settling on mildly disgruntled, he trailed after me. After walking through the automated door he looked around curiously. It was one of the superdrugstores that carried enough merchandise to cure the diseases of a small Third World country, then throw a party to celebrate, complete with wine, balloons, and barbecued weenies. Colors and noise, it was a lot of stimulation for a kid who was shuttled to the mall once a year to "act normal."

I nudged him as he stalled by the doors to stare at a woman pushing a stroller loaded with squalling twins. Accustomed to the sound, she absently reached down to smooth two nearly bald heads and kept moving. "Weird," Michael murmured, more to himself than me. "Seeing where they come from."

They, not we. Moving us both into an aisle, I lightly bumped his shoulder with mine. "I have pictures, tons of them. I'll show you where you came from. It's pretty much the same."

With a defensive folding of his arms, he studied the

shelves with a scrutiny more suited to emotionally moving art or really good porn than the feminine-hygiene products that were actually there. "What are we looking for anyway?" he asked with the avoidance of a pro.

We walked on, leaving the aisle of no-man's-land until we reached hair care products. "Anything your tree-hating little heart desires." I picked up two boxes at random and shook them in his direction. "And dye. Red or blond?"

He caught the implication instantly. "You must be joking."

"Blond it is." I put the red back with the rueful realization of why I'd picked the other color. It was more familiar to me than the brown Michael had now. Swiftly checking one way, then the other, I stuffed the small box into the wad of jacket I'd carried in over my arm for just that purpose. Belatedly, I glanced at the smaller figure beside me. "By the way, stealing is bad, okay? Don't steal." Considering, I added, "Or smoke. And don't drink and drive." Wait, he was seventeen. "Scratch that last one. Don't drink at all." It wasn't the entire summary of knowledge required for teens, but it was the best I could do at the moment.

"You're . . ." He shook his head. Apparently there were no words for what I was, and he let it go to pursue another subject. "Why are you stealing it? You have money."

"If anyone trails us here, I don't want them to know we've changed our looks." How I was going to change my appearance was more problematic. I had thought of cutting my hair, but that would only make my scar more noticeable. In the cosmetic department I found the answer: makeup specially constructed to cover scars. That, combined with a haircut, should change me enough to escape anything but a good, hard stare.

"Snack cake aisle is just down there, Misha." I pointed with one hand while tucking away the glass jar with the other. "That we'll pay for. Short of pretending one of us is pregnant, there's no way we can smuggle what you can eat out of here."

He gave me a look, one far too haughty for a seventeen-year-old, but he went. He always had been smart as hell, far too much so to bite off his nose to spite his face. I watched as he loaded up with box after box of empty calories. "I've created a monster," I groaned under my breath, deciding to pick up some vitamins before we hit the cash register. Kids took vitamins, didn't they? I remembered our housekeeper's buying them for Lukas and me after our mom died. I hadn't taken them, but I vaguely remembered a bottle of colorful characters on the bathroom counter.

We waited in line for nearly ten minutes. Sandwiched between a harassed lady with three sociopathic children and a teenage couple working desperately on making one of their own, I noticed Michael moving his weight from foot to foot. It was a minute motion, barely detectable, but it allowed me to pick up his discomfort. In the past two days with me he'd been exposed to more of the outside world than in two years at the Institute. He and the other kids may have studied it until their eyes watered; it wasn't the same. This was direct, unrelenting contact with a basically alien existence. It was enough to shake up even the coolest customer.

I dumped the items that I actually intended to pay for onto the counter. "Hang in there, *perrito*." As I'd hoped, it distracted him and he instantly turned a pale pink. "Maybe someday we can grab breakfast there again," I offered lightly. "The food was good and the company not so bad either."

The pink deepened. "Maybe," he replied, noncommittally.

I grinned at him, then transferred the flash of teeth at the cashier in the hopes of hurrying her along. She stopped tapping keys long enough to give me a smile back. It'd been a long time since I'd flirted, even superficially, with a woman. Long dark brown hair as straight as a fall of water, bittersweet chocolate eyes, and a tiny diamond piercing her nose, she was a good place to start, but she had to be eighteen at the most. She was too young, and this wasn't exactly the best time. I slapped down hormones that had been in hibernation for what seemed like years and passed over the cash.

I'd always known that saving Lukas would be saving myself, but to feel the internal thaw . . . to feel ice cracking over black water to let in the first ray of light in ten years . . . It was unexpected in its ferocity. I hadn't imagined it would be like this. I couldn't have imagined.

In college my scar and questionable family background hadn't held me back on the dating scene. At that time I'd used the occasional relationship and anything-but-occasional sex to forget my guilt over my brother's disappearance. After college I had only one relationship, Natalie. And after she left, I gave up on relationships altogether. I wasn't especially good at them, so who needed them? And sex was easy enough to find at Koschecka if I was in the mood.

I rarely was. When you're filled with guilt and rage it doesn't leave much room for the more healthy emotions . . . ones that were beginning to swell in me again. I gave the girl another smile, wistful and wicked, as she gave me my change and receipt, then prodded Michael into motion. "Let's go, kiddo. We have more shopping to do."

The shopping I had in mind took place in the parking lot. As with most places, the employees had a spot at the far end designated for their cars so the customers wouldn't be crowded out. Chances were a car stolen here would go the longest before being missed. I'd already gathered everything out of our old car and given it a quick wipe down. Now I stood casually on the back curb of the lot and made my choice—an old gray Toyota; it didn't get more nondescript than that, or easier to steal. I'd pulled a jimmy, a thin piece of flexible metal— an old tool for an old ride—out of my duffel bag as I automatically tested the door handle. It was unlocked, unbelievable as that was in this cynical day and age. Motioning Michael around to the passenger side, I started, "Remember what I said. Stealing—"

"Is wrong. Yes, I know." He put the drugstore bag in the back and then climbed in. His language was always so precise. I didn't expect it would last. He had picked up swearing from me; sloppy speech couldn't be far behind.

Within seconds we were on the road with no sign anyone had noticed anything out of the ordinary. The hours passed and I filled them telling stories of our younger days. Mostly Michael ignored them, staring out the window or leaning his head back and pretending to nap. But there were a few times I caught the gleam of interest sparking from the corner of his eye. He didn't want to believe because he was afraid to believe. I understood that implicitly. I'd become afraid to believe too in the past years. I refused to give up. Hell, I was incapable of giving up. Doing that would mean I'd as good as killed Lukas when I'd led him to the beach. I couldn't give up, no, but neither had I believed . . . not really. Not with any true faith.

Yet, here he was.

I looked over at him to see pale brown lashes resting on his cheeks, but there was an alert air to him that indicated he was still awake. I felt a rush of warmth that damn near embarrassed me. Excepting Natalie and maybe Saul, I couldn't remember the last time I gave a damn about anyone—and to this extent, never. This was my brother. This was family, true family; it wasn't that crap people like Konstantin tried to pass off. As for Anatoly . . .

"You talk about your mother all the time." With unfortunate timing considering my thoughts, his voice broke in quietly to be barely heard over the radio. "What about your father?"

Once again with the training . . . I could all but feel the

seat beneath me turn into a psychiatrist's couch as the kid spoke. I tried to ignore his still saying "my mother" as opposed to "our." Small steps; it was all about small steps. Instead I concentrated on another discomfort. Good old Dad. What in God's name could I say about him? I'd always known that the old Lukas, softhearted and innocent, would have been devastated when he eventually found out the truth. This Lukas wouldn't be. This Lukas very probably wouldn't give a shit. And he was far from innocent. None of that changed my reluctance to tell him the truth.

Finally, I settled on something that, while true, had nothing to do with Anatoly's career of choice. "He loved you. Called you his little Cossack. If he had a favorite, it was you." That had been the case with nearly everyone. Lukas had a quality then that I couldn't explain. It was like an inner light, the kind you see in people who devote their lives to something beyond them, those who have a calling. He would've been someone amazing, my brother, if he hadn't been stolen away. Now? Fuck amazing. That he was alive was more than good enough for me.

"He loved your brother more than you?" I don't think he could help the barb he inserted in the question. He was indoctrinated to home in on weakness and vulnerabilities. "That doesn't seem fair."

"I didn't say that, Freud," I said patiently. "You were special to him, but that doesn't mean he loved me any less." The fact that I had the love of a man who ordered men killed without a glimmer of remorse was something I'd never truly gotten a handle on. How do you feel about something like that? "You'll see that yourself when you meet him." And how exactly that would go I couldn't begin to guess. As certain as Anatoly was that Lukas was dead, he was bound to demand proof, DNA most likely.

"He's still alive?"

I wasn't surprised Michael had gotten the impression

that he wasn't. The stories I told were about him and me, about our mom and grandmother. Our father hadn't entered into too many of them. That was for two reasons. First, he hadn't entered our lives any more than he had the stories. He was a busy businessman; he simply wasn't around often. Second, I wasn't ready to spill the whole ugly bag of secrets just yet.

"Yeah, he's alive; just a busy man, that's all," I answered evasively. "Hard to reach."

"Is that who you were talking to last night?" The homey rustle of a Twinkie wrapper didn't take the bite out of the question.

"You heard?" I made a conscious effort to lighten my suddenly adrenaline-heavy foot on the gas pedal. "I thought you were asleep."

"I've gotten rather good at faking that over the years." Impassively, he took a bite.

"No, that wasn't Anatoly on the phone. I haven't been able to track him down yet." I tried to mentally reconstruct my half of the conversation with Dmitri last night and came up with some disturbing recollections. I'd mentioned loyalty, I'd mentioned Anatoly, and I'd said the word "dead." Talk about your triple threats. If Michael had caught any of that, overcoming his suspicion had just become a helluva lot more difficult. Unless . . . unless I came clean. Talk about the devil and the deep blue sea. Which was worse? A deceitful stranger or an honest criminal? I was a bodyguard, not a leg-breaker, but that still didn't make me as pure as the driven snow. There was no doubt about that, not in my mind.

And Michael wasn't going to make the decision any easier for me. He didn't ask any further questions to push me one way or the other. Finishing up his snack, he shifted his attention to the radio and surfed the stations without another word. Hours later, long and silent ones, I chose another hotel. We needed a bathroom, not only for Michael's peace of mind but for our transformations.

And it was mid-transformation when I told my brother the truth.

"Like a movie star," I commented with a grin, cradling the empty dye box in my hand.

Sitting on the edge of the bathtub, Michael scowled from beneath tufted hair covered in yellow goo. "I think I hate you."

"Only think?" I snorted. "Hey, I can live with that." I checked my watch. Per the directions on the box we had ten more minutes. It was enough. "Misha, I have some things to tell you." Resting the box on the sink, I added dryly, "And as luck would have it, you seem to have some time on your hands." What type of luck was something that only time would tell.

He caught a dribble of creeping yellow foam making its way down his forehead. "And I have you to thank." Meticulously, he wiped his hand on some tissue before continuing in the same charm school elocution. "Asshole." Catching my reaction before I could smother it, he sighed and reached for another tissue. "I'm not very good at that, am I? Cursing."

I could've said practice makes perfect, but I wasn't sure Michael would ever be able to pull it off. He wasn't a normal teenager and despite the Institute's effort to give him the façade of one, I wasn't sure he ever would appear to be one. "I'm sure you're loaded with other talents, kiddo," I came back consolingly.

Something about that hit an obviously sensitive area and his eyes darkened. "You were going to tell me something?"

"Yeah, I was." I boosted myself to a seat on the sink, scooting the dye box to one side. Taking a breath that somehow evaporated before it reached my lungs, I struggled for the right way to begin. "I told you how I've been looking for you all this time. How I hired people who'd made a career of searching for the missing . . . kids, things, info. Whatever. I guess what I didn't mention is how I paid for it." Leaning back, I rested my head against the cold glass of the bathroom mirror. I wanted to close my eyes, but that would've been the coward's way out. "I'm in . . . I *was* in the mob. Anatoly, our father, was in the *Mafiya* back in Russia before he emigrated. He kept up the family business here."

The eyes hadn't left me and I felt an itch of discomfort at the base of my skull. I didn't want to read disappointment in my brother's face, and there was no anticipating if I would or not. He didn't have a normal framework in which to slide this bit of information. Most things he would run into, no matter how mundane to the rest of the world, were going to be impossibly shaped puzzle pieces to him. It would be a while before things began to fit for him. Until then there wasn't any way to guess how he might react . . . to anything.

"After college, that same business was waiting right there for me. I needed the money, more than I could get from any ordinary job." I didn't make any further excuses. It didn't matter how it had happened or what had driven me; I'd made the choice. "And I stayed in as long as it took." That had been two days ago. Glancing at my watch, I stood. "Time to wash your hair. Give me a shout if it starts falling out in clumps." I went through the door and closed it behind me without a backward glance. I could wait on Michael's reaction. I could wait a good long time.

There was a pause and then I heard the shower running. There was the sound of water for about ten minutes and then ten more minutes of silence. Finally, I knocked on the door. "You still alive in there? Do we need to change your name to Kojak?"

"Who is Kojak?"

The muffled question had me turning the knob and opening the door. "Just an obsession of mine—old cop show."

A newly blond head turned in my direction. "You wanted to be a policeman?"

"Yeah, yeah. It's all very tragically poetic, I know."

The quip passed through lips suddenly numb. His hair was the color of a sun-bleached strip of sand, the white gold it had been the day he'd been kidnapped.

He turned back to look at himself in the mirror. "This doesn't make me him, you know." His eyes moved to mine in the glass. "I'm sorry, but it doesn't."

He was right. The change in hair color didn't make him Lukas. He was Lukas long before I'd picked up that box of dye. And I would keep telling him that as long as it took for him to realize it was the truth. But sometimes truth worked better in small doses, and tomorrow was soon enough. Sending him out to eat dinner, a few subs I'd picked up before checking in, I went to work on my own transformation.

Twenty minutes later my ponytail was gone. With the length gone, the short black hair had much more of a wave to it. With the curl and olive skin I looked more Greek or Italian than of Russian descent. I tried the scar cover-up. It would do. Unless someone was within six feet of me, I'd pass as smooth faced. Hell, girls would be mistaking me for a male model. I flashed my teeth at myself in the mirror. Yeah, they'd be falling all over themselves. The smile melting into a self-deprecating grimace, I decided there was little I could do about changing forbidding pale eyes. Vasily might have had puppy dog brown, but I had wolf amber; predatory through and through. Sunglasses would have to do the trick there.

In the room I discovered several discarded clear plastic wrappers and no sandwiches. Cocking an eyebrow at Michael, I said wryly, "Thanks for saving me one." I patted what I liked to think was a lean stomach. "You trying to tell me something?"

Still speeding through the television channels with the remote, he looked up. "Oh. That was rude, wasn't it?" He appeared disturbed, probably more from a failure in training than from the actual rudeness itself. Michael might not have excelled in his acting class, but I was confident he was an A student in all the rest. I had

my doubts that Jericho and his school had much sympathy for poor performers. It made me cold, the thought,
and it made me realize I still didn't know the purpose of
the Institute. If Michael didn't learn to trust me soon, I
was going to have to start pushing . . . a lot harder than I
wanted to. But for now . . .

"I'll survive." Gathering up the refuse, I dumped it in
the garbage can beside the bed. "But tomorrow you owe
me one big order of cheese fries. Which reminds me." I
searched until I found the vitamins I'd purchased at the
drugstore. Tossing him the sealed bottle, I ordered, "One
a day. Hopefully that'll keep alive the cells that don't
run purely on sugar."

After the painkiller incident I thought he'd appreciate a tamperproof bottle. "What are these?" He didn't
wait for an answer, instead reading the label, then the
ingredients. I was waiting for another Freud-channeled
crack. I could all but see it hovering on his lips, but he
resisted the urge. Maybe he thought of it as atonement
for eating my dinner. Peeling open the plastic seal, he
pulled out the cotton and chased down a pill with a swallow of soft drink. "You did a good job on your hair. You
look completely different."

"Yeah?" I ran a hand over the shortness of it, the feeling still peculiar. "Since I'm looking for a career change, I
figure I'm pretty enough to be an actor now. Maybe a
male model. What do you think?"

"I think . . ." He looked me up and down, then tossed
me the vitamin bottle. "I think vitamin B is supposed
to be excellent for the brain. It improves your thought
processes. Helps you make clear decisions."

"Biology, huh? Or the psychology of breaking it to
me gently?" I caught the vitamins. "You combined two
classes in one there. I couldn't be more proud." Reaching for the remote, I took it from his hand and switched
off the TV. "Time to turn in. We're up early." He gave in
with only a mildly petulant expression, a bare shadow of
the one I would've flashed at his age. Nearly a half hour

later I was on the edge of sliding into sleep when a quiet question ripped me back into stark awareness.

"Did you ever kill anyone?"

It wasn't a question you expected to hear in the dark while cocooned in a nest of blankets with a soft pillow under your head. That was a question for the unblinking and unforgiving harsh light of day—or never. Never would be good too. Rolling over onto my back, I studied the pattern of moonlight on the ceiling. "No," I replied simply.

I hoped it was true, but technically I couldn't be sure. I may have killed someone at the compound during Michael's rescue. I hadn't exactly been stopping to check any pulses. Nor had I particularly cared whether they'd had one . . . not for my sake. None of those bastards deserved to live in my book. But for Michael's sake, I hoped I hadn't been the one to kick them over the river Styx. It was bad enough to have an ex-mobster for an older brother. I didn't want to add the label of killer to that. I heard the rustle of sheets in the next bed as Michael processed my answer and then gave the response I wouldn't have had a hope of anticipating.

"I have," he said calmly.

Chapter 15

It rained during the night. A sheet of water had turned half of the parking lot into a rippling reservoir. A trick of the morning light made the depth of scant inches seem bottomless. When you're a kid, something like that is so . . . shit, "miraculous" is the only word. Just a little thing, but through a child's eyes it would be a lake so crystal clear that you could sail across glass to the distant shore. There would be trees that blazed autumn colors year-round, animals with the silver eyes of a benevolent moon, and amber gold grass would sing with every whisper of the wind.

It would also be a shore where children had never learned to kill.

I stepped into the massive puddle and broke the illusion. Water soaked through my sneakers as I popped the trunk to the car. My eyes burned from lack of sleep and even the rays of a cloud-shrouded sun felt like needles. Michael had slept a few hours, from what I could tell, but I hadn't. I don't think I'd once closed my eyes the entire night. Michael had finally come through with some hard information, as I'd wanted. Ask and you shall receive, right? Unfortunately, what he had told me was right on the edge of being more than I could handle. I'd once thought my brother had been taken by a sexual predator, a twisted perverse monster. I was wrong and I was right. There had been a predator. There had been a monster. But sexual abuse had nothing to do with the nightmare Michael had lived through.

There are all kinds of monsters.

Yeah, all kinds. And the one that had taken Michael was even worse than the pale slavering creepers with long probing fingers I'd concocted in my nightmares. Placing the duffel bag in the trunk, I slammed the lid with unnecessary force. The sound echoed through the deserted lot and sent a knot of birds screeching angrily toward the sky. Crouching, I checked the fasteners on the license plate to make sure they were tight. I'd switched the plates with another car last night just after we'd checked in. The original one was bound to be in the state cops' computer system as stolen by now. The Toyota was an older car without any of that satellite transponder crap that made life so difficult; I'd made certain of that. For some reason that thought tugged hard at my mind. Unable to catch the kite tail meaning of it as it flew, I gave up and shook it off. If I kept changing plates, I could get a few days before I had to get us a new ride.

"Here's your soft drink."

I looked up, startled by Michael's presence at my elbow. I'd sent him across the lot to a soft drink machine against the building. "Sorry. I was thinking." Taking the can, I popped the tab and took a swallow and reveled in the life-giving caffeine. "Thanks."

Rubbing a finger in the condensation tracking the metal of his can, he asked diffidently, "Am I still invited? Or should I catch a bus?"

The can dimpled musically under my clenched grip. He thought I'd desert him, that I was afraid of him. He thought I saw him through his eyes, as he saw himself . . . as yet another monster. Clearing my throat, I growled, "Get in the car, Freud, or you won't see sugar for a week."

The relief in his eyes came and went so quickly that it was possible I imagined it, but I don't think I did. When we were in the car, I rested a hand on the wheel. I could feel the weight of his gaze centered on the small bruise on the back of my wrist. I pulled my sleeve down farther to cover it. "A bus?" I said, hoping to divert his attention. Rolling my eyes, I started the car. "You wouldn't have the first clue how to catch a bus."

He frowned instantly. "I took . . ."

I finished the sentence with him. "A class." I laughed and after a second he smiled along with me. It was a small smile, and hesitant, but it was genuine. Sobering, I offered, "You're my brother, Misha. As far as I'm concerned, you walk on water. Nothing you could say or do will change that."

"Except sink?" The smile quirked, then disappeared as his eyes were dragged with obvious reluctance back to my bruise. "No one at the Institute can do anything good. No one who lasts."

He'd said that last night too. He'd said and done quite a few things. At one point he'd touched a single fingertip to my arm. I'd felt a numbness, then a brief sharp pain as blood cells ruptured beneath my skin. It was then that the story he'd told me seemed as if it could be true—true in the way that violence and disease are true . . . in the way that death and murder are true. And suddenly I wasn't a big fan of the truth as everything I'd known and believed exploded as thoroughly as my blood had.

"You're good, Michael," I said fiercely. "It's not what you can do that decides that. It's what you choose to do." It was a lesson that had taken me too damn long to learn. I didn't have a single doubt that he would learn it more quickly than I had, if he didn't know it already. Of course it could be I wasn't the best one to advise him on choices, because if one day we saw Jericho again, it was a good bet I would choose to make that his last day.

"I hope you find him." He saw the question on my face and elaborated pensively. "Lukas. You're a good big brother to him."

"I'm a good big brother to you," I corrected firmly. He wanted to believe, I knew he did, but he just couldn't make that leap of faith. Not yet. Considering what I now knew of his life at the Institute, the fact that he trusted me at all, even if only in the tiniest measure, was a miracle. That he was alive and sane was an even bigger one. One more and the pope would have him up for sainthood.

I, on the other hand, would never be mistaken for a saint. And with what I had boiling in me now after hearing Michael's tale, the chances of that happening dropped drastically. He'd said Jericho had made them special, and the son of a bitch had. He'd made them so special that most could kill with a mere touch. Some could do worse. Bodies had been warped from nature's plan. A little girl ... a very special little girl ... had nearly destroyed the flesh of my hand without laying a finger on me. If her hand had actually touched mine, I'd be missing that appendage now or I would be dead.

This same little girl had chosen to stay with the man who'd done this to her. The mental had been twisted along with the physical. And why not? That was much easier to do. Hadn't I convinced myself that my blue fingernails had nothing to do with a small girl with long blond hair? Hadn't I dismissed it as nothing at all?

I had told Michael about her. Her name was Wendy, he'd said, and Wendy was scary. What had felt like freezing cold was actually blood vessels constricting, cutting off the warming flow of blood. And she hadn't done it because she was afraid of me; Wendy wasn't afraid of anything. She simply enjoyed inflicting pain. She was one of the thirty children or so the Institute held. The number fluctuated. New children, usually around the age of three, were brought in when the numbers decreased due to graduations ... or other reasons. The kids who weren't working out, who didn't have a talent sufficiently powerful or destructive, were the ones who disappeared in the middle of the night.

Like Peter.

He wasn't the first of Michael's roommates to be spirited away not to be seen again. Peter couldn't do what Michael and Wendy could—not on a scale large enough to matter. No bruises; no blood; no, the most he could muster was a mildly painful tingle barely worse than a tickle. When it became apparent that was not going to change, Peter's time was up.

The names had triggered something in my mind— Michael, Wendy, Peter—and then it hit me. Michael verified it. All the kids were named Michael, Wendy, Peter, and John; lost children from the land of Pan. Jericho had quite the sense of whimsy—for a malignant cancer.

My Wendy, the angel carved from the ice of a grave, was actually Wendy Three. Peter had been Peter Two. Michael ... Michael was simply Michael. He was the first, no number needed, and he remembered no other name; no other identity. His first memory was of classes, meals in the tomblike silence of the cafeteria, and cradling white mice in his hand only to watch them die. White fur was stained with red as blood spurted from tiny mouths. "I cried," he'd said, so matter-of-factly. He had been so goddamn, heartbreakingly matter-of-fact. He cried ... the first time, but never again. Jericho didn't like tears and Jericho didn't like weakness. The mice progressed to rabbits to cats and then to pigs. Michael wore their blood blankly and without any outer emotion. That it shredded him like glass in places that couldn't be seen was something he didn't have to spell out to me.

It was some time before Michael learned to control the darkness that coiled and struck blindly within him. It was even longer before he was allowed to have physical contact with another human.

After Jericho forced him to kill a man, he didn't care if he touched another person as long as he lived.

It was a test, he had explained, as if it were perfectly normal. Sent on a bogus errand to carry a message to one of the gate guards, Michael was attacked by a strange man as he passed the building's edge. He was pinned against the wall with a knife to his throat. He had told me that if he'd had time to think, things might have turned out differently. But there was no time, only instinct, and instinct took no prisoners.

The man died. With Michael's hand spread on his chest, his heart stuttered, then burst like overripe fruit. It was a test . . . just a test. Jericho liked to see how his subjects performed in a variety of conditions. It accounted for the confusing reaction I'd received from Michael when we'd first rescued him. He kept asking if it was a test. He thought he had failed because he hadn't hurt me.

It also explained what had happened when I'd tended to his cut feet. Not used to that kind of attention, he'd kept his hand hovering over my head. He had been ready to protect himself. It was lucky for me that I hadn't made any sudden moves. Michael wouldn't have killed me, I knew that. He wasn't a killer no matter what Jericho had manipulated him into doing in the past. But he could've easily injured me in self-defense.

With just a touch.

"Um, Stefan? How long are we going to sit here?"

Jerking my attention back to the present, I grimaced. "Sorry." Putting the car in gear, I pulled out of the parking lot. "It's a lot for me to process. Things like this don't happen in the real world." The dark blue mark on my wrist mocked me. "I mean, sure, they can make designer fish that glow and splice jellyfish genes into a monkey, but this is people we're talking about. Kids." I'd seen that room in the basement and for all I knew it was one among many, but it was still hard to conceive. It was science fiction with a barbwire twist of horror. "How did that bastard do it?"

"I don't know." He shrugged, but I could see it was a question he'd thought about endlessly. "They were careful not to mention the science of it around us. I do know that they would take us downstairs. We'd lie on the bed and they would give us a shot or sometimes gas." Closing his eyes, he shook his head. "I never remembered anything after that . . . just waking up in my room. And I'd be cold. Freezing for hours."

I had to consciously relax my fingers clenched on the wheel. "How often?" It came out roughly and I cleared my throat. "How often did they take you down there?"

"Often enough I've lost count." The sun struggled through the clouds and made a halo of blond hair. "Once I woke up with an incision." Leaning forward, he touched the small of his back. "Here. But that was the only time."

The only time, as if its happening just once made it better. I tried to find something to focus on, something normal in a world that so unexpectedly was anything but. "My name." That was something and a good something at that. "You said my name."

Eyebrows now several shades darker than his hair winged skyward. "And?"

"It's a first," I grumbled. "Let me revel, all right?"

"You're awfully easy to please." He pulled at the bottom of his new shirt bearing the logo of a popular sports team. We'd purchased the purple and gold long sleeve jersey at the drugstore. He'd given me the same dubious look then that he was giving me now. "Are you sure you're a mobster?"

"Ex-mobster." It bore repeating, so I repeated it. "Ex."

"Where are we going then, Mr. Ex-mobster sir?"

Where were we going? It was a good question.

I was rapidly racing down my list of options. The first had been to get away scot-free. That was profoundly optimistic, I know, but one can hope, right?

Wrong.

The second possibility was one that had been lurking in the back of my mind well before we raided the compound. And I'd exercised it the night before last by calling Dmitri with the intention of finding a place to hide. He could've steered me to a safe house. Michael and I would have disappeared in the hairy bosom of the family for as long as it took. Konstantin, however, had managed to bring that plan to a crashing halt. Even dead, the man had the ability to bust the balls of everyone around him.

"There's a house," I said slowly, turning over the thought in my mind. "It's in North Carolina. It belonged to a friend of Babushka." A gentleman friend as our grandmother Lena had said with pursed and moral lips, I remembered with wry affection. "He left it to her when he died. Nobody knows about it now but Anatoly and me. I think that's our best bet."

"I bow to your superior judgment," he offered with suspicious blandness.

The kid was smart. God, was he smart. He was also a world-class smart-ass; far drier than I, but a smart-ass all the same. That had changed from our long-ago childhood, but I didn't mind the dig. We Korsaks were known for our mouthy quality. At least, to be more honest, I was. Regardless of our shared sarcasm genes, it was also another step down the road of recovery. It was a road that would probably never end for Michael, but that didn't matter—not as long as he kept making the journey.

"You come up with a better plan, kid, you let me know." Keeping my eye on the road, I leaned over and snagged the bag beside his leg. "Here. Read one of your books." I had directed him to pick out a few at the store. He had chosen three: a murder mystery, a Western, and a horror novel, to my surprise. I would've thought his life had been horror enough. Maybe in comparison, the novel would be a mild scare . . . a dark fairy tale. He chose the Western and began reading with one knee propped on the dashboard.

The cover was emblazoned with the typical square-jawed hero in a Stetson. On horseback he stampeded a herd of mustangs through a rocky arroyo. None of them had Annie's flirty ways or Harry's black-tipped ears. "Horses, huh?"

His eyes flickered sideways at me, almost with resignation. "I've dreamed of horses. All my life."

That straightened me in the seat instantly. "You know what that means?" He'd carried a memory with him. Jericho . . . the Institute . . . Neither had been able to take his past away from him, not completely. "Michael . . ."

"It doesn't mean anything." He turned his attention back to the book and turned a page.

"Doesn't mean anything? Jesus, Misha, if you were going to remember anything, that would be it." It was a huge part of when he had been taken. "How can you explain that away?"

"You've seen what I can do." He kept his eyes on the paperback. "Why do you think it stops there? Seeing something that doesn't belong to me, dreaming it—how is that any harder than turning someone's internal organs into liquid meat?" Turning a page, he read on.

Michael might think he didn't believe, but if that was the case, why had he told me? Why indeed. Heartened, I was about to turn on the radio, when without warning my thoughts took off on a tangent—a highly unpleasant one. I'd asked him when I'd first rescued him why they were training him, what their purpose was. He hadn't answered me then; he didn't have to now.

Trained to kill, but not as a spy. He was given a deadly ability, but not to use as a last resort. A normal boy had been warped into an engine of destruction, pure and simple.

"You're a weapon," I said quietly, my smile long gone. "A living weapon. They tried to make you into the ultimate assassin, didn't they? You and all the kids. Assassins who don't need knives or guns. For sale to the highest bidder."

He raised his hand and shaped it. Pointing an index finger at me, he dropped the hammer with a softly muttered *pa-pow*.

And he didn't raise his eyes from the printed page to look at me, not once.

Chapter 16

Five hours later, I nearly lost my brother again.

It was in a public restroom. Forget the eye-watering stench of the flowery disinfectant that was worse than the smell it was meant to cover up. Ignore the tile colored a puke green that made your stomach heave and gave you a desire to check the bottom of your shoes. Concentrate instead on puffy white feet, one in a cheap loafer, one bare and twisted to the side. Take a look at those as they show beneath the stall door. White, white skin splotched with purple veins and resting in a puddle of blood so fresh that the warmth of it steamed against the icy tile.

Yeah, take a good look. Here's someone in the wrong place at the worst of times, much like Michael found himself. I couldn't know exactly what that felt like to him, but I could hazard a guess. His stomach would be stretched comfortably full with a mystery-meat hamburger and an order of fries that would've foundered an elephant. I would bet he stopped at the mirrors over the sink, still startled by the blond hair that flashed at him from the corner of his eye. Maybe he looked at his reflection and tried, despite himself, to remember a young boy with the same blond hair. Or maybe he just groaned at the bleached mop and cursed me under his breath.

I'd take three to one on that second option.

With the door shut behind him, he didn't see the man who slapped an Out of Order sign over the universal little stick man that made the bathroom safe for penis-

carrying men everywhere. He didn't see it, but I did. And
that was something they did not expect. They waited until
I was around the corner buying Michael another apple
pie with a chocolate shake to chase it down. It wasn't the
brightest move on their part. My body may have been
around that corner, but my mind wasn't. I hadn't kept
Konstantin alive, no matter how temporarily, by standing around with one thumb up my ass and the other in
an apple pie. Jack fucking Horner I was not.

The sun hit the plate glass that lined the boxy building at the exact angle for a clear if phantom reflection of
the rest of the so-called restaurant. My eyes were glued
to it as I handed over a five to the cashier. As I paid, I'd
seen a veritable parade of the full bladdered. There had
been a pudgy old man in high waters and a white belt
who'd entered the restroom at an urgent clip. He was
followed by a man in jacket and jeans, and then by Michael. My brother now took any and every opportunity
at a toilet without leaves and bark.

I didn't think much of the guy in the jacket. We were
well into northern Florida by now and it had cooled
into the forties and fifties. A jacket was the rule here,
not the exception as in Miami. It was when the second
man, denim jacket and baseball cap, taped the sign on
the door with the speed and panache of Houdini that
I immediately realized just how many guns one could
hide in those jackets. The bastards had traded in their
khakis, forsaking the Gap for Wal-Mart.

They'd found us. In one damn day, they had found
us—*again*.

Leaving the shake on the counter, I shoved the boxed
pie into my pocket and walked to the bathroom. In a bit
of sleight of hand of my own I'd pulled my gun from the
small of my back and hid it against my leg as I moved.
Considering that I planned on making one helluva com-
motion when I passed through that door, that conceal-
ment would buy me only seconds at best before the cops
were called. But those few seconds could mean the dif-

ference between getting away and being stuck behind bars as Jericho walked out of the police station with Michael. It might be with real government ID, bought and paid for, or with the expertly forged kind. Either way, they'd be gone. It took ten years to find my brother; I doubted I would be able to find him a second time. And that was making the rainbow fantasy assumption I'd live out the week to even try.

Jericho wasn't that stupid and neither was I.

I kicked open the door hard enough to rip it from one hinge. There was an immediate reaction, in front of me and behind.

If life had taught us anything in the past few decades, it was that you could die violently in a public place long before you'd win the lottery. Psychos were everywhere. These fast-food fans were at the top of their class on that news headline. To the back of me I heard fish patties and cheap plastic prizes hit the floor as lunch patrons stampeded. Good for the herd. If the aerosolized fat in the air didn't kill them first, they just might survive.

The bathroom was fairly large. There was more than enough room for the two men to keep a safe distance from Michael. In the confines of the Institute he'd been obedient, but now he was an unknown. He'd gone along with his rescue and then ignored Jericho's demands to return with him. They may have thought he'd been confused, inexplicably gone rogue, or simply transferred his submission to me. It could be that I'd already been identified as his brother and his sudden stubbornness could be pinned there.

The speculations didn't matter. The two of them weren't about to let Michael get close enough to make contact with them—no way, no how. They had him blocked into a corner by the urinal. He had his arms folded with his hands tucked tightly out of sight. He had even less desire to touch them than they had to be touched. His life was at stake, yet he was desperate not to take the life of anyone else. That alone proved that Jericho, despite all his efforts, hadn't tainted him. Couldn't taint him.

One of the bastards aimed a peculiarly shaped pistol at Michael's chest as the other pointed a gun that was completely familiar and completely lethal. The explosion of sound that was the door shattering had their heads whipping around. Michael's eyes, as empty of emotion as his face, rose to meet mine. "I think I should've waited for the tree," he said with darkly forced cheer.

Hopefully, I'd be able to remind him of that later. For now I slammed a foot into the back of the first man's thigh before the startled expression had time to register on his face. Catapulting across the room, he crashed headfirst into the stall, but not before he'd pulled the trigger of his weapon. A dart flew through the air and hit the tile next to Michael's shoulder. That's why I hadn't recognized it. It was some sort of tranquilizer gun. Jericho would take Michael out permanently before he'd risk exposure, but if he could recover him alive, safely and secretly, that could only boost his profit margin.

The second kidnapper was turning, attempting to shift his gun in my direction. He did come close; I'll give him that. A definite A for effort, but I doubted that was much consolation. I fired the Steyr, and a bullet in his chest bowled him over backward. A fine red spray flew from his mouth to dot the white porcelain of the sink. I didn't know if he was still alive or not, and truthfully I didn't have time to wring my hands over it. The one who had cracked the stall like cheap cardboard was trying to climb to his knees. I could've shot him in the back easily enough. But the words I'd said to Michael came back to me: It's not what you can do, but what you choose to do.

I chose to beat him senseless.

Grabbing a handful of his short brown hair, I cracked his skull repeatedly against the tile until he stopped twitching. It was the lesser of the evils. Unconsciousness and a fractured face beat death hands down . . . from the point of view of the spit-bubble-blowing vegetable anyway. From my perspective, leaving any of Jericho's men alive wasn't exactly in my best interest, but that was the price you paid to walk the path of the righteous. Yeah, world's biggest frigging humanitarian, that was me.

"Come on, Michael," I rapped. "Let's go."

Inscrutable gaze on the fallen men, then on me, he flowed past me as insubstantial as a ghost. I followed behind him, my shoes flattening fries into greasy yellow skid marks. The restaurant was empty, but the glass doors were still swinging and people were sprinting through the parking lot. Taking Michael's arm, I held him back and moved ahead of him as we reached the doors. "Stay behind me." I scanned the lot with sharp, hard eyes. "And if I go down, run." I tightened my grip on him. "Okay? Run like hell and find a Saul Skoczinsky in Miami. He'll help you."

He pressed his lips together but reluctantly nodded when I gave him a quick prompting shake. "Don't go down," was all he said.

I'll do my best, kiddo, I thought silently. And then I hit the door and the ground running. Michael shadowed my every step. People were all over, running or starting their cars to career over curbs. It would be nice to think we blended in with them, but the guys inside had spotted us quickly enough despite our cosmetic changes. I didn't have any reason to believe we'd be any better off exposed in the bright noon sun. We bolted between parked cars, their colors streaking in my peripheral vision like those of a bad abstract painting. Within a few steps I had to shove one hero wannabe with a hunting knife out of my way. He landed on the hood of a shiny Ford T-Bird and slid across the ice-slick wax job to drop out of sight on the other side. I kept going without missing a step. His good luck was our bad luck; we were halfway home when disaster struck. The sound of the gun firing came as I was already falling. A searing pain tracked across my side as the world rolled from beneath my feet. And then, despite my silent promise to Michael . . .

I went down.

Thrown backward, I landed on the asphalt as the back of my head kissed the metal of a car door. Spots blossomed red and black across my field of vision, but I could still see the figure that slithered out from under the car opposite me. Cold black eyes measured me with sterile detachment. Jericho rose to his feet with a fluid grace that belied the brutal car accident of the previous day. There wasn't a mark on the man, not a goddamn scratch. I'd seen the blood on him; yet now he stood, whole and unwounded. It was disorienting, as if this were all a B movie and we were suffering a serious hitch in the continuity. Keeping a sleek semiautomatic pistol centered on my abdomen, he observed with a dispassionate charm, "Naughty. Naughty. It's not wise to take what doesn't belong to you." His scrutiny didn't flicker for a second from me as he raised his voice slightly. "Move, Michael, and I give him a scalpel-free lobotomy. That may or may not matter to you, but the two bullets that follow will be yours. One in each knee. You know from class that shattered kneecaps never heal quite the same."

And why not? Michael didn't need to walk to be able to kill. A kid in a wheelchair—who would possibly suspect him when the president of Timbuktu dropped dead of a heart attack while shaking his hand?

Head and ears ringing, I slid blurry eyes toward Michael. He'd seemed unafraid when trapped in the restroom, as cool and calm under pressure as any soldier. But that stoicism had fled. I knew he feared Jericho. As far as I could tell, that was the only thing he did fear, but dread of Jericho wasn't the emotion I was seeing now. "You're hurt." His face was as translucent as wax paper. "You're bleeding."

"Misha." The 9mm was still in my hand that rested on abrasive concrete. It would take more than a bullet in the ribs to make me turn loose of that. A cop didn't give up his gun and neither did I. Often enough it was all that stood between you and a headstone, for both the law-abiding and the somewhat less so. I was still in the game; I still had a chance to save my brother . . . no matter how small an opportunity it might be. "Misha, *ubegat. Nemedlenno.*" Run. Now.

Michael might have had language classes out his well-educated ass, but I was hoping Jericho was too preoccupied with playing the baneful God of Genetics to pick up your average Slavic dialect. Once again luck deserted me.

"He takes one step, *preyatel,* and I blow his foot to a thousand splinters of bone." He held out his free hand to his side, waiting with arrogant assurance for Michael to take it. It was then I noticed it was artificial, an artistic prosthetic detailed down to the fingernails and perfectly matched skin color. It explained how he was willing to let Michael clasp it; it wasn't flesh. It wasn't vulnerable. "I don't believe you want that," he continued deliberately. "I can use a temporarily damaged piece of goods, but I'm not at all sure you can."

He didn't know. He had no idea that Michael was my brother. How could that be? Years had passed, but the man had to guess that the family of even a much altered, long-renamed Lukas would still be looking for him. He couldn't think that we'd just give up—even if one of us had.

Anatoly might have moved on, but I never had. In all the time that had passed, I hadn't stopped trying to take care of my brother. That hadn't changed. From then until this very moment, it hadn't changed. "Misha, it's okay." My lips curled in encouragement as the blood spread on my shirt. "Now keep your promise."

I don't know what Jericho expected would happen. I didn't even know what I expected, not really. But I knew what I hoped, and Michael didn't let that hope die. He didn't let me down.

He ran.

It diverted Jericho's attention for the briefest second. I saw the flicker of disbelief cross the spare profile. Although Michael had refused to go to him days ago in the van, he still expected the boy to obey him. He couldn't believe that all the manipulation and all the training hadn't tamed Michael's inner core. He simply couldn't believe it. And when I shot him . . .

He believed that even less.

I wasn't able to lift my hand to fire. He would've seen the movement even before I made it. So I didn't move the hand; it wasn't necessary. My finger was enough. At that angle the best shot I could make was his leg. Crimson spurted from his shin and there was the flash of pearly white bone as he screamed. Hoarse, deep, and full of fury, it was the cry of a wounded predator. I'd watched enough Discovery Channel to know that only made him less predictable and a damn sight more dangerous.

Grabbing the door handle behind me, I lurched to a crouch. His gun was still pointed at me and I could see him pushing aside the waves of agony to focus on his target. I found mine first.

Gutshot isn't the best way to go. The pain of a torn stomach leaking flesh-searing bile doesn't begin to cover it. I wouldn't wish it on my worst enemy. For Jericho, however, I wished I had the time to send another slug in there to keep the first company. The close wail of approaching sirens told me that while it was a pleasant thought, it might not be practical. I had to get out of there . . . in one goddamn hurry.

The second time I'd shot him, Jericho had fallen onto his back. This time he had lost his gun, using his hand to try to stem the blood oozing from his stomach. The frozen stare had turned into one glossy with hate. Words, sharp and grating, were pushed painfully between clenched teeth. "I'll . . . kill you." Sucking in a breath, he closed his eyes and grinned with all the warmth of a toothy skull. "And if . . . I don't . . . Michael will."

Then again, how long did it take to pull a trigger?

The tackle of a speeding whirlwind made the question moot. Michael hadn't run quite the distance I'd

hoped. Arm wrapped tight around my waist, he dragged
me along with a strength I wouldn't have believed was
in his slim frame. I was still tempted to take another shot
at Jericho . . . the last shot, but as it was, I was lucky
to stay upright even with my brother's help. The bullet
wound in my side was taking a backseat to the throb-
bing in my head. From the dizziness, nausea, foggy vision, it was safe to say I'd bought myself a pretty good
concussion when my head had hit that car door. The si-
multaneous desire to puke and lie on the ground to die
wasn't too helpful in keeping my eyes open for Jericho's
flunkies, but I gave it my best shot. As we moved, from
behind I could hear a choked, ugly laughter. Jericho was
laughing. Through an agony that should've killed anything more coherent than a scream, the son of a bitch
was laughing.

   The sound was unnaturally chilling, the throaty cackle
of a hyena muzzle deep in warm entrails. Trying to block
it out, I picked up the pace as best as I could. "I told you
to run," I grunted. "If you think that's running, you can
kiss a track scholarship good-bye."

   "I guess I'll have to depend on my brain, not my legs."
His breath was fast but even against my jaw. "And I did
run—just not very far."

   "Kids these days." I could see our car. It was barely
fifteen feet away. As far as I was concerned, it may as
well have been fifteen miles. "They never listen." My
legs buckled as the muscles went from rubber to water.
How Michael kept me upright I didn't know. I had to
outweigh him by a good fifty pounds. Add one-twenty
to that and deadweight became a very real concept to a
skinny teenage boy.

   Savagely biting my bottom lip to the salty taste of
copper, I straightened and ordered legs I couldn't feel to
move faster. No one was more surprised than I that they
actually obeyed. As we fell against the driver's door, I
was already digging in my jacket pocket for the spare
key I'd found tucked under the sun visor. Pulling it free,

I tried to ram it into the lock. It was more difficult than it seemed as twin images spun lazily before my eyes. Double vision is less fun when it's minus the alcohol.

Michael snatched the key from my hand and slid it home. Flinging open the door, he stretched a hand to unlock the rear before trying to shove me into the backseat. I grabbed the edge of the door frame and resisted with a growl. "What the hell are you doing?" Icy sweat beaded my forehead and I swallowed convulsively. "You're all about the theory, remember?" I slurred. "You can't drive us out of here."

"Yes, I can." The next push was more forceful, not to mention more successful. I lost my grip and tumbled in. "I've been watching you."

Oddly enough, I didn't find much comfort in that. And I knew of a driving instructor whose leg still ached in rainy weather and who would probably agree wholeheartedly with me. Slamming my door shut, he climbed into the driver's seat. Two seconds later we were hopping curbs with the rest of the rabbits. Monkey see, monkey do might not be the best learning tool out there, but at least we were in motion. I couldn't guarantee the result would have been the same if I'd been behind the wheel.

As it stood now, I was hanging my head over the floorboards and trying my damnedest not to be thoroughly sick. The nausea was a living, breathing creature clawing its way upward without mercy. Air disguised as ground glass burned my nose and throat as a vise tightened on my head with every heartbeat. I still had the gun clenched tightly in my right hand, but my fingers were losing their grip. They slowly unlocked and the Steyr dropped onto the rubber mat below. I let it. I'd half forgotten what it even was. Something as familiar as my own face had suddenly turned so foreign as to be unidentifiable. That and the warm dribble against my neck and cheek had me blinking in confusion. "Is it raining?" I didn't need to see the puzzled look of worry that Michael shot at me over his shoulder to know it was a stupid question. Raining? Sure, because it rained inside cars all the time.

The hand I put to the back of my head came away red—poppy red like Natalie's freckles. Long-gone Natalie and long-gone Lukas; they were two of a kind. Squeezing my eyes shut, I clutched desperately at the raveled edges of consciousness. No. Not gone. Here. Lukas was here, and he needed help—my help. He was in trouble, and this time I could do something about it. This time I wasn't a boy trapped under a dead horse . . . even though I could feel the sand beneath me, the sun hot and liquid on my head. Sucking in a breath that didn't seem to want to go down, I opened my eyes and raised my head to see blond hair haloed by oscillating red and blue lights. It was Lukas . . . just as I remembered him.

"Lukas?"

The car jerked to the left as the blazing lights careened off to the right. I went with them, pulled along in their wake until I was lost. They flew around me, brilliantly glowing butterflies. I soared with them long and far until I sailed off the edge of the world. Beyond that, it's been said, can be nothing good. Beyond the end, I've heard, lies only the abyss. Beyond can be only darkness and monsters.

Big deal.

I'd already lived through both.

Chapter 17

In the tenth grade I played football. I wasn't particularly good or bad, but I was quick. Outrunning slow-witted assholes who wanted to rip me to shreds had come in handy later in life while working for Konstantin. But there had been one occasion, one game where I hadn't been quite fast enough. For that, I'd paid the price, and it was one that the three-hundred-pound gorilla who sat on my head was more than happy to collect. It was a feeling I would never forget. A giant fist had tightened on my head until I thought I could hear the literal cracking of bone. The pain was so intense that it froze the air in my lungs, turned thoughts into congealed mud, and sent jagged shards of glass splintering through my brain.

I would have given anything to be experiencing that cakewalk again.

"He needs a doctor."

Insistent; the words were very insistent, with a calm that sounded stretched to a jaw-locking tightness. There was a pause as I floated in an ocean of black agony, and then came more words. "I can't put him on. Are you even listening to me? Do you need the Merriam-Webster dictionary definition of unconscious?"

Lukas. It was Lukas's voice, and from the sound of it he was giving someone hell. Now who . . . ah. Random neurons collided with a spark. Saul. I'd told him to call Skoczinsky if he ended up on his own. Apparently the situation we were in was close enough to qualify.

I levered up eyelids that fought me every millimeter of the way. The slice of dusty yellow light that re-warded me was a cheerful ice pick drilling through the liquid mush that used to be my brain. Hissing with pain, I tried to cover my eyes with a clumsy and uncooperative hand.

The conversation continued unchecked as my heroic efforts went unnoticed. "He's been shot and he hit his head. He may even have a skull fracture, and the first aid I know doesn't cover that." I could guess how those biology and anatomy lectures went at the Institute. Here's the best location to inflict damage; don't worry about fixing it. It won't ever be an issue.

From the feel of the surface slick and cool beneath me, I was still in the backseat of the car. And from the sound of Lukas's rigid annoyance, he was right by my head. He was probably standing in the open door with his back to me, but I wasn't about to shift the water-melon substituting as my head to see, so I did the next best thing.

Holding up my hand, I croaked, "Phone."

Instantly Lukas popped into my view, his face directly over mine. From what I could see of the god-awful purple and gold shirt, it was stained to a darker color, almost black, from blood—my blood. He might disparage his medical skills, but it was obvious he had tried. "Stefan." His face brightened fractionally. "You're awake."

"More ... or ... less." Every single word was a molten lava of misery. "Phone."

He hesitated, then put the cell phone in my hand. "Better you than me."

Stubborn paranoia meeting paranoid stubbornness; talk about your rock and a hard place. Lukas and Saul were born to butt heads. I fumbled the phone to my ear. "Saul?"

"That is one smart-ass little shit, Korsak." Saul's voice, slightly tinny, stung my ear. "Are you sure you don't want to toss him back?"

"He's not ... fish." I wanted to be amused. I settled

on queasy. "Saul, we're in trouble." True enough, and the last thing I wanted to do was involve Saul. He'd done more than enough already, gone far above and beyond. Dragging him deeper into this mess was not the way to thank him. Unfortunately, I didn't see any way around it, not if Lukas and I were going to survive.

"Yeah, I gathered that from the Boy Wonder." He exhaled and I heard the sound of a hand rubbing over a face. "Tell me, Smirnoff. How bad are you, really?"

"I'm not dying." At least I didn't think I was. My eyes were beginning to focus with glacial speed. Through the car windows I could see a low, squat building and weeds as high as a man's waist. It looked as if Lukas had done a good job of finding us somewhere off the beaten path. "But Lukas is right. Think I need a doctor. Someone who can keep his mouth shut."

Saul's network of subcontractors was numerous and far-reaching. If anyone could come up with the name of a competent and ethically flexible physician, it would be him. "That's a tall order. Let me think a second. Where are you anyway?"

"North. Close to the state line." My legs were already bent and I used the leverage to try to push myself up. I managed to rise up on one elbow, but the effort had me soaked in sweat. "I don't know how they keep finding us. It's been twice now. They come out of nowhere."

"They haven't been trailing you?"

"No." As the arm supporting me began to shake, I felt two hands behind my shoulders bracing and easing me up to a sitting position. Twisting slightly, I leaned back against the seat and gave Lukas a grateful nod.

"The kid's tagged then," Saul said brusquely. "Hell, they microchip dogs and cats. It was only a matter of time."

Tagged. Shit. That was the thought that had slithered away from me when I was stealing our latest car. I'd wanted to avoid anything with a GPS, but here I was hauling around my own walking, talking homing device.

"Goddamnit." And I'd thought my headache couldn't possibly get any worse. "We're screwed," I said bleakly.

"Maybe not. If you can get to a doctor, he might be able to remove the chip as well as fix up your black and blue ass." I could hear the distant sound of typing. "And I think I have the man for the job. Okay, his name is Lewis Vanderburgh, better known as 'the Babysitter.' He lost his license ten years ago and just got out of the joint last February."

"The Babysitter?"

"Use your imagination," he ordered curtly over a thick layer of disgust. "Needless to say he wasn't too popular in the pen. He's done some research for me, medical crap, and he needs the money. Picked up an expensive drug habit on the inside."

"He sounds like a real winner."

"When you can afford to be choosy, we'll book you into the Mayo Clinic. For now it's Dr. Degenerate." He gave me the address. "Keep your eyes open and your back to the wall and you should be okay. He's a monster, but he's a weak one."

Monsters, monsters everywhere. Speaking of which . . . "Saul, I need you to get some information for me." I was fading, but this was every bit as important as finding a doctor. "Remember the scary son of a bitch from the van? His name is Jericho. I need for you to look up anything you can find about him and genetic research. Anything at all." I couldn't be more specific than that because I couldn't tell him what had been done to my brother. I couldn't tell anyone about that; not Saul and not my father. Protecting Lukas came first, even if that meant protecting him from the reaction of his own family.

"Jericho? That's all you got?"

"That's it," I confirmed, closing my eyes against the dizzying sway of tall grass bordering the cracked and overgrown parking lot. "I'll call you back tomorrow and see what you've dug up."

An exasperated growl echoed in my ear. "You'd better not think this is some kind of freebie—you got that?"

I smiled, the barest twitch of my lip. "Never."

Disconnecting the phone, I let it fall into my lap. I hung for a moment, suspended between consciousness and an endless somersault into the shadows of sleep. A touch on the back of my head brought me around. Opening my eyes, I saw a folded pad of cloth in Lukas's hand. It had once been a white sock; now it was a makeshift bandage stained beyond repair. It was a practical choice; the material was absorbent if not precisely sterile. Then again, what better place to grow penicillin?

"The bleeding's almost stopped." He regarded me gravely. "I should check your bullet wound."

I watched as he peeled up my sweatshirt with efficient hands meant to heal, not harm. "You did good, Lukas."

"Michael." He didn't look at me as he said it, keeping his eyes on my injured side. I think he knew how painfully sharp the reminder would strike me.

Sharp it was. He had very probably saved my life and at the risk of his own, but that hadn't changed a thing in his mind. He wasn't budging on the belief that he wasn't my brother. I'd come out of an unconscious haze with a lingering illusion that he hadn't shared. It was hard to let the image go, but I had to suck it up and do it ... for his sake. "Sorry." And I was, sorry as hell, but not for calling him Lukas. "Chalk it up to brain damage."

"Admitting you have a problem is the first step." He visibly relaxed when he realized I wasn't going to push him on the issue.

"I don't think there's a twelve-step program for stupidity." But if he knew of one, I was certain he would tell me about it. I looked down at the ugly furrow of raw flesh that rode just under my ribs. The bullet had carved a path that was bloody and nasty to the eye, but in reality only about half an inch deep. Some stitches or gauze packing with a healthy dose of antibiotics should take care of it. As for my head, my choices were more limited—either ingesting massive painkillers or being taken out back to be shot like a lame horse.

"Flesh wound," Michael murmured, more to himself than to me. "Lost a fair amount of blood." There were patches of white beside his mouth. After the experiments that had been forced on him, I wasn't surprised the sight of blood would be upsetting to him.

"It's not that bad," I reassured him. "I've done worse shaving."

"Even I know that's a cliché, and I've lived my life in a lab," he said dryly, a little color returning to his face. Disappearing momentarily, he returned with a shirt hanging from his hand. He folded it and pressed it against my side, although the blood flow was now sluggish at best. "You found a doctor?"

"Yeah, and not too far. Saul came through." It would be about two hours unless Michael had taken us farther than I'd thought. "By the way, where are we?"

"About twenty miles east. It's some sort of abandoned storage locker facility." He turned his head to take another look around. "I think. Things sometimes look different from the pictures and video at the Institute."

Life itself must look different outside those walls; it had to. As I shifted position against the unrelenting ache in my head, I heard the scrape of cardboard against cloth. Rolling my shoulder, I fished in my jacket pocket and pulled out a battered apple pie. "I almost forgot. Here."

He hung back in the open door for a second, then sat on the seat beside me. "Thanks." Taking the pie, he quietly opened it and took a small bite. "Did your friend know how they found us?" he asked eventually after working halfway through the dessert.

"He has an idea. Remember that incision you were telling me about?" I didn't wait for a response. It wasn't as if he were going to forget it. "Saul thinks Jericho planted a tracking chip in you."

"Oh. Like an animal." He crumpled the cardboard and deposited it with stony care in the plastic bag we'd been using for trash on the trip. "Makes sense."

It didn't make the kind of sense I wanted to contemplate, but in Jericho's eyes, yes, I could see that it would. I was hoping like hell that those same eyes were staring at a morgue ceiling right now. "Don't worry, kiddo. It's coming out. As soon as we get to that doctor, you'll disappear off their radar. For good."

He accepted it with a nod, then leaned back against the seat. There were smudges under his eyes and lines that didn't belong on the face of a seventeen-year-old. He looked as tired as I felt and we still had a two-hour trip ahead of us. "But how about we sack out first? Sleep for about an hour. Neither of us is in any condition to drive." I then added with the measure of pride he deserved, "Not that you didn't do one hell of a job getting us here. Damn impressive for your first solo attempt." His response to that wasn't exactly what I expected. Then again, few of his responses ever were, but knowing what I knew now, that wasn't surprising.

"It's strange." His eyelids fell. "You're strange."

"Yeah?" That wasn't exactly news. "How so?"

"I don't know." His respiration began to deepen as the exhaustion took its toll. "From the beginning you've treated me the same as you would treat Lukas, the same as you would treat your brother." He shrugged his shoulders minutely. "You've been so . . . patient. So harmless. Then today . . ." The words trailed away. Either he was at a loss for the rest or was losing the battle against sleep.

He'd seen me in action during his rescue, but that had been swiftly done and the majority under the cover of my darkness. Following that I'd been the big brother . . . a teddy bear. This morning, however, I'd become a teddy bear with teeth—teeth coated carmine red and anything but harmless. I was the guy who bought him apple pies, but I was also the one who shot men without hesitation. It was a dichotomy of darkness and light that would be hard for anyone, much less a kid, to absorb. And what made it more difficult was that the same duality lived inside him. His had been forced upon him while I had chosen mine, but it didn't change the fact we both straddled that bloodred line.

We were brothers all right, in more than genetics.

"I'm here to take care of you, Michael. To be on your side." I didn't know if that reassured him or not. For that matter, I didn't even know if he was still awake, but I repeated it all the same. "I'm here for you, nobody else."

The here-and-gone glimmer under masking eyelashes let me know he had heard. "I guess neither of us is harmless," he said softly. "The only difference is you use weapons and I am one."

"Don't get stuck on yourself, kid," I contradicted, sliding down a little in the seat. "Compared to most people I know, you're barely a fluffy hamster."

He laughed. It was barely audible and smothered in fatigue, but it was a laugh and not half as somber as I expected. Then he rolled over onto his side and this time did slip into a peaceful sleep. I wasn't far behind him.

Chapter 18

The double vision was mostly gone, but reading the map was still a bitch. Rubbing my eyes against the blistering pain, I directed, "Take the next exit, then go left."

Nodding, Michael announced, "I like driving. How much does a car cost if you actually buy one instead of stealing it?"

"Funny. Funny stuff." I tried to thread fingers through my hair but backed off immediately with a grimace. The curls were matted thick with dried blood. Pulling down the visor, I took a look at myself in the mirror. Jesus. I looked like the the lone survivor of a ketchup factory explosion. I couldn't check into a motel like this. I'd have to grab a shower at the doctor's place.

"Are you hungry?" With his hands precisely at ten and two on the wheel, just as the manual said, he glanced over at me. "I still have food from the drugstore."

My nausea peaked at the thought. "No thanks, kiddo." It might be a day or two before I could keep anything down. Concussions were good for that. Football had taught me that particular lesson and working under Konstantin had only reinforced it. "Maybe later."

That didn't seem to satisfy him and he checked the rearview mirror, then the side mirror, before turning his attention back to me. "Are you sure? You should at least drink something. You've lost blood. You need to replenish your fluid volume."

"Replenish, eh?" Holding my hands up in surrender as he slitted his eyes, I gave in. "Okay. Okay. There's a bottle of something down here." I retrieved the half-empty soft-drink bottle from the floorboards and opened it for a lukewarm sip.

Mollified, he let me drink in peace, although I had the suspicion he'd be pushing those snack cakes again in no time. After I finished drinking, I blew softly into the opening of the bottle. The resulting musical note accompanied the bass drum pounding between my ears. "I'm going to be okay, Misha," I declared lightly, unsure of the best way to approach a delicate subject. "I promise. I won't leave you all alone out here."

His hands tightened on the wheel until his knuckles stood in stark relief. Setting his jaw, he denied stiffly, "I'm not afraid to be alone."

Of course he was afraid to be alone. He'd gone from a tiny fishbowl to the wild blue ocean. And while he may have shared that tank with a piranha, that didn't mean there weren't predators out here as well; unknown dangers that lurked around every corner. Everything was strangely surreal, and nothing was quite like it was in the pictures and books he'd been shown. Naturally, he was scared. I'd have pissed my pants in his situation.

"I know you're not," I said agreeably. "I'm just saying." It was one thing to be aware of his perfectly justifiable fear but another thing altogether to shove his nose in it. No teenage boy would be accepting of that, free-range or lab raised.

"That's not why I came back for you." Stopped at a light, he studiously looked out his side window. "It's not."

I knew it wasn't, but that didn't stop the tiny verbal nudge I gave him. "Then why did you?"

"Good question." The light turned green and he fed the car more gas than was strictly necessary in a move that had nothing to do with inexperience. "That's a very good question."

Casa de Vanderburgh turned out to be quite the dump—big surprise. A squat block covered with stucco

that was crazed with as many cracks as a two-dollar
ceramic pot, it didn't precisely shout *House Beautiful*. The driveway was floating islands of asphalt shot
through with rivers of yellowed weeds, and the flower
beds hosted only dust and cola cans. The one spotless
and gleaming exception was the satellite dish on the flat
roof. Cleanliness might be next to godliness, but twenty-
four-hour-a-day porn beat lawn care hands down.

The twisted shit that stoked his engine couldn't be
found on television, not even satellite, but he was likely
making do with what he could get, poor suffering bastard. I choked down the growl that threatened to push
its way from my throat and closed the car door. This was
business. If I kept that first and foremost in my mind, I
might get through the next few hours without resorting
to violence. Saul wouldn't thank me for putting a source
in the hospital . . . no matter how much he deserved it.
As for paying his debt to society, ten years fell short . . .
by about ninety or so.

Resting my hand on the hood of the car, I waited until
the dizziness settled and then I headed for the front
door. I plodded the ten feet and every step felt mired in
the thickest mud. Michael hovered behind close enough
to catch me if I fell, but I managed to avoid the embarrassment. Standing on the concrete blocks doubling as
a poor man's verandah, I raised my fist and knocked on
the door. As we waited, I commanded, "Stick close while
we're in there. The guy's a . . ." I stopped and reconsid-
ered. Michael had had a psych course, true enough, but
how in depth they would've covered child molestation I
couldn't begin to guess. And it was not a concept I particularly wanted to get into while standing on a pedo-
phile's porch. I settled on an evasive, "He's a bad guy,
and he likes to hurt kids. I want you to be careful, okay?
Keep me between you and him at all times."

Technically, Michael was probably too old for Vanderburgh, but he did look younger than seventeen. He
had the self-possession and an intellect older than his

years but the appearance and naïveté that could have him passing for fifteen, maybe even fourteen. Worse, he was beautiful. If anyone had said that to me when I was that age, I would've squirmed with outrage. Beautiful simply isn't a word a guy wants applied to him. Good-looking. Hot, if it was a girl saying it ... sure, no problem, but not beautiful. Unfortunately for Michael, that was the word that suited him the best. He'd outgrow it eventually. In a few years he'd be the model type I'd joked about when I'd cut my hair. But for now he was a young David, pure as shining white marble and incandescent as the sun.

"Why? I can take care of myself, Stefan," he countered with an obstinate streak that was beginning to show more and more. "If I have to."

Maybe he could and maybe he couldn't. From what I'd seen this morning, he was in no hurry to hurt anyone, and that was all to the good in my book. It could be that might change when it came right down to the wire; I couldn't say. Regardless, I wasn't about to place him in a situation that required him to use an ability that he was so obviously ambivalent about; not if I could avoid it.

"Against assholes like this guy you shouldn't have to," I replied firmly before pounding on the door again. "So stick close."

"Who is it?"

The wary question was easily heard through the cheap metal of the door. "Friends of Skoczinsky's," I answered. "We need a doctor."

Silence. Then came a voice. "You have money?"

"I wouldn't be standing here if I didn't." The jamb was scratched and the grain irregular beneath my hand, but it was enough to keep me upright. "Now hurry up and open the door before I give it a new puke paint job."

There was the metallic chuckle of a lock tripping and the door opened, a rectangle of light in the dusk. Standing there in a dark blue robe over burgundy and white striped pajamas was Santa Claus. His pink scalp peeked through snow-white hair. His short beard was as curly as the cocker spaniel my mom had had before she died, and his eyes, half hidden behind bifocals, were the same limpid brown. Just how goddamn disturbing was this? Forget the better mousetrap; someone had built a better pervert. He was a malignant hook concealed in the bait of pudgy cheer.

Robe straining over the swell of belly, Vanderburgh looked me up and down. Full pink lips curved into a distasteful sneer. "You couldn't have made yourself more presentable first?"

He had a lot of gall. He hadn't wasted any spit and polish on the outside of his squalid shack, but he was bitching at me over some dried blood. I can't say that I was much in the mood to hear it, whether it came directly from old St. Nick's mouth or not. "And my money's just as dirty as I am," I drawled, "but I bet you'll take it just the same." Pushing past him without an invitation, I blinked. What he hadn't wasted on the outside he'd run wild with on the inside. There wasn't much space in the small living room, but what there was he'd filled with plush furniture, lamps of jeweled glass, and finely woven rugs that covered a dingy tile floor. The television was plasma and hung like a cherished painting in a place of honor on the far wall.

"Nice. I guess you don't shoot all your cash into a vein." I wanted nothing more than to sink onto that soft, soft sofa and sleep for days. But even if I'd trusted Vanderburgh enough to shut my eyes, it simply wasn't in the cards.

"No, a portion I spent on this." He lifted a pistol from his robe pocket and pointed it at me. It wasn't anything fancy—your standard .38 available at any pawnshop—but it would do the job as well as the pricier models. Those soft brown eyes had become small, hard stones. "Now, let me see the color of your money. And, gentlemen, credit cards are not accepted."

It wasn't an unexpected turn of events; business was

business. I opened up my wallet to flash the money at him. It was the only thing it held. My ID, genuine and fabricated, was hidden in a much more secure location. "There you go. Happy?"

He was. Six-gun-packing Santa clucked his tongue in satisfaction and laid his gun on the mosaic-inlaid coffee table. "Go to the back and try not to drip any bodily fluids on your way."

Nudging Michael ahead of me, I obeyed. The back room was twice the size of the living room. There were cabinets of drugs and supplies, a low bed with plastic sheets, and a portable X-ray machine. "Sit down." The esteemed ex-doctor waved a plump hand at the bed before pulling over a wheeled silver tray laden with instruments. He didn't bother to ask what the problem was or give a heyhowyoudo as I took a seat. He had no bedside manner whatsoever. Wielding a pair of surgical scissors, he put a hand on my shoulder, shoved me flat, and deftly sliced my shirt up the middle before I had the chance to slip it off. After a quick look, he grunted and went to work.

He cleaned the wound efficiently but without a whole lot of tender loving care. I gritted my teeth and endured it. Filling the raw channel with antibiotic cream, he covered it with a bandage and tape. "Hardly worth my valuable time," he grunted as he flexed gloved fingers painted with dabs of red. "Let's see if the head trauma is a tad more interesting."

At the head of the bed Michael bristled slightly but kept an even tone. "He has a concussion. Even I can see that and I'm no doctor."

There was an assessing look aimed at my brother, and it was one I didn't care for . . . not at all. "A concussion, you say. Aren't you the knowledgeable boy? Well, could be or perhaps it's more than that." Strong fingers mercilessly probed the gash in my scalp. "A slow bleed in the brain is a possibility, but without a CAT scan there's no reliable way of knowing." Cold, avid eyes moved from

Michael to peer at me over the top of crescent-shaped lenses. "Then again the fact that you haven't dropped dead yet can be counted a good sign."

"Thanks. That's a real comfort," I muttered.

If he noticed the sarcasm, he was unfazed by it. "You'll need stitches and IV fluids for the blood loss. Local anesthetic and painkillers are available at an extra charge."

Hippocrates would be so proud. "Give me the local and a bottle of pain pills. I prefer to dose myself." If there was any doping to be done, I didn't trust Vanderburgh to do it. "What about the dizziness and nausea?"

"They'll pass," he said dismissively as he reached for a syringe and a rubber stopper vial. "I can give you something for it until then. Of course, it'll cost—"

"Extra. Yeah, I gathered that." The sharpness of a needle bit at my skin and filled it with a cold, numbing liquid. I was glad he hadn't decided to shave a patch of my hair for the stitches. That would be taking my new look a step too far.

Michael was still at my side and looking less impressed with the ex-doctor all the time. He'd been fine through the dressing of the gunshot wound, but now at the sight of needles piercing flesh, a sliver of discomfort showed. That was only going to get worse when it was his turn. The memories made in the Institute basement were going to color anything medically related with suspicion and anxiety. I couldn't change that or erase the past, but I still had some minor tricks up my sleeve.

"Misha." Snagging his sleeve, I suggested, "Maybe you should check the car. Make sure you put it in park. With driving as shaky as yours, better safe than sorry."

"Shaky?" It wasn't outrage on Michael's face. He had his emotions far too battened down for something as overt as that. Control was the name of the game, and it was a game that had kept him alive longer than that poor doomed roommate of his. That type of ironclad restraint wouldn't allow for visible wrath, but it had no problem with annoyance.

"Why do you think I'm so nauseated? Forget concussion. It's car sickness. You drive like a drunken grandma."

The annoyance went from mild to a diamond-hard intensity. "I do not. And, by the way, I was not the one who ran over the statue of a large purple pig."

"Now you're just being petty," I rejoined. "That pig died for the greater good and you know it."

By the time Vanderburgh finished with the stitches, Michael had decided it wasn't worth wasting valuable oxygen to argue with me, as I was clearly insane. Bending down to examine the results, he relented, "It looks better. Quite a few stitches, but I don't think it should scar too badly."

"What's one more?" I asked wryly before sitting up. Within five minutes I had an IV going into the crook of my arm. I'd chosen the IV bag myself. As I'd said to Michael, better safe than sorry. "Okay, Doc." The man was no more a doctor than I was despite his years of med school, but I had even less desire to say his name. It was bound to taste foul, like rot. "Now we have a more complex problem." I explained, in very general terms, about the tracer planted in Michael. Being more specific wasn't to our advantage. The man would sell us out in a heartbeat if he knew whom to get the money from.

"Intriguing." Those repulsively fleshly lips pursed. "If it's not too deep, it may be possible to remove it. I'll need an X-ray first for location. That's going with the assumption that it has a metallic component."

"Yeah, here's hoping," I said, standing. Towing along the IV pole, I moved in front of the doctor. He'd left his gun in the living room, carelessly enough, but mine was still here with me. Retrieving it with one smooth motion, I centered it directly between his eyes. The muzzle indented rosy skin just below the V of silver-tufted eyebrows. "I'd just like to go over a few things with you first, Babysitter." I smiled. It wasn't a wolfish smile or that of a shark. It was merely a simple friendly one. After all, weren't we beginning a trusted doctor-patient relationship? Didn't I have Santa's best interests at heart? Sure I did.

"First, you perverse prick, look at him like that again and I'll kill you." I didn't bother to elaborate. He knew all too well which look I was referring to. "No warning. No second chances. Just a bullet to that squatting cancer you call a brain. Second, when you remove the tracer, you'll be a damn sight more gentle with him than you were with me." I pressed harder. "Are we clear?"

Those round eyes seemed to sink deeper into doughy flesh like oven-wizened raisins. He'd survived what couldn't have been a cushy prison stretch; he wouldn't scare too easily. But then again, I wasn't trying to frighten him. I was only giving him the unvarnished truth, and that could be more terrifying than any threat. "I'm not—," he started to deny. They always denied, his kind. Always.

"Are we clear?" I cut him off as a reddened bruise began to form beneath the metal.

He gave in to the inevitable. "We're clear," he said tightly.

"Great. Clarity is good for the soul." I let the gun drop to my side. "Michael, are you ready?"

He had been or at least he thought he had been until that moment. Looking at the hospital-style bed so similar to the one from the Institute, he came within a hairbreadth of losing it. It wasn't anything as noticeable as trembling or fear-sweat slicking his face. He simply went still. It wasn't a human stillness. It was the crouch of a cocky jackrabbit frozen under the gaze of a hawk; it was the inner core of a stone hovering on the lip of an avalanche. He wanted to move; he wanted to run, but I couldn't let him go. With that chip in place, it was only a matter of time until they found us again. He couldn't ever be free until he lay down on that bed.

Trailing IV tubing, I placed a hand on the back of his neck and squeezed lightly. "It's about time you kissed those assholes good-bye, don't you think?"

He exhaled, then gave a wooden nod. "I think. I do think." Making it to the bed under his own power, he lowered himself onto his stomach. The thin pillow was ignored and pushed aside as he used his folded arms instead. Despite his adult response, he'd never looked younger or more lost, not even when I'd plucked him from the heart of the Institute in the middle of the night. I dragged up a chair beside him, rested the gun in my lap, and ordered, "Get started, Doc. We don't have all night."

As he was pushing the X-ray machine in our direction, I reached out and pulled Michael's left hand from beneath his head. Simple human contact was something he'd been deprived of most of his life. Here was hoping it could help him now. "Squeeze it as hard as you want, kiddo. It won't break."

A green and blue stare reminded me that actually it could, if he wanted it to, or worse. But he remained quiet and let his hand lie loosely in my grip. It was only after the X-ray was developed and his bare lower back was swabbed with Betadine with meticulously professional care that his hand swiveled in mine and tightened until my bones creaked. "Butch and Sundance," he offered in a barely audible whisper.

It was a distant echo of a long-past conversation, one he didn't remember and one I couldn't forget. Swallowing thickly, I asked, "What about them?"

"They showed us the movie. Along with others, about all sorts of things. So we'd be convincing, you know? We'd be able to have normal conversations." His cheek rested against the sheets. "If we had to."

I don't think he expected that occasion would've

arisen—kill and get out; chatting rarely required. "What about our favorite outlaws?"

His eyes shut as a needle delivered the same local anesthetic used on me. His voice had thinned but was still solid. "When they jumped."

On the run from the posse, they'd sailed off the cliff hand in hand, going down together toward an uncertain fate. "Yeah, I remember." The soft drip of the IV hung in the background. "So which of us do you think will hit the water first?"

"You. Your legs are longer."

I admitted with a small laugh, "You've got me there."

He didn't speak again throughout the rest of the procedure. It was done in a relatively short time although it had to feel much longer to Michael. The chip wasn't implanted too deeply and was plucked free to lie bloody and innocuous on a sterile drape. It was small, one-third the size of my pinky nail. A tiny bathroom adjoined the room less than four steps away and I promptly flushed the tracer down the toilet. Let them follow that straight to the nearest waste disposal plant. I only wished I could see them stumping through the steaming muck.

Acutely conscious of my eyes on him, Vanderburgh sealed the inch-long incision with some sort of skin adhesive and covered it with a bandage. Backing away as I helped Michael sit up, he muttered something about getting our pills together and sidled over to a glass-front cabinet. I changed my mind about using the shower. I wasn't turning my back on this piece of shit for a second, much less ten minutes.

"You doing okay?" I asked as Michael rearranged his shirt and stood.

He nodded. "It's still numb." Even when the local wore off, it should only be mildly sore. "But I feel . . . lighter. It couldn't have weighed even an ounce, and until today I didn't even know it was there." His hand unconsciously moved to cover the unseen bandage. "It's stupid, I know."

"You're a lot of things, kiddo, but stupid isn't one of them." Putting away my gun, I grabbed a square of gauze and used it to quell the gush of blood that welled when I pulled out my IV. I accepted the piece of tape Michael scrounged for me from the pile of supplies on the counter and used it to fasten the gauze to my skin. The grinding headache was still present, but I felt slightly better. The fluids had lessened my light-headedness, if nothing else.

"Antibiotics and pills for pain and nausea. Follow the directions on the label," Vanderburgh commanded curtly as he extended a clear plastic bag filled with three brown bottles in my direction. I took it, opened all three bottles, and extracted a pill from each.

With my other hand gripping his thick wrist, I placed the pills, red, purple, and white, on his palm. "Dry or with a glass of water. Your choice."

His fingers closed over the pills. "What?"

"I'm just not a trusting man, Doc. Go figure. Now take the goddamn pills."

Opening his hand back up, he stirred the tablets with a finger, then took the red and purple ones. Swallowing them dry, he opened his mouth to reveal an empty pink cavity. The white pill he crushed underfoot. "I think perhaps we can find you a different pain pill."

"Yeah, that's what I thought." The gun at my back positively itched to be used. Despite my recent career, I wasn't prone to violence. I did what I had to do, but I hadn't liked it. I would've liked hurting this man. I think I would've liked it quite a bit.

Once he'd demonstrated the new pills were safe, it was payment time. Meanwhile, Michael had moved with alacrity back out to the living room. He may have survived the experience, but it was unlikely he wanted to hang around that medical environment any longer than he had to. By the time I finished passing over the cash and followed, he'd had time to hide Vanderburgh's gun and start messing with the man's VCR/DVD player.

Yeah, he'd hang on to the VCR part as long as he could. No doubt some of his best stuff hadn't made it to DVD or Blu-ray yet.

I took note of the now-empty coffee table and was duly impressed. Vanderburgh probably wouldn't rush out to shoot at us as we drove down the street, but there was no need to leave him the option, and Michael hadn't. "Let's go, kid."

"Okay." He dropped the tape he was shifting from hand to hand and stood from his squat. As he walked toward me, he passed close to Vanderburgh—much closer than I liked and much closer than he normally would have. I'd noticed in the store and restaurants that Michael had a large sense of personal space—not surprising considering what he'd been through. That he was voluntarily violating it now made me wonder . . . until I saw his hand brush Vanderburgh's robe below the tie. It was the lightest of touches with the most drastic of consequences.

The old man's face went an unpleasant plum color and the portly figure of the former doctor fell to his knees with a choking gasp. Fat hands paddled desperately before settling on his crotch, cupping with exquisite care. "What?" Air whistled through his open mouth. "What—what's happened?"

What indeed.

"Good-bye, Dr. Vanderburgh," Michael offered politely before exiting from the front door. He didn't look back at his handiwork, although I did. Vanderburgh had fallen onto his side and curled up, an obese and tearful fetus. He could cry the proverbial river; it wasn't going to equal one of the tears of his victims.

Trailing after my brother, I closed the door behind us and cut off the pants and sobs issuing from behind us. "Misha." I watched as he fished the keys from the pocket of his sweats.

"Mmm?" He inserted the key into the lock.

"All right, Mr. Casual. What did you do?" I demanded.

"Cut off the blood flow to his testicles. Permanently." Opening the door, he looked at me across the top of the car. "You were right. He's not a nice person. Not nice at all." Then he disappeared behind the wheel.

The tape. Michael had seen something on that tape that had given him a glimpse at Vanderburgh's blackened soul and that glimpse had given new meaning to the phrase "blue balls." Once in the passenger seat, I took one of the pain pills. After swallowing, I said in the best big-brotherly tone I could manage through my pounding headache, "You really shouldn't destroy a man's balls."

"No?" The car started, the sound only ratcheting up the pain in my head a notch.

"No." I closed my eyes.

"Even if they deserve it?"

He had me there. "Well . . . yeah, the son of a bitch definitely did. There's no denying that. But I don't want you getting hurt in the process."

"It doesn't hurt me." He sounded so certain, but I remembered just last night how he'd told me he and the others at the Institute couldn't do anything good and how in the morning he expected me to discard him as tainted and leave him behind.

I rolled down the window an inch and let the cold air play over my face. I was getting tired, damn tired, and the twilight chill would help keep me awake. "Funny. You didn't seem so sure of that when those assholes had you trapped in the bathroom."

"That's different."

I opened my eyes the better to see in his face exactly what it was he was trying to say. "How so?"

"He hurts kids. Normal kids," he amended. "Kids who can't protect themselves."

"Yeah, they can't protect themselves like you can,

but that doesn't mean you're not normal." He rolled a darkly disbelieving eye in my direction but didn't comment. "But that's not what I'm talking about," I added. "I want to know why you'd do something for faceless strangers that you won't do for yourself." It wasn't as if there was much he could've done in the face of two guns, but even if the men had been unarmed, I still doubted he would've "laid on the hands," so to speak. I'd seen his face. He wouldn't have done it ... not then anyway.

He shrugged with discomfort that wasn't as concealed as he thought, but I didn't let it go at that. "Misha. Give. Why wouldn't you protect yourself? You wouldn't have to kill, God no. But you could give a little of what you gave to the doc. So why not?" I could understand his never wanting to use what he had in him. I might think it unrealistic, but I would understand. To use it for others and not himself, though, that I couldn't.

There was the squirt of cleaner on the windshield and the swish of wipers. He watched them with fascination before reluctantly bowing to the inevitable. "Because"—he paused—"because I'm beginning to wonder if I don't belong in a cage after all."

That woke me up quickly and thoroughly. Glaring, I reached over and thwapped him lightly in the back of the head. Startled, he looked over at me with wide eyes. "Say something stupid like that again and you'll never see an empty calorie again as long as you live. No cakes, no candy bars, nothing. You'll be cut off."

He was smoothing the back of his hair as I talked and entertaining the thought of giving me a dirty look. I could see it as clear as day. "Don't bother," I warned. "Bottom line, kid. You don't belong in a cage. No one but no one is going to say that, not even you. Got it?"

"Guess I had better, hadn't I?" he answered with what seemed to be only mild irritation. After a few minutes of the only sound being the tires on the pavement, he said quietly, "I wouldn't have given up. I wouldn't have let them take me without a fight." The dusky purple light filled the car, making him increasingly hard to see . . . as if he were fading away. "I just don't know if I could hold that part of myself back once I started to use it in a situation like that. All the adrenaline. Fighting for my life." I thought I saw his face work in the darkness. "I won't risk killing again. I can't. I still remember how it felt . . . with that man's heart beneath my hand. How it pounded; then the muscle melted like wax. I could feel it scream and die even through his chest." He stopped, and I wasn't sorry he did. Hearing that wasn't doing either of us any good right now. There would be time to talk about it later. When we were free and safe, we'd talk about a thousand things until he was at peace with every one of them.

"Then you don't have to." End of story. "Leave the violence to me, Misha. I'm already used to it."

He had something to say about that; I didn't have to see him to know the wheels were spinning in his head. But winter air and determination aside, I dozed off before he was able to get the words out. Against a concussion and a pain pill, consciousness was a lost cause. Michael woke me up when we stopped at a gas station and I cleaned up as best I could in the grubby bathroom. The paper towel dispenser was empty and I scrubbed away dried blood with wet toilet paper. There wasn't much I could do about what was matted in my hair, but hopefully I would pass a brief inspection at the motel.

I did. It was a small, run-down place with only ten rooms and a small gravel lot. The guy behind the counter had blond dreads decorated here and there with rusty metal hoops. If he had noticed the condition of my hair, it would only have been to give me a thumbs-up. The room was even worse than the outside, but it didn't matter. With a thin, rock-hard mattress and a dingy cracked ceiling, it was the Ritz-Carlton as far as I was concerned. I fell into bed as if it were feather stuffed and covered with silk sheets. I was gone in an instant, and I dreamed. Like Michael's, my dreams were of horses. There was also the beach with churning waves and a sky as improbably blue as an Easter egg. There was no strange man; no gun. There were only horses that lived to canter into the water and boys who never learned to live without their brothers. They were good dreams.

The best.

Chapter 19

"Saul, you're giving me a headache."

That wasn't entirely true, but he was adding to my already existing headache.

"Giving you a headache?" Outraged and louder than the voice of God booming down on Moses, it had me yanking the phone from my ear with desperate speed. *"Giving you a headache?* I've got Pudgy the Pervert crying to me from his hospital bed that his balls have been cut off. Have you ever heard a fat ex-con cry? It's no goddamn fun."

"I didn't do anything to the man's sack, okay?" I repeated with weary patience for the third time.

"The balls are gone, aren't they? And my business relationship with the dickwad isn't looking too good either. He might be a bastard, but he was handy to have on the roster."

"He still had balls when I left, Skoczinsky," I growled. "You can't blame that on me." On Michael maybe, but I was thoroughly innocent. As for the missing balls, either the hospital had amputated them or Vanderburgh had botched a do-it-yourself home job.

"I know you, Korsak. You had something to do with it." He'd said my name on a cell phone, the least secure connection in the world today, which broke his rule of "protect the client." He was pissed all right. There was a groan that turned into an aggrieved sigh and then a reluctant question. "He wasn't doing that shit again, was he? With the kids?"

"I have no idea," I answered honestly.

"If he was, I would've driven up to hold him down while you made with the cleaver. You know that, right?" I did know, but he didn't wait long enough to hear my confirmation. "Ah, hell, balls or not, he can still work. And speaking of work, I've got that info you wanted."

Fumbling for the bottle of pills on the nightstand, I wrestled with the stubborn cap. "Yeah? Lay it on me."

There was the rustle of papers and Saul became even louder as he cradled the phone between shoulder and chin. "John Jericho Hooker. Forty-seven years old, raised in Massachusetts. He's a doctor several times over, medical and otherwise. He has doctorates in human and molecular genetics and biochemistry. Started college at the tender age of fourteen—a genius brat apparently—and hasn't looked back since. Genetic replacement and manipulation—what there is to know he practically wrote the book on. What his peers felt wasn't worth knowing is where he got into trouble."

This sounded promising. Getting up, I filled a glass at the bathroom tap while Michael showered. "How so?"

"Two words. Human chimeras."

Okay. I got one of those words, and that wasn't so bad. I was the king of partial credit in college. "Come again?"

"Human chimeras, obviously. Surely you've heard of them, Korsak. Big college-educated mob guy such as yourself." Then Saul dropped the lofty tone and admitted, "Yeah, I'd never heard of them either. Apparently there are more things in Heaven and Earth, just like my bubble gum wrapper said. A human chimera is the result of twins, mostly identical but occasionally fraternal, intermingling in the womb. Blood or other genetic material mixes between the two of them. One twin usually dies in the womb and the twin left has the building blocks of two instead of one. Sort of like human to the second power, I guess."

All right. It was vaguely interesting, but was it pertinent? The jury was still out on that one. "And what's this have to do with the man in the moon?"

"Hooker is one. A natural chimera—and damn proud of the fact. He did a lot of groundbreaking work, so says Google, that's the backbone of the field of genetics today, but his true passion was for chimeras. He was of the opinion that his humans squared should be stronger, faster, smarter . . . everything we are, but only much more so. Now, the fact that he wouldn't submit proof of that was really no big deal. It was a pet theory; all scientists have them. It was when he started into the psychic crap that eyebrows began to rise."

A single cold finger climbed my spine as if it were a ladder. Psychic. I didn't know exactly how to classify what Michael and the other Institute children could do, but it had to occupy some twisted corner of the psychic realm. "Psychic? What the hell?"

"I know. As we said in the van, he's a goddamn fruit loop. He calculated that if they would be stronger and faster, they would also have a heightened psychic ability. Of course, if he'd ever bothered to demonstrate all those abilities himself, maybe he wouldn't be the pariah he is today." I heard him yawn. "Shit, maybe I'm a chimera myself. Twice the sexy jammed into one body. Now that's a science project worth the bucks."

"Bucks? How about cents?" I replied absently. Michael had come out of the bathroom. Bare-chested, he was wearing a pair of my jeans that bagged ridiculously on him and a towel hanging around his neck. My eyes went instantly to the incision on his lower back. He'd said it hadn't hurt when he'd gotten up this morning, and now I could see why.

It was gone.

The only sign the surgery had ever taken place was the thinnest of silvery lines, nearly invisible to the naked eye. I felt my mouth go dry. Stronger or faster, I didn't know if there was truth in that or not, but Jericho had certainly proved resilient. It had to be the same resiliency that Michael was exhibiting. The recollection of his tattered feet from the night of the rescue hit me. The next day he'd said they were fine when I'd asked and had seemed puzzled by the question. At the time I'd thought he was reacting to a concern he was unfamiliar with, but it could've been simple confusion over what he thought a pointless question. Of course they'd been fine, no doubt completely healed.

Turning, he blocked my view as he dumped the towel and pulled on a long sleeve T-shirt. He caught me staring and raised his eyebrows in question. Shaking my head, I strong-armed my attention back to the phone conversation. Saul was still indignantly jabbering about my cheap shot and I interrupted without mercy. "So, you say he's a pariah. Then what's he been doing lately?"

"Once his pet theory became his only theory, he literally dropped out of sight. The scientific community probably wasn't very sorry to see him go. The chimera line was on shaky ground, but then he went over the edge. Psychic research isn't any more accepted now than it ever was, not when it comes to the big boys. These are the guys who have their eyes on the Nobel, and they don't have the patience for anything that isn't one hundred percent for that goal."

"Then there's nothing else? About the kids or the compound?"

"Nada. For nearly twenty years he's been off the radar. Forgotten except for textbooks and old articles." There was the explosive pop of a soft drink can being opened and then a long slurp. "But with what was in that room we saw there, he couldn't have been up to anything good. And that's above and beyond kidnapping kids."

"Was there anything in the news?" Saul had made the 911 call the night we'd broken in, but I hadn't heard anything on the radio over the following days regarding captive children held in a walled compound.

"Not a thing. Not a damn word. And if that doesn't scream government connections out the ass, I don't know what does. I even sent one of my people out there to take a casual look. It's still locked up, but the guards are gone. I'm betting everyone else is too. They've pulled up stakes."

And taken the children with them. I had my brother back, but there had to be more than thirty families out there whose sons and daughters and brothers and sisters were still missing—worse than missing. While I wished we'd been able to take more of them with us, I realized it might not have been so simple. The thought of that tiny porcelain Wendy on the loose in public was bone-chilling. As she skipped down the sidewalk, her fair hair floating behind her like spider silk, her huge eyes would be wax doll empty as people collapsed in showers of blood all about her. Wendy was a victim, I knew that, but was she a salvageable one?

I didn't think she was. I really didn't. But some would be like Michael or Peter. Some could be saved. But without the help of the authorities, I couldn't guess how a large-scale operation like that could be pulled off—not now at any rate, but I wouldn't forget those kids, and I didn't think Saul would either. "Keep your ears open, Saul. Just in case. Okay?"

He promised he would, then hung up. Damn, I'd forgotten to ask if he knew how Jericho had lost his hand. The information probably wouldn't be useful, but you never knew.

"What did you find out?"

Damp hair neatly combed, Michael was sitting cross-legged on the other bed opposite me. Skin pink, eyes bright, he was apparently healthy as a horse. Yeah, a horse whose racing was done in healing, not on the track. Scrubbing both hands across my face, I filled him in on what Saul had told me. That Jericho was involved in genetics wasn't news, but the chimera aspect was. I mentioned the stronger, faster, and smarter, keeping the accelerated healing to myself. I wanted to discuss that separately.

Michael was a chimera; that couldn't be avoided. The question was whether he had been born one or whether genetic manipulation had taken place after he was kidnapped. Saul had mentioned a chimera could be found by way of a blood test. If Michael was a natural chimera like Jericho, that information could've been obtained surreptitiously from the hospital where Lukas was born or from his pediatrician. I had a hard time buying that natural chimeras had always been among us and no one had noticed their so-called superhuman qualities. Maybe Jericho had been the first of his kind, a new breed of chimera. And it wasn't that far a jump to believe Jericho could have used his knowledge of genetics to somehow force other normal chimeras into the same mutation. That had led to the creation of the accelerated healing and fatal talent for cellular destruction, although so far Jericho hadn't shown any signs of the latter. That must have been an "improvement" that he stumbled upon during the process. He'd made something amazing and frightening, half wonderful and half dire. He was a cruel god, Jericho.

"Smarter," Michael mused. "Yes, I can see that."

"Uh huh, I'm sure you do." As for stronger, he had seemed stronger than a kid his age should be when he dragged me to safety across the parking lot, but not freakishly so. I stood and felt my joints howl from the drug-heavy sleep of the night. "I'm going to grab a shower, Einstein. Try not to formulate any theories while I'm gone."

"Just as well. I'm not sure that any theory could explain you."

Smart-ass kid.

The hot water eventually loosened up my muscles enough that I was able to gingerly wash my hair. But first I simply stood there, head hanging while I leaned with my hands against the mustard yellow tile. The water poured over me and whirled down the slow-working drain. It was hypnotic . . . liquid glass spinning in lazy rotations until it was swallowed from sight. It wasn't as soothing as it should've been. Jericho was still out there. I'd hoped the son of a bitch had died there on the asphalt, in midmaniacal laugh. But now . . . I was less optimistic. Even with Michael's chip gone, I didn't like the idea of Jericho's still trolling the waters looking for us. It might take him longer to find us, but it was by no means impossible. It could be done.

Hadn't I done it?

It had taken years and years to find Michael, but I hadn't had government help or at least not the kind Jericho had at his disposal. I didn't think it would take Jericho as long—not nearly.

By the time I finished showering, shaving, and dressing in jeans and socks, it was nearly a half hour later. Feeling slightly more alive, I walked back out into the room to see Michael watching porn. "Holy shit!" I bounded over to the TV and turned it off. The directions for the play-for-pay channel were labeled clearly on top of the television. They were easy enough for a self-proclaimed genius like my brother to comprehend. "You little *otradbe*."

"Brat?" He blinked with an innocence that was suspect at best. "A curiosity about the human body is natural in a teenager my age."

"So's an ass kicking. You wanna place bets on which is the more natural?"

As he lay on his stomach with pointed chin resting on folded arms, his air of amused disdain couldn't be missed. He'd seen all I had done and was yet willing to do to keep him safe. To say that put a serious kink in any future disciplinary threats I might make was putting it mildly. That I was thoroughly screwed was the more accurate assessment. Giving in was not in my nature, though, and dumping the batteries of the remote into my hand, I tossed the device back to him. "Knock yourself out."

"Foiled again," he said, grinning. "How will I ever

cross nearly three feet to turn it on manually? It boggles the mind."

"Silicone rots the brain, kid. Hang in there. We'll find you a nice girl closer to your age and basic chemical makeup." Tossing the batteries into the nightstand drawer, I gathered up the first aid kit for a bandage change.

Either taking pity on me or being more curious about what I was doing, Michael ignored the television for the moment and sat up to watch me work. Sitting on the edge of my bed, I began to strip away the wet bandage from my side. When the graze, red and puffy, was revealed, he immediately frowned.

"Something's wrong."

It seemed all right to me, a little inflamed, but there were no other signs of infection and no fresh blood on the bandage. "What? It looks okay."

"It hasn't healed at all." He moved in for a closer look. "It should be nearly half closed by now." Brown brows met in an ominous scowl. "That man. That *doctor*." His mouth twisted as if he wanted to spit the word. "He did something, didn't he? Poisoned the wound, infected it."

The prime opportunity to bring up the healing issue had just appeared. "Whoa, Misha, you're jumping the gun there." I looped fingers around his wrist and squeezed gently. I'd never been one for physical displays of affection. Mom had been, Lukas too. As a child, he had been all about spontaneous hugs and football tackles. I'd taken more after our father in that respect, but if ever someone needed some tangible affection in his life, it was Michael. And changing my ways hadn't turned out to be as difficult as I might have imagined it to be. "You don't know, do you?"

He didn't. It was plainly seen in his puzzled and wary expression. "Know what?"

Jesus. Where to start? And how could he not be aware of a difference between us that was so fundamental? "Your back. It's healed already, right? I saw it."

He nodded, still perplexed. "Of course it's healed. It's been almost twelve hours, and it was a small incision to begin with."

Releasing his wrist, I stalled a little as I squirted out a generous wad of antibiotic cream onto a square of gauze. I wanted to phrase this in a way that he wouldn't feel any more to the left of normal than he already did. "It's like this, kiddo." I applied the cream and hissed at the raw bite of it. "Your average Joe takes a while to heal. Something like those won't completely scab over for days; it's too big. And it won't fully heal for weeks." If I were lucky. "It seems, along with the extra dose of smarts you seem so sure you received, you and the other kids have some kind of accelerated healing. Jericho too." Holding the gauze in place, I nodded at him to rip me off a few pieces of tape. "See? You can do something good. Pretty damn miraculous in fact."

Independently of the rest of him, his fingers mechanically tore off sections of tape and handed them to me. "I don't under . . . I didn't know. We heal more quickly?" His gaze moved to the bruise that he'd given me. There, on my wrist, which wasn't covered by a shirtsleeve now, was more evidence of what I was telling him.

"And then some." I taped the gauze into place and began to clean up the supplies. "About ten times faster at least."

"We didn't seem any different from the people in the movies." The statement was both stubborn and wistful. It reminded me of when at the ripe age of six I'd found out there was no Easter Bunny. I'd denied the truth and yet mourned it all the same. Miraculous or not, this was simply one more thing that set Michael apart from the rest of the human race. In his eyes, that wasn't anything to celebrate.

"The movies?" I gave a nostalgic smile of my own. "No, I guess not." When he watched the hero get shot in one scene and scale fences in the next with only a tiny bandage as a memento, why wouldn't he think that was just the way things were? After all, that was the way he was. As for his education, I'd already reasoned it was aimed at making the perfect assassin. The body's mechanisms of overcoming trauma, not to mention the timetable involved, had probably been low on the list of classroom topics. At best, it was irrelevant; at worst, it might cause sympathy for the prey. Maybe it was something they told them before "graduation." Maybe they never told them at all. I couldn't begin to second-guess the twisting paths of Jericho's reasoning. The sick son of a bitch . . . making children over in his own image, but not for a longing for his own kind. No, he'd made them to be killers; made them to sell. Bastard.

"It's a good thing, Misha," I reiterated. "I swear." Picking up the shirt I'd laid out, I put it on and winced as the action pulled at my side. "Trust me. Right now I'd love a little bit of that myself."

He didn't look as though he believed me, but, more than that, he was regarding me with something very close to betrayal. "You—all of you." He wrapped his arms around himself and said grimly, "You're all so *fragile*. So breakable. No wonder it's so easy to hurt you."

"We're tougher than you think," I countered immediately. What I meant, of course, was that *I* was. Michael had lived years without anyone to rely on, his whole life from his incomplete memory. Now he was asking himself how he could possibly depend on me. Hell, I could trip over a curb and die when I hit the pavement, right? Fragile . . . never in my life had someone entertained that notion about me. "I've stayed alive these past few years in a business that doesn't exactly pull its punches, kid. I might heal a little slower than you, but I do heal."

He didn't look convinced, and I didn't think words would change that. Only time would prove to him I was here to stay, healing impaired or not. I couldn't completely reassure him, but maybe I could cheer him up. The batteries went back in the remote and I handed it over with a sigh. "Go on. Just take it in small doses, would you?"

I made calls while he surfed. He gave equal time to naked women and a documentary on ancient Egypt, but from the stiff punching of the remote buttons, he still had enough attention set aside for less pleasant considerations. Keeping a concerned eye on him, I dialed my cell phone. I knew tracking down our father wasn't going to be anything but difficult, but it didn't make the futile call after call any easier to endure. Most of the numbers I'd memorized two years ago at Anatoly's order either rang endlessly or were disconnected. I was hoping he would show up at one of the numbers still working. On the run himself, he nevertheless had the resources and the manpower that would make our chances at survival a little less grim.

"The landlines are too easy to trace, aren't they? That's why you use your cell phone."

Twenty useless minutes had passed when Michael's quiet question came from the other bed. Calling it quits for the moment, I switched the phone off and rubbed a hand across a grumbling stomach. "Yeah. Cells can too, but it's more difficult, especially when you're on the move and they're disposable. That's why I picked up a few when we stopped for the dye." I bent down with care and felt for my sneakers under the bed. "You want something to eat?" There was an unnecessary question if ever I'd asked one, but Michael didn't need someone else taking complete control of his life . . . telling him where to go and when. He needed to be included in decision making, at least as much as was possible in our situation. Independence was important to any seventeen-year-old; it would be doubly important to him.

We missed breakfast but caught lunch in a small café. Close to Gainesville, we drove on in to find a strip mall with restaurants, stores, and a putt-putt course. Volcanoes belched smoke and water dyed turquoise tumbled over rocks as wildly colored plaster jungle animals crouched frozen to swallow golf balls whole. Gracious enough to let me drive this time, Michael ogled it the second he climbed out of the car. "That's . . ." Craning his neck for a better look, he tried again. "It's . . ."

"Tacky? Hideous? A crime against God and nature? What?"

"Amazing," he breathed.

We ended up playing for more than an hour, and he beat me every time. I consoled myself with the fact I was a wounded man, but the reality was that he would've beaten me anyway. By the time I dragged him to the café, I was disgruntled, my stomach was devouring itself, and I had a fast-growing phobia of artificial grass. After dual orders of bacon cheeseburgers, old-fashioned malts, and steak cut fries, we hit the bookstore.

"What are we looking for?" Michael asked curiously. "I haven't had a chance to finish the ones we bought at the drugstore."

"This is for work, not fun." I dug out a sheaf of bills and passed it over to him. "I want you to pick up something on genetics. Anything that might help us understand more about Jericho and what he's done to you and the other kids."

He didn't exactly brighten—that wasn't the right term—but his focus definitely sharpened. "You want me to do research?"

"Who better than a smart-ass . . . I mean, a smart guy like you?" I grinned. "I'm going to grab a chair and take a break. Come and get me when you're done. Then we need to haul some ass." I'd wanted to buy him some more clothes, but with the miniature golf excursion setting us back, we really didn't have the time. And leaving Michael alone in the store while I shopped elsewhere wasn't something I was willing to do. The chip was gone and Jericho was hopefully down for a few days at least, but it didn't matter. Life had taught me all about careless moments. I wasn't going to have another.

The road to Hell . . . shit.

I fell asleep. It wasn't hard to understand how it could happen. Hard to forgive, but not hard to understand. The physical trauma of being shot the day before combined with a full stomach and an hour of swinging at golf balls took me down like a Mack truck. When I woke up ensconced in an overstuffed armchair close to the front windows, I felt a momentary ripple of confusion. It was one of those where-am-I flashes that bounce through your brain like a manic Ping-Pong ball. It was similar to the mornings when the alarm clock rang shrilly and you couldn't begin to comprehend what was screaming at you.

But there was no alarm this time—only low voices, glossy covers, and a chair beneath me that was patterned with roses and hummingbirds. The smell of cinnamon and coffee hung in the air and a sports magazine was lying across my knees. That same magazine slid to the floor in a heap when the world abruptly slid into place and the confusion disappeared in the face of stomach-plummeting fear. I'd fallen asleep and left Michael unguarded. I'd . . . Jesus Christ.

Before I headed into complete panic, the gleam of a familiar head of blond hair had my head whipping toward the window. Michael was outside. Talking to another kid who was about thirteen or fourteen, he appeared to be in one piece. Safe. He was safe. The air was just air again, not heavy unbreathable chunks, and I headed for the door with a chest that ached only slightly. Although it took only seconds, by the time I reached Michael, the other boy was already gone. But he'd left something behind.

"What the hell is that?"

He'd given me one damn good scare and it put a snap in the question that I ordinarily would never have used with him. Then again considering what he held in his hand, I couldn't be one hundred percent positive about that.

"A ferret." Hoisting the cage to eye level, he gazed

fascinated at the creature through the crosshatch of wire. "That boy sold him to me for only thirty dollars."

"Only?" Beady black eyes and a glimmer of pointed ivory teeth turned in my direction to regard me with an ill-favored stare. "It's like the fairy tale. I send you out for a cow and you come back with magic beans. Worse yet, stinky magic beans with sharp teeth."

Another ill-favored glare came my way, this one blue-green. "Are you saying he smells bad?"

"He doesn't exactly smell good, now does he?"

"And you're making the assumption that you do?"

This was getting us nowhere in a hurry. Switching topics, I said more harshly than I intended, "I told you to get me when you were done with the books. I can see how that might sound like 'traipse up and down the sidewalk like a bulls-eye with legs,' but use some goddamn common sense, would you?" Immediately, I regretted lashing out. These past few days had been Michael's first taste of freedom. It was easy to see that he would want to do some exploring on his own, and he hadn't strayed far.

The faintest wash of dull red stained his neck as he said stiffly, "You were tired. I thought I'd let you rest for a few more minutes."

Suddenly, regret was kissing cousins with the sudden unshakable belief that I was an utter asshole. "Ah, damn it." Morosely, I rang a blunt fingernail off the metal of the cage. "Welcome to the family, Stinky." Jerking my finger back, I barely avoided a nasty bite.

Michael recognized it for the apology it was and unbent enough to correct me. "His name is Godzilla."

I groaned aloud. "That's encouraging."

He tilted his head curiously. "Why is that?"

That must be one of the movies that hadn't made it to the Institute. "Godzilla is the big lizard that ate Tokyo. Famous movie monster, and from what I can tell, he had nothing on this little fur ball." There was a bag of books at Michael's feet and I retrieved them. While I did so, I offered gruffly, "I'm sorry for snapping, kiddo. I was worried."

"I know." He gave me one of his rare smiles. It took a lot of imagination to call the stoic quirk of lips a smile, but I saw it for what it was. "Babushka."

"Granny, my ass." I grumbled on in that vein as I steered him through the parking lot, stopping only to swipe another license plate for our car. Michael didn't hear a word of it. He was too involved in a mutually rapturous conversation with his weiner-shaped weasel. It would chitter happily at him while he clucked a musical tongue back. For me it had nothing but murder in its tiny brain, but apparently my brother passed some sort of muster known only to plague-carrying ankle-biters.

I was surprised Michael would want a pet, especially one so similar to the lab animals that had died in his hands. Then again, maybe having one would help him get past that; help heal the parts of him that didn't knit as fast as his skin and bones.

Redemption in an overly musky ferret; stranger things had happened.

Chapter 20

Tokyo might've been half a world away, but I was right here to terrorize, and that was more than good enough for Godzilla.

"Okay, that's it," I snarled. "This time that half-digested hair ball took my gun." The bedspread twitched at the bottom and I saw a toothy grin bared at me. Somewhere under there in no-man's-land were my Steyr—unloaded, thankfully—four socks, a pair of underwear, and my comb.

"I think I saw a public service announcement about gun safety just this morning." Sprawled on the bed, Michael turned a page. "Carelessness and tiny paws just don't mix." And that was the sum total of his sympathy as he continued making his way through one of the science books that we'd bought yesterday. This one was about the thickness of a phone book, but he'd devoured the majority of it, taking in every single word like a human sponge. Lukas had been a bright kid, bright as hell, but this . . .

Smarter, faster, stronger.

I hadn't seen any signs of the faster yet, but as for the rest . . . I felt an uneasy ripple tickle the base of my brain. Saving Michael was first and foremost in my mind always, but when he was safe, what then? There were many Jerichos in the world, in intent if not talent. If any one of them sniffed out Michael's capabilities, we would be on the run all over again—perhaps for the rest of our lives. It wasn't what I wanted for my brother.

But that was another worry for another time and pre-mature at best. We might not survive long enough to see an existence beyond Jericho. Or beyond the damn ferret for that matter, a distinctly evil squeak had me adding to the thought.

I slid my foot under the bed to feel around for my gun. In retrospect it wasn't the most intelligent move to be made. The sensation of a miniature bear trap clamping on my big toe had me hopping backward and swearing loudly. If the lamp hadn't been bolted to the nightstand, it's hard to say what I might have been tempted to do. Two dots of scarlet bloomed on my sock as a length of charcoal fur flowed past me to perch on Michael's head. Under a black mask a wet, pink nose wrinkled derisively at me.

Damn rat.

As I used the opportunity to retrieve my belongings, Michael lifted up a finger and scratched the chin of his new best friend. "You should be more understanding, Stefan. Hoarding is probably a natural instinct for the ferret. Isn't that right, Zilla?" The polecat made a con-tented sound, a cross between an eep and a purr, before draping bonelessly over Michael's skull for a nap. "I re-ally do need to get a book on ferret care and their hab-its. Maybe we could stop tomorrow?" He'd lowered his voice in deference to the snoozing spawn of Satan.

I didn't know which was more annoying: that he whis-pered for his pet but stomped around like a drunken lumberjack in the morning when I tried to sleep, or that he wanted to take time out of fleeing for our lives to get a how-to book on his carpet shark. "Yeah," I said with blatant insincerity. "I'll put it right at the top of my to-do list." Securing my weapon against thieving paws, I zipped up the duffel bag and jerked my chin at his book. "You find out anything interesting yet?"

He scooped the ferret into his hands and sat up to place it carefully on a pillow. Stretching, he then traced his fingers across the glossy pages and said, "Everything in here is interesting . . . in its way." As if the thought unsettled him, he closed the book firmly and pushed it away.

"A little too close to home?"

"Maybe," he admitted reluctantly only after I started to reach for the book. "No, it's all right." The volume was swiftly retrieved before I could get a grip on it. "This is me. This is my history. I want to do this." That he embraced, but my part in it he refused point-blank.

"I'm a chunk of that history too, Misha, believe it or not."

Before he could deny or give me a sympathy that was unwanted and unneeded, I sat down beside him and pulled off my sock to examine the puncture wounds in my toe. "You used to drive me crazy, you know? Typical little-brother stuff." I brushed a thumb across my skin and wiped the drop of blood away. "You stuck to me as if I had Velcro on my ass. When I first kissed a girl, you were there, hiding in the bushes. I think your exact words were 'Eww, cooties.' Funny, how thirteen-year-old girls don't appreciate that. Or thirteen-year-old big brothers for that matter." Balling up the stained material, I tossed it over onto my bed. "Then there was the time you thought my bike wasn't snazzy enough, boring navy blue not being your favorite color. So you painted it purple . . . with a couple of yellow stripes. And I yelled at you." I sent my other sock the way of the first. "Not much of a surprise, considering. But you were hurt. You'd done something to make me happy, and I yelled at you for it."

I still had that bike. It was in my condo storage unit. It was one of those things you simply couldn't look at, yet couldn't throw away.

"Did you ride it that way?"

Surprised, I laughed. "Um . . . yeah, I did. For a while."

I'd forgotten about that. We'd lived in an actual neighborhood at that time, with sidewalks and huge houses on postage stamp–sized lots. I'd tooled up and down our street on that clown cycle to universal howls of laughter. Mom had been alive then and she'd gently coerced me into it, saying it was the only way to cheer up Lukas. "It was pretty humiliating, but I guess I don't have any right to complain." As understatements went, it was a goddamn doozy, but Michael didn't challenge it. Why would he? As far as he was concerned, it had nothing to do with him. If he didn't accept that he was my brother, then he could hardly blame me for his life with Jericho.

"I never had a bike." There was a bag of pretzels beside him and he dug for a handful. "But I prefer cars anyway. Purple, yellow—the color's not important as long as they're fast."

"A potential speed demon—that's all I need," I remarked with a roll of my eyes, accepting the snack bag he passed me. He was joking, I was fairly sure. The times he'd driven, he'd been very careful to stay within the speed limit even before I'd explained that the last thing we wanted was to be pulled over by a cop. "Hey, it seems I'm always the one doing the talking, telling the tall tales. Let's hear some from you." I didn't know if he was ready for that, but I wanted to give him the opportunity. He'd already told me about the classes, the training, the experiments, but he had been careful to keep it impersonal and at arm's length as if it had happened to someone else. If he had expended even an ounce of emotion in the telling, I'd missed it.

"You don't want to hear my stories." He leaned forward to deposit a pretzel by the sleeping ferret's head. "Boring, all of them. Eat, sleep, go to class—not much entertainment value there."

"I'm not a demanding audience," I prompted. "So lay it on me." At his continued silence, I nudged him with my shoulder. "I know they won't be happy stories, kid, but don't pull any punches. I want to know what you went through at that hellhole."

"At the Institute." His head dipped and fingers

wrapped around a strand of hair over his eyes. Tapping those knuckles against his forehead, he exhaled. "It's been only days. I can't believe it. When I wake up in the morning it takes me a minute to remember that I'm not still there, but the rest of the day"—he shook his head— "the rest of the day it seems forever that you showed up in my room dressed up like a Hollywood ninja."

That had been last night's cheesy movie. That was one thing Michael hadn't gotten his fill of at the Institute. He would watch a movie on any subject—good, bad, or just plain freaky. I let the ninja remark, damaging though it was to my ego, sail past and I waited for him to go on.

"I didn't think you were there for me. Not for one minute, not for one second. You were just another test, one I couldn't pass. Jericho had made it clear I wasn't doing too well. Graduation was coming up for me, but I wasn't living up to my potential."

I could hear the quotes around the last word. "How many graduated before you?"

"A few. I'm the oldest now, but it doesn't go by age." He released his hair and dropped his hands onto his knees. Lifting his shoulders slightly, he let them fall in a small shrug so precise, so controlled that any casual element was lost. "But I wasn't going to make it. I'm not as obedient as the other students, and I don't like to kill. I'm good at it, but I don't like it." Pitch-black humor came and went in his face. "Your Wendy will probably graduate before she turns eight."

Not my Wendy, thank God. That was a thought I didn't want to contemplate, and it led me to others of a similar nature. What if I'd opened Michael's door to find that he was like that little girl, his brain as twisted as his genes? What if taking him into an unsuspecting world hadn't been feasible? As I'd said, they were thoughts not worth thinking.

"You? Disobedient? The hell you say."

With a jaundiced air at my mockery, he revised. "Maybe it would be better to say unenthused."

There was the crunch of teeth against rock-hard bread and I swiveled my head to see the drowsy ferret clutching the pretzel in its peculiarly adept paws as it nibbled. The sight reminded me of my earlier curiosity. "Jericho, do you know how he lost his hand?" Since he healed at the same breakneck pace as Michael, I would've thought, short of chopping the appendage off, any normal damage would heal.

"John." He frowned and got to his feet. "It was John." Moving over to the window, he fiddled with the blinds. Fidgeting was uncustomary behavior for Michael. He was so routinely sanguine, in his way as unflappable as our father was—or as Konstantin had been. Like both of them, he lived deep inside himself. But whereas my father and former boss came by the trait through the slow erosion of their finer human emotions, Michael had developed his out of a sense of survival. It made sense, that inner retreat; for him it had always been far safer there.

"John?"

Opening and closing the slats, he let in the dim yellow illumination of the security lights that bathed the parking lot. "He was the only one older than me. He was my first roommate, the first person I can actually remember in my life." He kept his back to me as he talked, still gazing out of the window. "Aside from Jericho."

I remembered how he said they numbered the children, identified them as the experiments they were considered to be. Wendy had been Wendy Three, and Michael had said he was the first with no number necessary. "The first John then."

"The first one," he affirmed. "And the only one. There were no Johns after him. Jericho retired the name, I guess you'd say."

"He retired John too, didn't he?" I asked quietly when he fell silent, lost in the golden haze drifting through the glass.

He didn't answer and that in itself was answer enough.

"He was like Jericho in a lot of ways, same features, same hair and skin. The eyes were a different color, of course, but the same shape. They looked as if they could've been"—he struggled for a moment and then settled on a word—"related." The concept of family, of father and son, brother to brother, was almost a myth to him. It was something to be read about in books and watched in the endless stream of movies, but not something that he'd seen close up in the walled-off microcosm that had been his world. No wonder he was having such a difficult time with it, and me, now.

"A miniature Jericho? Now there's a scary thought," I commented with utter sincerity.

"No. On the outside they were similar, but on the inside John was nothing like Jericho. Nothing like me either." There was self-recrimination there, a thin brittle layer under a glittering frost of calm. "John wanted to be free. He always wanted to be free. I can't remember how many times he tried to escape. He wanted me to go with him, but I never would. Not the first time. Not the last time." The blinds were closed with a savage snap. "He kept asking me why. Time after time. When the lights were out for the night, he would whisper it so they wouldn't hear. Why? Why won't you come?"

"And what did you say?"

"Where would we go?" he responded evenly.

It was the question of a prisoner serving a life sentence. Only this prisoner had been a child, one with no memory of anything but the cage he lived in and the monster that ruled it. Where could we go that Jericho wouldn't find us? Where would we ever fit in? How could we survive in an outside world as inexplicably alien as a distant star? I wasn't sure that I would've been any different if the situation had been reversed. John must have been unique in that respect, with a will that was as superhuman as the rest of him. Poor damn kid.

"How old was John?" I let the rest of the question

hang in the air, implied. How old was he when he made the last futile attempt?

"About twelve."

Only twelve. Jesus Christ.

Michael gave up on the window. What he wanted to see wasn't there; wouldn't ever be there. "He slipped out of bed one night and just . . . never came back. I didn't think he had made it, though. I never thought that. And when I saw Jericho two days later with his hand missing, I knew for sure. We can heal fast, but we can destroy even faster. John didn't make it." He swallowed, but his voice remained calm. "But at least he took part of that son of a bitch with him. It was afterward that Jericho wouldn't let any of us get close enough to touch him or the teachers anymore. They carried stun guns in case any of us tried."

"What about Wendy?"

"Wendy's the first of her kind." Weariness peeled his face like an apple, leaving pale vulnerability in plain sight. "She's the only one of us who doesn't need to touch. For her they keep tranquilizer darts, and even that might not work. But Wendy likes it there, and she likes what she's being groomed to do. She doesn't kill because they make her. She kills because she wants to."

It was a grim end to an even grimmer conversation. I had more questions, but they could wait. Michael had had enough for the night whether he realized it or not. "Yeah? Well, I like what I can do too. And that's boss your scrawny butt around." Standing, I picked up the pair of sweatpants he liked to sleep in. He had laid them out with anal-retentive neatness on the bed in preparation for bed. I wadded them in hand and tossed them in his direction. "Bedtime."

He caught them as he wavered between dignity and indignation. "I'm not a child."

But he was, and one so wounded that I was amazed he managed to be the bright, inquisitive, and fundamentally good person he was.

"Would my hanging you by your ankles until you begged for mercy prove any different?" I grinned wickedly.

"You wouldn't dare." He meant it too. He still harbored the suspicion that at some level I feared what he could do to me if he chose. As if he would do to me what he refused to do to those who tried to attack him. In so many ways he was damned brilliant, but in other ways he had serious catching up to do. Trusting me and trusting himself—he'd get there. I'd make sure of it.

I didn't actually have to follow through on the threat. Once I was close enough to swipe at his ankles, he gave in and went to get ready for bed. His heavy step was enough to let me know the push had been necessary. He wouldn't admit it, but talking about his friend—perhaps the only friend he had ever known—had taken a lot out of him. It had drained me, and I'd only been doing the listening. One childhood mistake had led to years of pain that couldn't be forgotten or erased.

It was my mistake and Michael's pain.

The sound of brushing teeth brought me out of my self-pitying funk. "Be sure to floss," I called out as I moved to set up the first aid kit on the table by the window.

Leaning through the door, he said indistinctly around a mouthful of foam, "Once again, I've got to ask. You were in the Russian mob? Really?"

"Believe it." I unscrewed the top of the antibiotic cream. "I threw guys down and committed vicious dental hygiene on them against their will. They called me the Flosser. Don't make me do the same to you."

"Mmm hmm. Frightening." With complete unconcern, he disappeared back into the bathroom.

If he hadn't been exhausted, the remark would've been much more biting, I knew. He was coming along. He truly was. I changed my bandage with now-practiced hands. The wound, too, was coming along. Not with the speed Michael would've shown, but for your average person who got shot in the side, it was doing well enough. As for my head, it still ached, but not as fiercely. I'd put away the pain pills that morning. A little pain was worth enduring to keep your edge. The dizziness and nausea had mostly faded as well. They only popped up once or twice a day at the most, usually in the face of Michael's enormous and not particularly selective appetite. That kid would eat anything, and I did mean anything—the more grease the better.

By the time I finished cleaning up, Michael was in bed with the ferret paws up on the pillow beside him. Walking over, I switched off the lamp. "'Night, Misha."

He was already gone, one hand tucked under the pillow. Except for the rat, it was a warm and homey scene straight from the past. We hadn't shared a room when we were younger; the age difference was enough that I wanted my own. But there were times I'd walk in and find Lukas asleep in my bed with one of my comics clutched in his hand. Kid brothers . . . What could you do?

Pulling the covers up over his shoulders, I sat on the edge of the opposite bed and watched him sleep. It probably wasn't a first for him. He'd as much as said the Institute either watched or listened to him, John, and the other children at night while they slept. I was still thinking about the lost John and wondering. He had the Never Never Land name, but it was also Jericho's. And then there was the resemblance Michael had mentioned. Could it be that Jericho had done his malicious work on his own flesh and blood, his own namesake? That might explain the abolishment of the John designation. That was a definitive sign of personal interest, personal offense.

Personal rage.

That was telling. He did have emotion. It was doubtful that any of them were the good kind, but they did exist and that could reveal weaknesses in him. Another thing it revealed was that if Jericho would kill his own family, the things he would do to us were worth avoiding—very much so. That wasn't news to me, by any means, but it was an unpleasant reminder.

Didn't life just love to hand those out?

Chapter 21

"No luck?"

I looked up from the cell phone in my hand to see Michael sitting balanced on the overlook wall. We were currently stopped at a national forest in Georgia, and I couldn't have pried Michael away with a crowbar. He was in awe of the massively tumbling waterfall below. The breathtaking sight along with the rushing sound and rising rainbow mist enthralled him. It was something to see, I admitted, and the view Michael was getting was even more spectacular because he was seeing it for the first time. It wasn't just the waterfall, but everything that went along with it: wild, green nature in general. Institute field trips had consisted of places where people—victims—congregated. This was something entirely new and pictures in books hadn't done it justice. Leaning so far over the edge that I'd had to restrain the urge to grab a handful of his shirt, my brother had watched the violent storm of water for nearly a full hour. Hair gone damp and floating on the wind, he finally was able to tear himself away long enough to watch my last futile call.

"No. Reception here is for shit." It was true, but there was a bigger truth behind it. I could have had a tower up my ass and it wouldn't have made a difference. Anatoly wasn't to be found. We hadn't kept the closest contact since I'd graduated college, just the occasional call or holiday visit, but he had made it clear that if I needed him I'd be able to track him down. That I was finding it so difficult wasn't a good sign. The feds must be hot on his heels for him to go under this deep.

"Who are you trying to call?" With face flushed from the chilled air, he was bundled in a jacket with the sky behind him in a brilliant blue backdrop. Except for an unusual inner stillness and eyes too old for his face, he looked like any other kid on vacation.

"Didn't I tell you?" I asked, surprised. At the shake of his head I stretched out my legs and lay back on the picnic table. "Jesus, talk about your scrambled brains." The sun was distant and its warmth nonexistent, but I closed my eyes anyway and pretended I was back in Miami soaking up the rays—or maybe in Key West. It would be in the seventies there, almost perfect. I might be the first generation out of the home country, but cold had never been a friend of mine.

"Did that happen before or after you hit your head on the car?"

"Punk-ass kid," I said with sleepy equanimity as the light glowed red through my eyelids. "I'm trying to reach Anatoly. Our father," I amended, opening my eyes to slide my gaze his way.

"Anatoly." A sneakered foot sketched a triangle in the dirt, as precisely equilateral as if he'd used a ruler. "You don't call him Dad? In the movies . . ." He stopped himself, having already learned the hard way that movies weren't as accurate as they could be.

"When I was younger." Much, much younger. I hadn't exactly lived the *Brady Bunch* family life, particularly after the kidnapping. We had our share of dysfunction, same as anyone else. It hadn't been too noticeable before Lukas was taken, with merely a father who worked far too much and secrets a child couldn't penetrate. Later, I'd either become more cynically aware or Anatoly had tried less to hide his business. If my brother had still been around, I don't think I would've ended up in that same business. I hadn't cared enough to stop it from happening and my father had seen it, oddly enough, as a way of keeping me safe. In his realm, he felt he had control.

"He's used to being in charge. I guess it's rather like having a father who's a general in the army. He's a boss first and a parent second. That's not to say he didn't— doesn't—love us. In fact, he thought the sun rose and set in you. The day you were born he passed out Cuban cigars as if they were candy and named you after his father." The memory was so fresh that I could all but see the blue balloons floating, cheerfully proclaiming "It's a Boy!" for anyone who cared to know. "It didn't matter that you were practically a carbon copy looks-wise of Mom and her side of the family. He saw something in you, something special."

And he hadn't been wrong.

Lukas had been born special, but not the kind of special that Jericho embraced. His was a rare but completely natural special, a shining quality that made a father beyond proud, a mother doting, and a seven-year-old boy think his new baby brother was the best kid in the world, even if the butterball didn't do anything but eat and poop.

"Anyway," I forged ahead before Michael could comment on how our father loved Lukas, not him. "Anatoly's on the run from the government. They have more indictments against him than they did Capone. But if we could find him, he knows more about going under the radar than I ever will, not to mention the money he has socked away in off-shore accounts. That kind of cash would take us far from here—far enough." Sitting up again, I turned off the phone. "And he'll want to see you . . . to see his son. He won't be able to believe I found you." Even in my imagination, I couldn't picture that scene in my head. "He just . . . won't believe it."

"Why not?" The triangle disappeared beneath the erasing scuff of a sole. "Why wouldn't he believe? Wasn't he looking for Lukas too?"

How do you tell a boy his father had given up on

him long ago? And he had. Anatoly had lost hope with a speed that had seemed shocking to a fourteen-year-old kid. It still seemed just as shocking to a twenty-four-year-old man. So, how do you tell a boy that? How do you tell him he was assumed dead by everyone but me?

You don't.

"I think he trusted the authorities to do their job. More than I did at any rate," I temporized. "Weird as shit, I know, considering his occupation, but the FBI did write the book on missing kids. It's what they do. And I'm sure he had his contacts working day and night for a long time." I didn't remember if that had been the case or not, but it must have been. The first few weeks after Lukas had been taken were still hazy to me. Emotional trauma, I guessed, but there hadn't been any therapists to verify my self-diagnosis. Anatoly, old-school Russian and old-school mob, didn't believe in that kind of thing. Still, whether I remembered or not, I knew Anatoly would've pulled out all the stops for his missing son . . . whether he had hope or not. He loved Lukas. Criminals could love. They killed, they stole, but they were capable of love—in their way. It was a mental litany I'd repeated doggedly more than once or twice during my teenage years. Some days I had even believed it.

"But you kept looking yourself—personally. Long after a lot of people would've given up." This time it was a circle he traced, as geometrically perfect as a soap bubble. "Why?"

It was a difficult question with an easy answer. I searched because he was my brother, but that wasn't the whole truth. I also searched because I had been the one to lose Lukas, and "personally" wasn't the word for the way I took that. "I'm smelling more Freud here, kiddo," I dissembled as the wings of a bird beat overhead. "There's a leather couch and two hundred bucks an hour in your future; I can see it now."

I may as well have been talking to the wind for all the notice he took. "You blame yourself." He may have been watching me. I didn't know; I didn't look. "You think it's your fault."

This was a topic that needed no discussion. I'd discussed the hell out of it with myself for the past ten years. Yeah, I had it down to a real art. Putting the phone in my pocket, I didn't so much change the subject as ignore it altogether. "You finished that last book in the car, didn't you? Find out anything that could help us out?" This time I did meet his eyes and with a gaze as bland as oatmeal and impenetrable as a vault.

He studied me for a long moment, then, to my relief, let the matter drop. I had the uneasy feeling, however, that we'd be circling back to it soon enough. "Yes, I'm done. I'm not sure it'll be helpful or not, though."

"We'll never know until you spit it out." I swung my arm in a classic director's gesture to point at Michael. "Go."

And go he did.

He'd learned a lot from those few books, enough that he could've taught an introductory course in genetics. It was something I could see with astonishing clarity. Blazer and tie, chalk dust on his hands, and an unquenchable passion for knowledge etched on his lean face, he would be a college professor who had the freshmen girls hanging their panties on his office doorknob; my brother, the intellectual stud muffin.

The more high-tech details went in one ear and out the other for all the foothold they gained in my brain, but I didn't try to rein in Michael. Much of the miniature lecture was over my head, true, but I enjoyed his enthusiasm. Most of his inner self was so locked down that watching him cut loose, even over something as dull as science, was a kick. After tossing off esoteric terms such as polymorphism and pseudogenes with machine-gun rapidity, he finally began to slowly wind down. "It's as we thought," he summed up. "A customary chimera is simply a person with genes from their brother or sister intermingled with their own. No special powers. They're ordinary people . . . like you."

To give him credit, there wasn't any condescension in that statement. Considering all he could do, it was rather remarkable that he didn't consider himself more than human rather than less. If I could get him to see that he was neither . . . that in the ways that counted he was as human as anyone, I would be content. "Ordinary like me." I shook my head sadly. "How awful for them."

"I said ordinary, not normal. If they were like you, they'd be anything but," he said straight-faced. "Anyway, I think you were right about Jericho. He must've been a mutation, the first chimera to have the healing ability and the increased intelligence. As for stronger and faster . . ." He frowned. "He is strong and fast, but I don't think much more so than, say, an athlete. Nothing in the supernatural range, at least."

Thank God for small favors, I thought with relief. I thought he was probably right. Michael himself had seemed strong when he'd pulled me into the car after I'd been shot, but it could've been the strength of adrenaline.

"I'm guessing he studied his own genetic makeup and found the mutation. He determined where he was different from other chimeras, and that was his starting point to making more like him. I can see that." This frown was deeper than the first and ripe with confusion. "What I can't see is how he made the leap. Altering a few replicating cells, that's possible. Altering an entire person, I can't begin to guess how he could do that. There's gene replacement therapy, but the books didn't really cover that in much detail, but enough to know the scientific world isn't quite there yet. To treat a disease, yes. To remake a whole new person . . ." Shaking his head, he finished his thought, saying with self-disgust, "I'm smart, but I'm not that smart. I just don't see how it could be done. It seems impossible."

"You're smart enough. We just need better books," I contradicted before bringing up a more difficult subject. "What I really want to know is whether Jericho's process is reversible." I saw his shoulders immediately tighten at the question as his face smoothed out to the mask I'd seen that first day in the Institute. "Not for you, Misha," I clarified immediately. "You're fine the way you are. Hell, perfect in my book. I wouldn't take that healing trick away even if I could. And as for the other, you wouldn't hurt anyone who didn't deserve it. I know that as well as I know anything in this whole goddamned world."

He remained silent, but his shoulders relaxed slightly. Standing, I walked over to him, scattering puffs of red dirt as I went. Sitting beside him on the rock wall, I said quietly, "It's the other kids. I know some are like you, Peter, and John. But some are like Wendy. If someone can't undo what Jericho did to them, they won't ever be free." Rescuing the children was a premature thought at best, but I wanted to keep it in mind. Even if it were possible, it could be a long time before anything could be arranged. Maybe years. Regardless, giving up on the kids without even thinking about what could be done for them seemed the worst sort of betrayal. And they'd been betrayed enough in their short lives. I didn't know if I could help them, but I wasn't going to forget them.

"Just something to think about," I added, bumping his shoulder with mine. "You ready to go? Grab lunch? You're too skinny, kid. We need to fatten you up."

His lips curved. "Bab . . ."

"Don't even say it," I warned, cutting him off with a scowl. "I'm nobody's grandma, not even yours."

"Uh huh." It wasn't as literate as the majority of his responses, but combined with the amusement that softened his features, it got the point across.

We were back in the car and on our way before Michael asked seriously, "You honestly wouldn't change me if you could? You wouldn't want me to be normal?"

"You are normal." I shot him a grin as I turned his previous words back on him. "Just not ordinary."

"That would make me extraordinary then, right?" Reassured, he slid quickly from uncertainty into the home base of cocky smugness; professor to teenager in less than sixty seconds flat.

"Don't push your luck," I said without any real heat. But all the while I was thinking that he wasn't far off the mark. Not far at all.

Chapter 22

Lunch turned out to be more exciting than I'd planned. It wasn't the fun fest that had ended up with me shot in a parking lot, but neither was it hot dogs and a football game on the big screen. It just goes to show that it's true what they say. No good deed goes unpunished, "unpunished" being the euphemism for many things. It could be a mild inconvenience or it could be a royal ass kicking. My punishment lay, as it usually did, somewhere near the ass-kicking end of the spectrum.

Picking up the pregnant girl was my first mistake.

Several minutes into the ride, Michael spoke up. He'd been busy entertaining the malevolent Zilla. Out of the cage and creating havoc, it was a must-buy option for every car—air, power locks, carnivorous eel with fur. And then there was the odor. What genetic manipulation had given Michael in healing and supersmarts, it had obviously taken away from his sense of smell in the worst sort of robbing-Peter-to-pay-Paul scenario.

"I was thinking," he contemplated as the ferret perched on his shoulder. "One of the books mentions a Dr. Bellucci who . . ." He stopped and reached over to tap my arm. "Stefan, there's a girl."

I'd already seen her. She was standing nearly half a mile past the park entrance. On the gravel shoulder she stood prim and proper as a princess attended by her royal hound. They matched, the two of them. Woven into two thick strawberry blond plaits, her hair was nearly identical in color to the red-gold color of the dog sitting upright beside her. An unusual dog, it looked as if someone had wrestled Lassie to the ground and given her a marine buzz cut.

The girl was wearing jeans, a long lavender sweater, and a thigh-length white jacket trimmed in blatantly fake fur. Some Muppet had apparently given its all in the name of fashion. Together, she and the dog were pretty as a picture and completely out of place in the middle of nowhere. Those were the first things you noticed. That she was about nine months pregnant came as a surprising distant second.

"What's she doing out here?" I muttered, my foot automatically easing up on the gas as we approached her. One hand was resting on the dog's smooth head while the other was held shoulder height in a breezy thumbs-out. She was hitching. The princess was actually hitching, dog and all.

"Are we stopping?"

"Not hardly," I retorted, getting my foot back under control. Feeding the car gas, I steered us into the opposite lane to give the girl a wide berth.

"But"—his head swiveled to keep her in view—"she's pregnant, and she's out here alone."

"And that's a big fat clue, isn't it? No pun intended." Hearing the engine of our car, she turned to face us while waving her thumb with almost-imperious demand. Royalty all right, even if only in her own mind. I swung the wheel even wider. "This is an urban legend in the making. Why doesn't she have a cell phone? Everyone has a cell phone. Her *dog* should have a cell phone. Maybe she's not even pregnant. She could have accomplices hiding in the woods, a gun in her purse, or an armed dwarf under her shirt. Who the hell knows? She could rob us and leave us for dead. Maybe even feed your damn rat to her dog. The possibilities are endless, kid."

"All from a girl and her dog? And I thought I had trust issues." He returned the ferret to its cage. "I'll clean out the back."

I was about to tell him there was no point, but at that moment in the rearview mirror I caught sight of the girl leaning over, clutching her stomach, and the happy hitching thumb gone. Even the dog looked worried.

Fuck. Fuck. Fuck.

And just like that we were saddled with a hitchhiker. I didn't kid myself. I would've kept driving and called her a cab—hell, no cabs out here; I'd have called 911. I would've let the local sheriff give her a ride, but with this . . . and in front of Michael. I'd told him I'd been a criminal, and I'd told him I would change. Passing up a pregnant girl at the side of the road possibly in labor didn't make me appear particularly changed, but change I would. I'd promised Michael and I'd promised myself.

In other words, I was screwed—on the path to all that's good and goddamn righteous, damn it, but still screwed. The knowledge didn't improve my mood any when I pulled over. Michael rolled down his window and said, "Um . . . are you . . . you know . . . all right?"

The insistent tone he'd taken with Saul and the critical one with the ex-doctor had disappeared under this newly diffident one. I'd found a weakness in Mr. Extraordinary. He was shy around girls; how relentlessly common and mundane. How would he ever live it down? I smothered a grin as one pink-nailed hand found the window opening with entitled assurance.

About nineteen, the girl had a heart-shaped face—which I'd thought a trite phrase every time I'd read it—twilight blue eyes, that one as well, and a sudden and complete lack of labor pains. With pale skin free of makeup and only the lightest gleam of gloss on her lips, the princess was as beautiful as in any fairy tale or Miss Universe pageant, depending how your media tastes ran. She smiled and drawled in an accent as thick as clover honey as she addressed Michael's concern, "Oh, that? That was just a little bit of indigestion. Goes with the territory. But right now, sweetie? I'm finer than frog hair." I could all but hear Michael's heart clunking against his ribs.

I couldn't help but take the teasing shot and said lightly, "*Crashennui*." The tips of Michael's ears flushed red at the remark. He was smitten indeed.

Studiously ignoring me, he asked her, "Do you need a ride?"

"That would be fabulous." The smile and the drawl became even broader. "You boys aren't killers or perverts, are you?"

Rarely in life is fifty percent a passing score, but it was the best that Michael and I could do between us. If she didn't call us on that, I wouldn't call her on her slightly overdone modern-day Southern belle act. She was playing us, although maybe modern-day Southern girls did say "finer than frog hair." I wasn't a Georgia guy; so I couldn't say. But she was conning us. It probably was for a simple ride and not anything more sinister, on par with a pretty woman flirting her way out of a ticket, but that didn't quell my suspicion completely. You never knew with people. You just never frigging knew. I did try to keep in mind she was just a teenage girl, but my faith in innocent girlish appearances had faded considerably in the past week thanks to Jericho's Wendy.

"Not so much that you'd notice," I replied in a lazy drawl of my own. "But we can call someone to come get you if you'd rather."

"Oh, no. This'll be just fine." Before Michael could get out to open the back door for her, she'd already helped herself. The dog jumped in before her and she scooted with a heavy grace into the seat behind it. "I'm Fisher Lee. Fisher Lee Redwine. This is Bouncing Blue Blossom. *The* Bouncing Blue Blossom." If thinking up names like that was what this girl did in her spare time, way too much spare time just reached a new standard of measurement.

Blossom, *the* Blossom, gave a soft yip when she heard her name, then curled up on the seat and dozed off immediately.

I held back a hand over the seat and waited until hers slid into mine. Shaking it briskly, I said, "Nice to meet you, Ms. Redwine." I was far less concerned with the etiquette of introduction than I was with checking out her stomach to see if it looked authentic. Paranoia, suspicion; call it whatever. It had kept me alive thus far. Wendy wasn't the only member of the fairer sex in my lifetime who had demonstrated deadly tendencies. One of the strippers at the club had once stabbed her boyfriend in the bathroom and then had calmly gone out to work another set. I'd been the one to find him. Facedown on the tile with his blood spider-webbing around him as it flowed along the path of the grout, he hadn't been dead, but he probably wished he had been. She'd taken him down with a deep wound to the belly and then she'd gotten creative. The surgeons had stitched his face together like a patchwork quilt. Other parts of him weren't so easily pieced together. She'd flushed those down the toilet.

It could've been that he'd deserved it; it could've been that he didn't. I had never asked, but it was a lesson I hadn't forgotten. Anyone could be dangerous—absolutely anyone.

"What should I call you handsome fellas?" Fisher asked as she pressed hands to the small of her back and stretched. "Besides my saviors?" The Georgia accent had the *R* sound fading before it hit the air.

"Nick and Albert," I answered promptly before Michael could let slip our real ones. I wasn't positive that he would have, but hedging my bets was a longtime habit. "You can call the kid Al." Beside me Michael made an almost inaudible snort to let me know he had caught the Einstein reference.

Turning back, I took the car back out onto the road. She looked genuinely pregnant, but not being precisely an expert in the field, I kept a sharp eye on the rearview mirror. "We're headed toward Waycross. We can drop you off there." Can and would; a philanthropist such as I had to have his limits. The sarcasm sounded the same in my head as it would have out . . . sharp and edgy. I didn't like risk where Michael was involved, and thanks to the past, I wasn't wild about the unexpected. What was setting up camp in my backseat definitely qualified as one, maybe both.

"Waycross is fine. It's a little one-horse town, one and a half at the most." She smiled and patted the mound of her stomach. "Just like me. Horse and a half, right here."

"What . . . mmm." Michael cleared his throat, the redness in his ears fading to a pale pink. "What are you doing out here? All by yourself, I mean."

"Oh, honey, y'all wouldn't believe it if I told you." She must have slipped off her shoes as up popped two feet on the console between my seat and Michael's. The toenails were painted to match her fingernails, a pearlescent rose. Wiggling her toes, she asked Michael, "Albert, would you be a doll and rub my feet? They haven't been the same since Junior here hit his seventh month."

The flush was back and it spread to the rest of Michael's face with the speed of a wildfire. Frozen, his eyes darted from the feet to me and then back again. I had to admit, even slightly swollen they were very pretty feet. Snorting, I took a hand off the wheel to grab his and place it on a foot. "You heard the lady, Big Al. Get to work."

If I'd seen anything more amusing than a profoundly pregnant woman flirting with my brother, I couldn't think of it offhand. But I wasn't going to let that stop me from giving Miss Fisher Lee a good, hard verbal shove. "Go on with your story, Fisher." I gifted her with an encouraging and completely insincere grin over my shoulder. It made my teeth hurt. "We're interested. Goddamn interested. Couldn't be more interested if we tried."

Michael was touching the pink and ivory feet with acutely cautious fingers. For all the force he was using he might have been massaging a creation formed from the most delicate of blown glass. I've heard the old cliché before . . . a thousand times at least. But now was the first time I had felt it as opposed to only hearing it. Clichés make us cringe for a reason, and it isn't from the banal repetition. It is the unbearable truth of them. I watched Michael touch smooth skin with a normal embarrassment and a not-so-normal wariness, and I honestly didn't know whether to laugh or cry. He wasn't scared simply because she was a gorgeous, if rather round, girl. He was afraid he might accidentally hurt her. I'd seen his control over the past week and it was unshakable, but with that kind of power, how could you not have the occasional doubt slither through your mind? If a foot rub could help him overcome that, then I was all for it.

"Aren't you sweet? Taking such a concern." Unlike mine, Fisher's sincerity was bona fide or at least it seemed to be from her good-natured tone. "Good guys like you make up for dirtbags like my boyfriend. Albert, honey, you can rub a little harder. I'm tougher than I look."

I heard Michael's convulsive swallow as loudly as if it had come from my own throat, but he obeyed and increased the pressure. The contented sigh that ruffled my hair from the backseat indicated he had hit the spot. "It's the usual sad, sad story," she said with a carefree air that was belied by a faintly bitter undertone. "Cocky guy, stupid girl. Junior doesn't have a chance. With his parents, the poor kid will probably have to repeat preschool three times." There was another sigh, this one much less content. "Can't say I didn't make my bed, though, and whining won't change a thing. We had one last big fight and I told him to stop the car and let me out. Great guy that he is, he did. Took off and didn't even look back."

Pink nails flicked through Michael's hair. "You get a girlfriend, sweetie; you treat her real nice, okay?"

On that note Michael's blush progressed to full-blown, spontaneous human combustion and he hurriedly finished with the massage, "I'm not sure a girlfriend is the best idea for me."

"Oh, well, a little boyfriend then." Untroubled, she fished a piece of hard candy out of her coat pocket and popped it into her mouth. "Just be sweet to whoever you end up with."

"That's not what I . . . Never mind." The conversation was too close to home for Michael and he turned in the seat to face the front. It was debatable whether he would ever trust himself enough to allow the creation of a bond—sexual, romantic, or both—with a girl or woman. That same uncertainty applied to the bonds between family . . . between brothers. Eventually, when we were safe, I could look into providing him with DNA evidence proving that we were related, but that still might not do the trick. Michael had to allow himself to believe, and I wasn't sure he was emotionally capable of that—not now; perhaps not ever.

It was not the best of thoughts and I let it wash away under the bright chatter that flowed out of Fisher like an endless stream of sticky, sweet molasses. She talked about her worthless boyfriend, her cheerleading days, her plans to go to college after the baby was born, but mostly she talked about Blossom. Blossom this and Blossom that. The dog ignored it all, even the tale of her rescuing seven children from a burning building while still wearing the blue ribbon from her last dog show. I didn't believe any of it for a second, but it made for a good story.

It wasn't long before we had to stop for lunch. Waycross was only twenty or so miles, but it turned out a hungry pregnant woman could be a cranky one. The honey in her voice began to turn to vinegar after she finished off the last of her candy. We ended up at yet another barbecue joint. They sprinkle the landscape of the South like a savory-smelling, greasy-fingered Milky Way. This one was lacking a purple pig out front, which was probably for the best. A repeat of that scenario might have PETA all over my ass, and my ass was fairly well booked up for the moment, although we hadn't seen any sign of Jericho in the past two days. Then again, I really hadn't expected to. The fastest of supernatural healers wasn't going to shake off a bullet to the gut and a shattered leg that quickly. And I doubted he would send a team after us that he couldn't head himself. Jericho was the hands-on type.

"Here! Stop here." A hand pounded the back of my headrest. "I've heard of this place. It's supposed to be best round these parts."

Best round these parts . . . who could argue with that? I pulled into the parking lot that was nothing more than a patch of bald, red ground. And there we were at Annie's Big Fat Fannie. There was a blinking neon sign in the window that let us know just how fat that fanny was. It was a simple design: glass tubing twisted into two pinkish red curves that buzzed cheerfully as we walked to the door. If Annie's fanny was indeed as large as indicated, the food they served must be good. Inside there were mostly booths with red and yellow plastic seats and a few scattered tables. We chose a table to accommodate Junior's girth, but I did maintain enough control of the situation to choose one that gave me a clear view of both exits.

Fisher didn't care one way or the other. She dived headfirst into the menu as she waved one frantic hand for immediate service. By the time the waitress—obviously not Annie as the fanny was flat as a pancake—arrived, Fisher had picked out three lunch specials. Two were for her and the other was for Blossom who was still snoozing along with Godzilla in the back of the car. Michael and I put in our own orders, unmanly single servings, and a few minutes later were provided with pint-sized jars full of iced tea garnished with a frozen peach slice. Fisher ignored hers and made her way through a basket full of fried biscuits slathered with apple butter.

"Someone who can out-eat you, kid." I kicked Michael's ankle lightly under the table and tipped the fruit into the tea before taking a swallow. Not too bad. "I never thought I'd see the day."

"Even the best of us have off days." Clearly challenged, Michael reached for a biscuit, only to have his hand swatted away.

"Sorry, sweetie," Fisher apologized. "It's you or Junior, and Junior always wins."

"I see." He shook his fingers as if they stung. Fisher must pack quite a punch, I thought with amusement. "It's too bad Junior hasn't learned about sharing yet."

"Kids, kids, come on now," I admonished. "Play nice. I'll get another basket." Rising, I went to the counter to ask for more biscuits. By the time I returned, the two had come to terms and they promptly divided the new basket between them. Licking a finger, I philosophically dabbed at the three or four remaining crumbs. "What was that you said about sharing?"

Michael didn't blink an eye at his hypocrisy. "I don't recall."

"Yeah. Plead the Fifth. Toss me under the bus." The gun in my back waistband dug into my flesh and I leaned a few inches forward away from the ladder-back chair. "You have family in Waycross, Fisher?"

"My great-gramma Lilly-Mae." Biscuits gone, she rubbed the end of her braid across the curve of her cheek. "She's amazing. Everything you can think of, she's done. She ran moonshine with her brothers back when she was younger than me. She worked the farm all by herself when her first husband died. Then, when she lost it, she became a stripper. And not just to survive, but because she thought it sounded like fun." The blue eyes glittered with laughter and pride. "And that was in the old days when they'd run you out of town for something like that. She remarried more times than I can remember and ran for mayor when she was fifty. She didn't win, but they still talk about her campaign . . . even twenty years later. They say she threw the best 'we lost' celebration ever. There were buffets, clowns, belly dancers, and even an elephant. The guy who won left his own victory party to go to hers."

"Sounds like quite a lady."

"She is. She'll take me in. I've always been her favorite." She grinned cheekily. "I'm a troublemaker just like her."

I had no problem believing that. Despite myself, I was actually coming to like . . . to tolerate Miss Fisher Lee. She was somewhat obnoxious and more than a little pushy, but she was entertaining. And despite my earlier reservations, I now thought she was good for Michael. I was more than willing to be everything and everyone I could for him, but realistically he was going to have to learn to accept other people in his life. It was the only healthy option. I didn't break him out of the Institute only to let him enclose himself in walls that while different, were just as isolating.

The barbecue was excellent, in every way as good as the biscuit crumbs. I curved a protective arm around my plate to fend off the rampaging piranhas. Finishing every bite but the pickle, I slid the slice of dill onto Michael's plate. He was developing a fondness for things sour that rivaled his love of sweets. See the human trash compactor, only fifty cents. Walk this way and don't stick your fingers between the bars.

"I think I'll have me a piece of apple pie." With a hand resting on the swell of her stomach, Fisher looked up at the waitress and added, "And don't be stingy with the à la mode, sugar. Give me a bowl on the side. I'm eating for two."

"What's your excuse?" I murmured to Michael as he ordered the same.

"Youth," he retorted without hesitation. "When I'm old like you, I'm sure I'll have to cut back."

Twenty-four . . . old? Punk-ass kid. Unfortunately, I had to admit there were times I felt much older than my true age. A culture of violence and a past full of regret will do that to you. That aside, this was not one of the times I felt like reaching for a walker. This was a good time. I was enjoying myself as I watched the dessert duel, and with bemusement I saluted Fisher as she finally finished two spoonfuls ahead of my brother. "The king is dead. All hail the queen."

The queen laughed and gathered up the sauce-stained doggy bag for Blossom. She then went to stand by the front door and plugged a quarter in a gumball machine. As she blew large purple bubbles and tapped her foot impatiently, I came to the conclusion I was picking up her and Junior's tab. After I forked over the twenty-five bucks, grumbling under my breath that I wasn't a god-damn charity, the three of us stepped out into the winter sunshine.

That was where I lost considerably more than lunch money.

She was walking, waddling really, ahead of us by ten or fifteen feet. The parking lot was empty except for a few parked cars. The white fur trim of her coat waved sea anemone tendrils in the brisk breeze and her hair was as bright as the smile she gave us when she turned around. The metal of the gun she pointed at us was bright too, like a mirror. It was a cute little chrome revolver held in a cute little hand. It was also a steady hand, I noticed— rock steady.

"I almost feel bad, you know?" She tossed a braid over her shoulder and cocked her head coquettishly. "Ah, who am I kidding? Robbing y'all's going to be the most fun I've had all day."

My first thought when she'd gotten into the car was that she was playing us, if only a little. But somewhere between foot rubs and stories about a crackerjack grandma I'd let even that mild suspicion drift to the back burner. I'd forgotten the lesson of Wendy and the stripper at Koschecka and gone with the conclusion that the ride and a free lunch were all that Fisher was after. Too bad deductions such as that came from thinking with my smug ass instead of my empty head. In my business, I'd made my living outthinking predators, and yet here I stood . . . taken down by a pregnant girl in braids. Trying to live the straight and narrow—I wanted to be better for my brother, but being better could get us both killed.

I could try to get her gun before she shot Michael or me, but I had serious doubts. Her peaches and cream complexion was high with bright color and the grip she had on her weapon was as practiced as that of any three-time loser. Her eyes met mine with the same lighthearted cheer she'd shown since we'd picked her up. There were no reservations, no guilt, but worst of all . . . there was no fear. She didn't care that someone might leave the restaurant and see her or that someone could drive by and call the police. Being utterly amoral and completely fearless . . . There was no deadlier combination.

"What do you want?" I asked neutrally. "My wallet? Fine. Take it." There was a little less than seventy dollars in there. She was welcome to it. Slowly and carefully, I pulled my wallet from my back pocket and tossed it at her feet. I could've tried for my gun hidden under my shirt, but what then? Shoot a pregnant girl? Granted, she was a sociopathic, thieving pregnant girl, but that wouldn't make pulling the trigger any easier.

"I love men who share," she purred, discarding the bag of food to one side. "Albert, sweetie, pick that up and hand it to me real careful like. I'm not quite as limber as I used to be."

I didn't need to see the questioning look Michael gave me to know what he was thinking. With one touch, just one, a thousand or so cells would suicide and the gun would fall. It could potentially work; she certainly wouldn't be expecting it. But it wasn't worth it, putting Michael through that, not over less than a hundred bucks. It just wasn't worth it to me, and not to him either, whether he knew it or not. I gave him a minute shake of my head. "Do as she says, kiddo. Exactly as she says."

For a moment it seemed as if he would protest, but he didn't. He only nodded, walked forward to retrieve the wallet, and placed it in her free hand. "Good boy. Such a good boy," she cooed before shooing him backward. "All right, scar face, now lift up your shirt."

So much for the specialty makeup I'd swiped under bright drugstore lights, but that was the least of my concerns. Losing my wallet and the money in it was nothing. Losing what was under my shirt would have much more serious consequences for my brother and me.

"Why?" I asked bluntly.

"You're a shady one, Bubba." A pink tongue touched cat quick to her upper lip and she winked. "I know my kin when I see them. And people like us have secrets we don't keep in our wallets. Now get that shirt up before I turn it red, hear?"

I heard. Giving in to the bitter inevitable, I pulled up my shirt to chest height and revealed the money belt around my waist. It was there that I kept every penny I hadn't paid to Saul. There was nearly fifty thousand dollars along with all of my fake ID in that belt. I couldn't keep it in the car. I'd stolen our transportation easily enough; there was no guarantee someone else might not do the same.

"Jackpot," she breathed, eyes locked on my waist with naked avarice. "Baby needs a new pair of shoes. And it looks like he's going to get them, a whole store's worth." Waggling the revolver, she ordered, "Fork it over. Now."

There was only one way out of this that didn't involve gunfire and blood, and it sucked. It sucked thoroughly, but I didn't see a way around it—not one I was willing to involve Michael in at any rate. Gritting my teeth against a cold rush of anger, I released the buckle on the belt and held it out to her. Her gun unwavering, she took a step forward and snatched the thick strip of nylon out of the air as it swung back and forth. As she did so, I heard an excited barking. It was Blossom. She was rid-

ing in the back of a pickup with her front paws propped
up on the tailgate in true time-honored country style.
The truck pulled up not quite ten feet from us, stopping
just behind Fisher. The pickup itself was a dusty reddish
brown or brownish red; it was hard to tell. Either red
with brown mud or vice versa, it was completely nondescript. And so was the guy behind the wheel.

Dirty blond hair under a baseball hat, denim jacket,
and a two-day beard, he could've been any good old boy
in a two-hundred-mile radius. The deer rifle pointed at
my head was the only false note. Through the open window the man showed white teeth any Gulf shark would
be proud of. He didn't take good care of his truck, but
he loved his teeth. Or he loved his meth and those were
dentures. "You think good thoughts, fella." Calling to
Fisher, he added, "You 'bout ready, honey?"

Here was the boyfriend who had supposedly left a
pregnant girl high and dry on a lonesome road. In reality he was her partner in crime, although I had the feeling she would wear the pants in any relationship. They
might be maternity pants, but she was the boss. On that
front I had no doubts.

"Coming, doll baby." She hefted the money belt to
feel the weight. Her eyes were brilliant with pleasure.
"Boys, boys, you've been so good to me. Better than
even Gramma Lilly."

Gramma Lilly, my ass. Her lies had been consummate,
her acting flawless. She'd put Meryl Streep out of business. There was no Lilly. But if there were, I would've
hoped she didn't have life insurance naming her grand-
daughter as beneficiary. The old lady wouldn't have been
long for this world if that were the case. I remembered
with perfect clarity how Fisher had pointed out the restaurant for its great food. That the gun-toting boyfriend
would be meeting her here was only a bonus to the best
barbecue in the tri-state area. Who knew how many
times before they'd pulled a stunt like this. Who knew
how many people out there were as stupid as I was.

"Yeah, it's been our pleasure," I said with tight-lipped venom.

"Now don't be that way." She backed toward the truck and punctuated the remark with the cocking of the revolver. It was unnecessary. The damn thing was double action; she could pull the trigger at any time, no preparation necessary. "I was sweet as pie to you. Told you some good stories, flirted with the boy. It was like a dinner and a show. You should be thanking me, not being all pissy."

"Yeah," I gritted as she began to back away. "I'm a real bastard."

Her partner put his rifle down to open the door for her and take the belt from her hand. Then he opened his door and stood within the opening to keep us covered while she climbed awkwardly into the passenger seat. When she had closed the door and settled in, she rested her arm out the window, cheek lying against shoulder, and watched us—just watched. I could see the thought swimming beneath the blue violet water of her eyes, a silver fish circling and circling.

To kill or not to kill?

It wasn't Shakespeare, but it had a certain poetry that held my attention all the same. Her finger caressed the trigger as a dreamy smile curved her lips. She'd reapplied her lip gloss at the table after finishing her pie and ice cream. I'd caught a whiff of the pink stuff as I watched the tube glide across her mouth. It had smelled like strawberries. Realistically, I was too far away to smell it now, but I did. I smelled it as strongly as if I stood in the middle of a field of berries ripe for picking, sweetly tart and warm from the summer sun. It's strange what you think of when a bullet is seconds away from shattering your skull.

I was going to have to try for my gun. I wouldn't make it in time, that was a given, but I had to try. Just before my hand began to move Fisher made her decision. "What the hell. You did buy a lady lunch." Blowing us a triumphant and gloating kiss, she and the truck disappeared in a cloud of red dust. I didn't know if the chalkiness in my mouth was from the free-flying grit or was merely the taste of my own idiocy. As I stood there minute after minute, unmoving, the taste grew stronger instead of fading.

It was definitely idiocy.

In the choking thick silence came Michael's wary voice. "I'm guessing calling the police is out of the question." I didn't blame his caution. My mood was less than pleasant.

"Pretty much," I said shortly, eyes still riveted on the dissipating dust.

"And her name probably wasn't really Fisher Redwine."

"No." I felt the muscle in my jaw spasm and that was when the calm broke. "Goddamnit, goddamnit, goddamnit." I kicked the dirt, sending a spray of earth flying. It didn't make me feel any better, so I tried again—and again. Then with temper spent for the moment, I turned to Michael and gave a rueful sigh. "This, by the way, is why we don't pick up hitchhikers."

"Yes, I see your point," he offered gravely.

Scrubbing a hand across my face, I said wryly, "And you thought I had trust issues before. Just wait." I wrapped an arm around his shoulders and gave him a quick, hard squeeze, trying to reassure him things weren't as bad as they really were. "You ain't seen nothing yet."

"Two of a kind." He allowed the embrace for a second, forgetting momentarily that he was an island unto himself, then subtly shifted to pull away. "We're in trouble, aren't we?"

"We've been in trouble for a while, kid," I countered lightly. "What's one more drop in the bucket?"

"Stefan." His gaze was uncompromising. "Don't."

He was right. Not only was trying to protect him from this pointless and dangerous; it was also insulting to his intelligence. He knew as well as I did that this

wasn't a drop; it was a fucking waterfall. "Yeah, trouble
is a good word for it. They took every penny, and we're
not getting very far without money." The door to the
restaurant opened and five people came spilling out,
their voices magpie loud. It was getting a little crowded
out here, and I started toward the car. "Shoplifting
and boosting a car is one thing," I continued quietly.
"Knocking over a gas station or a bank is a different
matter altogether. That'll get us shot or in custody in
no time. We can't risk it."

"What will we do then?"

"Give me a while. I'll think of something." It wasn't
as if I had much choice. Our backs were to the wall. If I
didn't come up with a plan and quickly, Jericho wouldn't
have to put any effort into finding us. We would fall right
into his psychotic lap. "Have faith." I didn't put any
thought into the words; it was automatic—just something you say. It made Michael's response, murmured
under his breath, that much more gratifying.

"I do."

Chapter 23

When you're a kid, there are miraculous things in the world. Even a tiny bit of ice fluff can seem more like magic than a part of nature. Growing up mostly in southern Florida, I hadn't seen a lot of snow, but there had been the occasional vacation to Colorado or New York. The memory of the first flake cradled in my hand was as distinct as the edges of the ice crystal had been soft. You knew then that every snowflake was different, every one a uniquely carved diamond.

You forget that. I'm not sure when, but somewhere, sometime the knowledge fades away. It's bad enough losing sight of the singular nature of snow, but that's not the worst of it. You even forget the myriad lacy patterns exist. You forget that anything lies in the white drifting from the sky. It was only crumbs from God's table; misshapen wet pearls before an invisible swine; just snow. And because you've forgotten, you never look anymore.

Michael still looked.

South Carolina had been hit with an unlikely snowstorm. It seemed to be happening more frequently these days. Excessively bad winters, global warming messing with weather patterns; who knew? It didn't matter. The result was a seventeen-year-old's nose pressed nearly to the palm of his hand as he studied a melting snowflake.

"They really are all different."

I leaned over his shoulder and took a look for myself. It was nearly gone, a victim of body heat. Only the barest tracings remained, a transparent filigree that disappeared as I watched. "So they are." I hefted the snowball I held behind my back and then dumped it down the back of his shirt. "Here's some more to study."

By the time we were done, the empty lot behind the motel was witness to an epic battle, a hundred flying snowballs, and one lopsided snowman. It was fairly juvenile play for an ex-mobster and a kid who ate books on genetics as if they were Pop-Tarts, but it was one of the best hours I'd spent in years. Michael caught on quicker than I would've thought to the idea of rough-and-tumble. There were a few hesitations on his part, but those ended with one spectacular tackle that had me face flat. My brother's weight on my back kept me sputtering in five inches of snow until my nose was in danger of frostbite.

The heat in the room took care of that quickly enough. As with all cheap motel rooms you could either freeze or swelter. Our thermostat was stuck firmly on swelter. I dumped my snow-covered jacket on the carpet and ran a hand over my wet hair. "Okay, track is out, but I'm thinking there's a football scholarship in your future."

"I didn't hurt you, did I?" In contrast to my sloth, Michael had carefully placed his jacket on the one rusty hanger in the shallow depression in the wall that passed for a closet. "Your side?"

He'd done a little forgetting himself. The fact I was in the state of delicate health shared by the rest of humanity had escaped him for a little while. "I'm okay, Misha." I slapped my stomach lightly. "Healing up just fine." It was true. The bullet wound had scabbed over and rarely ached.

He accepted the statement with only mild skepticism and went for the phone book. "Supreme or double pepperoni?"

"Whichever is cheaper." We had about seventy dollars left after paying for the room. It was money I'd previously given Michael. If something happened to me, he would have enough to keep him safe and holed up until

Saul could reach him. We were lucky Bonnie and Clyde hadn't thrown him down and strip-searched him; if they had, up shit creek would've been more than a quaint little saying. It would've been our life. As it was, the money would barely be enough for gas and food to get us to our first destination. We were now facing not one but two detours on our way to North Carolina.

The first was necessary, but the second I had my qualms about. It was Michael's idea and it was a good one, but I didn't know whether we had the time. I had the instinct to go to ground, dig a hole, and pull it in behind us. And it was getting stronger all the time. The sooner we arrived at the house in North Carolina, the happier I would be. But Michael was right, as much as my gut hated to admit it. The more information we had about Jericho, the better. To that end, we were going to visit a Dr. Bellucci.

My brother had started to tell me about Marcos Bellucci seconds before we'd spotted our pregnant downfall at the side of the road. The man had been mentioned in several of the books we'd purchased. He had worked along the same lines as Jericho had, before Jericho's theories had split away from the mainstream. He'd even coauthored a few papers with our favorite monster. But as their scientific outlook began to diverge, so had their professional relationship. Dr. Bellucci had spent a considerable amount of time refuting Jericho's work after that. He kept it up for quite a while, even after his newly ordained rival dropped out of sight. Michael thought if anyone knew something that might help us, it would be Bellucci.

Like I said, he was a smart kid.

The scientist lived in St. Louis, about twenty hours from our first stop, which was Boston. As I had called number after number looking for Anatoly, I'd given serious thought about calling his allies in the business. Uncle Lev, Uncle Maksim, and others had popped in and out of my childhood for birthdays and special oc-

casions. They weren't related by blood, not my parent's
blood at any rate. Associates of my father, these uncles
came and went like the tide. With vagaries of the business and shifts in loyalty, the faces changed, but the
birthday presents showed up all the same. It wouldn't
do to show disrespect to Anatoly Korsak.

Calling the uncles about my father wasn't too risky—
not really. Anatoly might be on the run, but he still had
a power with the older crew. It was fading the longer he
was gone, but it still existed. They would be willing to
give me any help they could in finding Anatoly. Unfortunately, the simple fact was they probably had no help
to give. If Anatoly hadn't given me concrete information
on his location, he certainly hadn't given it to them. But
while they couldn't point me in Anatoly's direction, they
could give me another kind of aid.

Money. They could give me money.

Uncle Lev was my father's oldest friend, one of the
few uncles who'd remained steadfastly present and
mostly unshot throughout my childhood. He was also
the only "uncle" who had felt like genuine family. If I
could depend on anyone, it would be him. I didn't bother
to call ahead. His phones had been tapped since before
I was born. It wasn't as if I needed directions anyway.
I'd been to his house once or twice for his daughter's
graduation and wedding. Point the car to the richest part
of town and you were there. Easy. But deciding what I
would tell him about Michael wasn't so easy. Lev had
been at Lukas's first birthday and every one following
until the kidnapping on the beach. He was godfather to
both of us, and I knew he'd welcome my brother back
with open arms. It might be good for Michael, seeing
firsthand that someone besides me accepted him as family. Then again, it would raise a thousand questions, the
majority of which I couldn't answer, not even to Uncle
Lev.

I was distracted from my thoughts by the sensation of
a cold and wet nose against the skin of my ankle. Look-

ing down, I saw a sinuous body beside my foot. The head was invisible, hidden under the bottom of my jeans. "Michael," I growled, "your damn rat's two seconds away from being flatter than that pizza you're ordering."

Hanging up the phone, he moved over to scoop up Godzilla. "He isn't a rodent," he said with imperious indignation. "Ferrets are actually members of the—"

"Satan's inner circle would be my guess. Too bad he wasn't ripped off along with all of our money," I said, cutting in before he went any farther. I was learning that to let Michael start lecturing on a topic was to lose massive chunks of time. It had been not even a week since I'd pulled him from that place, but the change in him in those short days was nothing short of astounding. He had gone from withdrawn and indifferent to insatiably curious and not a little mouthy.

I loved every minute of it.

But there were limits to human patience, as well as human ears. And I wasn't precisely in the mood for a biology lesson about my least favorite animal. Living with it was enough benevolence on my part. Sitting on the edge of the bed, I toed off soaking wet socks and wriggled bone-chilled toes. My sneakers weren't made for this type for weather. "We should be in Boston by late tomorrow night. You stocked up on rat food?"

Deciding my thirst for ferret knowledge was nonexistent, he labeled me as unteachable and gave up on the subject. "And this uncle Lev who's not really an uncle will be glad to see you?" came his doubtful question.

"Yeah, he will be. He's a . . ." I stopped, unsure of exactly how to finish that sentence. I'd wanted to say that he was a good guy, but it was hard to say that about a man who made a living off the blood and thievery of others. "He's loyal to Anatoly. He's like family. Sort of." The curve of my lips was apologetic. "Sorry it's not more of a normal family for you, Misha."

"Not your fault." His eyes focused on me long enough for me to catch the flash of automatic rejection before they dropped to the remote he picked up from the table. "And not my family."

That merry-go-round again—it still showed no signs of stopping, but I hadn't given up the hope it might at least one day slow down. "You're a stubborn little bastard." I sighed as I twisted and flopped back onto the pillows. "Just like me, believe it or not. If that's not a family trait, then what the hell is it?"

"Annoying?"

I laughed. It was something else how in the middle of this huge mess the kid could make me laugh—really something else. Rubbing the back of my hand across a five o'clock bristle that just wouldn't quit, I admitted fondly, "You've got me there."

Considering the loss of our money and the tripling of our travel time, I should've been in the worst of humors. But I wasn't. I might be on the run and broke as hell, but I was still ahead of the game. I was still worlds away from the nightmare the last ten years of my life had been. Then I couldn't see the light at the end of the tunnel. Now I could.

It was enough.

The light chose that moment, not surprising, to wipe the complacent smile off my face with a few seemingly innocent words. "Stefan, I was wondering." He paused casually. "Have you ever had sex?"

Okay, perhaps his words were not so innocent, depending on how rigid your upbringing or how high your monthly porno budget. Covering my eyes with my hand, I gave a groan straight from the grave. "That's a big subject change from Uncle Lev," I pointed out hoarsely. "What brought this on?"

"This and that," he answered with irritating cheer. "There's my natural curiosity of course. We talked about that a few days ago."

Yes, we had. And I'd given him the remote to the TV; free educational rein as it were. You would think that would satisfy him, but no.

"And then Fisher . . . that girl, whatever her name was, was . . . you know. Her eyes . . . her mouth. At me."

I didn't have to uncover my eyes. I could feel the heat of the blush fill the room. "Flirting," I filled in hastily before he stumbled on.

Recovering smoothly, he said, "Flirting. She was flirting with me. That sort of thing isn't done at the Institute. Flirting. Intercourse. It isn't allowed."

Intercourse. Jesus. No, I couldn't imagine that it was. No horny teenagers were going to splash around in Jericho's carefully crafted gene pool. Although it wouldn't have been too long before he arranged something himself, a *breeding* . . . simply to see what it might produce.

"I know the mechanics of course." He was relentless, horrifyingly relentless. "That was in the biology books. But I was curious about the specifics. So, if you have had sex . . ."

"Yes," I spit out somewhat defensively before rolling over and covering my head with the pillow. My voice muffled, I went on. "I've had girlfriends, and I've had sex." And please God, I begged internally, conveniently forgetting my semiagnostic ways, let that be the end of it. Naturally, it wasn't.

"Really?"

At the fascinated tone in his voice, I flinched. Then with resignation I lifted the pillow just enough to gaze at him with one reluctant eye. "Yeah. When I was twenty-one, just like the law says."

Confused, he tilted his head to one side. "Law?"

"It's like drinking," I lied without the slightest compunction. "You can't drink or have sex until you're twenty-one. We'll buy you a book before then. A really explicit book with all the gory details. I promise. The Kama Sutra two point oh."

"Oh. I see." Settling onto his own bed, he leaned back against the headboard and gave me a look of overt sympathy. "If you're a virgin, Stefan, you don't have to be embarrassed or make up stories. Maybe we could both buy a book—or a movie. There seem to be lots and lots of movies. If we watch enough, we're bound to learn something."

I had been neatly wedged into a corner by a psychologically adept, offensively trained brat-on-wheels. It wasn't as if I didn't want him to know the big picture beyond simple anatomy. And it wasn't as if I hadn't been involved in my share of locker room exchanges with my high school buddies. Hell, one of my bases of operation for the past three years had been a strip club. I hadn't had a girlfriend since Natalie, but that didn't mean I didn't get laid now and again. The thing was . . . I was Michael's brother, not his father, and I didn't want to get this wrong. It was important.

But if he didn't have me to ask, then who did he have? Retreating completely under the pillow, I surrendered. "Jesus. All right. Ask away."

"Great." The thin layers of cotton and foam insulating my ears did nothing to hide the triumph. "Let me get a pen and some paper. I want to take notes."

Notes—he was going to take notes. This was shaping up to be a long night.

A long, long night.

Chapter 24

The skyline of early-morning Boston was reflected in the rearview mirror along with a pair of seriously blood-shot eyes—my eyes. We'd reached the city at about two a.m. and slept in the car in a parking lot surrounded by a cluster of office buildings. The fifteen dollars we had left to our name wasn't going to put us up in even the worst fleabag. But the lack of sleep wasn't caused by the cramped quarters. It was Michael and his questions. They'd lasted most of the previous night and all of the following day. I should've actually bought him a book on the subject as I'd threatened, or two or a hundred of them, but I doubted that would've saved me. Somehow he had even managed to elicit details about the relationship between Natalie and me, and that was something I had refused to talk about to anyone.

It wasn't sexual particulars he was after, which was good. I was an open book on all my other exploits, but Natalie had never been that. I'd loved her. At least it was as close to love as I could manage in the midst of my fixation with finding my brother and my obsession for redemption. I couldn't give her my entire heart, but that wasn't by choice. I simply didn't have it to give. I did give her all that I did have. The small slice that was still open for business belonged to her—completely.

I bought her daisies every day. Sometimes it was a bunch tied with a ribbon. Sometimes it was only one. She was a daisy girl. Roses seemed too pretentious for someone as honest and down to earth as she was, and tulips didn't have her life. They didn't explode with light and energy. They didn't throw their arms to the sky and gather in the sun. Nat and daisies were two of a kind in that respect. She was all about color, too, my girl. All our sheets were covered with whimsical patterns—fish, flowers, flying birds, diving dolphins. And every set was so tacky and garish that you were in serious danger of going blind at the sight of them.

I'd never claimed to love Natalie for her subtle taste. I loved her because of her lack of taste and for her freckles that spread like a wildfire in the summer sun. I loved her for her homemade caramel milkshakes, the best in the world, and for her tuna casserole, the absolute worst. And when she dragged that dog from the pound home for my birthday, I groaned and threw up my hands, but that was on the outside. On the inside I kept right on loving her. I'd told her before that I liked Labs, and that's what she brought home. It had three legs, a tongue too big to fit in its mouth, and produced a gallon of slobber every five minutes. She named it Harry after my long-gone horse and gave it my spot on the couch.

With that, if possible, I loved her then even more. I loved her as much as I was capable. That was the key word, wasn't it? Capable.

It wasn't enough. When I finally broke down and told her what I did . . . what I had become since college, it was over. She could've handled just that, I think. Make no mistake; she would've dragged me by my ear out of that life and across the country if that's what it took to break away. Innately honest and stubborn as all hell, she would've put my career to bed, for good, and before I could have taken another breath.

But it wasn't just that. Natalie had known all along that she owned only a piece of my soul. Unreservedly, she had given me all of hers and waited patiently for me to come around.

I never had.

I hadn't put her first. I was good at the daisies, but I'd

never put her first. She wouldn't have minded that. She would've understood. But I had never made her equal to my obligations either—never. It hadn't even been close. It was one strike too many. She could've easily reformed me. I hadn't ever cared about the business other than how the money from it could help me find Lukas. But while getting me on the straight and narrow would've been a piece of cake for Crusader Nat, she couldn't force me to free up the rest of my heart. And she knew it.

I knew it, too. I hadn't blamed her then, and I still didn't. She didn't leave me; I gave her up. I threw her away. I couldn't make room for her in my life. There was Lukas and only Lukas. All Natalie ever had from me was the leftovers, the table scraps. Lukas came first, last, and always. Finding him was the only thing that had mattered. I'd made that choice before I had ever met Nat. When she was gone, I tried to tell myself that my only mistake had been to lead her on, to give her hope for a relationship I wasn't equipped for. Yeah, that's what I told myself.

I was wrong.

Lukas . . . Michael wouldn't have begrudged me love while I searched. Generous of spirit and with a basic goodness he wasn't yet aware of, he would've been happy for me. The denial wasn't his; it was mine.

Jericho had stolen more than my brother on that beach. He'd stolen me too. He had hollowed me out, scooped out the important parts, and left a shell of brittle ice masquerading as a human being. When his man had left me for dead on the sand, he hadn't been far off the mark. Not far at all.

I missed Nat. I missed her every time I saw a scraggly daisy blooming in the weeds, every time I saw a red kite flying high enough to block out the sun. I missed her when I bought boring white sheets and when I bypassed the dog food aisle in the grocery or when I bought thin, overly sweet fast-food milkshakes. I missed her and hoped she was someone else's daisy girl.

I missed her and knew I'd never see her again.

So when Michael had asked me about love and relationships, things that were much harder than sex to explain, Natalie was the only place I had to go. It was a painful place, but it was a worthwhile one too. She deserved to be talked about, my girl, and Michael deserved to know there was glory in this life if you weren't too damaged or too afraid to accept it. I talked long enough that my throat was sore. I didn't want him to make my mistakes. It was a mistake no one should have to live with.

Michael had seemed to sense how painful a topic it was and thanked me before curling up in the backseat to leave me with my memories and my regrets. The sweet and the bittersweet; that was what life was all about. He slept for nearly six hours. I'd slept for maybe three, but for once my dreams were . . . nice—melancholy, but good.

"I thought your uncle Lev would be happy to see you. I thought you said he would welcome you with open arms and a heated house." Jarring me from thoughts of kites, daisies, and freckles, a disheveled blond head popped up from the backseat and a sleepily disgruntled face peered at me from a cocoon of blankets. "It's cold, in case you haven't noticed, and I have to use the bathroom. This isn't any better than that tree incident. In fact it's worse."

To his confusion, I handed him an empty plastic soft drink bottle I grabbed from the floorboards. "No, kiddo, *now* it's worse."

As comprehension flooded his features, I yawned and turned back around to watch the snow slowly pile on the hood of the car. I ducked automatically as the bottle returned, whizzing by my ear. I'd noticed Michael, like me, wasn't much of a morning person.

"Absolutely not," he said evenly. "No way."

I shrugged and yawned again, rubbing at my eyes.

"It's your bladder. Besides, if you save up, I'll teach you to write your name in the snow."

With a glare as chilly as the air inside the car, he leaned over the seat and retrieved the bottle. I kept my back to him to give him some privacy. "And, smart-ass, Uncle Lev will be glad to see me. I just didn't want to show up in the middle of the night. He'll know something's up. If he thinks I'm in trouble, he'll be all over us, asking questions, and trying to get us to stay. We can't afford that."

"Why not?"

I hadn't gotten very specific with Michael on how exactly I'd left my earlier employment. It had been difficult enough to tell him what little I had about my life in the *Mafiya*. "I told you how I quit the mob to come after you," I started slowly, jangling the keychain that hung from the ignition.

"I remember."

Of course he remembered. What had it been? Four, five days ago? "Well, it's not the type of job where you give two weeks notice and they throw you a going-away party. Konstantin, the man I worked for, wasn't exactly boss-of-the-year material. He could've made things difficult for me if he'd wanted." From day to day it was hard to guess his mood. From distantly amused to coldly murderous, Konstantin was rarely predictable in the depths of his violence. He wouldn't have hurt me, not once he heard my reasoning. He still respected Anatoly too much for that, but he could've slowed me down while I laid it all out. That I couldn't afford. "So, I simply took off. Disappeared. I could always explain myself later if I needed his help. I show up with my missing brother, Anatoly's lost son, and all's forgiven." Leaning my head back on the seat, I massaged the back of my neck. "But on the day I left, someone killed Konstantin. Shot him. For his ex-bodyguard, yours truly, that doesn't look too good."

"Won't your uncle Lev believe you're innocent?"

"Do you?" I asked lightly and far more casually than I felt.

There was a moment of thought, the sounds of shifting blankets, and then, "I do. You don't seem to like hurting people. You're good at it, but you don't like it." His voice dropped to a barely audible murmur. "Not like Jericho." A hand came over the seat before I could comment to thrust a capped and newly warm bottle into my hand. "Here. There's no room back here."

Right. Sure there wasn't. But encouraged by his belief in me, I decided I could probably put up with a little urine. Putting it in our trash bag for later disposal, I returned to the conversation. "Uncle Lev will know I didn't do it, but that doesn't matter. If we're there more than a day or two, it'll get back to Miami via the grapevine, and Konstantin's son will send some people after me. They won't be as scary as Jericho, but that doesn't mean they can't do us some damage all the same." Damage was a nice euphemism for "kill us and dump us in the harbor."

"All right. That makes sense, I guess," Michael accepted doubtfully. Cheek to cheek with him, a sleek ferret head poked free of the blanket to fix me with a nearsighted glare. "But it's still cold. And it's still your fault."

"The logic of a true student of the sciences," I grumbled, but I started the car and set the heater on high. "We'll find someplace to clean up and head to Lev's. That reminds me; I have something for you."

He took the glasses I retrieved for him from the glove compartment. I'd lifted them yesterday at a gas station. With cheap wire rims, the lenses were tinted tawny brown, but not nearly as dark as most sunglasses. Michael would be able to get away with wearing them inside without raising any eyebrows.

Releasing his death grip on the blanket, Michael

turned the glasses over in his hands. "What are these for?"

"Your eyes," I said matter-of-factly. "You can deny you're my brother until the end of time, Misha, but if Uncle Lev sees your eyes along with the blond hair, he'll have something to say. And we don't have time to get into that with him." Nearly twenty years older than Anatoly, Lev was basically retired. He had a few of his old crew who still hung around, but they were like him, in their early seventies and not as quick with the brass knuckles as they used to be. They might put a crimp in Jericho's style, but they wouldn't be able to hold him back for long.

I could see that Michael wanted to say something. Eyes distant under the fringe of unruly hair, he chewed at his lower lip before opening his mouth, only to shut it again. "Something wrong?"

He shook his head slowly at the question. "No . . . no. I'll wear them." Slipping them on, he raised both eyebrows. "How do they look?"

"You're practically a movie star there—Brad Pitt all the way." The glasses did work well enough at obscuring the differing color of his eyes, making them both appear an indistinct color, maybe brown, maybe hazel, maybe gray. "Just keep them on. Hey, we could always dye your hair again. There's a whole rainbow of colors out there we haven't touched on."

He promptly retreated back into the blankets. "And let's keep it that way."

"No guts, no glory, kid." The car had warmed up and I plowed it through the drifting snow. Not only would Lev be glad to see me, but he would feed us breakfast as well. It had been just over a week since I'd tasted home-cooked food, but it felt like years. I was looking forward to eating off china instead of from a paper bag.

By the time we swept through the wrought-iron gates that guarded Uncle Lev's house, we were fairly presentable courtesy of the now-familiar gas-station-bathroom sponge bath. Michael was in jeans and a navy blue sweatshirt, the dressiest thing we'd managed to pick up for him along the way. I'd put on a black shirt and a pair of gray slacks that were miraculously unwrinkled from a week in a duffel bag. We weren't exactly suave by any means, but neither did we look like we were living out of our car with nothing but a ferret and a half-empty jar of peanut butter.

I didn't recognize the guy at the guard shack, and he fixed me with a suspicious glower until he received the all clear from the house. I was unimpressed. From the size of his gun, he had something to prove; at least Michael would have said so.

Parking the car on the rosy brick drive that circled before the front of the house, I climbed out into the lazy drizzle of snow. I shoved my chilled hands into my jacket pockets and started around the car. Michael joined me and stood looking up at the house with a slightly awed expression. It was something to see; there was no doubt about that. Three stories high with a multitude of leaded glass windows and masses of winter-brown ivy, it could've been shipped stone by stone from jolly old England. There were even miniature gargoyles on the roof that spouted water nonstop during the rainy season. It was a testament to the overblown, and Uncle Lev through and through.

As we stood at the door, I gave Michael a last once-over. "You ready? Comfortable with the story?"

He didn't appear nervous, but considering the past ten years of his life, this was definitely small stuff and not to be sweated. "Nephew of the girlfriend you don't have. Fairly simple. And if I forget, I've written it on my hand."

I almost looked at the palm he overturned, but caught myself at the last minute. "To think I took a bullet for you," I snorted as I pressed the doorbell. "And this is the thanks I get. Lip from a snot-nosed kid."

Looking over at me, he haughtily pushed up the glasses with one meticulous finger. "The privilege is all yours."

I swallowed the automatic groan that came to my lips as the door was thrown open by Uncle Lev himself. "Stefan, *krestnik*. My absent godson come home to roost," he crowed as he pounced on me. Well, pounced can be a relative term when it's applied to a man just shy of three hundred pounds. Pudgy hands seized me and patted me vigorously on the back before giving my cheeks the same treatment. "You've cut your hair. Finally, and after all the times Anatoly nagged at you." He beamed at me and ran vain hands over his own hair. Slicked back and shockingly black for a man his age, it must have left a nice charcoal imprint every night on his pillowcase.

"Yeah. It just got to be too much trouble." I reached out to sling an arm around Michael's shoulders. "Uncle Lev, this is Michael. He's my girlfriend's nephew. I'm running him up to see New York for a few days. She insisted. Male bonding and all that."

Black eyes glittering with good cheer, Lev took Michael's hand and pumped it. "Nice to meet you, young man. Come in. Come in. You delicate sunbirds can't handle true weather."

In the cavernous foyer, I shook the snow out of my hair and took in the vision that was Lev Novikov. It was barely eight o'clock; yet he was already dressed in a snowy expanse of shirt with suspenders of deep blues and purples. His tie matched perfectly and the creases in his pants were knife sharp; at least they were until they reached the swell of his stomach. Both chins were damply clean and gleaming with aftershave. He was a big man, but Lev had made his way through four wives, all of whom had adored the overgrown cherub up to and even after the divorce.

"You're looking good, Uncle," I said, grinning. "Working on wife number five yet?"

He returned my grin with a sly one of his own. "I've a

few *damskee ygrodnik* in mind, angels all." Clapping his hands, he went on briskly. "Now, you're just in time for breakfast, and I'll hear no arguing on the matter."

Behind him an unassuming figure stepped forward to take our jackets. Dressed in dark gray, he wasn't British and his name was Larson, not Jeeves, but he fulfilled Lev's desire for a butler all the same. He'd worked there nearly twenty years and had seen things that guaranteed him a paycheck miles above that of any other domestic servant.

We walked across marble floors in the traditional checkerboard black and white and found ourselves in a dining room in royal reds and rich gold. The table was already set for three. No time had been wasted once the call had been received from the guardhouse. There were servers massed with eggs, sausage, bacon, and fried potatoes. There were also *plushki*, a type of cinnamon bun, and *bleeny*, Russian pancakes with honey and jam. Crystal pitchers of orange, raspberry, and apple juice topped it all off.

"Sit, boys. Sit." Lev waved an expansive hand. "Stefan, tell me what you've been up to. Are you still doing *byk* duty? Tschh, you could do so much better than . . . ah . . ." He gave Michael a glance and finished circumspectly, "You could do better. I wish you'd let me pull some strings for my favorite godson."

He had to know Konstantin had been killed. Lev might be retired, but he'd have to be in the ground not to have heard that news. This was his way of hinting around for a bit of private discussion time.

"I think it's safe to say those days are behind me, Uncle Lev," I said neutrally as I took a seat and began filling up my plate as my brother did the same beside me. It would be best to keep up the pretense that Michael was in the dark when it came to my career, at least as Lev knew it. Muddying the waters was the last complication I needed at the moment. "We could talk about it after breakfast, if you want."

"Good." He poured himself a glass of juice. "It's always a smart thing to keep your options open, Stefan. Your father would be the first to say."

"Speaking of which"—I swallowed a bite of *bleeny* that melted in my mouth like spun sugar—"have you heard from Anatoly? I've been trying to contact him."

"No, no. Haven't much expected to, what with . . . you know." He waggled long curly eyebrows that bunched and leaped like black and white striped caterpillars.

The feds. I nodded and stabbed a fork into a piece of sausage. "I know. I was just hoping."

"I'm more than happy to step in until your father can be here, *krestnik*. That's what godfathers are for." His large head turned to take in the sight of Michael already cleaning his plate and loading up with seconds. "Look at the little *ytenok* go. You've a man-sized appetite in that skinny body, little one."

"Yes, sir. I'm a growing teenager." He said it so earnestly that I was forced to smother a grin behind a swallow of coffee. That grin turned into a silent groan as I saw a small furry head peek from Michael's jacket pocket. I should've known he wouldn't leave his beloved vermin in the car.

The rest of the breakfast passed amiably. Uncle Lev told me his daughter was expecting twins and that his son-in-law still wasn't half good enough for her. Considering he'd broken the legs of one of her boyfriends while she was in college, it was actually high praise. He also laid out his plans to travel to Europe in the summer on a three-week singles cruise and invited me with arm-waving enthusiasm. I said, politely, that I would think about it. After we had finished plundering and pillaging the table, I sent Michael off to one of the entertainment rooms while I got down to business with Lev.

The minute Michael disappeared out of the dining room, Lev leaned his not inconsiderable weight back in the chair and folded his hands over the girth of his stomach. Lips pursed, he shook his head woefully. "Stefan, Stefan, Konstantin could be a real *zasranees*; no one knows this better than I. But tell me you didn't pop one in the back of his head."

I pushed my plate away. "Uncle Lev, you know better than that."

Shrewd eyes measured me and then he sighed. "I do. You're smarter than that and also a little too soft, I'm thinking."

Unoffended, I let the corner of my mouth quirk upward. "Is that right?"

"Now, my boy, don't take it badly. I always thought you too good for this life. You and your brother, God keep him. Same as my Katya. Your father and I have worked hard in this country. If you choose a better life, how could we not want that for you?"

I wasn't sure Anatoly completely agreed with him, but I nodded nonetheless. "I've pretty much decided you're right. I thought I'd take a little time off. This trip came up with Michael and seemed perfect. I know Konstantin would give me grief about it. He thought I was a little soft too." I gave a humorless smile. "So, I went without telling him, and then I found out he was killed the day I left. Talk about some shitty luck." The last portion was the only truth to my tale and more true it could not have been.

As stories went, it was thin, thread-fucking-bare, in fact. And I wasn't sure if he would buy it or not. I know I wouldn't have and Uncle Lev was certainly more devious minded than I was. He'd had nearly a half century more practice. Either way, after a hissing exhalation of doubt, he let it go. "So, you want I should straighten this out for you, Stefan? Call Konstantin's boy to stop being a *moodozvon* and look elsewhere for the shooter?"

"He wouldn't listen. Fyodor has even more balls than Konstantin and a whole lot fewer brains. But if you want to try, I'd be grateful. Just wait until I leave, okay? I wouldn't mind more distance between him and me before you call."

"Fedya always was stubborn." He clucked his tongue against large, overly white teeth. "He'll take some convincing, of that there's no doubt. But I'll keep working at him until he comes around. Now, what can I really do for you, Stefan? I know you didn't stop by just to have me intercede on your behalf. You wouldn't give Fyodor the satisfaction. You're a little stubborn in your own right, *krestnik*."

"Me, Uncle Lev?" I spun a fork in a lazy circle on the cherry surface of the table. "Say it ain't so."

"Ahhh." He shook his head and flapped a hand. "I may as well be talking to my third wife and she was deaf as a stone."

"She must've been. She was married to you after all." I grinned at his growl and ducked my head beneath the swat he aimed at it. It had always been harder to reconcile Lev than my father to the world in which they lived. I'd been sixteen when I'd finally caught on to my father's business. I'd had my suspicions since Lukas's disappearance; the men who'd shown up in the house during that time had had a rougher edge to them than the usual guards who had patrolled our grounds, and that was saying something. But I hadn't come out and asked the big question until two years later. My father concluded if I was old enough to ask, then I was old enough to hear the answer.

It hadn't surprised me—not for a second.

My father had fit into that picture with ease, but I'd had more trouble pushing Uncle Lev into it. He was jolly, cheerful, coddling, more like a Jewish mother than a Russian gangster. It was similar to having schizophrenia, trying to balance the doting adopted uncle and the man who postponed a meal only if he had to personally kill someone. At sixteen I tried not to think about the latter. At twenty-four I still tried, but with much less success.

"Actually, Uncle Lev, I need to borrow some money. Once I drop the kid off in New York with his relatives,

I'm going to take a vacation. Wait until things cool down or until you talk some sense into that asshole, Fyodor. I had some with me, but . . ." I tugged a short lock at the nape of my neck and groaned. "I was robbed. By a girl, a pregnant girl, can you believe it?"

Lev laughed, his belly rippling with good cheer and good food. "You've always been such a sober young man since . . . since the trouble. It's nice to see you joke."

"Yeah, I wish." Glumly, I dumped the fork onto my cleanly polished plate. "She and Bubba Shitkicker cleaned me out. I'm lucky they left me my nads."

That was apparently more entertaining than my developing a sense of humor. He chortled until his face turned beet red and I honestly feared a massive coronary wasn't far behind. "A girly. A pregnant *keykla*. Ah, Stefan," he choked out.

"Jesus, it wasn't as if I could *shoot* her," I protested darkly.

The color intensified to liver purple and he had to sip at his half-empty glass of juice to recuperate. He sputtered and wheezed for several moments before wiping his perspiring face with his silk napkin. "No more, Stefan. No more. You'll be the death of me with this. How much do you need?"

"Forty, fifty. How ever much you have to spare." I handed him a fresh napkin to replace his soaking one. "Michael and I need to get back on the road within the next hour or so."

In your ordinary family, asking for so much might be suspect. Uncle Lev didn't think twice. He could drop three times that on a Friday night in Atlantic City and not blink an eye. "I've sixty-five in the safe I think." He finished mopping at his neck. "It's yours. But I want you and the boy to stay for lunch at least. Such a skinny *pateechka*. He needs fattening up and I want to catch up on old times with you, Stefan. It's been, what, two years now? Shameful behavior, ignoring an old man that way."

I recognized the unrelenting glint in his eye and gave

in as gracefully as I could. Four or five hours wouldn't hurt, and it would be a chance to unwind in a place of relative safety, even if for just a short time. "Okay, okay. We'll stick around for lunch. Maybe I'll kick your wrinkled old butt in a little poker."

"Ha," he barked gleefully. "If you remember a tenth of what I've taught you, you can keep the sixty-five. No payback. No interest. Consider it a late Christmas present."

"And if I don't remember?"

He reached over and patted the back of my hand. "Let's not dwell on your certain doom. It'll only ruin the game."

Uncle Lev always had been one for card sharking. When he said doom, he meant it. He'd taught me a little over the years, but it was only a fraction of what he was capable of. The man could cheat you out of your briefs and you wouldn't know what hit you until the cool air fanned your ass. It was a lesson I was able to relive several times over the next few hours. The unsympathetic audience at my elbow didn't make it go down any more easily.

"Are you sure you want to do that?" Michael peered over my shoulder at the cards in my hand as I prepared to discard two. "Statistically speaking your chances of making that combination aren't too high." He had gone from knowing nothing about the game of poker to knowing more than enough to criticize my playing. And he wasn't shy with his opinions.

"I'm sure," I groused, tossing the cards down on the table. Lev and I had joined Michael in the entertainment room to expose him to the finer art of gambling. Surrounded by overstuffed couches, jewel-toned rugs, and more electronics than a NASA mission control room, I was being thoroughly humiliated in front of my brother who seemed to be enjoying every second. He had even torn himself away from the giant flat-screen television to take in the spectacle.

Moments after I was dealt my new cards, plump arms were sweeping away my chips. "You should've listened to your friend, Stefan," he chortled. "He's a nose for this you've never quite had."

A hand hesitantly laid itself on my shoulder as Michael did an about-face from disparaging to stubbornly supportive. "He's not that bad. He only needs a little work on the theory."

"Psh. He's terrible." Lev stacked the chips and dealt again, this time dealing Michael in. "But he's my godson all the same, and I'm happy to see your loyalty to him." He winked and gave him a generous share of what had once been my chips. "You're a good friend, little Michael. Probably better than he deserves. Let me tell you what this one got up to when he was your age. It will curl that blond hair of yours."

"It will?" Michael picked up his cards but kept his eyes riveted on Uncle Lev. "Was he bad?" He spared me a quick, bright glance, tongue firmly in cheek.

"Ah, so bad. So very, very bad." And he was off. Assuming Michael was as young as he appeared to be, he mostly told of the scrapes I'd gotten into at ages thirteen and fourteen. That was the time period before my brother had disappeared. Following that, I hadn't gotten into much trouble; the will simply wasn't there. Before then . . . there were no holds barred. I had detention so often that I had a permanent reservation for the desk by the window. It was all in good fun, I thought, but the custodian who had to chase the five chickens out of the gym hadn't agreed; neither had the biology and chemistry teachers whose labs had to be decontaminated by biohazard units. Then there had been the hiding in an empty locker while the varsity cheerleaders changed. That had made me and Angelo, my best friend, cocks of the walk for the entire seventh grade. It was all typically harmless kid stuff. Anatoly had laughed it all off the few times a teacher had ever been able to pin him down on the phone. He would've done the same if I'd been caught loan sharking during recess.

"Where did you get the chickens?" Michael asked with interest.

"None of your business." I watched with gloom as the last of my chips disappeared.

"What did the cheerleaders look—"

"Don't even finish that sentence," I warned him.

Throwing in the towel, I watched as the two of them battled it out on the gaming field of honor. It wasn't long before Lev realized Michael could hold his own in fair combat. It was an opportunity for the old man to impishly begin a lesson in cheating. First he showed off his simple overhand shuffle, a finger break, then a false cut. Following that, he used a double undercut to move the ace of spades back to the top of the deck. I'd seen it all before, but it didn't stop me from whistling in appreciation.

"You haven't lost your touch, Uncle Lev."

Michael was watching it all with a quiet and, if I wasn't mistaken, mildly larcenous fascination. "You could make a lot of money this way, couldn't you?"

"Sure," I drawled. "If you didn't mind being beaten to a pulp when you got caught."

"If you were clever enough, you wouldn't get caught." He held out a hand for the cards. "Sir, could you show me that last one again?"

That's all I needed, Michael trying to score us pocket change at every gas and lunch stop, all in the spirit of an interesting experiment. Hoping to distract him, I rose, stretched, and checked my watch. Nearly four and a half hours had passed since breakfast. "When's lunch, Uncle Lev? We really do have to get going soon."

"Spoilsport," he grumped. "I'll go check on the cook. She's been temperamental lately. I should never have *traykhate* her. It wasn't worth a late lunch."

As he trundled out the door, Michael said curiously,

"I don't recall that word being covered in my language class."

"And it's not going to be covered here either, Junior. So don't hold your breath."

He ran through the cards in a fairly decent imitation of Lev's last move. "Why do you do that?" he asked matter-of-factly.

"Do what?"

His eyes narrowed at me from behind smoky glass as he shuffled silently.

"Okay, okay. Maybe I'm a little overprotective," I admitted grudgingly. "I think I'm entitled." But much more than that, I was obligated.

He continued to manipulate the cards without speaking, his fingers growing swifter with each pass. Finally, he said, "It wasn't your fault, Stefan."

I felt my mouth go dry. "What?" This was not a road I wanted to travel.

"Your brother's being taken. It wasn't your fault. From the way you described, it was planned, right? The beach was mostly inaccessible; he had a getaway car available. It was planned," he repeated. "If it hadn't been then, it would've been some other time. Some other place. You're trying to make up for something you didn't do." To someone who's not your brother was the unsaid tag on that statement.

"Misha." I shook my head and tried for a smile, only to fall short. "Now just isn't the time, but . . . thanks." I didn't think it would ever be the time for that discussion if I could avoid it, but I realized what the effort said about Michael. He had been locked away in a place of rigid authority and people who could've passed as robots for all the emotion they showed. That he could still reach out to someone was extraordinary, and I wasn't about to slam a door in his face.

He dipped his head in acknowledgment and began to meander about the room, still putting the cards through their paces. From the bookshelves to the stereo system to the massive collection of DVDs, it all received a thorough examination. "I like this place. Is your house like this?"

I snorted. "You wish, kid." Actually, I didn't have a place to live anymore. Going back to the condo at any time in the foreseeable future wasn't an option. I'd suspected that before I left, even without the added complication of Konstantin's death. I'd taken everything important to me, which hadn't been much. The majority of my money was for finding my brother. Material things hadn't meant much, except as unnecessary expenses. But Michael hadn't been allowed ownership of anything in the Institute. Of course the bright and shiny things in life were going to fascinate him. "But don't worry. Whenever we settle in one spot, you can fill up your room with anything your greedy little heart desires."

"Anything?" He moved to the window that faced the back of the property and looked over his shoulder at me with impudent challenge. "Honestly?"

"Anything that doesn't come from an adult bookstore," I amended.

He turned to look out the window, but I heard the indistinct mutter of "Issues, issues." As he tilted his head, his attention was caught by something other than giving me a hard time. "There are fountains and a maze. It looks . . . nice . . . with all the snow. Peaceful."

"It's always prettier when you're watching it from someplace warm, eh?"

His lips moved in a sheepish curve. "Strange how that happens." Shifting to get a better look, he said, "There's your uncle Lev. He's talking to some people."

Puzzled, I walked over to join him. It was Lev. I only caught a glimpse of him before he disappeared back into the house. The four people he had been talking with began to walk to their cars. All of them were obviously servants. One was the cook; I recognized her from previous visits. The man was Larson, and I didn't know the other two—housekeeper and maid probably. But why would they all be leaving so early in the day?

It was a stupid question—colossally, monstrously stupid.

"Hide."

The air was so clear and sharp, I was vaguely surprised it didn't cut Michael's face when he turned to look at me. "What?"

I gave him a hard push toward one of the couches resting against the side wall. "Hide!" Without further question he ran and pushed behind the piece of furniture, slithering out of sight. My gun had found its way into my hand, I couldn't recall how. It was remarkably similar to a magic trick. Abracadabra. There it was, clenched in a grip carved from bone. My fingers should've ached. Maybe they did ache, but I didn't feel it.

The crystal knob of one of the double doors began to slowly turn, and I stepped smoothly to the wall beside it. Lev had closed the door behind him as he'd left. He could not have possibly carried his weight up the stairs in the seconds that had passed from the sighting of him via the window, but I called his name nonetheless.

"Uncle Lev," I said with laughter that passed through my throat like chunks of regurgitated ice. "Give me a hand, would you? This kid has me pinned to the floor. Thinks he's some sort of wrestler."

Wasn't that a disarming picture? Michael and I rolling around in horseplay, laughing and joking.

A perfect target.

The door was kicked open in a shower of splinters and a gun fired, chewing up the antique rug in the center of the room. It was Sevastian, my old adversary from back in Miami. The bastard. It didn't surprise me. Only he would be overconfident enough to fire at what he couldn't see. As cocky as he may have been, he wasn't entirely mindless. He saw his mistake instantly and was already turning his weapon toward me when I shot him.

I took the chest shot. It was the easiest. With broad

bands of muscle that rippled even through the covering of a thick black sweater, he was built like a bull, and when he fell, he shook the floor as heavily as one. Swiveling, I jammed my shoulder against the door to slam it shut. There was a resounding crash as someone hit the other side face-first. Yanking it back open, I straddled the fallen body and swung my foot into the shaking chin in a hard kick. And that was it for number two. Pavel had always been Sevastian's shadow. Sevastian went first and Pavel mopped up what was left, which usually wasn't a whole hell of a lot.

An arm came across my throat like an iron bar and my thoughts of Pavel vanished instantly. The crushing pain managed to cut through the layer of numbness that sheathed me. "I knew you'd fuck up one day, Korsak," came the gravelly voice in my ear. The accent was still thick after fifteen years out of Moscow and he slipped into the Russian that came more easily to him. *"Segodnya etot den."* Today's that day.

I could feel his blood, hot and plentiful, soaking the back of my shirt. I should've known one bullet wouldn't take the son of a bitch down. I started to bring my gun up to try for an awkward shot, but his other massive hand fastened around mine. The bones in my wrist creaked to the point of breaking as it was bent backward in an unforgiving grip. Before I could shift weight to try and throw him off, a knee hit the back of my thighbone and buckled my leg instantly. Sevastian had once been in the Russian army, and what he'd learned there trumped anything I'd picked up in my few working years. The fall was over before I knew I was going down. Sandwiched between the floor and a hulking mountain of flesh, my lungs expelled every molecule of air, leaving me wheezing desperately.

Ripping the gun from my hand, he flung it across the room. With his arm still around my neck he tightened the pressure until yellow and black spots washed across my vision. With all that air forced out and now with no

way in, if I didn't do something within the next few seconds, Michael would be on his own. He might be the
fastest healer around, but I didn't think that would save
him from a bullet in the heart or brain. He was a boy, not
a vampire. He wasn't going to rise from the dead, and
Sevastian wasn't one to leave witnesses any other way.

Feebly I raised my hand up and behind me to scrape
uselessly against his face. He chuffed a laugh stinking
with the copper of blood against the back of my neck.
The bastard's lungs were filling up. Without medical
help he'd be dead in fifteen minutes. It didn't matter;
I'd be dead in five . . . and that was a blue-sky estimate,
a best-case scenario. If he let me asphyxiate, it would be
minutes. If he snapped my neck, it would be seconds.

My hand continued its path up his jawline, the motions
as fragile as those of a newborn child. "You're barely
struggling," he said in a clotted whisper, switching back
to English for my benefit. He knew my Russian wasn't
as fluent as his, and he wanted me to understand every
word. "It's so much more satisfying when you struggle. I
want to feel you flop under me like a fish out of water. I
want to feel every twitch as brain cell by brain cell you
die, traitor." A hard prodding at my hip told me what I'd
always suspected. Death was the ultimate hard-on for
Sevastian. Twisted and sickly perverse as he was, neither
women nor men held much attraction for him. Killing
was all. He lived it, breathed it, and if he could somehow
make death itself tangible, he would probably fuck it.

The choking hold on my neck eased slightly as he
cajoled, "Stay awake, Stefan. Stay and try just a little
harder. Perhaps then I won't rip that boy limb from limb
when I find him."

I barely heard the words. The roaring in my head
had followed the curtain of spreading black before my
eyes. My only concern was my traveling hand. Sevastian ignored its progress even as it touched his ear. He'd
always had well-shaped ears, I thought dimly as my capacity for coherence began to unravel. It was peculiar to

see: his bullet-shaped head, Neanderthal brows, soulless and cloudy eyes combined with a delicate seashell curve of ear that any woman would've been proud of. Whether Sevastian was proud of them, I didn't know. It was, as they say, moot.

I ripped the left one from his head.

There was a scream that managed to rip through the haze surrounding me and the weight rolled off my back. Weakly pushing up to my knees, I sucked in air that seemed as thick as syrup. It rebelled in my throat, refusing to push past and inflate my lungs. I could feel the sensation of woven wool under my hands, but I couldn't see it. I couldn't see anything. With a last-ditch monumental effort I struggled to expand my chest and pull in air. It worked; a teaspoon of oxygen managed to trickle down into my lungs. That short, choppy breath was followed by two more and then by a brutal kick in my ribs. I was thrown what felt like several feet and landed hard on my hip and shoulder. Fragments of light and color were returning to my sight and I spotted the glittering chrome of my gun barely out of reach. Lunging, I snatched it from the floor, rolled to my side, and fired.

And missed.

If this had been the movies, I would've hit him right between the eyes, and that would've been that. Conquering hero prevails. Popcorn and a cold one for everybody. But this wasn't a movie. This was crappy real life, and I missed the son of a bitch. He was moving faster than any lung-shot man had a right to move, and I still had the vision of a ninety-year-old glaucoma victim. Ideal circumstances it did not make.

Sevastian had lost his gun as well when I'd shot him in the chest. With one blood-covered hand clamped to the side of his head, he was using the other to reach for his own weapon on the floor when my bullet passed him by a good six inches. I fired again. This time I did hit him ... in the shoulder, but the wrong shoulder. The blow knocked him nearly sideways, but that only lined his gun up on me all the faster and he was already firing. Right up until the moment he dropped, boneless as a jellyfish, I thought I was dead. I knew I was; I knew it for an irrefutable fact. I could all but feel the bullet in my throat instead of in the floor that had claimed it; yet here I was alive, whole. And I owed none of that to myself.

Michael looked down at Sevastian impassively. "He's not a particularly nice man either."

He wasn't wrong. First a child molester and now a hit man, Michael was being exposed to people who weren't any better than those who kept him in the Institute. It wasn't the most smoothly run escape to ever come down the pike. My talents, assuming I had any, apparently lay elsewhere.

Once again pushing up to my knees, I tried from there to get to my feet. Sevastian's chest was still rising and falling, albeit slowly and unevenly, which meant Michael hadn't killed him. Relief weakened my legs almost as much as the lack of oxygen. Putting that burden on him even to save my life wasn't remotely what I wanted. Unfortunately, Michael seemed destined to do for others what he wouldn't risk doing for himself. "You . . . okay, Misha?" I gasped roughly as I tried for more air.

He blinked and moved to my side to brace me. "I should probably be asking you that. He nearly killed you."

The bastard had certainly given it his best shot. "Nah." I rubbed the back of my hand across my eyes, clearing the last of the swirling flecks of light. And breathing, the breathing was slowly coming along. "I had it under . . . control . . . the whole time."

With an openly skeptical look generated by the croak of my abused throat, Michael nodded and said dryly, "I'm sure."

His mask of equanimity didn't fool me. The tawny glasses emphasized the faint pallor of his skin and the fingers of one hand were curled tightly against the palm. It was the hand, I would bet, that he'd used to touch

the back of Sevastian's neck. Michael had left his hiding place behind the couch and used what Jericho had
given him—no, what Jericho had *forced* on him—all to
save my miserable ass. Taking him by the shoulder, I
urged him toward the door. Sevastian and Pavel usually
worked as a pair. There shouldn't be anyone else lying
in wait for us, but I tucked Michael behind me all the
same. "What did you do to him?" I murmured, my eyes
flickering back and forth for any signs of a nasty surprise
that would indicate Sevastian had changed his MO to
include a backup team.

He didn't have a chance to answer as Lev appeared
in our sight as we stepped over the unconscious body
of Pavel. Waiting in the hall with hands clasped in their
familiar position over his belly, he watched us come into
sight with only a bare widening of dark eyes. "Stefan."
He gave a small smile laced with a lively curiosity. "It
seems you're not so soft after all."

"Yeah," I said remotely. "Seems that way." The numbness I'd first felt as I'd realized his betrayal had dissipated. What was left in its place wasn't as desirable—not
goddamn nearly. "Five hours." The time we had spent
waiting for the lunch that Lev insisted we stay for. "That
was more than enough time to stick Sevastian and his
tag-a-long on Konstantin's plane, wasn't it?" He must've
called Fyodor the minute the guard at the gate called
to the house to announce us. Before we even made it
through the front door, we'd been given up.

"The weather nearly spoiled their trip, but they landed
right before the airport shut down." He looked at Pavel
sprawled spread-eagle in the doorway. "But I suppose
you've ruined their trip just as much, eh, *krestnik*?"

"Don't call me that." The moment the words left my
lips I regretted them. They were stupid, and they were
pointless. The things I had thought about Lev, the illusions I'd embraced, were knives . . . slicing away pieces
of me. I'd known who my uncle was, but I hadn't ever
accepted he was that same person with me. I'd thought

I was exempt from his darker side. I'd thought I was family.

I'd thought wrong.

"Stefan, Stefan." Lev rested his chin on his chest as he contemplated me with a mockery of melancholy affection. "It's just *zapodlo*; you know that."

Just business, my ass. I didn't bother to respond to the excuse as I raised my gun to point unwaveringly at his head. "The money. Now."

He sighed and rippled his massively rounded shoulders in a minute shrug. "Very well." Walking with surprisingly dainty steps for such a large man, he turned and moved toward the study.

Michael stepped up to my side as we walked the long stretch of hallway. I could see the confusion that furrowed his forehead, but I was still surprised when he asked Lev the quiet question, "How could you do that?"

Lev shook his head as he pushed open the study door. "Child, you've no idea what's even happened here."

My brother ended that misapprehension instantly. "I am not a child, and Stefan didn't shoot that man. You know he didn't. How could you betray him?"

Pausing in the doorway, Lev looked back with an air of patronizing bemusement. "Whether he shot him or not doesn't matter, little Michael. It doesn't matter at all." Then his eyes met mine and he scolded, "Talking out of school, Stefan. You know better."

The safe was flagrantly visible on one wine-colored wall. There had been no effort to hide it. Who would be suicidal enough to rob from the Russian mob? Plump fingers agilely punched in the combination and Lev went on with his lecture. "Talk, talk, talk, but did you tell your little friend that your father has vanished like a ghost? Did you tell him the rest of us are dependent on the goodwill of those in power?" The bronze metal door was opened to reveal several drawers. "I'm retired, Stefan, and I'm happy to be so. Making waves is no way to ensure I'll enjoy that retirement. Konstantin was to take your father's place. Now Fyodor will." His smile was knowing. "Quite the coincidence, yes? But no matter. I'm loyal to the family. Fyodor is the family now. You, Stefan, are only a tiny piece of it. And, so, I did what I had to do. Loyalty to the family is all."

He had done what was necessary to maintain loyalty—his loyalty to himself. I didn't care anymore. I didn't care in the slightest. And if I repeated that to myself often enough, it would be true. Prodding his back with the gun, I said coldly, "Great. I couldn't be prouder. Now give me the goddamn money." Jerking my head at the ornate desk in the center of the room, I told Michael to find some manila envelopes to put the cash in.

At the touch of metal against his spine Lev had given an almost imperceptible twitch as he remembered what he'd said only minutes ago. I wasn't so soft after all. Now as he pulled stacks of bills from one of the drawers, his air of placid composure began to fade. "I'm still the same man who took you to see Santa, *krestnik*. I'm still the one who held your hand at your mother's funeral. That hasn't changed." His eyes were wise, wistful, and full of lies. "I did all I could for you; you must know that. But in the end, there is only so much that can be done. Even for an uncle who loves his godson."

"Yeah, I'm a lucky guy," I commented with empty detachment. "I'd count my blessings, but then I'd be here all day." I took the envelopes from Michael with my free hand and shoved them into the soft mound of Lev's stomach. "Fill them up fast enough and maybe I'll leave you with some blessings of your own to count." My lips peeled from my teeth in a parody of a grin as I added flatly, "Maybe."

He filled the envelopes quickly and silently after that. When he was done, I handed them to Michael before directing him to the door. "Wait in the hall, Misha. I'll be right out."

I expected him to hesitate at the tone in my voice. I barely recognized the sound of it myself, abraded hoarseness aside. He didn't, though. Flashing me a look of confidence, he faced Lev and said with excruciating politeness, "Good-bye, Uncle Lev. I'd say it was nice to meet you, but then I'd be a liar." He hefted the load in his arms and finished with unusually savage bite, "Just like you."

Once Michael was out of sight, I stared at the man who had done more to shape my childhood than my own father. He had taken me to see Santa when I was six, as he'd said. And like Saint Nick, Uncle Lev had been nothing but a myth. All this time, he had been just a story I'd been stupid enough to fall for ... even though I was a man who should've known better. "Have a seat, Uncle."

Obeying at a snail's pace, he settled himself slowly on a couch of buttery leather and eyed me with false sympathy. There was some genuine concern there as well, but it was reserved for him. "What, Stefan? What do you do now? Shoot me? You know better, and so do I."

He was a liar, a killer, and maybe as much of a monster as Jericho. He was also a seventy-year-old man who had acted as family toward me my whole life. It hadn't meant anything to him, but it had to me. As much as I would've liked to deny it, it had meant a helluva lot to me. After what he had done, hating him should've been child's play. A nice black hatred sizzling with acid and bile would've made things so much easier. And I wanted easy now. I was tired of hard, and I was tired of family that disappeared ... one way or the other.

"Shoot you?" I walked to the desk, picked up the phone and base, and tossed it into the hall. "Why would I want to shoot a toothless old wolf like you, Uncle?" I asked grimly. "Your day has been over for a while. All you're good for is carrying tales to men more powerful than you." It was true. He was a fat spider; poisonous, but if I avoided his web, I'd be safe enough.

Ripping one of the curtains free, I tore it into pieces and tied both of his thick wrists tightly. He hissed disapprovingly as I squatted and used the remaining material to do the same to his ankles. "Those are silk, Stefan. That's no way to treat a beautiful thing."

"Criminal of me, I know. How will I ever live with myself?" The house was old, a historical masterpiece, and the doors all had the large keyholes equipped with baroque keys. I would lock Lev in the study and Michael and I would be long gone before he was found. He'd done us the favor of sending his help home; the house was empty except for him and the unconscious and dying hit men.

"I think you'll do just fine, *krestnik*." Resigned to the situation, he leaned back and let his eyes fall to half mast. "You've more *yaitsa* than I gave you credit for. Anatoly will be proud. That is, he will be if he's alive and you yourself live to see him again."

"If I do, I'll be sure to pass on your regards." I tied the final knot.

Under a naturally ruddy complexion intensified by a high-fat diet and an enlarged heart, he paled slightly. I might have balls of steel, but my father's were titanium. While I wouldn't kill an old man, Anatoly would stop and make a point of it.

"Enjoy that wave-free retirement, Lev." I picked up the Steyr from the floor and tapped the muzzle on his knee. "However long it lasts."

Rising, I moved toward the door. Behind me the couch creaked alarmingly as Lev shifted. "Stefan," he called urgently.

I kept going.

"Stefan, my heart medicine." He was referring to the nitro pills he had been taking for nearly a decade now. Too many *bleenies* and too much vodka had finally caught up with him over the years. "I might need it. It's in the master bedroom."

"Is it?" I paused in the doorway to look back at him. "That's too bad, Uncle Lev. It really is." Quietly pulling the door shut, I locked it.

And then I walked away.

Chapter 25

"I like this one. Can we keep it?"

I shut off the engine and snorted ruefully as Michael ran a reverent finger across the dashboard. "Life should be so easy." We were in the middle of a snowdrift-covered mall parking lot in the SUV that Sevastian and Pavel had rented at the airport. Our own car was beginning to flounder in the snowstorm and I wasn't one to look a gift horse in the mouth, especially when it had four-wheel drive and was sitting unlocked in Lev's driveway. It was about time we switched cars anyway, but we couldn't keep this one. Too bad. It was nice, with leather seats and a stereo system that could be heard in the next state. It also had GPS written all over it, but we had a few days to find another car before the rental place figured out no one was bringing this one back.

"It would be a nice change." Breathing lightly on the passenger window, he drew a cartoon face in the fogged glass. It had a ferocious scowl and familiar curly hair.

"What?" I reached over and wiped away the unflattering if accurate portrait. "The car or life?"

"Both," he said with a teasing quirk of his lips. Then more seriously he said, "About what happened at the house . . . I'm sorry." The words came out rather awkwardly, as if he'd never said them before. Chances were he never had. If one of the kids in the Institute had reason to be sorry, I would be surprised if they were given the opportunity to apologize. Jericho was bound to embrace a zero tolerance policy with a vengeance.

"Sorry?" I echoed blankly. "What do you have to be sorry about, Misha? I'm the one who got us into this mess. Hell, you saved my life back there."

"That's not what I meant." Two fingers softly stroked the ferret's head as it peeked from Michael's jacket pocket. "I'm sorry about your uncle Lev."

"Yeah?" My jaw tightened and I made a conscious effort to relax it. "Don't worry about it, kiddo. Like the man said, it was only business. It's my fault for forgetting that."

"It is? When you were five or six? I know I would've been thinking that while sitting on Santa's lap."

I raised my eyebrows at his sarcasm and ignored the meaning behind his comment. I knew I'd started out young and innocent, and I didn't blame the naïve kid who'd loved his uncle Lev. But not blaming the blindly stupid adult who should've known better was a little more difficult. "Had a class on Santa too, did you?"

"All the major topics were covered." He was still wearing the glasses, but they had swooped down to balance on the end of his nose. It made it easier for him to shoot me an exasperated glance over the rims. "You're changing the subject, aren't you?"

"No, I'm ignoring it altogether." I leaned the seat back, looked at the roof for a moment, then rolled my head toward Michael. "You never did say what you did to Sevastian to take him down like that."

He pushed the glasses back up, trying very hard for casual. To give him credit, he almost made it. "Stopped the blood flow to his brain, just for a few seconds. It's harmless. Mostly."

"You knocked him out," I said with instant and strong approval. Michael had done the only thing he could to save me. I wasn't going to let him start second-guessing or blaming himself now. He'd shown a lot of restraint with Sevastian, a good deal more than I had. "Good idea. You really did save my life, you know. Again. It's getting to be a habit of yours, making me look bad." I grinned at him. "I guess I owe you, huh?"

"I guess you do." He looked toward the mall and opened the car door. "And there's no time like the present to discuss payback."

I groaned and climbed out on my side. "Okay, okay. But no porn."

The snow was still falling heavily and it covered Michael's hair in seconds as he agreed with a long-suffering sigh. "Very well. No educational materials, but you're sincerely stunting my social growth."

"I'll try and live with myself," I grunted as the snow accumulated under my jacket collar with the touch of cold fingers. That was the reason we were here. The thin coats we'd purchased in Georgia weren't doing the job. We needed the real deal. We still had our trip to St. Louis ahead of us before we made our way to Babushka's old house, and it wasn't getting any warmer. A mall was the perfect place to buy heavier clothes and go relatively unnoticed if anyone came looking. I doubted anyone would. I was fairly sure Sevastian and Pavel were alone and Lev didn't have the men he used to.

If Michael was familiar with anything in the outside world, it would be malls. Full of people, the majority of whom didn't see beyond the nearest sale or the slice of tepid pizza they were shoving in their face, it had been the perfect location for Institute field trips. No one would look at a group of kids twice, no matter how strange they might be. Inside the doors I handed him a wad of cash and drawled, "Go wild. Just no purple." I'd already had enough of the grape-colored shirt I'd bought him only days ago. It had seared my eyes for the last time.

He accepted the money, only to ask dubiously, "What should I get then?"

"Whatever you want." I knew it had to be unnerving for him. In his life, all that he could remember, he hadn't been given the chance to make decisions—any decisions. He'd done well in the bookstore, but there he'd had fairly specific guidelines. This was different; this was being adrift. He had to find his way, though, sooner or later. I nudged his shoulder. "Hey, you bought the rat without any help. This will be easy in comparison. No teeth. No stink." I gave him a light shove. "Now go. Just make sure you get us both coats and a couple of sweaters."

I kept him in sight as he shopped. I wanted to foster independence but not at the expense of having him snatched while I wasn't watching. Jericho was like the monster you knew was under your bed when you were little. You could turn the lights on and peer under there to see only a lost and dusty sneaker. You could know for a fact you were alone, but the second the lights went out again, it would be back. Its hot breath would pant fetid and foul in your face. The jagged claws would weave through your hair to lightly scrape your scalp. Logic meant nothing to childhood monsters.

It didn't mean anything to Jericho either.

I knew he couldn't have followed us. The tracking chip was gone, and we'd made our way across several states. We were safe, at least for a while. Even if he was capable of finding us again, it would take time. He wasn't going to come rushing out of the crowd to my left with that bone-jangling laugh. He wouldn't be waiting around the next corner to take Michael from me as he had before. I kept telling myself those things, kept looking under the bed for all I was worth, but it didn't reassure me any more than it had when I was four.

Michael stopped in front of a store teeming with teenagers. There were artsy black-and-white posters and faceless mannequins draped in clothes the Salvation Army would've thrown out. I sat on a bench, went to work on a chocolate chip cookie from the food court, and watched the show. He leaned closer to the glass to peer through at a price tag, then jerked upright with outrage as it registered. "It's a trap, Misha," I murmured under my breath around a mouthful of crumbling dough. "Run. Run for your life." Although Uncle Lev was still lurking inescapably in my thoughts, I couldn't help but be entertained as I watched my brother.

Moving to the next store, Michael studied the window display for several minutes before deciding to go in. I smothered a smile at the suspicious set of his shoulders. The ways of the world remained mysterious to him, and the ways of retail were mystifying to us all. Relaxing as he went from store to store, I was ready for more than a cookie by the time he finished up. He'd taken about an hour, but considering that he had to develop his own likes and dislikes in that time, I couldn't complain. I was curious to know what he'd picked out, though. I had the kid pegged for dark blues and grays, clothes that wouldn't stand out; a combination of post-Institute syndrome and being a fugitive on the run.

"What'd you get?"

He deposited two large bags on the bench beside me and reached into one to whip out a shirt. There were blues and grays; I'd been right about that. There were also white, black, green, all coalescing into a picture . . . a face. It was a long sleeve shirt of a slick, heavy material and it was covered with a psychedelic, watercolor portrait of Albert Einstein. I'd seen the type before, retro funk and usually decorated with a rock star or famous actor. This was definitely a new twist.

"Isn't it great?" Michael shook it out so I could get a better look. "What do you think?"

"There are no words," I said honestly.

"I have one with Sigmund Freud too." He folded Albert carefully and put him back into a bag before rummaging again. "Where? Oh, here. See?"

Unless the eminent and penis-obsessed psychiatrist had had a sex change operation not recorded by history, Michael had grabbed the wrong shirt. There were blond hair, cleavage, and a wide ruby red mouth. Marilyn Monroe. At least he had an appreciation for the classics.

"Well," I said in contemplation as I sucked the last of my Coke through the straw, "that'll let the girls know you're open for business."

Michael looked down and flushed before hurriedly shoving the famous blond bombshell back out of sight. "Er . . . it was on sale." It was his first solo shopping trip and he'd already nailed the ultimate excuse.

"Damn, kiddo." I couldn't help myself. I had to laugh. It came out a bit strangled through my aching throat, but it was genuine. "You've got the worse taste."

He stiffened, not seeing the humor in the situation. "You told me to buy whatever I wanted."

"Hey, come on." Pushing the bags aside, I took a handful of his jacket and pulled him down to sit on the bench. "I think it's perfect. You landed on your feet and hit the ground running. You're you, Misha. No matter what those bastards tried to do to you, you're still your own person." I tossed the cup into the garbage can a few feet away and gave him a wicked smile. "And that person just happens to have crappy taste."

Michael relaxed with my words, hopefully recognizing the good intentions behind them. It didn't stop him from peppering me with vengeful comments about my wardrobe as we walked back to the food court. Monochromatic man was the kindest thing he had to say. I liked black. So sue me.

We were halfway to the food court before Michael finally laid off my clothes. I seized the opportunity to ask, "You did get me a coat, didn't you? And sweaters?"

The smirk on his face was pure, unadulterated evil. "Trust me. I wouldn't forget you, Stefan."

He refused to show me the remaining contents of the bags as we sat down to eat our mediocre Chinese food. Instead, he tortured me with vague hints and sly remarks until finally he went quiet and concentrated on twirling noodles around his fork. It was a strange silence, almost wistful.

"Are you wishing you'd bought more sweaters for

yourself now?" I toed the bags at his feet. "Nice, sensible, boring sweaters?"

"No." He rolled his eyes. The glasses had been discarded in his pocket for the moment, but I had thoughts of contacts for him in the future. His bicolored eyes were simply too distinctive. They would be remembered by anyone who saw him up close.

"Don't come crying to me when Albert doesn't keep you warm in the snow." I speared a mushroom off his plate, popped it in my mouth, and chewed. It hurt to swallow, but not too badly. Sevastian would be hurting far more—if he ever woke up. Appetite waning, I dropped my fork and pushed the plate away. "Brings back memories, doesn't it? This place?"

Michael took a long look around. The crowd was sparse. The snow had kept most people home and it was a weekday, but it was still a mall. "It does," he admitted reluctantly. He toyed with his food, knotting the noodles into neat little piles. "They drugged us, you know. On the trips."

"Drugged you?"

"Not so much we couldn't function." The fork kept moving. "They wanted us to interact, wanted to see if we could pass for normal. They gave us just enough to slow us down in case we tried to escape." The tines of the plastic fork bent under the pressure and broke against the plate. "Not that any of us ever tried. What a waste."

I knew what he was thinking, that his fearless friend John would have made the attempt . . . that he wouldn't have let the chance go by. But John hadn't lived that long. "Actually it wasn't." I piled our plates on the tray for disposal. "That last field trip is how I found you. One of the girls who worked there spotted you. She's one of Saul's. He's had your description out to his network for years now."

"She recognized me?" he asked doubtfully. "How?"

"Your eyes. Your age. Faces change in ten years, but there aren't many kids out there who fit both of those." I stood and dumped the contents of the tray into the garbage can beside our table. "Face it, kid, you're unique."

The expression that shimmered across his face was partly wary and partly something I couldn't identify. "Stefan—"

"I know," I interrupted with a tug of the hair at the nape of his neck. "You're not my brother. You can keep telling yourself that, Misha, but it's not going to make any difference to me. Now, you want to hit the pet store for ferret food before we go or just toss the rat out the window?"

He sighed but went with the change of subject. "The pet store. I like Zilla. It's nice having someone around I can have an intelligent conversation with."

"You certainly bitch like a brother," I grumbled affectionately under my breath. I might have lost my uncle, but I still had family and it was right here with me, bad taste and stubborn nature included.

"I remember that girl. The one who saw me." Michael hoisted his bags and followed me. "I was off from the group a little. She tried to sell me a hat." His voice took on a longing note. "She said I was . . . um . . . hot."

I slung an arm around his shoulder as we approached the doors. "We have to get you a girlfriend, kiddo. We really do."

Chapter 26

The trip to St. Louis was uneventful. I could see myself saying it. I could hear the words as if I had. The trip was uneventful. Uneventful.

Yeah, it would've been nice.

The bastard hit us from behind. It wasn't Sevastian, soaked in blood, or Jericho looming dark and menacing against the white background of the blizzard. It was just some random son of a bitch who couldn't drive. Maybe he'd forgotten to put on his snow tires or maybe he wasn't paying attention. Six of one, a half dozen of the other—it all equaled a world of hurt for Michael and me.

The roads were covered in a thick slush growing more treacherous by the moment, but they were still passable. The streetlights had flickered on early as a combination of the storm and approaching dusk conspired to make the gloom midnight thick. It was one of those helpful streetlights that we hit head-on. The blow from behind was massive and the SUV leaped forward as if swatted by a huge paw. We slid into what felt like a never-ending spin, swapping the front of the car for the tail God knew how many times. There are things to do in that situation, I know, but given that I was from Florida, they weren't exactly second nature to me. Tapping the brakes, turning into the curve, it all sounds good. But when you're caught in a whirlwind of metal and glass, it's not that easy. To give credit where credit is due, they might not have been meant for collision conditions.

Hitting the pole was almost a relief to the sickening

motion. The airbag against my face muffled the crunch
of metal and the wind-chime splintering of glass. There
was the taste of chalky powder in my mouth and a faint
burning of my skin, but that was overshadowed by the
searing band—the seat belt—slanting diagonally across
my chest. "Michael?"

Coughing at the talc, I shoved at the white material as
it deflated. "Michael, you okay?"

He was fighting with his own airbag with panicky un-
coordinated movements. "He's here," he choked. "He's
here." Lunging at the door, he struggled with the handle. I stopped him with a hand on his arm, not that he
would've gotten far with his seat belt fastened.

I'd already checked the rearview mirror to see the
man who had hit us. He was a big, bearded lumberjack
in a delivery truck. "No, Misha. No. It's not Jericho. It
was just an accident."

He was still pushing at the door, and I moved my
hand from his arm to his shoulder to give him a gentle
shake. "Listen to me, kid," I said firmly. "We were in a
wreck. Somebody slid on the ice and hit us."

It finally seemed to penetrate and he sagged under
my hand. "An accident?"

I nodded. "Just a dumbass who rear-ended us. That's
all."

Michael had been so calm and composed since his
rescue, even when facing down Jericho in the parking lot
where I'd been shot, that I was momentarily surprised
by his distress now. But the sudden shock of the collision
had shaken me, and it was bound to have disoriented
him. Then I saw the trickle of crimson winding its way
down his face and it was all the more clear. Swiping my
thumb across the welling of blood in his right temple,
I revealed an inch and a half laceration. He must have
struck his head on the side window when we hit. The
new tightening in my chest had nothing to do with the
pressure from my seat belt.

Michael blinked at his blood on my hand and exhaled

a steadying breath. "Oh." He rubbed at his forehead with the back of his hand, wiping blood away. "It's okay. I'm a fast healer, remember?"

Who was reassuring whom here?

"You guys okay?" A cold reddened face appeared at our demolished windshield. A thick brown beard bristled around a mouth chapped by the elements and large gloved hands were clapped for warmth. "Goddamn, I'm sorry. The truck got away from me. Frickin' weather."

Pulling the sleeve of my shirt over the heel of my hand, I carefully mopped at Michael's still sluggishly bleeding cut. His pupils were equal. There was no bloody discharge from his nose or ears. Those were all good signs. All those overwrought medical shows on TV said so. "We're fine," I said brusquely. "Now go away."

Suffering patiently under my makeshift first aid efforts, Michael allowed his eyes to meet mine. He knew as well as I that we were in trouble—big trouble.

"Fine? The boy's bleeding." The man pulled a cell phone out of his pocket and started punching buttons. "I'm calling 911."

An ambulance and police—that was everything we didn't need. I was in a stolen rental car with a kid I couldn't prove was related to me, and I still had no idea of the extent of Jericho's connections with the government. The scrutiny of the authorities, no matter how casual, was something we couldn't afford. Grabbing a rumpled and worn shirt from the backseat, I folded it, put it in Michael's grip, and manipulated his hand to the cut. "Hold pressure there, okay? I'll be right back."

I undid my seat belt and opened the door to climb out. My legs felt oddly anesthetized, as if I were walking on unbending lengths of wood. My dismal expectations were fulfilled. The SUV was totaled. It wasn't moving another inch, much less carrying us away before the police arrived. Big trouble had transmuted into catastrophe.

While I was taking stock, Paul Bunyan had just gotten through to the operator to report the wreck. Instantly I swatted the phone out of his hand and wasted no time in kicking it out of sight into a distant pile of snow. He gaped at me, his breath puffing white clouds in the air between us. "What the hell did you do that for?"

I ignored him and turned to examine his truck. It seemed fine except for a bent grille and a few dents, but then I saw the right tire was deflated. The crumpled fender had punctured it. Things just kept getting better and better. Around us the street was empty. Since we'd left the mall the storm had only gotten worse. Not many people were risking the roads. Swearing, I moved back to the car. I leaned in and said regretfully, "Misha, I'm sorry, but we have to go." Our transportation was trashed and Bunyan's truck wasn't any more mobile.

With the wad of cloth still pressed to his head, he gazed past me out into the curtain of snow and sighed. "Seems about right." He was pale but had returned to his familiar collected self, the confusion having cleared. Whether it was his accelerated healing or pure force of will, I didn't know. Knowing Michael, it was a combination of the two, with a heavy emphasis on will.

"Put on your new coat. I'll get all our bags." All that I could carry.

"I said, what the hell are you doing?" A meaty hand fastened on my shoulder and spun me around. "That kid is hurt. You're not taking him anywhere."

When you needed one, Good Samaritans were nonexistent, a myth. But try to flee a hit-and-run from the victim end and you were tripping all over them. "Look, pal." I peeled his hand from my shoulder. "I know you're trying to do the right thing, and that's great. But this isn't your business."

"When you drag a hurt kid off into a blizzard, I make it my business." The scowl was full of righteous anger and his fists were clenched at his sides. He was a good man trying to do the right thing; it wasn't his fault it happened to be at the worst possible time.

"I don't want to hurt you," I offered sincerely. I ex-

pected the comment to be in vain, and it was. The guy
was nearly four inches taller than I was and had at least
sixty pounds on me. He wasn't threatened by me in the
slightest, and it showed.

"Buddy, the hurt that's going down is going to be
all over you. Now get away from the car and the kid,
you hear me?" The fists were coming up now, and I
didn't wait to see if he would have second thoughts. A
true Good Samaritan rarely did. Truth, justice, and the
American way—for them it wasn't only a comic book
code; it was a way of life. It was admirable, courageous,
and inconvenient as shit.

I laid out Mr. Admirable with a quick blow to his
spreading gut and a hard clip behind his ear. It was easy.
A Good Samaritan didn't stand a chance with a professional bad guy. He went down instantly, an over-the-hill
Goliath toppled by a highly disreputable David. The
snow and slush cushioned his fall and I quickly turned
him over to keep his airway unblocked. He wasn't unconscious, only profoundly dazed. He'd come to in a few
minutes, long before he became hypothermic. By then
we'd be on our way; desperate and directionless but on
our way. "Sorry," I murmured, stripping off his thick
wool scarf and shoving it under his head. "The boy will
be all right. I promise." I doubted he heard me, but then
again, wasn't I really saying it more for my sake than
his?

"Stefan?"

Michael's voice drifted to me through the hush.
"Coming."

He was wrapped in his new coat, the price tag still attached to the sleeve. It was a dark blue ski jacket with a
hood that framed his face. The cut on his head, although
angry and red, had stopped bleeding and once again I
was grateful for the unusual healing speed of the chimera. "Here."

He was holding out another coat in my direction
as well as a ski jacket—the one he'd been teasing me

about over Chinese food. His threats weren't idle. It was purple, the same purple, in fact, of his hideous shirt. The precise color I'd hoped not to see again and I was going to be wearing it for a while. "What a pal," I snorted as I slipped it on and zipped it up. "Did you happen to get me matching gloves?"

"They're in the pockets." His eyes brightened despite the line of pain creasing his forehead.

A wonderful thing, revenge . . . when you're not on the receiving end of it. Tossing pride and masculinity to the winds, I put them on and gathered everything I could carry from the backseat of the SUV. I had to leave the books, food, and most of the clothes, but everything else fit in my duffel bag. "You have the rat?"

He patted the front of his coat. "I have him, but he's not happy."

The weasel could join the crowd. Our circumstances didn't have me jumping for joy either. I slung the strap of the bag over my shoulder, moved up the street away from the cars, and scanned the area around us. We were in an industrial area with warehouses, chain-link fences, and empty lots. Everyone had left early trying to beat the weather; the parking lots were deserted. It's an often-overlooked yet basic fact of the car theft business: It's hard to steal what isn't there. I didn't see any alternative; we were in for a walk.

"We have to get moving, kid. You up for it?"

Barely ten feet away from me, he was nearly lost to sight behind a veil of white, but I saw his nod. He joined me with head down against the gusting wind. As he reached my side, I saw he had a bag from the mall in his hand. "Misha." I shook my head, hating to deliver more bad news. "You'll have to leave it. We have to move fast and you're already hurt."

He gave an obstinate thrust of his jaw. "No. I can handle it. It doesn't weigh much."

True, it was only clothes. It couldn't weigh more than five pounds. But trek a mile or so through knee-deep

snow in whiteout conditions and those five pounds
would soon feel like fifty. On the other hand, I all too
easily saw that pile of mall trash through his eyes. Aside
from the ferret, it was the first thing he'd bought just
for himself. It was the first step on a road that led to
independence, something he hadn't dared imagine for
himself back in the Institute. And now I wanted him to
throw proof of that treasured step aside. Michael had
lost so much in his life. Damned if I wanted to add one
more thing to that list, no matter how much of a burden
it was at the moment.

"Goddamn, you're stubborn." I snatched the bag
from his hand and scowled at his knowing expression,
wise beyond his years. When it came to Michael, I had
sucker written all over me. In a few years, if we survived,
I'd undoubtedly be signing over everything I owned to
the kid with a glazed and sappy look in my eye. "I'll take
Einstein and Freud. You just concentrate on staying upright. Now come on." I took a step, then looked over
my shoulder and ordered seriously, "Hang on to me. I
don't want to lose you in this. Popsicles don't make good
brothers."

His hand fastened on to the back of my coat. "You
won't lose me."

There was a promise I intended to hold him to.

We'd taken only a few steps when I heard the faint
groan and bellow of our Good Samaritan coming
around. I increased my speed while monitoring the tension of Michael's hold on me. Within seconds we were
out of sight in the whiteout conditions. Safe from discovery from Bunyan or any cops that would soon arrive,
I concentrated on slogging through the snow. Murderous colleagues aside, I missed Miami. I missed the sun. I
missed the warm air. Here there was only what felt like
the next ice age. It abraded skin and numbed face and
limbs.

I followed the walls of the looming buildings when
I could. They shielded us to a certain extent, but not

enough. We had coats and gloves, but we were still in
jeans. The snow pushed its way up my pant legs to pack
tightly against my skin, and sneakers did nothing to
keep my feet from aching fiercely before losing feeling
altogether. We kept moving for nearly thirty minutes
before the district began to change from industrial to
residential.

"You still kicking, kiddo?" Michael's grip on my
jacket hadn't wavered, but the weight of it had increased.
I'd slowed accordingly, as much as I could, but taking a
break had been out of the question. The weather had
deteriorated rapidly. The snow was falling harder than a
warm-blooded creature like me thought possible; it was
knee-deep and drifting dramatically in the fierce wind.
Boston seemed determined to give the Antarctic a run
for its money.

"Walking is hard enough." He sounded winded.
"Kicking . . . out of . . . the question."

I looked back at him to see his face drawn with cold
but resolute. He was shorter than I by a few inches and
was having a more difficult time. What was knee-deep
for me was almost thigh high on him. I stopped walking
and turned to face him. "Seriously, Misha, you okay?"
I lifted his hood an inch or two to see that his cut had
scabbed over. It was like time-lapse photography; I
could practically see the healing taking place.

"I'm fine. Just tired." He made an aggrieved face.
"And cold. It was never cold at the Institute." He was
waxing nostalgic for his prison; that couldn't be a positive sign.

"Yeah, I hear that place was like a Caribbean resort."
I pulled his hood back into place and hefted the plastic
bag with a leaden grip. "Buck up. We're almost there."

"Almost where?"

I shifted and pointed across the street at the nearest
possibility, a house that huddled as an amorphous shape
in the storm. The porch light twinkled dimly in the murk,
hopefully advertising that no one was at home. "There."

His hand latched on to the duffel strap across my back. "Why there?" He was trying so desperately not to lean against me that I made up my mind. The possibility was now a dead certainty. We had come as far as we could go. If we were lucky, the place would be empty. And if we weren't lucky, it wasn't as if it would be the first time that day. I would deal with it.

"Because it's the closest." I started across the street, keeping the pace slow and easy.

"With logic like that . . . how can we go wrong?" Breathing heavily, Michael plodded at my side, lacking the strength for the sarcasm that the statement deserved. I switched the bag to my other hand and grasped his arm with a supportive grip. I expected him to be mulish as always and protest that he didn't need any help, but he didn't. I was beginning to suspect his improved healing ability used up a considerable amount of energy when it was in full swing, as it was now. "If it's the closest," he murmured, stumbling a bit, "why doesn't it feel that way?"

"Bitch. Bitch. Bitch," I said with grimly determined cheer as I steadied him and kept us both moving. "I'm showing you a winter wonderland and this is the thanks I get." Dropping my hand from his sleeve, I wrapped my arm around his shoulders and took the majority of his weight. "You liked it fine when we were building snowmen at the motel."

"I've changed my mind." He leaned heavily against me, his legs beginning to shake. "Snowmen suck."

My lips curled despite our situation. Cursing, pornography, and obstinacy; under that shockingly mature façade the teenager just kept breaking out, bit by bit. "I guess maybe they do," I said placatingly as we reached the front of the house. Two-storied and sprawling, it was separated from the others on the street by a large lot and a literal wall of trash. Old tires seemed to make the majority of the divider, but I was only guessing by the shapes under the snow. The house itself was old and in a better neighborhood would've been considered a historical treasure. Here it was one more pile of crap two or three years away from being condemned, razed, and replaced with a parking garage.

Warped and uneven, the ancient wood of the stoop was as rippled as the incoming tide. But it was somewhat protected from the icy onslaught by a shingled overhang. That left the surface clear enough that Michael breathed a sigh of relief to be on more or less solid ground. Knocking sharply on the door, I kept an eye on him as he rested against the wall of the house. "Don't lean too hard," I advised. "You might take the wall down."

"There was a crooked house. . . ." His smile was equally as crooked as he began to regain his breath. "A lady was reading nursery rhymes to the children at that bookstore."

"Clowns and nursery rhymes, the two creepiest memories of any childhood." I knocked again in case some elderly person as decrepit as their house was meandering their slow way down from the top floor. When that didn't happen, I stripped off my gloves, pulled out a card from the wallet I'd taken from Pavel before we'd left the mansion, and went to work. I wished I had something more high-tech than that asshole's credit card.

The card, despite being maligned, did the job. A few jiggles had the old lock giving way with a rusty creak and then we were in. Closing the door behind us, I sneezed immediately. The dust was thick in the air—dust and something far worse for my sinuses. I sneezed three more times and didn't have to rely on the winding motion around my ankles to identify the type of fur floating in the flickering lamplight. Cat.

"Ah, damn it." I rubbed at my stinging nose with the back of my hand.

"What's wrong?" Snow was sliding off Michael and melting into a puddle on the wood floor. There were so many other stains—cat urine from the smell—that I didn't think we needed to worry about one more.

"I'm allergic to cats." I carefully nudged away the one now gnawing at my shoe. It was gray with black stripes, a huge puffball of long hair, pumpkin orange eyes, and rampant feline dander. Another one, white with a lashing tail, sat at the bottom of the stairs curving up to the second floor. The third was yellow, hugely obese, and curled around the base of a lamp. The lamp sat on a table that rested against a wall covered with patterned paper. With roses, roses, and more roses under the yellow film of age, cats, and paper flowers, this place had old lady written all over it. I wondered where she was. Maybe she was staying with her kids until the storm blew over.

"You're not much of an animal person, are you?" Michael pushed his hood back and bent over to give the tabby a pat on its head. "Nice kitty."

Feeling another sneeze coming on, I buried the lower half of my face in the crook of my arm to muffle the wet explosion. "That nice kitty is suffocating me," I said nasally before straightening. "Stay here. I'm going to check out the house and make sure we're alone."

I did a quick run-through of the place. Everything was old. The furniture, appliances, rugs—all dated to several decades before my birth. Even the quilts on the beds were faded and worn; the afghans raveled and covered with fuzz balls. It definitely belonged to an old lady. Two bedrooms, a bathroom with a claw-foot tub and cloudy mirror, and a sewing room made up the second floor. After a quick look around, I concentrated on scooping up two blankets, a quilt, and a pillow before heading back down the stairs.

Michael was sitting on the bottom step, leaning against the wall. He was fast asleep and he wasn't alone. One of the cats had seized the opportunity to curl up in a convenient lap. Annoyed at the competition, Zilla had crawled out of the ski jacket and was currently racing up

the banister. I let it go. If anyone was a match for three
cats, it would be that damn ferret. "Misha." I shook his
shoulder lightly before shooing off the cat. "Come on."

His eyes opened, just barely, and he allowed me to
shepherd him to the couch in the living room. The cush-
ions sagged from years and years of use, but he didn't
seem to mind as he dropped onto it. He could've used
one of the beds upstairs, but if we had to make a sudden
getaway, being on the ground floor would be best. As
Michael slithered out of his jacket and with clumsy fingers worked on removing his gloves, I helped him with
his shoes. The laces were too encrusted with ice and
snow to untie and I didn't even try, simply pulling them
off. The socks went too, a sodden pile on the rug. "All
right, kiddo. Down you go."

He obeyed without argument, showing me how exhausted he truly was. Michael had shown that he wasn't
one to let me fuss over him, at least not without some
self-deprecating or distancing remark. But now . . . he
was like a tired five-year-old, obedient and docile. It
brought back memories. God, did it. Lukas had been
able to sleep anytime, anywhere. There had been many
times I'd hauled him from an unconscious heap on the
floor to lift him into his bed without waking him. His
name had changed, but inside he was still Lukas. It was
like they said. The more things change, the more they
stay the same.

In the here and now I slid the pillow under his head
and piled on the blankets. "Sleep for a few hours. I'll
keep an eye out." His eyes closed, but his mouth twisted
downward. A hand slipped out of the blankets to move
his thumb back and forth across the rough texture of the
worn cotton in a self-soothing motion. It wasn't sleep. It
wasn't even a good imitation. I thumped his chin lightly
with a finger. "I said sleep, not mope."

With eyes still closed and a voice thick with a fatigue
he couldn't completely fight, he said softly, "I told myself
I couldn't get attached."

Confused, I eased from a crouch to a sitting position on the floor. "Misha . . ."

He ignored me. "After John . . . I couldn't do it. Wouldn't. People go away; they die. I knew . . . know better than to get attached to anyone." There was anger underscoring the words, anger and resignation. "Why did you make me?"

Ah. Damn. The kid could make me happy as hell and rip me up inside all in one fell swoop. Trust was a ridiculously hard step for even the well-adjusted. For the rest of us walking wounded, it was nearly impossible. But Michael had already demonstrated that impossible wasn't a word that applied to him. That didn't make the wonder any less for me. He was coming to accept me, to trust me. And because of that, he now was also terrified of me. The one person he remembered relying on had left him . . . had died. It was one thing to be deserted by someone you cared for; it was a completely different circle of Hell to be abandoned by your family . . . by your brother.

"I'm your family, Michael. I won't leave you," I promised. "And I won't die. Not until I'm knee-deep in dentures and adult diapers."

"You can't know that." His eyes opened, and the challenge in them was clear.

"No?" I rested my shoulder against the couch. "I knew I'd find you, didn't I? I know lots of things. I knew you'd get me a god-awful ugly coat. Hell, I'm practically psychic."

He gave a disbelieving snort, pulled the blanket back over his shoulder, and rolled over to present his back to me, physically. It was too late to accomplish the same emotionally. I rearranged the blankets over his shoulder and received a brisk smack of my hand for my troubles. Sighing, I sat back and took my own jacket and shoes off. As I worked, I said firmly, "I moved Heaven and Earth to find you, Misha, and I'm not giving you up. If I have to live forever to prove that to you, so be it. If Dick Clark can do it, so can I."

Under the quilt his shoulders relaxed. It was probably from an approaching sleep that couldn't be denied,
but I took it as a positive sign nonetheless. I stood and
looked down at him. "A couple of years and you'll be
sick of the sight of me. You'll change the locks while I'm
at the store. I'll be homeless."

He didn't hear me. Breaths deep and even ruffled the
threads of the fraying patchwork cloth by his mouth.
With the lightest of touches I brushed his hair aside.
The wound was half healed. By morning the skin of his
forehead would be smooth and untouched. It made me
wonder. I'd made the sincere if unrealistic promise to
stick around until the end of time, but how long would
he live? Would he age at the same rate as your average
human or would the ravages of time be wiped away by
Jericho's genetic tampering? For that matter, if he had
children, would he pass on to them his heritage? Would
they be like Michael?

Questions for another time, I thought, as the yellow
cat appeared to wind around my ankles. This time was
spent on more important things . . . such as watching
over my brother as he slept.

And sneezing.

Chapter 27

St. Louis was gray and miserable with an icy rain that wouldn't relent. It didn't bother me; it was better than the snow of Boston. I didn't even mind the monotonous swish of the windshield wipers, although the nauseating country music station Michael had become so fascinated with was beginning to wear on my nerves. As I had predicted, he'd recuperated from the accident completely by that next morning and was just as anxious as I was to hit the road. To that end, we'd taken the car sheltered in the attached garage. It was an older sedan, but with not too many miles on it—an only-to-church-on-Sunday car.

The car ran and that's all I cared about. I left eight hundred dollars for it on the kitchen table under a cow-shaped creamer. Head down, the porcelain bovine grazed placidly on the field of greenbacks. I'd given a self-conscious shrug at Michael's curious look and said nothing. He'd seen me steal a few cars now, but this one belonged to an old lady who wasn't exactly living in the lap of luxury. She needed transportation for herself and the dander-ridden fur balls.

Unfortunately, Michael found his own fur ball before we left. There were . . . one big happy family again— Stinky, Sneezy, and Country Joe. I looked over as Michael gazed dreamily out of the window, his lips shaping the words of a song we'd already heard three times in the last two hours. "Why country, kid?" I asked with a nearly physical pain. "Seriously, why?"

"You mean you don't like it?" He unwrapped a candy bar and inhaled the scent of chocolate as if it were a fine wine. "It's great. Every song is a story and in every story the singer has worse luck than we do. How can you not appreciate that?"

There was something to be said for that, but I'd suffered enough twanging in the past few hours to last me for the rest of my life. "I don't know. Maybe my bleeding ears are the problem." I switched the station and then sneezed. "Goddamnit." We'd left the cats behind, but they hadn't left us. The upholstery was covered liberally in a layer of white, gray, and yellow hair, and I hadn't stopped sneezing since Boston.

A froth of tissue was automatically passed my way. "We should've bought another box." Michael returned to his candy bar. "Or five, although I'm not sure it would help. The mucous river cannot be dammed. See the villagers flee in fear."

I kept one steady hand on the wheel and blew my nose. "Smart-ass."

"Smart as they come," he confirmed with haughty cheer around a mouthful of nougat and chocolate.

My comeback was buried in my next sneeze and Michael used the opportunity to ask a question. "Do you think this man will know anything about Jericho? Anything that can help us?"

It had been his idea to begin with, but we all needed some reassurance once in a while. "I don't know. I'm hoping. From what you said, this Bellucci has a real hard-on for sticking it to Jericho and his theories." At his mystified expression, I clarified. "He hates him." I wadded up the tissue and dropped it in the cup holder. "The funny thing is that friends may come and go, but people tend to keep track of their enemies. It's screwed up, but there it is."

The rain continued to beat in a lulling rhythm on the roof of the car as Michael contemplated my rough and ready wisdom. Apparently it called for the fortification of another candy bar. I let him get halfway through it before saying, "I have a question of my own."

Michael shrugged lightly in permission, but there was a hint of uneasiness in the gesture. He knew I was bound to continue in the same vein and Jericho was far and away not his favorite topic. I couldn't blame him. The thought of being strapped to the table in that bastardized excuse for a medical room was horrifying enough. But picturing Jericho bending over me with gleaming teeth rivaled by the glitter of the metal instruments in his hand stitched my bowels with a needle and thread of ice. Worse than that, though, would be not knowing when or where your moments in the basement would come.

Michael had said it hadn't hurt that much, that he'd been sedated for the majority of it. Did that matter? Hell, no. It might be that loss of control made the experience more unbearable. You couldn't prepare and you couldn't resist. It would be like falling, falling, and never having a chance to grab on to anything. Michael had forgotten a lot of things in his life. It didn't surprise me he'd as soon forget this as well. I only wished our situation could have allowed him that luxury.

"You said Jericho was grooming you and the other kids to be assassins," I started. "That he was going to sell you."

His nod was hesitant and wary, a far cry from the indifferent reaction he'd shown the last time this topic had come up. Trust; it was all about trust. Unconsciously or not, he was now letting me see flashes of what churned inside him.

"How'd that happen? How did they go about it?" There had to be some way to obtain more obvious evidence that the government was turning a blind eye to Jericho's setup. Saul had thought it obvious, but I still wanted to be sure. "Did people come in and"—Jesus

Christ. I gritted my teeth to finish the disturbing question—"pick you out?" Like a stray dog at the shelter or a ripe melon at the grocery.

They did.

But from what Michael said, the children never saw the "shoppers." The ones near graduation were shepherded into a room with mirrored walls to be looked over by invisible eyes and then sent back to class. The next day one of the students would be gone. It wouldn't be based all on appearances, I was sure. Blending in to a certain population might be necessary, but obedience and temperament would be considered as well. And that last one would be the reason Michael had only heard about the inside of those rooms, not seen them. Michael may have been obedient on the surface, but his temperament wasn't that of a killer. As he'd said before, it was a toss-up as to whether he would've seen graduation.

The only thing I was accomplishing was to stir up bad memories for Michael, and I gave up on the subject for the moment. Proof might not exist in either direction. If it didn't, we would probably spend the rest of our lives on the run. Jericho we could evade, with luck, but the government was a different matter. Then again, Elvis had been doing it for more than thirty years.

We stopped at a gas station to check the phone book for Dr. Marcos Bellucci's address and buy a street guide. He lived in a fairly ritzy area, not quite up to Uncle Lev's standards, but nice enough. There were quiet streets and trees that would cast wide pools of shade in the summer. Now they bowed morosely under the drizzle. Michael shared their opinion of the weather. As I parked the car on the street, he made a face at the rain spattering against his window. "We should've bought an umbrella when we stopped for the map."

He was such a cat with his distaste of the cold and wet. "Manly men like us don't use umbrellas," I instructed, switching off the car.

"We don't?"

"Nope."

"Why not?" he asked curiously.

"I don't know, kid. It's an unwritten law. Kind of like the one that says we don't wear shirts with Einstein on them," I drawled.

I could see he was contemplating throwing the rest of his candy bar at my head, but at the last moment he decided it was too precious to waste on the likes of me. Folding the wrapper carefully around it, he stored it in the glove compartment. "Next store we come to, I'm getting an umbrella," he said firmly.

"Afraid to get wet, Misha? Think you'll melt?" I teased.

"That's not what I want to use it for," he shot back.

Either he wanted to hit me over the head or insert it in places rain gear simply wasn't meant to go. Both choices caused mental images that had me wincing. Pocketing the keys, I climbed out of the car and was instantly soaked. The houses on this street were all close to the curb. The majority of them were prewar and two and a half stories high with elaborate lacy moldings and stained glass. They were nearly as pristine as they must have been when they were new. With a definite pride of ownership, the neighborhood was the type that would abound with professors, artists, overgrown houseplants, and a thousand flavors of tea.

Resting a hand on the wrought-iron railing, I walked up the stairs that led to the sidewalk. "Get a move on, kiddo."

With coat pulled over his head and a scowl darker than the lowered sky, Michael followed. When we both stood on the porch, I rang the bell. I could hear the faint ripple of musical notes through the front door. I heard a murmur at my shoulder. "What are we going to tell him?"

I glanced over to see an annoyingly dry brother, his

hair and face untouched by the rain. But was he manly like me? I didn't think so. "We? I thought the resident genius would come up with a good story."

He barely had time to flash me a vexed look when the door opened to reveal a wiry man in a charcoal gray sweater and black pants. Equally black eyes took measure of us from behind rimless glasses. "Can I help you?"

I held out my hand and gave my best professional smile. From the blanching of his skin, apparently it was a shade too much of my old profession. I tried to tone it down, from wolflike to that of a friendly German shepherd. "Dr. Bellucci? I'm Peter Melina, freelance journalist. I was wondering if I could have a few minutes of your time."

He shook my hand cautiously. "Ah . . . perhaps you should've called first. What's this about?"

"An article I'm writing regarding the ethics of genetic manipulation," I responded smoothly. "Specifically the ethics of a certain Dr. John Jericho Hooker."

At that, his caution disappeared and a crusading light blossomed as red patches high on his knife-sharp cheekbones. "That bastard. He's done as much to sully the name of the field as Mengele." Pulling off his glasses, he used them to wave us in. "Come in." After looking me up and down, he added, "I'll get you a towel."

I closed the door behind us and waited obediently on the small hooked rug as Bellucci disappeared down a hall. Beside me Michael was entangled in the vines of an amorous potted plant. Pushing them aside with exasperation, he whispered to me, "If you're a journalist, then who am I?"

"An eager-to-learn high school intern," I replied absently as I looked the place over, taking in the polished wood, high ceilings, painted ceramic tile, and the lush quiet that came from an empty house or really thick walls.

"Clever," he said. "You're a good liar."

"And I didn't even have to take a class." Lying well wasn't a talent most boasted of, but there were times it did come in handy. The fact that Michael probably had in all actuality suffered through such a class only made me want to put Jericho in the ground all the more.

Bellucci returned with a thick towel and handed it to me. Thanking him, I dried my face and scrubbed at my hair to blot up the water. "We can talk in the study," he offered, and led the way, sliding paneled doors open to reveal what looked more like a sunroom than a study. The walls were only a framework to support the many windows. In fair weather the room would be awash with bright sun. It was nice. I could picture lying on the large leather couch and taking a nap in that bright spill of light.

Instead I sat on it and took a small notebook from my pocket to rest on my knee. I'd bought it with the map at the gas station, having already formed a vague idea of the story I was going to feed the scientist.

"Dr. Bellucci, this is Daniel," I said in introduction as Michael settled on the arm of a nearby chair. "He's an intern. Actually, he's my sister's kid, but he is on his high school paper. I had my arm twisted to let him tag along." I gave a sheepish shrug of my shoulders. "Family. What can you do?"

"Helping your nephew is admirable," he said, but it was obvious neither his heart nor brain was behind the statement. The entirety of his attention was on Jericho. He was Bellucci's bête noire, as a distant junior high school English teacher of mine would've pompously labeled him. Our good friend Fisher Thieving Lee would no doubt have called him the stick in his craw. Whatever you wanted to call him, from the moment I mentioned the name Jericho, he was all Bellucci could think about.

"What brought you to me?" He carded his fingers through wiry salt-and-pepper hair with an energy that seemed less nerves and more the fire of a man with a cause. "Outside certain academic circles you don't hear

Hooker's name much anymore. He's been a forgotten man since he dropped out of the public eye." Setting his mouth grimly, he amended, "Forgotten except by me."

I leaned back, sprawling with casual comfort in my best imitation of a seasoned journalist. "I read a whole stack of books. Well, skimmed them—most were thicker than the phone book. Some had articles that quoted your opinion on your former colleague. He was quite the bad boy of genetics, according to you. It seemed like a good look back, what with all the cloning brouhaha being pretty much over now and the stem-cell matter being the new target." Michael had donned his glasses again, but I could see the humor in his eyes. I would bet he thought he would never see a pretentious word like brouhaha pass my lips—junior high detention had been proctored by our librarian. As for taking credit for his research, I was sure I'd pay for that later on.

"Colleague." Bellucci tasted the word and found it bitter from the twist of his lips. "Try friend. The son of a bitch was my friend."

"And what changed that?" I opened the notebook and fixed him with an expectant and sympathetic gaze. From the feel of the contortion that sent my face into, as with my smile, I should've practiced the expression in a mirror first.

"Two words. Human experimentation." He enunciated the last so clearly, I could hear the pause between each syllable.

"He experimented on people?" I didn't have to fake outrage. It wasn't precisely news, but my fury hadn't faded since day one of discovering what that maniac was up to at the Institute.

"It wasn't quite as simple as that," Bellucci denied, beating a tattoo with his fingers on the arm of the chair he'd chosen. "He started on himself. You're familiar with his rare genetic makeup? That he's a chimera?" At my nod, he continued. "He wanted to prove something that simply wasn't true. And when he couldn't, he de-

cided to make it true." Sighing, he got to his feet and
paced across a rug brilliant with a jungle print. Candy-
colored birds and cheetahs peeked from emerald green
foliage. "But he couldn't. Chimeras are nothing more
than people with a little extra DNA. He wouldn't accept that, though, and that's when he started with the
pregnant girls."

Apparently Jericho had held back more than the true
nature of the experiment to Bellucci. He also hadn't revealed his healing abilities. "Pregnant?"

He nodded with a grimace. "He figured if he could
accomplish the manipulation he had in mind in utero, it
would be merely a series of extrapolations to achieving
the same in those already fully formed."

"And what exactly were the accomplishments he
hoped to make?" I doodled something on the pad, non-
sense basically, to give the impression I was actually taking notes.

"Faster, smarter, stronger." There was a pained crease
between his eyebrows. I wondered what would happen
to that deepened line if he knew the "improvements"
Jericho had actually ended up making instead. "Non-
sense, all of it." He sat back down and tapped a toe rest-
lessly on the floor. "They were volunteers. He did pay
them money. They knew more or less what he was doing
to the fetuses, what little they could understand, but the
women were poor . . . desperate. Many of them were
drug users, which didn't precisely lend any kind of cre-
dence to the experiment results, human trial violations
aside."

"Then what the hell was he thinking?" I asked for appearance's sake. I knew precisely what he'd been thinking, and science had been only half of it. "No one would
touch him or his work after he was found out. He had
to know that."

"You would think." Shaking his head, he repeated
with a soft incredulity unfaded by time. "You would
think." He stood and walked to the expanse of windows

to stare blindly at the rain. "John was the most determined person I'd ever met ... will ever meet. He truly
didn't believe there was anything in the world he couldn't
do if only he wanted it badly enough. Maybe he thought
he was too smart to be found out. Maybe he thought the
ends justified the means. Maybe he was completely out
of his mind." His shoulders hitched in a dismissive motion. "Could be all three. We'll never know."

"But he did get caught, right? If he hadn't, we
wouldn't be sitting here talking about it. How did that
come about? Who was the first to discover he'd strayed
from the path of the scientific straight and narrow, so to
speak?" I had a suspicion on that score that was easily
confirmed by the iron-rigid set of his spine.

"Why, his closest colleague of course." His voice was
deceptively calm. "His friend. The one he nearly turned
into an unwitting collaborator. We helped each other out,
you realize, on various projects. One would lead and the
other would come in later to help with the paperwork
and publishing end of it. We'd done that for years. By
the time I waltzed obliviously into that last experimental trial, John was too far gone to save. So far ..." Sighing heavily, he turned away from the outside world. "He
wasn't even ashamed. There wasn't the slightest iota of
guilt in him over what he'd done. I tried to reason with
him, but it was futile. He simply couldn't see where the
line was anymore. Couldn't even understand *why* there
was a line. I had no choice but to turn him in."

"And then?" I prompted quietly.

"And then nothing." He took his seat again, loosely
clasping his hands in his lap. "By the time administra-
tion managed to get off their collective wrinkled asses
to confront him, it was too late. He had disappeared and
all evidence of the project had disappeared along with
him."

"The women?"

"The same. They were invisible people to begin
with, living on the outskirts of society. Many of them

lived in missions or with other lost souls. Not one of them ever showed up at the lab again. I'd copied a few names before I blew the whistle. I used that to try to find some of the women, but I never did. They had vanished just as thoroughly as John." The nervous energy was draining away now, leaving a bitter emptiness in its place.

"Did any of them have their babies before the project was blown open?" I shifted and leaned forward. This would've been nearly fifteen years ago. Had the first genetically altered chimeras been produced then?

He shook his head. "No. The farthest along was a woman at eight months. I never saw the results of John's work."

Until now, I thought, as Michael continued to follow our conversation with a blank face. What Jericho had learned to do to children before they took their first breath, he'd adapted to those already born natural chimeras . . . not yet genetically manipulated by a monster.

"What do you think happened to those children?"

"After they were born?" The intertwined fingers tightened on one another. "At best, nothing. At worst, congenital defects that would make thalidomide seem like party punch. Genetics, as a science, wasn't yet advanced enough then that we could do even half of what John was attempting. It still isn't. He thought he was a god. I'd never noticed that before. He was my friend and arrogant as hell, yes, yet I never noticed that he thought himself a god." He paused and cleared a suddenly tight throat. "But I imagine those poor damn children proved him less a god and more a fiend. If they grew up capable of coherent thought or purposeful movement, I'd be surprised."

I didn't argue the label of monster; after all, I'd thought it many times myself. But Bellucci was less accurate with the rest of his assessment. Jericho hadn't crippled his subjects, not physically or intellectually. There were other damages, to be sure, but for all that he was a monster, he was a monster who knew his business.

I closed my notebook. "No one has seen him since, have they?"

"No. He disappeared so very well that I have to wonder if he didn't have some sort of help. That and the fact the majority of what happened was kept out of the papers." The wide mouth thinned to a knife-edged gash. "And I was bound by a nondisclosure agreement. The university would've ruined me if I'd spoken up." There was a broken-glass glitter behind his eyes. "Odd. I've kept quiet all these years; yet I still feel ruined. It hardly seems fair, does it? I wrote my articles, of course, refuting everything John ever theorized, but it wasn't enough. It won't ever be enough."

"So why open up now?"

The question seemed to amuse him, but it was a bleak and dark humor. Lifting a hand, he tapped the base of his skull. "Brain tumor," he said matter-of-factly. "Supratentorial glioma. I have six months . . . *if* I'm very, very lucky. There is little anyone could do to my life now that this rampaging package of cells hasn't already done, nondisclosure agreements be damned."

It made sense. He was stepping away from the game and wanted to clear his debts before he went. It was human nature. It was only too bad it wasn't our nature to settle things before it was on the verge of being too late. "Two last questions, Dr. Bellucci, if I may." Placing the mock notes into my jacket pocket, I asked, "Do you think if Hooker hadn't been found out that he would've been able to do what he'd planned in the beginning? Do you think he could have gone on to substantially change the genes of a person after they were born?"

"Genetic replacement is a reality for us now." He continued to unconsciously rub the juncture of his neck and skull. "Unfortunately, the amazing medical miracles we were so sure it would bring about have been accompanied by problems nearly as adverse as what we

were trying to cure. As for John . . . normally, I would
say his chances were low. What he was aiming for was
worlds beyond what the scientific community is doing
now. Still"—he dropped his hand and used it to make a
throwaway gesture—"this is John we're speaking of and
that alone makes it almost conceivable. I'm not saying
he would've accomplished any of his goals, mind you;
they were far too improbable, not to mention insane.
But I do believe if he'd continued on with the resources
we had, he would've advanced genetic replacement considerably—in theory if nothing else."

Insane and brilliant was a mix that hadn't done the
world any good throughout history. "Did Hooker have
any government connections, contracts? He vanished,
as you said, so thoroughly. I have to wonder if he had
professional help."

Once again he was out of the chair. This time it was
to pull the drapes, squinting as if even the dull gray light
hurt his eyes. "I wondered that myself, but truthfully I
don't have the slightest idea. Although it would be hard
to imagine John voluntarily taking up with an organization with far more rules and regulations than academic
research ever dreamed of." He pressed a knuckle against
his temple and gave a pained grimace.

The interview apparently over, I followed his lead
and stood. "I appreciate your time. We can show ourselves out if you want."

"No, no. I'm fine." He moved over and shook my
hand. "And I appreciate it far more. The chance to get
this off my chest means quite a bit to me."

We were nearly at the door when I remembered one
more question I'd wanted to ask him. "Did Hooker have
any family to speak of? Children maybe? A son?"

Michael had commented on how closely his John had
resembled his namesake, Jericho, and I'd wondered if he
had performed his twisted magic on his own blood. Had
he tried to create an even darker version of himself?

"Son? No. John was an only child and had no other

family after his parents died. He didn't marry and had no children that I knew of. Not before he disappeared anyway. Why?"

"Just curious," I answered somewhat truthfully. In the foyer a wet figure almost collided with us as it came through the front door wrestling with an umbrella and an armful of yapping dog.

"Gina." Bellucci leaned in to take the white bundle of wet-dog smell away from what turned out to be a short, squat woman in a raincoat. "Let me help you."

"Thank you, sir." Stripping off her coat, she revealed no-nonsense black polyester pants paired with a plain white blouse. She was either a housekeeper or a nurse, although Bellucci didn't seem to be in need of the latter yet. "Priscilla quite took her time with business. I'll have to towel the little beast off." After carefully wrapping both her umbrella and tightly folded coat in plastic bags she obtained from the top shelf of the closet, she reclaimed the still-barking dog and whisked it off. Not a single drop of water hit the floor during the process.

"Good help is hard to find," Bellucci said ruefully. "But anal-retentive help is priceless." He shook my hand again and let us out onto the porch. "Let me know when the article comes out, would you?"

I nodded. "Of course. As soon as I finish it and send it off, I'll let you know."

Eyes distant, he said quietly, "Hurry." Then he closed the door, leaving us to the rain.

Protected from the weather by the overhang, Michael and I stood in silence until he finally said, "That was a lot of big words on your part. Are you okay?"

"My head hurts, but I'll try to struggle on," I replied dryly. Actually I was struggling, but it was in an effort to keep afloat above a wave of pessimism. What we had learned had given us something of a background on Jericho, but it hadn't given us anything useful to our situation. The issue of government ties was still a mystery and Jericho had no family he might keep in contact with, which left us with no way to trace him. And while we did know now how it all began, we didn't know the answer to the more important question.

How it would all end.

Chapter 28

The beach house was mostly as I remembered. It was a little shabbier, with a few areas of peeling paint and warped wood, but otherwise it was the same. A sprawling affair on stilts, it looked identical to the majority of the houses up and down the coast. There was an outside shower to spray off the sand and salt and a deck with chairs of weathered wood to watch the sunrise over the dunes. The ocean itself was hidden behind those same swells of sand and could be seen only from the windows on the second floor. You could hear it, however, no matter where you were . . . inside or out. I'd spent the majority of my life listening to the sound. In many ways it had been one of the few constants. Maybe now I could learn to enjoy it again.

"Can we go see?"

I dropped my duffel bag by the stairs leading up to the house and gave Michael a shrug and half smile. "Why not? It's definitely worth seeing." The Institute hadn't been too far from Miami, but that didn't mean Michael had had the opportunity to see the ocean—not that he remembered.

Leaving Zilla in the car, he took off toward the dunes. I zipped up my jacket against the biting wind and followed with less enthusiasm. When I crested the slope, slipping and sliding with every other step, I wanted to turn away from the sight. Gray water under a gray sky; it wasn't like that day. That day had been all blues. Blue overhead along with crashing waves the color of a million shattered marbles was what I'd seen then. Gray or blue, it was all the same. It was where I'd been the moment life had fallen away beneath me. Sitting on my horse's back as the water soaked my jeans, I had watched blue meet blue as water met sky. I'd watched that instead of watching Lukas, and . . . here we were.

It was why I lived in a condo on the beach. I wouldn't let the impulse to close my eyes defeat me. I lived by the ocean; I swam in it, because I wouldn't let myself forget. I didn't deserve to. Seeing the waves fall was the same as seeing Lukas do the same. I wanted to look away, this time as all times, but I didn't.

And because I didn't, I was lucky enough to see Michael's expression. He stood on wet sand in brine-soaked shoes and stared without blinking. This time water met sky in his eyes. I draped an arm over his shoulder. "Big, huh?"

"Big," he agreed softly.

We stood for a long time in the presence of that which should've made me feel very small. It didn't. Standing next to Michael, I suddenly felt big, and as whole as I'd ever been. In a place that echoed the beginning of a nightmare, the nightmare finally ended. And it felt right that it happened that way, an inevitable circle.

After a while the cold drove us back to the house. Inside the smell of damp and must wasn't nearly as bad as I had expected, but I still cracked a few windows. As I worked, Michael roamed about exploring. He would stop here and there to peer at a framed picture or pick up a seashell collecting dust, although even that wasn't as bad as I thought it would be. Maybe Anatoly had a cleaning service come in once every few months to keep the place from falling apart. Being what he was didn't change the fact he'd respected Babushka Lena and, in turn, would respect her treasures. "Pick a bedroom, Misha," I prompted. "There're four of them upstairs."

He looked up from the abstract pink and purple curl

of abalone shell nestled in the palm of his hand. "I get my own room?"

He sounded like a five-year-old, simultaneously thrilled and apprehensive at the prospect. If he was afraid, I didn't blame him. Jericho had decorated many of my dreams in the past week and a half, propelling me from a sweat-soaked sleep with my hand searching desperately for my gun more times than I cared to admit. And Michael had ten more years of that evil bastard to contend with than I did. The things that he dreamed of I couldn't even begin to guess. If he wanted to bunk with me until he was ninety, I wouldn't hold it against him.

"Maybe," I answered noncommittally. "Tell you what. You take a look. If two of them are in good-enough shape, then take the one you want. If only one is livable, then sorry about your luck, kiddo. You'll be stuck with me for a while." That left him an out. If he found only one to be acceptable, we would go with that and there would be no embarrassment on either side.

"Okay." Carefully placing the shell back in a cloudy glass bowl, he headed for the stairs. It was circular, a wrought-iron monstrosity that showed the red bloom of rust. At the top and out of sight, he called down, "You know you're not half as clever as you think you are, but ..."

It had been obvious all along that my college psych classes were sadly lacking compared to the ones he had been exposed to, but I kept on trying. Yeah, I kept on trying, and I kept on getting shot down, I thought ruefully. "But ... ?" I prodded, flipping the switches to check the lights. The utilities had been kept on all these years in the name of Babushka's long-gone gentleman friend. It was just one more way of keeping the place untraceable. "But what?"

There was a pause and then, "Thanks." Footsteps creaked overhead as he hurried away from the stairs and toward the bedrooms. He wouldn't want to get caught up in a wave of gooey emotion or anything.

God forbid. I allowed myself a small grin and headed back out to the car for our stockpile of groceries. We'd switched roles, Michael and I. When we were kids, he'd been the open one. Every emotion he felt he wore on his face, so clear and bright that it couldn't be missed. Hell, you would know what he felt before he knew himself. I'd been more like our father in that respect and, to be honest, I still was—aloof, a little distant. But not with Michael. He needed to know how I felt, and he needed it pretty badly. It was the only evidence he'd been able to accept so far that I considered him family . . . no matter what he considered himself. Photos and stories were suspect, but emotion couldn't be faked. Michael was too damn smart not to see through anything that wasn't completely genuine.

Turned out he picked out two bedrooms for us. I wasn't surprised, and I couldn't have been any damn prouder. What did surprise me was the pang of separation anxiety I felt. I was worse than any overprotective mom waving good-bye to Junior on the first day of kindergarten. But I bit my tongue and stood in the doorway to watch as he shook out the sheets. Apparently the cleaning service had skipped this bedroom. Dust billowed in huge clouds and I waved a hand in front of my face. "Sleeping on a bare mattress isn't that bad." I coughed. "Maybe you should give it a try."

Blond hair sticking up in dusty spikes, he shook his head. "No. I'm done with sleeping in cars and going to the bathroom in bottles. No bare mattresses either."

"Aren't you the picky one? Wanting clean sheets and real bathrooms. You're like a little girl." I ducked as the sheet was snapped in my general direction. "I never did teach you to write your name in the snow, but we've got a whole shitload of sand out there to practice in." Another fierce snap of the sheet expelled me from the room.

That evening I made my first home-cooked meal in months. In the condo, I lived mostly on takeout. Natalie had managed to get me involved in cooking despite myself—mainly by threats or promises. Both involved kissing, soft touches, and the occasional brisk swat to my ass. Needless to say, after Natalie had her wicked way with me, a Cordon Bleu chef had nothing on me in motivation, if not talent. Since she had left, I'd done much less cooking, but you never really forget how to make a tuna casserole.

Michael regarded the steaming pile of cheese, fish, and crackers on his plate with a dubious frown. "What's wrong with hamburgers? I like hamburgers. And pizza."

"This is healthy." I didn't know what they'd fed him from that place before I snatched him, but the kid now had a love of junk food that was passionate, if not borderline obsessive. I sat down at the kitchen table and dug into my helping. "Growing boys need healthy food once in a while." I knew it was true. I'd read it in a magazine.

Spearing a chunk of cheese with his fork, he stretched it out from the plate in a near-foot-long streamer. "Healthy. Useful in grouting tile maybe, but healthy?"

"And what do you know about grout?" I grumbled, taking a bite and swallowing. It wasn't that bad. It wasn't that good either, but it rose above the grout standard.

"There's a book in the bathroom." He moved his fork in a different direction, snapping the cheese like an old rubber band. "And lots of fuzzy green grout."

It was another black mark against the not-too-accomplished cleaning service. A haphazard dusting seemed to be the best they could do. "Eat your food or the next thing I fix will be fuzzy-grout casserole."

With a long-suffering sigh he stuffed the forkful into his mouth and chewed with such grim resignation that I may as well have served him fried roadkill. "You know, I could learn to cook. Just to help you out. A way to thank you for everything you've done for me."

"Yeah, you're a real humanitarian, pizza boy," I scoffed. "Now eat."

Before he finished with the meal, I knew more about

the clogging effects of cheese on the heart than I cared to. But the next time we came across a cheeseburger or loaded pizza, I was sure I would hear about nothing but the glowing health benefits. After dumping the dishes in the sink like true bachelors, we set up camp on the couch and turned on the TV. Without cable there were only three channels and two of them were full of snow. We were living in the dark ages here. I skimmed through them, then switched off the television in disgust. "Hang on. I think there might be a checkerboard in the closet."

A checkerboard and books on bathroom repair were the sum total of our entertainment here. I didn't mind the change from the bright lights and greased poles of Miami. I didn't mind it at all. The closet was stocked with boxes and broken vacuum cleaner attachments, but I sifted through it to find the red and black box. Beneath it I found a photo album, one that had belonged to Babushka Lena. I hesitated for a second, then piled it on top of the checkers box. Placing them on the table next to the sofa, I sat down and lifted the album into my lap. "I know you're not much for photos." I moved over until I was shoulder to shoulder with Michael. "But I thought you might want to see some of me when I was less frightening to the naked human eye."

He cocked his head doubtfully at me. "Less frightening? I'm not sure I can picture that. Are you sure they're really you? They can do amazing things with computer effects."

"Funny. You're a funny guy. Bet you scored an F in that class," I said sourly. I riffled through the book and stopped at one I recognized of myself. About two years old, I was trying to ride the family dog. Lying across his back with my arms around his furry neck, I was bare-ass naked and grinning like a loon. "The traditional naked-butt baby picture. A favorite of grandmothers everywhere."

"I do pity the dog. He probably never recovered from the trauma." Michael's finger stroked the glossy surface. "What breed was he?"

"A mutt, Lab with a dash of Saint Bernard, I think. I cried like a baby when he died." I elbowed him and added, "Tell anyone that and I'll have to kick your bony butt."

So underwhelmed by the threat that he didn't even feel the need to roll his eyes, he reached over to turn the page himself. "Who's that?"

"Our . . . my mom." She'd been caught in the act of nothing in particular. The only occasion was a trigger-happy kid with a new camera, namely me. I didn't recognize the background—a slice of muted wallpaper and the leaves of a potted plant. It wasn't the kind of thing a young boy paid attention to. Mom was looking over her shoulder at me, startled but with the merry and indulgent smile that rarely left her face. She had always been so happy. I'd wondered more than once over the years if she knew what her husband did for a living. How could she not? She was a grown, intelligent woman; after years of marriage she simply couldn't be that blind. Yet . . . somehow I thought she was. It could be I didn't want to believe she wasn't as picture-perfect in her purity as I saw her to be as a child. And it could be the sun rose in the east and set in the west. With the incredibly obvious bit of psychoanalysis out of the way, I just looked at the picture—looked at it and treasured the feeling it sparked in me. I might be a thug and worse, but damn if I hadn't loved my mother.

Pale blond hair caught in a loose French braid and high Slavic cheekbones joined with blue eyes and porcelain skin. She wasn't a beautiful woman; she was more than beautiful. The cheekbones were a shade too sharp, the eyes a little too round, and the mouth overly generous. But it all came together in a shining whole—much like it did in Michael. His features weren't as much like our mother's as I remembered; time had changed him from a male copy of Anya to his own distinct person. His eyes were more almond shaped and his mouth not as wide, but he had the same inner . . . hell . . . light, I guess you'd say.

"She's pretty." He looked as if he wanted to touch the photo but pulled back his hand before he made contact.

Maneuvering it free of the protective plastic film, I handed it to him. He started to shake his head, but I wouldn't let him refuse, pushing it into his hand. "Keep it."

"But . . ."

"I know, kiddo. You don't have to say it," I said patiently. "She's not your mom. But she was a great mom, the best, and I don't mind sharing." I knew Michael wouldn't accept anything less than rock-solid evidence, something that couldn't be denied—like Anatoly, he'd want to see the DNA results. One day when our situation cooled down I hoped to get that for him. But that could be years and until then it was going to have to boil down to a leap of faith. Unfortunately, that was the one thing the Institute had been ill-equipped to teach.

Still, he did take the picture. Resting it carefully on his knee, he asked, "What about the one of you and the dog? Whenever I have trouble sleeping, I could use that to laugh myself into unconsciousness."

"All right, you snide little punk," I growled. "Just for that you get to see Babushka Lena in a bathing suit, all five yards of it."

Over the next half hour, we made our way through the rest of the album and Babushka fulfilled my threat, showing up several times in beachwear that had been outdated even in the fifties. It was one of Lena's early albums, put together before Lukas had been born. The majority of the pictures were of a preschool me wreaking havoc. Only in the last pages did I start to age upward . . .

five, six, and finally seven. And in the very last picture I was shown sitting on the edge of a hospital bed. With an awkward armful of blanket and baby, I looked wary, amazed, and not a little horrified.

Michael studied the slightly yellowed window to the past with a blank face. Then, almost reluctantly, his lips curled. "Nice button."

I shook my head and gave a combination groan and laugh. "Mom made me. You should've seen the matching shirt she wanted me to wear. Luckily her water broke in the gift shop and I escaped with my dignity." The button pinned to my thin seven-year-old chest was blue and white with the traditional I'M A BIG BROTHER written cheerfully across it. "Mostly."

Before he could point out how far from the truth that was, I changed the subject with a suggestion. "Want to take a run on the beach?" I hadn't been able to keep up my usual exercise regimen the past few weeks, and that wasn't good. When you're on the run for your life, you need to actually be able to run.

"In the dark?" Michael glanced over at the slice of plum-skin dusk peeking in under the blinds.

"The moon will be out soon. There'll be enough light to whip your skinny ass into shape." Dumping the album onto the table, I stood. "I'll grab my shoes." When I came back down the stairs, I pretended not to notice him slipping two pictures into his jeans pocket. The first would be the one of Mom I'd given him, and I felt safe in betting the second was of a petrified boy holding a wet baby.

We walked along the water's edge until the moon rose high enough to reveal the dips and swells in the sand. Quicksilver light made the sand glow an oddly brilliant gray, and our footprints shadowed hollows of inky black. The moon itself was huge, the pumpkin-sized globe you seemed to see so much more often as a child. The glitter of the stars faded to pinpricks beside its brilliance. Blowing out a breath that curled and steamed as white as the breakers, I called out to Michael, "You ready?"

He was about twenty feet ahead of me, looking out to sea as the water washed over pale bare feet. I'd told him it was too damn cold, but what did that mean to a kid who couldn't remember ever seeing the ocean or feeling it on his skin? I let him enjoy the moment and trusted in his common sense to stave off frostbite.

Waving an acknowledging hand at me, he retreated farther up onto dry sand to put on his socks and shoes. As he tied the last laces with quick jerks of his fingers, he raised his head to look at me and opened his mouth. It was easy enough to make a general guess at what he was going to say. Let's go or, knowing Michael, I don't like to run. Running is sweaty and annoying. Whichever it was, the words didn't materialize. The gun I pointed at him had them melting away.

He didn't jump to his feet or lunge to one side, but instead he stayed frozen in place. His face smooth and calm, he mouthed silently, "Behind me?"

I gave an infinitesimal nod and fired a split second after he threw himself forward. The man behind him disappeared from sight, leaving nothing but an ominous dark spray on the sand. Dressed all in black, he had been crouched behind a low dune to blend perfectly with the background of night-shadowed beach grass—well . . . almost perfectly. As with most things in life, almost just wasn't good enough. I had seen him. I'd seen the whites of his eyes gleam as he watched Michael . . . only Michael. Concentrating on your target is good; focusing on it to the exclusion of all else gets the back of your head blown into the sea oats.

Every time I thought we were safe—every goddamn time.

I didn't have to tell Michael to run. By now it was more than second nature, for both of us. As was the taste of tin in the mouth and the adrenaline pulsing through the veins like an amphetamine poison—a familiar icy hand that clamped down on the back of the neck. It was like an old friend now . . . an old, hateful friend. I caught up with Michael and gave him a shove toward the dunes. There would be more there, I knew. There was no way around that, but fleeing down an empty beach was suicide. They would drop me in the sand. As for Michael . . . they would either kill or capture him, depending on whether Jericho thought him salvageable or not.

Killing would be kinder.

The grass, sharp as blades, beat at our legs. It stung even through my jeans as we fought for footing in our flight. And when I fell, it sliced open my palm with surgical sharpness. As I struggled to my knees, the hand that had erupted out of the sand to snare my ankle was joined by the rest of its owner. He matched the other one, with identical clothes and carbon-copy overconfidence. The night-vision goggles he wore would've protected his eyes from the sand, but they didn't do anything to guard from the heel I jammed into them. With hands clawing at the now-shattered goggles, he flipped over onto his back with a strangled yell. Using his stomach as a springboard, I took off after Michael. A crude and fast move, it was effective enough, judging from the sound of vomiting that followed me.

Michael had paused when I had fallen, and I hissed urgently, "Go. Go!" He ran on until a form came boiling out of the darkness to tackle him about the legs. Considering what Michael could do to him, the son of a bitch was brave to make the attempt. Considering the scream that came out of him, that label might be posthumous. But Michael hadn't changed his mind about using his abilities to save himself. To save me he would break his own rules. For himself, it was still an emphatic no. The kid was too good for this . . . too goddamn good by far.

I reached them and tossed the limp attacker off Michael with one well-placed kick. "What did you do to him?" I grunted as I grabbed a handful of his shirt and pulled him to his feet.

"The same thing I did to that doctor, only this time I used my knee." His hair a ghostly beacon, he rubbed a hand across his forehead. "They're everywhere, aren't they? It's hopeless."

"Only if we give up." Hand still wound in his shirt, I towed him behind me into a haphazard speed. "And I'm not giving up on you, Misha. Now move your ass."

We'd gone only a few more feet when a bullet kicked up sand at our feet. I missed the muzzle flash and fired in several directions. It was useless, and more bullets hit around us as we raced through the vegetation. We had no choice but to head back to the beach at the water's edge. They'd formed a line between us and the house; there was no way around them. I didn't know how long we'd last if we took to the water to swim down the coast, but I was afraid we were going to find out.

"Can you swim?" I demanded between panting breaths as we cleared the grass.

There was the glint of teeth as he smiled. "Theoretically."

The repeat of his remark from one of our first escapes had a spurt of dark laughter locked in my throat. I only hoped his theory worked better in water than it did in cars. I hoped . . . God, I hoped I lived to see him swimming to safety. I hoped to see him grow to be twice the man I was. I hoped to see him happy and free.

Of course, none of that was going to happen. If God existed, he didn't seem to be listening. Did he ever? Instead of God, it could be there was only inescapable fate. And fate seemed to like things tidy. What began on the beach should end on the beach. What was born in blood and pain should die the same way. God might be ignoring this particular sparrow, but fate was watching with lascivious interest. It couldn't fucking wait to see what went down next.

That would be me.

I heard my thighbone break. The sound was so clear. The snap of a tree branch underfoot; the cracking of ice in a spring thaw—I heard that, but I never heard the gun that fired the bullet. And I don't remember falling; I knew only that I was lying on the ground with the taste of sand in my mouth. I couldn't feel my leg. There was a slow warmth spreading across my skin, but no feeling ... no pain. Not yet. Shock took care of that. It also took care of my thoughts. They moved in staggering circles as my hands made vague motions in the sand, trying in vain to turn me over.

"There you are."

The gloating voice was fatally familiar. I pushed up again as my brain convulsed desperately to grasp what was going on. This time with a leg that was worthless deadweight, I managed to turn onto my back and braced myself, barely, upright on my elbows. Where was he? There was nothing but darkness and a leering moon that all but blocked out the sky.

"All I wanted to do," the voice floated on, "was to make others like me. With a few minor improvements of course." There was a laugh rich with mock self-deprecation. "I do get so lonely."

Jericho. It all came back; a river of fetid knowledge—fear, rage, and despair. The only hope I had left was that Michael was in the water. I didn't see him. He had to be swimming away—he had to be. As for me—I was dead. It was inevitable. I had seconds, maybe minutes, before Jericho killed me, but if Michael made it out of here, then death was something I could live with. That would look good on a T-shirt. Death was something I could live with. The bile black humor twisted itself onto my lips before a spasm of coughing sent sand from my lungs. "Come out, you son of a bitch," I rasped. My gun ... Where was my gun? It had flown from my hand when I fell. Surreptitiously I felt beside me, running fingers through grit for the comforting feel of metal. It was over for me; I accepted that, but my last breath would be spent trying to take Jericho with me. "Come out," I repeated. "What the hell are you afraid of?"

"Certainly not of a common thief." He materialized out of a mass of night and moon shadows. He was a shadow himself, lit only with lunar streaks along the planes of his face. "You took my Michael. You took my property. Cheaters never prosper, haven't you heard? And neither do thieves." He hadn't lost his gun. It was still securely in his hand and trained on me.

"Thief? You're the one who stole him. Stole a little boy," I spat. "Did you think you could just take him and walk away?"

"Steal? I didn't steal him. Like any good baker, I made him from scratch." The grin that carved across his face was as brilliant and cold as the moon overhead.

He wasn't making any sense. None. The man was insane, but I would listen to his psychotic ranting until the end of time if that gave Michael more of a chance to escape. "How did you find us?" My hands still searched futilely for my weapon.

"A friend." He crouched down well out of reach and rested his gun hand on his knee. "An old, old friend who sold you a sad, sad story. I hear you'll let him know when the article comes out. Could I get a copy? Since it is about me, it seems only fair. I could frame it for my office."

I should've felt stupid. I didn't. I felt worse. It was idiocy that couldn't be equaled; it was carelessness miles beyond criminal. Bellucci had spun his tale of righteous anger, betrayal, and redemption, and I had swallowed it all like a spoon-fed baby. I'd watched the person who had no doubt planted the tracer on our car and my only thought had been regarding the ugliness of the wet dog she'd been carrying. It hadn't once crossed my mind that Jericho needed a confederate in the legitimate science world. What better way to get access to cutting-edge new developments that had yet to see the light of the published world? Bellucci was the perfect silent partner. He could feed Jericho information, equipment, and get a nice slice of make-your-own-assassin pie. Even better, he could write outraged refutations of Jericho's work and show himself to be Jericho's most devoted rival. If anyone investigated Jericho, where would they go first?

Right.

Jericho's early-warning system had been our downfall. "College pals," I said bitterly. "Colleagues. And now you torture children together. Isn't that . . ." The pain started. I was talking and breathing, and suddenly that was over. A malevolent butcher set up shop and went to work carving my thighbone into a thousand sharp-edged ivory knives. I gasped raggedly for air, then pushed through the black wave that washed over me. "Isn't that . . . too . . . much togetherness?"

"You bore me." Dismissive, he stood and walked close enough to kick the foot of my injured leg. As kicks went, it wasn't much. Fairly gentle, more of a hard tap than anything, it was nevertheless enough to have the salty copper of blood flooding my mouth. "I thought you must be clever to have gotten this far, but close up . . . I simply don't see it. Although removing his tracking chip wasn't completely idiotic." He tilted his head as if truly considering the exact measurement of my stupidity. "Surprising such a thought would occur to you. But even more of a mystery is that Michael stayed with you. He's not much for killing, more's the pity, but I fully expected him to take his leave of you quickly enough. Surely he wouldn't have balked at a short coma for his kidnapper."

My tongue almost refused to cooperate, numb from where I'd bitten it to keep from screaming in pain. "Not a kidnapper." My hands fisted in the sand felt like the only thing holding me to consciousness. "He's mine."

"Yours?" The bass of his voice was colored with derision. "And here I thought he was mine all this time. Pray tell, dead man, how is he yours?"

He still didn't know? He still hadn't figured out who I was? "I'm his family," I snarled weakly. "His *family*, you bastard."

"Oh really?" The curve of his mouth was ripe with

superiority and an amusement I couldn't understand. "And how do you figure that?" He held up a hand and took a few steps back. Blood did tend to spatter a long way. "Never mind. I haven't the time or inclination to play this little game." Raising his voice slightly, he called out, "I see you, Michael. I've seen you watching all along. It's all right, you know. Watch all you like. I rather enjoy the thought of your watching your 'savior' die. You can watch at my side if you wish."

No. Damn it, no. He listened when I told him to run. He always listened, but then he always came back.

"Michael." He drew the name out cajolingly. "You cannot deny your Maker, boy. If history has taught us nothing, it has taught us that."

I didn't see him. I twisted my head back and forth desperately. Maybe Jericho was wrong. Maybe he was doing this to torment me, to make my final moments as wrenching as he could. That was all it was; it had to be. When I finally brought my eyes back to those glossy black ones, I tried hard to hold on to that hope. It wasn't easy in the face of the poisonous dark gaze fixed on me as I labored to sit upright in the sand. I wasn't going to die lying flat in the sand, as if I were just waiting for it.

"Shy, that one," he mused. "An odd quality in death incarnate."

"He's not." I knew that as well as I'd ever known anything. "He's not death."

"Death enters through a thousand doors." The gun extended toward me. "He's only one. In time I'll have all one thousand. And when all my doors open on the world, I alone will hold their keys."

Then he fired.

The waiting is the hardest part. You learn that from nearly day one. You could be a child waiting for a cookie or a shiny new bike, or a cavity-ridden teenager waiting and dreading the jab of Novocaine with a needle that has no end. You could ask one of a million people waiting for outcomes both good and bad, and they would all tell you the same thing. Anticipation is a bitch; everything else is downhill. Is that true or not? I didn't know, because what I expected, a bullet to the chest, didn't happen. But God, I wish it had.

Time didn't freeze. My life didn't riffle before me like the pages of a badly drawn comic book. None of the clichés held true. My heart didn't even have time to pound at a faster, more agonizingly painful rate. By the time you hear the gunshot, it's too late for that. The bullet has already found its mark. If you're the one hit, a beating heart may be a moot point. If you're not the one cradling lead, a living heart isn't what you want anyway—not anymore.

I looked down at the armful of deadweight, almost puzzled. So, it was God after all, not fate. It was God, and his sparrow had fallen from the sky to rest broken in my lap. Strands of bleached hair were cool against my arm, as cool as the liquid flowing against my chest was warm. The bullet had entered his back and exited his chest to rest in my shoulder. And the blood—the blood was everywhere. It flowed like a river out of him and onto me. I could even smell it on his breath—his shallow, fading breath.

"How could you do something so stupid?" I choked, the words ugly with anguish. "How could you do something so goddamn stupid?" His eyes were only colorless shadows in the moonlight, but I saw him in there still. Aware, he was with me, but beginning to drift away—far away. "Misha." I rested my forehead on his. "Why?"

"For my brother," he said simply.

The whisper brushed against my cheek and I watched as the life—the light—began to spill from his face. His skin went so transparent that dark lashes were a brutal contrast when they came to rest—and stayed at rest.

Jericho had known where he was. Charging him would've been futile. Instead, Michael had charged me. He'd thrown himself in front of me to take the bullet—my bullet. I pulled him close and blocked out the smell of blood with the scent of shampoo in his hair. Green and herbal, it took me from the beach to an endless field of grass and clover. It was a place without the stink of copper and the fly of fatal lead, a place without despair.

"Isn't this annoying?"

There was the hiss and purr of sand under approaching shoes. Obviously, he'd overcome his distaste of wearing his victim's blood, but it didn't matter. I didn't open my eyes as he came. I didn't care. I'd found what I was looking for. After all these years, I'd found it. Damn if I was going to watch Jericho end it all.

"All my time wasted. All the delayed graduations, not to mention moving the entire Institute. Then there's the money lost." The footsteps stopped. "But nothing compares to the inconvenience. Nothing approaches the arrogance of your thinking you could interfere in my affairs." The muzzle of his gun pressed hard against the top of my head, digging into skin and flesh. "My *work*."

"Pull the trigger already, Frankenstein," I said without emotion. "Just fucking pull it."

I felt the air ripple as he leaned closer. "I should take you with me. You remember that examination table in the basement? I could take you apart on one just like it, piece by piece. I could make it last days, weeks if I wanted. No constructive purpose of course." The laugh hit my skin with an unnatural heat. "Simply for fun. No?" The metal moved to my forehead as I remained silent. "That's all right. This is fun as well."

This time I heard the shot. It rang gray and sharp as a titanium bell. I felt the muzzle disappear from my head and I wondered at how easy it was; so very easy. There was no pain; no degrading of consciousness. I could still hear the roar of the waves, could still smell the leafy scent of Michael's hair. I even felt the ground shudder as a body thudded against it.

"Stefan? Son?"

I opened my eyes to see a face that was a near mirror image of mine. Lines of age, a scattering of white hairs in the black, it was me at sixty. Strange, considering I'd just died at the age of twenty-four. At least I thought I had. "Dad." I licked dry lips. "Dad, what—what are you doing here?"

"Saving your ass apparently." He holstered his gun and crouched down beside me. "What the hell is going on, Stoipah?"

My eyes left him to fix irrevocably on a fallen dark figure. Barely three feet away, Jericho sprawled in a boneless huddle in the sand. Lids only half closed, he stared blindly at nothing. His chest didn't move and the white of his teeth was obscured by blood, inky black as the sky above. Anatoly's shot had blown out the majority of his throat; he would've died instantly. He must have fallen on his gun, because there was no sign of it. And that was no good. I needed it—needed it badly.

"Give me your gun," I grated.

Eyebrows pulling into a confused V, Anatoly said gruffly, "He's dead, Stefan."

"Give me the goddamn gun."

With no further argument, he shrugged and slipped it into my hand. I cradled Michael with one arm and emptied the clip in Jericho's head at point-blank range. The shape of his skull changed to something misshapen and horrific. Now the outside of the son of a bitch reflected what lurked underneath.

As my father retrieved his gun from my hand, there was the stir of moving figures around us. It was Anatoly's men. Jericho's were either bodies cooling in the grass or long gone. "Have them cut off his head," I said harshly. That was what was done with vampires, although he was worse than any undead movie monster. Jericho wasn't coming back this time, not unless he could grow a new head. "Cut it off before they dump him."

"Stefan . . ."

"Cut it off!"

"All right. Whatever you want. We'll decapitate the bastard. The boys will enjoy the overtime." Two of the men, vaguely familiar, drifted up at his snap and dragged off the body.

I felt something in me break at the sight, something hard and dark and bitter. It cracked and shattered beyond repair, and I wasn't sorry to see it go. Pressing a hand to Michael's back, I felt the blood seep through my fingers. "Misha?" Nothing. "Dad, we need . . . We need help." It was the voice of a child, not that of a seasoned thug or newly minted killer. It was the voice of a teenage boy begging his father to make it all right. Please, this time make it all right.

"I've already sent Aleksei for a doctor. Stefan, what have you gotten yourself into?" He maneuvered out of the crouch to sit beside me. From the corner of my eye I vaguely noted that the white in his hair was more prevalent than the last time I'd seen him, the shoulders a hair less broad.

I ignored his question. I didn't have the kind of time or coherence it would take to explain all of it. "I was looking for you," I said distantly, because everything was distant now—everything except Michael. Lifting him higher in my arms, I could feel his breath against my neck; slow, so slow.

"I heard. That's why I came to the house. We were in town getting some supplies, but I've been staying here for the past few days." That explained the odd pattern of superficial cleanliness. "I knew you'd eventually show up here if you were in trouble." His hand touched my leg and came away stained with blood. "I also heard about Lev," he said with a smile etched out of ice. "My good and loyal friend Lev. I'm sorry to say that in the future, retirement isn't going to agree with him." Wiping his hand on his pants, he touched Michael's arm. "And who is this?"

"Lukas." It was a bizarre lightscape of ebony and silver that surrounded us. I shouldn't expect him to recognize his lost son in those conditions, but unrealistically enough I did. "It's Lukas. I found him."

"Stefan. My God, Stefan." He leaned back in shock, wiping blood and sand absently on his pant leg. His hand shook. In all my life I hadn't once seen his hand shake. "Stefan," his response bleak and implacable, "he's not your brother."

It stunned me, that he didn't see it . . . didn't believe me. "He is," I countered sharply. "He's Lukas. I know my brother. It's him."

"Ah, what an *esportet*." He ducked his head to rest it in his hands for a moment; then he raised his face to me. It was a mask, a jangled combination of sagging grief and ruthless angles. "Stefan, you saw him. I looked up as we were getting in the car. Your face was in the window. You saw."

I saw?

I saw. . . . God, I had.

I *had* seen it.

How could I forget that? How could I forget the small figure swathed in a blanket? Blond hair showing beneath a flap of wool, the thin arm hanging limp. Hours after my brother had disappeared, I had looked out my bedroom window to see my father riding away with his body cradled in his lap.

I remembered the weeks after Lukas's disappearance being hazy, distant. I just hadn't remembered precisely what had triggered those layers and layers of shock. I thought it had been Lukas's being taken in front of me. I was wrong.

"When you . . . forgot, I thought it for the best," Anatoly offered with a thread of pain even he couldn't hide. "No one could know inside or outside the business. No one, and you were young, hurt. . . . You might have said something." He sighed and rubbed his eyes. "I buried him with your mother, in secret of course. I let the police go on thinking he was still missing. I let everyone go on thinking that. Because if anyone knew how he had died, they would know whom to come to when I put every one of those bastards into the ground. Which is what I did." Satisfaction was a cold comfort, but apparently he still embraced it. "The entire Gubin family paid for what they did to Lukas. Every last one of them, from grandfather to the last son." And no one was the wiser. No one came to arrest Anatoly and none of the other *vors*, *Mafiya* bosses, came looking for a vigilante father out of control. "And in the years after, you didn't seem to want to remember. You *refused* to remember."

Nothing more than a snatching gone wrong. It was a common way to negotiate between rival factions. Lukas had died on that beach. I should've known it from the sound his skull made when it hit the rock. I should've known. His kidnapper had probably dumped his body not far from the beach when he realized Lukas was dead—when he realized my brother was dead. My brother . . .

Michael's breath hitched and slowed even further. Lost to the world, he felt light in my arms . . . insubstantial as a ghost. Lukas's ghost, long gone. "Misha, I'm here," I whispered, but his eyes remained closed.

The eyes . . . and then came another memory, this one not as old. It was a sickening flight back to a dark hallway and a little girl named Wendy. There had been something about her eyes, barely seen in the dim light of the hall. When I'd told Michael that he had Lukas's eyes, he'd gone still—distant and still. And when he'd talked about his friend John's resemblance to their captor, he had said that of course his eyes were different from Jericho's. *Of course*. Why hadn't I picked up on that? All the children had bicolored eyes. It had to be an unforeseen result of the genetic manipulation. I couldn't believe Jericho would've wanted such a visible marker on his product if he could avoid it. Assassins should be anonymous.

I'd pointed out to Michael that he had my brother's eyes, and he had known it wasn't the proof I thought it to be. He'd kept trying to tell me and I'd kept cutting him off. Or he'd cut himself off . . . because wouldn't it be nice to believe it was true, for a little while, before ruthlessly dragging himself back to reality? But in the end it hadn't mattered. When it came down to the wire, he hadn't been able to deny me.

I'd told him over and over. I'd inundated him with stories and so-called evidence he didn't want to hear. I'd given him a life and a family he had never asked for. I'd given him a hope he didn't even know he wanted, a hope he didn't know he desperately needed. It was up to me to decide if what I had done would save him or destroy him.

Michael believed now. And, by God, so would everyone else.

"He's my brother," I said with finality. Where the hell was that doctor?

"Stefan, what is this dream world you've concocted? This fantasy? What are you thinking?"

"He's my brother," I repeated flatly. "He's my brother and your son. And if you ever say he isn't or do anything to cause him doubt, I'll walk away and you will never see me again."

"Stoipah, what . . ."

"Never."

Chapter 29

Michael lived.

It surprised all of us, including me, and I'd seen him do some damn remarkable things in the healing department, although none were as miraculous as this. I survived too, more or less. The bullet that had passed through him and into my shoulder was nothing. As for my leg, a little fancy orthopedic surgery put it back together. I'd limp in cold weather for the rest of my life; it really wasn't that high a price to pay, considering the work was performed on the second floor of the beach house by an alcoholic surgeon with shaky hands. I felt lucky to have a leg left at all. Beggars can't be choosers, and neither could those of us on the run.

The recuperation, Michael's and mine, gave me time to think. Jericho had never conquered genetic replacement at all, on himself or anyone else. All his successful work must have gone on in the same way it had begun ... with embryos. Perhaps he did it with surrogate mothers. Or, hell, for all I knew, he could've learned to grow the kids in jars in a lab. Regardless, as he'd said on the beach, he'd made them from scratch. I'd wondered if John had been a relative of Jericho's, his son maybe. Now my best guess was that Jericho, the ultimate egotist, had cloned himself. If he couldn't have that fucking festive power of killing with a touch, he'd make another Jericho that did. Only it hadn't turned out that way. John had had a mind and a will of his own. He'd had a soul; made in a lab, of man and not nature, and he'd had the soul Jericho had lacked. Funny how things worked out—funny enough to break your goddamn heart.

Naturally, toward the end, Michael was up and around before I was, but in the beginning . . . heavy doses of painkillers and an unswerving belief in him were all that kept me sane, although that sanity was something my father would have debated.

Anatoly did as I asked; it wasn't as if he had much choice. I was deadly serious in my threat to him. If he made one misstep, said one wrong word, I would've been nothing more than a memory to him. I can't say he came across as World's Best Dad, with a mug and shirt on order, once Michael woke up. That had never been him to begin with, but he tried, in a cautious way, to include Michael. If not as a son, he treated him as a rarely seen nephew, with courteous and cautious charm. My father was nothing if not charming . . . when he wanted to be.

As for Michael, he kept his distance. He'd just embraced a brother; he wasn't quite ready to welcome a father with open arms. It was for the best, all the way around.

But when it came to me, it was different. In his eyes, I was his family. And he committed himself to that in the same way he committed to any project or endeavor, be it research or finding the best fast-food burger ever made. He did it with a wholehearted and stubborn ferocity. It was a humbling thing to see. It made it difficult for me to mourn Lukas. I should have, but in the bright light of day I couldn't. To my conscious mind, Michael was my brother, recovered memories and unfeeling reality be damned. It was only when I slept and the nightmares came that I was able to give Lukas his due, and I gave it to him over and over again.

Those nightmares in turn brought to mind Michael's dreams, the ones of sun and horses that he'd mentioned. They hadn't been his dreams at all; they'd been mine. Or, a more comforting thought, they'd been Lukas's.

He'd had a heart, Lukas . . . far bigger and better than mine was. If he could've sent a message of hope to another lost boy, he would have. And if anyone could have received that gift, it would've been Michael. Jericho had tried to accelerate psychic growth in his subjects, and he'd succeeded in the darker areas. It could be he had as well in ways not measured in dying cells or exploding organs, but in light and luminous promise.

What had happened might never be explained, and that was all right. Faith in the unknown can be a tenuous thing for people like me. It was best to let it be what it was—a warm glow close enough to be seen and just far enough away not to be marred by a skeptical touch.

But faith went only so far. With the Institute still out there, even without Jericho at the helm, I thought it prudent to continue to play rabbit for a while, hiding from any unseen hawks. When the national news carried a piece on a noted St. Louis scientist disappearing, it only cemented my determination.

In a time of hypersecurity, there were still certain borders that were crossed easily and anonymously enough if one had the cash. With what Anatoly gave us when we left, that wasn't going to be a problem for a long while. He made me swear to stay alive long enough for him to find us once he wrapped up business for good. I said I'd do my best, but I had my doubts that my father's elusive day would ever come. I hoped it would. Michael would want a father someday, and a retired crime boss might be better than nothing at all—at least theoretically, as Michael would say.

Weeks passed, then months, until one day I was sitting at a small table in the hot sun when a suitcase was deposited unceremoniously beside my feet. The dust cloud from it hung in the unmoving air as Saul dropped wearily in the chair across from me. Dressed in an impeccable if impractical white silk shirt and pair of eggplant purple linen pants, he lifted a straw hat from his head to wave before his sweat-beaded face. "This place

is like the Everglades on steroids," he said with wheezing outrage as he ducked a large mosquito. "Jesus, even
the bugs are pumping iron. The women though . . . Nice.
Very nice."

"Nice to see you too, Saul," I said dryly, moving my
cane out of his way and leaning it against the table. Michael, who stood at the cantina door, was flirting shame-
lessly with our waitress. In addition to fluent horny
teenage-ese, he spoke flawless Spanish. Me? I tended
to point and grunt a lot. When Michael caught sight of
Saul, his face hardened perceptibly into a scowl and he
started for us. He'd become rather protective of me,
punk-ass kid that he was. I waved him off and flashed
an "okay" sign.

Saul caught the exchange and raised eyebrows over
five-hundred-dollar sunglasses. "Hmmm. He's grown.
He must eat you out of house and hovel." Commandeer-
ing my untouched beer, he finished off the bottle in four
parched swallows. Afterward, he pulled a handkerchief,
an actual English gentleman's handkerchief—which I
was positive they hadn't made since my grandfather's
time—from his pocket and fastidiously mopped sweat
from his neck. Finally, he relaxed, put his feet up in the
spare chair, and said calmly, "I have the information you
wanted."

I knew he had. He wouldn't have come all this way to
deliver bad news. But the statement still had the power
to make my pulse jump and my eyes narrow. "You found
them?"

He nodded and cracked a triumphant grin. "They can
run, but they can't hide. I found them, Smirnoff. I found
those bastards and I found the kids."

We hadn't forgotten the others, Michael and I. It
might take years to be able to go after them, but now
we knew where they were. Now we had a start. "Thanks,
Saul," I said with grim satisfaction. "Thanks a whole helluva lot."

"Yeah, yeah. Thanks are nice, but I'll wait for that

bonus you promised before I get too excited." He grunted as he gestured desperately for another beer. "So, Bolivia, eh? It's not exactly a vacation spot to the stars, is it? What brought you here?"

"Butch and Sundance," I said obliquely, a faint smile hovering on my lips.

He gave me a sideways glance and, fearing the heat had gotten the best of me, held up two fingers for the waitress. She ignored him and, not put off in the slightest by the ferret on his shoulder, continued to give Michael the undivided attention of a pair of stunning dark eyes. His hair was brown again and it suited him. Certainly most of the local girls seemed to think so. Snorting in disgust, Saul turned back to me and commented, "He looks good. Healthy, happy. You guys getting along all right? Like each other okay? Hugs all around?" He grinned again at my exasperated groan, all humor and blinding white teeth. "What? You're family. That doesn't mean you're obligated by law to love each other."

The exasperation faded as I watched Michael laugh and take the girl's hand in his own. He took it with ease. There was no hesitation; no concern that he might lose control and hurt her; no fear that he was a monster. He held her hand as if he were nothing more than an infatuated teenage boy.

"What's not to love?" I said simply. "He's my brother."

ROADKILL
by

ROB THURMAN

It's time to lock, load—and hit the road...

Once, while half-human Cal Leandros and his brother Niko were working on a case, an ancient gypsy queen gave them a good old-fashioned backstabbing. Now, just as their P.I. business hits a slow patch, the old crone shows up with a job.

She wants them to find a stolen coffin that contains a blight that makes the Black Death seem like a fond memory. But the thief has already left town, so the Leandros brothers are going on the road. And if they're very, very lucky, there might even be a return trip...

R0030

ALSO AVAILABLE

DEATHWISH
by
ROB THURMAN

*In a nightmarish New York City,
life is there for the taking...*

Half-human Cal Leandros and his brother Niko are
hired by the vampire Seamus to find out who has
been following him—until Seamus turns up dead
(or un-undead). Worse still is the return of Cal's
nightmarish family, the Auphe. The last time Cal
and Niko faced them, they were almost wiped out.
Now, the Auphe want revenge. But first, they'll
destroy everything Cal holds dear...

"A subtly warped world."
—Green Man Review

Available wherever books are sold or at
penguin.com

R0008

MADHOUSE
by
ROB THURMAN

Half-human Cal Leandros and his brother Niko aren't exactly prospering with their preternatural detective agency. Who could have guessed that business could dry up in New York City, where vampires, trolls, and other creepy crawlies are all over the place?

But now there's a new arrival in the Big Apple. A malevolent evil with ancient powers is picking off humans like sheep, dead-set on making history with an orgy of blood and murder. And for Cal and Niko, this is one paycheck they're going to have to earn.

"Stunningly original."
—Green Man Review

ALSO AVAILABLE IN THE SERIES
Moonshine
Nightlife

Available wherever books are sold or at penguin.com